*Deck the halls with boughs of holly...*

Adam Markland wanted Holly Hall—
in his halls, his home and especially in his bed.
Only, with the lovely decorator's aversion
to lawyers, it would take a miracle....

*'Tis the season to be jolly...*

David Blade and his son had nothing to be jolly
about...until Jean Young came into their lives
offering the gift of love.

# DECK THE HALLS

*'Tis the season...to fall in love!*

Relive the romance...

**By Request**
Two complete novels
by your favorite authors!

**MARGOT EARLY**

says she's written romance fiction since she was twelve. (Her first hero and heroine were kids as well, solving a mystery together.) She's been writing ever since— humor, features, scripts, as well as fiction. In fact, Margot met her husband at a "murder mystery" for which she wrote the script. He played an undertaker, she played a nun. In a matter of hours, he told her he was falling in love. Margot lives in Colorado with her husband and son.

**HEATHER MacALLISTER**

lives in Texas with her electrical engineer husband and two live-wire sons whose antics inspire her humorous approach to love and life. She writes for both the Harlequin Romance and Harlequin Temptation lines, finding the main difference between her stories for each is that her Harlequin Romance heroines find love, but love always has to go out and catch her Temptation heroines. But in the end, of course, they all live happily ever after.

# DECK THE HALLS

## MARGOT EARLY
## HEATHER MacALLISTER

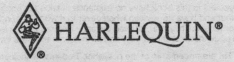

HARLEQUIN®

TORONTO • NEW YORK • LONDON
AMSTERDAM • PARIS • SYDNEY • HAMBURG
STOCKHOLM • ATHENS • TOKYO • MILAN • MADRID
PRAGUE • WARSAW • BUDAPEST • AUCKLAND

HARLEQUIN BOOKS

by Request—DECK THE HALLS

Copyright © 2000 by Harlequin Books S.A.

ISBN 0-373-21712-9

The publisher acknowledges the copyright holders
of the individual works as follows:
THE THIRD CHRISTMAS
Copyright © 1994 by Margot Early
DECK THE HALLS
Copyright © 1990 by Heather W. MacAllister

This edition published by arrangement with Harlequin Books S.A.

Visit us at www.eHarlequin.com

**Printed in U.S.A.**

# CONTENTS

**Their own Christmas angel...**

# The Third Christmas
## Margot Early

# *PROLOGUE*

*Santa Barbara Harbor*
*December 6*
*Three years past—the year without Christmas*

DIVE CONDITIONS were bad. Immersed in the murk, his view constrained by the edges of his scuba mask, he watched the dark unidentifiable shadows beneath the ship and the docks. There was nothing there, neither shark nor mariner's ghost nor the other thing, and yet he watched, afraid it would come back. Watching helped him forget the tangible threat, the police diver at his elbow. But that was all he could forget.

Behind his eyes, the colors came—brown mostly. Stormy charcoal green. Red. His heart started screaming again, and his breaths grew shallow.

The scene changed, a bad cut, and through his mind reeled the old scratchy film of unwanted remembrance, set against an unchanging backdrop. The arctic seascape that haunted his dreams. Icy abyss as far as he could see. Cold, so cold. *Full fathom five, thy father lies....* And mother.

And now, thought David, my lover. Skye—my wife, my hell.

The shriek rose inside him again, and he quelled it. He concentrated on trying to drive some warmth into his limbs. Even underwater, he knew it was December. The temperature of the harbor was indifferent to shock and horror, and he was cold, but he wouldn't leave while the divers worked under his ship, while they might find something.

Listening tensely to the whooshing and bubbling of his regulator and the endless creaking of the docks, he sought another distraction. The dark void with its specters and its taunts offered too little, and too much, and her voice wouldn't leave him.

*Death is a wild night, David, and a new road. I'm not afraid of death.*

God, she should have been, with her damned Emily Dick-inson quotes.

*He* should have been.

David peered through the soupy water at the police team searching the three-foot screws beneath his ship. They had found something.

Physically, he felt no reaction. His heart had never stopped pounding, nor his mind racing, not for hours. Psychically, he felt a flicker of fear.

He was twenty-eight years old, and today he had become a veteran of an ugly war. Whatever was in the props couldn't be worse than what he'd already seen. But he didn't want to see any more.

Still, he kicked toward the blades.

Immediately one of the divers turned, holding up two hands. *Stay back.*

He stopped, wondering what they would do if he suddenly dove. He knew the harbor better than they did. He could get away. Maybe.

But he had no intention of fleeing, nor of spending his life as a fugitive. Chris needed him, this minute and for years to come. For now, David was glad Jake had taken him down to the marine supply, away from the cops. It was Saturday and Santa Claus was on hand at the wharf, but

Chris had received that news with apathy. David didn't blame him.

*What goes through a three-year-old's mind at a time like this?* he wondered. Nothing that would be improved by seeing his father handcuffed and marched away.

David doubted that would happen, but he hadn't been willing to chance Chris's witnessing such a drama. He'd already seen more than anyone ever should. For a moment, David envisioned detectives grilling his son and felt impotent rage. Could it happen?

*They have nothing,* he told himself again. Not even a body, and they wouldn't get one. He wasn't a prisoner, and he wouldn't be.

The anger surged through him again, mingling with other emotions he didn't want to touch with a ten-foot pole. *How had it happened?*

The panic returned, a baseball-size thing in his throat, alien to him as fear. The colors came back. The shape in the water coming at him.

A diver at the keel was swept to one side by the power of the current, and David refocused on the police operation, his view now unobstructed.

He saw what they were removing from the screws.

MINUTES LATER, on the gusty aft deck of the ship, a diver handed the evidence bag to the technician from Forensics. "That's all we found." He shrugged. "You might get an order from the judge and put her in dry dock, but I don't see the point. There's no body—or parts. Frankly, it's hard not to doubt his story."

Struggling to hang on to the blowing piece of paper on his clipboard, the tech tagged the bag. "This is something, anyway." He eyed the dark sky, the gray-green water and the masts of the sloops rocking in the next marina, their stays banging in the whistling wind. "Those boats make a racket in this weather, don't they?"

No one answered. Keough from Homicide, his Lieutenant Columbo coat flapping like a sail, watched a red tinsel garland loosen itself from a nearby dock piling and drop into the water. It reminded him of party decorations on the morning after—though Christmas was still almost three weeks off. For the living.

Reaching to his throat to ease an extra inch of breathing room into the reindeer tie his daughter had given him years earlier, Keough glanced incuriously at the evidence bag. True, it was something—but not nearly enough.

Keough was far more interested in David Blade, across the deck, who was staring at a woman on the stern of a cabin cruiser two slips away. The woman was shedding her scuba tank beneath a canopy strung with colored lights. Seeing her scrub brush and scraper, Keough decided she was a bottom-cleaner. Unusual line of work for a woman. Blade might be thinking the same thing, but probably not.

He would have other things on his mind. His son, maybe.

Or his wife.

Or the uniforms all over his ship.

Without looking at his colleagues, he asked, almost rhetorically, "So, what do you give the wife who has everything?"

The diver was the one who answered.

"A push."

# CHAPTER ONE

*December 3*
*Three years later—the third Christmas*

DON'T THINK OF YOURSELF as a bottom-cleaner, Jean. You're a slime warrior, ridding boats in the Santa Barbara Harbor of a disgusting scourge. It's a noble calling.

Jake Doherty's words had cost him an extra fifty cents a foot, Jean reminded herself as she scrubbed thick slime from the keel of his Chinese junk, *Lien Hua*. Slime warrior. Her arm ached, a scumlike film clouded the view through her mask, tar clung to her hair, and her forehead throbbed. The slime warrior should be home studying for her cetacean-development final—unless she wanted to spend her life cleaning boat bottoms. And despite her dean's list standings, that was looking like a possibility.

Baby nuzzled her cheek as though attempting to kiss away her headache, and Jean, drawing as deep a breath as her ancient regulator allowed, ran a gloved hand over the dolphin's smooth underside. *Baby*, she thought, *you make this worth it.*

Baby was the best thing that had ever happened to her, and this filthy job kept them together. It seemed to Jean they were two of a kind: Baby, dishonorably discharged from both the U.S. Navy and Marineland and ostracized by her own kind; Jean, unable to find the diving work she coveted yet hating to work on land—and always feeling so different for it.

Baby slid along her side in an affectionate caress as Jean attacked the last square foot of slime on *Lien Hua*'s keel. Minutes later, holding Baby's dorsal fin, she gratefully accepted a lift to the surface.

At the top, she dropped her mouthpiece, breathed the tar-scented winter air and reached her arm around Baby, brushing her lips over the dolphin's smooth, warm skin. "Thanks for the ride, sweetheart." Reluctantly releasing Baby, she inflated her vest and pushed back her mask, in no hurry to haul herself out of the water at the dock. There was no diving ladder on the *Lien Hua*—more justification, Jean told herself, for charging two dollars a foot.

Still, she took a moment to rescue one of Jake's holiday decorations from the drink—Baby's work undoubtedly. Since Thanksgiving, Baby had been disarranging Christmas trimmings all over the harbor. Anything that looked like it might make a good toy was irresistible to her, and this time the casualty was a string of bells made from red and green pop cans. The bells had been draped along the starboard side of the *Lien Hua,* clinking faintly in response to the breeze, but Baby had been dissatisfied with the intermittent effect. Earlier, Jean had seen her attempting to ring them herself by hitting them with her snout. Now the entire string was floundering near the surface of the water. Jean gathered up the cans and slung them over the gunwale, then left the side of the junk and made her way to the dock, Baby chattering beside her.

Jean whistled back, mimicking Baby's clicking sounds as best she could and knowing it was a sorry attempt at communication. Swimming backward as Baby nosed her face, Jean said, "You're my best friend in the world, pretty thing."

Her tank bumped the dock, and Jean turned clumsily to reach for weathered wood. Instead, she grabbed a worn running shoe—with a foot inside. A warm, full-grown male foot and not Jake Doherty's.

"Sorry." Moving her hand to the dock, she squinted up at the tall figure standing over her, a black cutout against the cloudless sky. As he crouched beside the water, blocking the afternoon sun, Jean's heart gave a lurch.

David Blade, head of the Blade Institute of Marine Exploration.

"Jean."

The shadows hid his eyes, but Jean knew what was there. Small lines etched in the corners, telling of days spent on the sea watching distant horizons; irises of deep brown, shades darker than his sun-tipped hair and closely trimmed beard.

Today a long-sleeved rugby shirt hugged his broad shoulders, and the long legs of his canvas pants were splattered with old paint, dried splotches of white that suggested he did his own maintenance on his ship. Staring through dripping lashes at the promise of muscle beneath the worn fabric, Jean thought stupidly, *He knows my name.* And an instant later, *Why is he here?*

"I need a diver. Would you like to work on my ship?"

She set her scrub brush on the dock. "Bottom-cleaning?" It always was.

"Bottom-cleaning," he said. "I'll help you, and we'll get her scrubbed as fast as we can. I'm leaving for Baja the week before Christmas."

With a team of divers, no doubt, thought Jean. Why couldn't she find that kind of work? Once she had suspected the episode in Mexico of damaging her credibility, but it had happened years ago—and the story couldn't have reached the ears of *every* employer to whom she applied for diving work.

She didn't respond immediately and David said, "I hope you can help. Everyone else is working salvage."

He was more candid than tactful. Jean said, "I charge a dollar-fifty a foot." Her voice was shaky—fatigue, of course. *It's just like any other job,* she thought. *The only difference is he heads the Blade Institute.*

It was a big difference. The small but prestigious research institute founded by David's father, the late undersea explorer Christopher Blade, had once led the field in oceanic research. Though the institute had dropped in size and prominence over the past few years, it was still highly respected.

David said, "Can you start tomorrow?"

"I have a cetacean-development final at noon. I can come after that."

"You're a student."

"I'm a student till tomorrow. Then I graduate in marine biology with an emphasis in cetaceans." She sounded like a talking résumé, but David didn't seem to notice. Probably all marine-biology students spewed their credentials at him on first meeting.

Jean was wondering how to mention summa cum laude and the K. L. Sayles Award when Baby nosed up beside her, pushing an inflatable ring imprinted with the image of a Christmas wreath. Putting her beak through the wreath, Baby tossed it at David's feet. It bounced off his shins, hit Jean in the face and plopped back into the water.

Jean was grateful that if anyone had to witness the dolphin's playful mischief it was David Blade. Who better to understand Baby's antics and her constant demands for attention than a man who had written two books on cetaceans? For once, Baby might prove a career asset.

But David hardly glanced at the animal. Scooping the wreath from the water, he dropped it onto the dock beside him and asked Jean, "Want a hand up?"

Jean considered. If she said yes, he might think she was weak. If she said no, he would think she was hard to work with. The fact was, she welcomed the help. "Um. Yes. I can do it myself, but—"

"I know you can."

Jean let him take her arms, and he lifted her from the water and sat her on the edge of the dock. In his shadow, Jean stripped off her tank and fins, stood up and tripped over the inflatable wreath. She crashed into David and clung to his arms to steady herself—and to keep from tumbling into the harbor. Jean heard his quick intake of breath and felt the heat of him and the hardness of his muscles before he set her back from him—as one might a dog who had rolled in dead fish. The contact left his clothes wet, smeared with slime and tar.

"I'm sorry," Jean said at once. "Would you like me to wash them for you?" It sounded absurd, but it was the best reparation she could envisage on the spot.

"No." The word was curt and decisive.

Flushed, Jean peeled off her diving gloves. David Blade was taller than he'd seemed from a distance, and she felt small beside him. Fine hairs all over her body rubbed the inside of her wet suit as his gaze absorbed her.

As the only female diver working in the harbor, Jean was used to getting the once-over from employers who seemed to wonder if she had the muscle for the job. She did. At five-six and 115 pounds, she was no linebacker, but she was a strong swimmer, an experienced diver and a second-degree black belt in tae kwon do. Quick and agile enough to stand on a dock without falling over her own feet and slamming into the nearest man.

David Blade's scrutiny felt unforgiving. Imagining the grimy picture she made, Jean turned toward the water to squeeze out her thick, sun-singed braid. Tar was clumped in the loosened golden strands. She was a mess, and she wanted to get away from David Blade's eyes. It was impossible not to think of his sleek, beautiful, debutante wife, now three years dead. No one would have caught Skye Haverford Blade covered with slime and tar.

Baby rolled onto her side and waved a flipper at Jean. As Jean halfheartedly waved back, David frowned at the dolphin. "Your diving buddy?"

Jean heard the criticism and knew she deserved it for violating the number-one rule of scuba safety: *Never dive alone.* Of course, with Baby she wasn't exactly alone, but the dolphin wouldn't be much help if her equipment failed. On the other hand, at only ten or fifteen feet below the surface, how bad could things get? She shrugged. "It's just bottom-cleaning."

The reaction was all in his eyes, which darkened. "I must have misread my dive manual. I don't recall any special clauses regarding bottom-cleaning."

Coming from a man who'd logged more hours underwater than the *Nautilus,* the comment was scathing.

Before Jean could reply, he added, "No one dives solo from my ship."

Jean smiled stiffly. "It will be nice to have your company." Like diving with a twelve-foot shark.

David did not return the smile. Instead, he picked up the wreath at his feet and pulled the plug, releasing the air from inside. As he deflated it, evoking a whistling chatter of complaint from Baby, he glanced again at the dolphin and said, "They don't make good pets."

Jean was speechless. Baby was not a pet, and David Blade, of all people, should know that. Reading his books,

Jean had perceived him to possess a sympathy with marine mammals that bordered on mystical. He was wise, aware and compassionate. He was a kindred soul.

He was folding the inflatable wreath into fourths.

Watching her toy shrink, Baby cried loudly.

Jean nodded at the wreath and asked David, "Is that yours?" His ship, the *Skye,* was berthed less than a hundred yards away in the next marina, which could explain how Baby had retrieved the ring so quickly.

"It belonged to my son."

Belonged? The past tense implied that either his son was history or the wreath was. Since as far as she knew, the little boy she frequently saw sitting on the deck of the *Skye* was alive and well, David must mean he planned to confiscate the wreath. For what? Letting Baby have it?

David reached for her tank. "I'll take your gear to the *Skye,* since you'll be working there tomorrow. That will save you lugging it to the marine supply and back."

Jean was surprised he knew her habits. But then, he also knew Jake Doherty, who ran the marine supply. She said, "Thank you. You don't have to do that."

He reached for her mask. "When's your final over tomorrow?"

"I'll be here by three-thirty."

"Marina D. I'll meet you at the gate."

"Okay." Jean looked toward the *Lien Hua,* a study in flea-market Christmas decor. Her diving bag and beach towel were on the junk, and she had to retrieve them before heading home.

She turned back to bid farewell to David Blade, but he'd already left. The gate at the top of the dock clanged shut behind him as he strode down the boardwalk toward the next marina. Gone.

Jean stared after him, stunned by the abrupt departure.

He hadn't even said goodbye. Marking the cold, purposeful strides of his retreating figure, Jean told Baby, "I think I should have charged two dollars a foot."

Baby whistled and dove, then leapt from the water and landed with a splash. Her late-afternoon exuberance was predictable as clockwork—like the cries that would follow Jean when she left the marina. Both were pleas for her to stay. *Pay attention to me, Jean.*

*Oh, Baby,* thought Jean. The dolphin seemed so vulnerable in her solitude. It was always hard to leave her. Jean knew she should be home reviewing the embryonic development of *Globicephala scammonii* and other cetaceans, but instead she sat down on the edge of the dock and slid back into the water. At least David had saved her some time by taking her gear to his ship. She could spend that time with Baby.

David Blade. No wonder she didn't feel like studying. He was a distraction to ruin anyone's grade point average. As Baby surfaced near her and blew a long sighing breath from her blowhole, Jean said, "He's even better up close, isn't he, Baby? Mean, but cute."

Baby lifted her head from the water and released a faint whistle.

Jean echoed the sound and reached her arms around the dolphin to hug her, but she was still thinking of David, of the times she'd surfaced in the harbor after a dive and found him watching her and Baby from the deck of the *Skye.* And of the other times they'd passed each other on the waterfront and his eyes had lingered on her as though he wanted to speak.

She told Baby, "Now we know what he wanted to say, don't we? *I must have misread my dive manual.* That was so embarrassing, Baby."

Especially because he was right. Baby was a genius at

chasing off diving partners, but that was no excuse for going down alone. And Jean couldn't blame David for resenting her recklessness. Nobody wanted to drag a body out of the harbor, and he'd already suffered his share of that kind of grief.

Three years earlier, a few weeks before Christmas, Jean had been on one of her first diving jobs when the *Skye* pulled into the harbor with a police escort. Curious spectators had crowded the dock as David Blade and some other divers entered the water at the *Skye*'s stern. Jean and her diving buddy had taken more trips to the surface than usual to watch the commotion, and soon the owner of the boat they were working on, just three slips away from the *Skye*, came back to fill them in. Jean still remembered the tremor in the man's voice.

"That's a homicide team. His wife fell overboard out at the islands."

Jean and her partner and their employer had watched until the divers surfaced, David Blade with them. On the *Skye*'s diving platform, he'd dropped his tank and pulled off his mask, turning at the sound of two different camera shutters. On his feet instantly, a tall and bearded Poseidon in neoprene, he had snarled at the photographers, "Get off my ship."

The shutterbugs fell over each other getting out of his way.

Feeling like another spectator, Jean had cleared her mask as another diver surfaced at the stern of the *Skye* with something in his hand. A plastic bag. Forensic evidence.

From the newspapers the following day, Jean learned the divers had removed a grease-coated bikini top and some strands of dark brown hair from one of the screws. The story was on every front page on the south coast and many across the nation, beneath macabre headlines,

PUBLISHING HEIRESS SKYE HAVERFORD
DISAPPEARS FROM SHIP
HUSBAND QUESTIONED

David Blade told police he had seen his wife fall from
the bow and had cut the engine as soon as he could. The
details were sketchy, as though the papers had found the
story in its entirety too ghastly to print, and Jean's mind
wouldn't let go of the questions. Had Skye been sucked
under the ship and killed by the propellers? The possibility
was horrifying. She had seen the props on ships the size of
the Blades', and she knew their effect on the water and
everything around them. And if her body had gone into the
screws, the man at the helm probably would have felt it—
and the sensation would stay with him till his dying day.
Jean didn't know how anyone could live with it.

The articles taken from the propeller that day were all
that ever surfaced of Skye Haverford's remains, and with
no body there were no answers. Free to go, David Blade
had left Santa Barbara for an expedition near Fiji, then gone
on to a long project in Antarctica. And two and a half years
later, when the *Skye* at last returned to her berth, Jean noticed David again. His reappearance was the most intriguing change in her life of diving and study and tae kwon do
since the day Baby showed up at her favorite surfing spot.

Now Jean asked Baby, "Do you think all that time at
the south pole made him so...glacial?"

Baby responded with a series of clicks.

Jean said, "True. Someone should thaw him out, and it
should be me."

How many times had she imagined he would ask her to
clean the *Skye*'s hull? Too many to count. But her version
had never included David's hefting her onto the dock like
a net of fresh catch or her tripping and falling on him and

smearing slime and tar on his clothes. Remembering the look on his face when she'd offered to wash them, Jean gave a quiet moan that faded to bubbles as she let herself slide briefly under the water.

None of it was supposed to happen that way.

In her imaginings of their meeting, she was always ready to go down for a dive, though not in her usual guise. Her hair long and loose, she would look like something assembled from the pages of *Professional Diver,* the *Sports Illustrated* swimsuit issue and *Elle.* Cool, collected—and somehow both chic and sexy, like her sister Cecily. David Blade was always shirtless—as she'd occasionally observed him from a distance—and he always opened their conversation by confessing, "I've been watching you for months. You do things for a wet suit I didn't think were possible."

Later he would suggest she accompany him on a year-long expedition to some distant, exotic diving location. Sometimes it was to see the giant squid of the Humboldt Current, other times to the reefs of the Red Sea. Always she impressed him with her competence as a marine biologist and her sensitivity as a woman. After long afternoons diving, they would lie on sandy beaches in little clothing, and he would say things like, "I never dreamed I would fall in love with a research assistant. I have to tell you, Jean. No woman's ever made me feel this way." *This way* meant possessed of insatiable desire for her, a desire they would repeatedly attempt to quench.

The recollections and her encounter with David now seemed mortifying. She'd better get home and study. She was not David Blade's research assistant, lover or consort. She was still the Goddess of Slime, and like every other oceanic explorer around, David Blade apparently thought scraping hulls was the upper limit of her employment potential.

"Tomorrow," she told Baby, giving the dolphin a last stroke before climbing from the water, "I'm going to prove him wrong."

ERIKA BLADE WATCHED her brother remove a bottle of tequila from a high locker behind the bar, uncap it and take two quick swallows. Then he stood staring out the salon's one clear-paned starboard window at the next marina. He took another drink.

She said, "Good day?"

David started, then stared at the wheelchair that had soundlessly entered the salon. Meeting Erika's eyes, he said, "I'm going to put sleigh bells on that thing."

"Why not?" Erika laughed, setting the brake. "'Tis the season." There were few secrets between them, and she nodded at the bottle he held. "Speaking of which, is that why? The holidays?" Or the time of year, she wondered. It was almost St. Nicholas Day—again.

"You know better."

Erika wasn't sure of that, but she let it slide. "Individual glasses are more sanitary, unless you're planning to finish it."

He turned the label to face her. In black permanent marker, across José Cuervo's imprint, was scrawled the word "mine."

Erika smiled. "My brother the lush." He wasn't, fortunately. David cared too much for his son to damage any of their lives that way. And he had too much self-control. Still, as he capped the bottle in his hand, Erika wondered if it wasn't some sort of anesthetic for him, a quick fix for difficult moments in the day. There was pain there.

Watching him tuck the bottle back into the locker and secure the door, Erika changed the subject. "What happened to your clothes?"

He looked away. "I was helping a diver out of the water."

Erika did not ask which diver. She had eyes. And so did her brother—for the harbor's prettiest bottom-cleaner. She suppressed a smile, imagining a host of scenarios that could be responsible for the tar on his clothes. Any of them would be good for him.

David asked, "Where's Chris?"

"Reading. Number five or six of *Hank the Cowdog*. I think he wants to live on a ranch."

"I hope not." David smiled. "Next you're going to say he wants a horse for Christmas."

Erika recognized a perfect opening. "No, but I've been thinking about a puppy or a kitten."

David drew back almost imperceptibly. Then he reached for an object lying on top of the locker and unfurled it for Erika. The deflated wreath. He told his sister mildly, "Let's work on getting him to take better care of his toys for now."

Erika said, "My God, David. He's a kid. Surely you're not upset because he was playing with that dolphin. It's probably good for him."

"I doubt it. And we've covered this before. No pets." He started to leave.

*Slam*, thought Erika. The door was closed. That was David. One minute warm and almost loosening up, the next shut down, maximum security, closed for the duration. In the last few years, he'd become a master of protection, building barriers around all three of them. Too late, reflected Erika. We're already damaged, and David is broken.

He paused over the hatchway that led to the galley. "I have a diver coming tomorrow. We're going to work on the keel."

"Good," Erika said pleasantly. "Is there anything I can do to help?"

David's back was to her, and he closed his eyes. What it must cost her to say that, to say it so sincerely and serenely when he knew as well as anyone that she must long to be in the water, too, even bottom-cleaning. He forgot to answer. He wanted to tell her he loved her, that he wanted her to have the use of her legs again as much as she wanted it—maybe more. But Erika knew that.

When his silence became long, she said cheerfully, "I'll keep Chris out of the way. How's that?"

David turned swiftly, remembering her question. He met her eyes. "You do help. Every single day."

And because his throat suddenly hurt from the truth of the words and because he couldn't look at her any longer without seeing himself, he started below to the galley.

"David."

He looked back.

Erika's eyes were steady, but she chewed on her bottom lip for a moment before she continued. Instinctively he realized whatever she had to say was going to be bad.

"You know I'm going into rehab over Christmas."

"Yes." He faced her, unconsciously bracing himself on the edge of one of the lockers.

"I don't think I'll come back—here, that is."

His insides felt as if they were falling a mile. Not come back? When he spoke, it was an incredulous whisper. "Erika."

She looked unhappy, undoubtedly for giving him pain. "It's not you," she said. "Or Chris. You're the only family I have. But this is for me. I think I've leaned on you as long as I should."

Stalled two steps down the companionway, David backed against the locker on the starboard side of the stairwell. His eyes were keen. "Or maybe you mean I've leaned on *you* as long as I should."

Erika threw him a tender smile, the beauty of which her crooked incisors seemed only to enhance. She said, "Maybe I do, David."

His heart sank. It must be hard as hell for her to take this step. But if she walked away, she was going to leave a mess behind. His mess, which she had politely waded through for three years. He thought of Chris and all Erika had provided for him. A female role model and a great caretaker when David was working. What was he going to do now? Chris was only six.

Erika read his thoughts. "Get a nanny. You can afford it, and it will be good for him."

"A nanny?" David straightened up. The idea made him feel as if he was choking. He asked Erika, "Should we get one who'll decide to cast off while we're away from the ship like that girl down in Newport? Ten thousand dollars worth of damage to the boat. Remember? Or maybe we should get one like—who was it—the Averys' nanny, down in Baja. Went off with her boyfriend, and the kids burned down the condo."

Erika rolled her eyes. "I'm sure there's more to that story than we've heard. You and I both know that even on a bad day Chris wouldn't play with matches. And Jennifer Avery—"

She didn't finish, but that was Erika. If she couldn't say anything nice, she shut up. This time, David wished she'd continue. Jennifer Avery's husband, Michael, was a marine-biology professor at the university and had recently applied for a grant from the Haverford Trust. David had mixed feelings about the proposal and would have liked to know more about the man.

In any case, Erika was right about the nanny story, which he'd heard secondhand. There was probably more to it.

But a nanny for Chris!

Lost in thought, he murmured more to himself than to Erika, "A nanny." He couldn't picture it. *He'd* never had a nanny, and neither had Erika.

But they'd had a mother.

He became conscious of Erika watching him. Her smile was long gone, and he knew she was worried. Not about Chris, but about him, about how he'd get along without his big sister on board.

He turned and met her eyes gamely. "A nanny. Good idea." Before she could suspect his true feelings, he turned again to go below.

"David."

"Yes." He paused, but didn't look back.

"A wife might do as well."

"No, thank you. I can always fire a nanny." He dropped into the galley and hurried to his cabin.

# CHAPTER TWO

THE NEXT AFTERNOON Jean found him waiting in the sun on a bench outside marina D. He was leaning against the window of the boardwalk espresso shop, which was painted with a holiday scene—a sailboarding Santa Claus whose saucy wink seemed to say, *I see you when you're sleeping; I know when you're awake—thinking about David Blade.*

Jean was nervous, a state that worsened as David, his expression remote, stood up to greet her.

She said, "Am I late?"

He glanced at his diving watch. "No."

Jean looked down at her short denim skirt and white sweatshirt, sorry she wasn't already suited up.

He said, "You can change on the *Skye*." Crossing the boardwalk, he opened the gate with his key card and ushered her into the marina.

The dock seemed gloomier than those surrounding it. All the boats were deserted, many were covered with tarps, and not one was decorated for the season. Swinging her dive bag beside her, Jean scanned the water for Baby, but the dolphin was nowhere in sight. David said nothing, and only the slapping of rigging on masts and the splash of waves accompanied their footsteps as she followed him down the dock to slip 23.

There, the black-and-white hull of an eighty-foot ship loomed over them, a colorful array of flags streaming from her mast on the fly bridge. Following David down the narrow walk alongside the berth, Jean read the name printed in utilitarian block letters on the side of the bow: *Skye.*

The infamous ship that had killed the woman who bore its name. *Sad,* Jean thought, remembering. In her musings the previous night, she had wondered if perhaps unhealed grief was behind David's gruffness.

Her pale green eyes lifted to his, but he had already jumped aboard. He held out his hand, and Jean took it. Clasping his long, strong fingers, tanned brown and hardened by work, she allowed him to help her onto the ship. The gangway was narrow, and she balanced precariously between David and the ship's railing as she held her dive bag clear of the immaculate sides of the cabin.

"Careful." David steadied her, then dropped her hand and led the way to the aft deck. Her stomach flooded with heat from their close proximity, Jean took a deep breath before she followed. He was an occupational hazard.

It was a relief to turn her attention to the ship.

There was varnished wood trim everywhere, from decks to doors, unusual on a vessel used for scientific expeditions. But the *Skye* was legendary. Steel-hulled, she boasted powerful twin engines and a false nose, which housed an underwater observation chamber, a feature that interested Jean immensely.

Yet every utilitarian quality was matched by something rare and lovely. A diving platform at the stern gave way to a teak deck, and several of the triple-paned cabin windows protected stained glass. As she followed David aft, Jean saw a hammerhead shark captured in one frame, narwhals in another. Two colorful wind socks blew beneath the canopy, and a Jolly Roger waved over the stern, grinning insolently at the star-spangled banners on other boats.

Jean had noticed the pirate flag in the past. She was occasionally a reader of pirate fiction, and the emblem attracted her, hinting that David possessed a romantic soul—

or at least a good sense of humor. In the past twenty-four hours, she'd ruled out the latter. As for the former—

A small boy peered around the edge of the cabin, grounding her flight of fancy.

"Hi, Chris." David reached out to touch a head of fine hair the same wet-sand color as his own. "Jean, this is my son, Christian. Chris, this is Jean. She's going to help me clean up *Skye*."

Ah, thought Jean. The owner of the wreath.

The boy, whom she judged to be about six, melted against his father's side, buried his face, then chanced a look at Jean with solemn dark eyes. She was surprised by his shyness. Often she had seen him sitting on the aft cushions of the *Skye* watching Baby, usually in the company of a woman in a wheelchair Jake Doherty said was David's sister. Jean told David, "He looks like you."

David glanced down at Christian, and the two made identical faces and simultaneously shook their heads. "We don't think so," David said. "But thank you."

Jean met Christian's dark brown eyes, so much like his father's. "Hi, Chris." She realized her heart was beating faster than normal. It was ridiculous that the appearance of a child should make her anxious, but it did. Had her mother been right? Had that disastrous time in Mexico said something about her she wasn't prepared to face?

At least David's son seemed well behaved. In fact, Christian Blade appeared unusually reserved for a boy his age, not that she had much basis for meaningful comparison. He was wearing a black turtleneck and blue jeans, a sober ensemble that matched his demeanor.

David asked him, "Where's Erika?"

His sister, thought Jean. Jake had said her name was Erika.

Christian detached himself from his father's leg and shrugged, nodding toward the cabin. His eyes never left Jean.

David squinted at the sun dropping below the canopy and turned to her. "I'll show you where you can change. We don't have much daylight."

Baby's cries answered his words, announcing her arrival at the *Skye*'s berth. Jean whistled to her, then felt the sudden heat of David's gaze and remembered what he'd said about dolphins as pets. Blushing, she said, "I'm ready."

Without a remark or so much as a glance, David opened the nearest cabin door and steered Jean inside. Christian raced away to the stern and settled on the aft seat to look at Baby as his father let the door swing shut behind Jean.

Thinking again of the inflatable wreath and wondering what had become of it, she said, "Your son's quiet."

"Very." David indicated the enclosed area where they stood. "This is the diving alcove."

Jean noted scuba tanks, a compressor and a locker marked Masks and Fins. Two surfboards were mounted to a rack on the vestibule wall.

He opened another door, and Jean followed him down stairs carpeted in plush blue to a spacious cabin sensibly furnished. The chairs and matching couch were understated and looked comfortable; even the koa end tables blended rusticity with elegance. Along both sides of each clear window were stained-glass images, now dramatically lit by the sun and framed in the same rich, dark wood as the bookcases and cabinets that edged the walls. The bar and stereo console were mounted to withstand the high seas, as were two globes, one on each of the forward lockers: the Earth and the moon.

"The salon," said David. He continued below to the galley, but Jean paused to admire a watercolor hanging over the aft companionway. The portrait showed a striking brunette with brilliant blue eyes standing in a tide pool.

Skye.

Jean remembered pictures of the heiress in the news after her death. Now she stared at the portrait, captivated by the woman's half smile, until David spoke from the galley. "The engine room's beneath your feet. The access is under these stairs." He indicated the ladder down to the galley.

Her eagerness to see the vessel momentarily triumphed over her curiosity about Skye Haverford. Abandoning the watercolor, Jean followed David into the depths of the ship.

The galley was soled in teak. By the time her sneakers touched the wood, David had ascended another set of steps to a door labeled USE OTHER DOOR. Jean glanced around as she crossed the companionway. The galley was shipshape and well equipped yet homey, with a child's drawing of a rather unhappy-looking snowman taped to the refrigerator and a note on the espresso maker—FIX NOW. At a spot low on the wall, eye level for a six-year-old, hung a pasteboard advent calendar with the first four doors opened, revealing seasonal images. The offering for December fourth was a pair of silver skates.

When Jean reached the top of the stairs, David propelled her into a sunlit teak-and-koa cabin. "This is my cabin. You can change in here."

The room was masculine, tasteful and personal. A quilt appliquéd with dolphins and whales covered the queen-size berth, and a rag throw rug brightened the teak sole. Bookshelves, map table and a mounted rolltop desk—all of exotic woods—lined the walls beneath the windows. Like the windows in the salon, the clear panels of these were edged by stained glass. The lockers were tightly secured, the space immaculate.

"Come out whenever you're ready." David nodded toward a set of steps aft. "That door will put you in the wheelhouse. The hatch goes to the deck. Do you need anything?"

Turning, Jean shook her head at him. In the close quarters, it was hard not to stare and harder not to admire the details of him, particularly his eyes. The whites were immaculate, almost supernaturally clear, the irises dark as black walnut. He was an extraordinarily handsome man.

He said, "I'll meet you on deck. I'll take care of the tanks." And he left.

Alone, Jean kicked off her sneakers and peeled off her clothes as she pored over the photographs on the walls. She recognized Christopher Blade in one, David's son, Christian, in another. Examining the photo of his father, she remembered that Skye's death had not been the first major tragedy in David's life. At nineteen, he was sole survivor of the wreck of the *Siren,* his father's scientific-research vessel, which hit an iceberg near Greenland. He had lost both parents and the ship that had been the family's home, then gone on to revitalize the Blade Institute until it rose like a phoenix from its briny grave.

As she pulled on her black tank suit, Jean looked for a photo of Skye Haverford Blade but found none. In fact, there were no photos of women in the cabin, only the images in the four stained-glass panels. A mermaid, a geisha, a dark-skinned island beauty and a golden-haired pirate's wench. The words of an old song played through her mind. *In my ship I've sailed around the world, looking for a woman like you....*

As she examined the windows, Jean noticed a word etched into the wood beneath the mermaid: "Skye." There was something tortured in the crudely carved letters, and her heart twisted. Jean wished she'd paid more attention to the news three years earlier, but Christmas had been depressing enough that year. With her own parents dead only sixteen months, she had identified with what David and his son must be suffering. She'd avoided the media coverage and tried to tune out her classmates' morbid jokes about the mishap.

Realizing she was lingering too long in the cabin, Jean hurriedly zipped up her purple-and-black wet suit. Then she piled her clothing into her dive bag and carried it with her as she retraced her way through the boat.

David was in the salon, his wet suit peeled to his waist, and with him was the woman in the wheelchair. For the first time, Jean saw a second door from the deck to the salon, this one equipped with a ramp. Another ramp created a second companionway leading aft.

Pausing in the shadows at the foot of the galley stairs, Jean found her gaze riveted unwillingly on David's lean, muscled torso—and a long, symmetrical, crescent-shaped scar on his back. It was a deep, ugly, sinister-looking thing, and Jean had seen another like it in a diving magazine. Shark bite. Undoubtedly she would find its mate on his chest when he turned around.

Brother and sister were too deeply absorbed in debate to notice her presence, and as Jean sensed the tension in the room she became loath to announce herself. Instead, she listened, not intending to eavesdrop, as Erika said, "David, he belongs in school."

"He doesn't want to go, and I don't want him to. He's three levels above his class academically—more in some subjects—and there's nothing he can get there that he won't get here. Except a lot of grief."

Erika's voice was calmer than his. "He's lonely, David. He needs friends."

"He's growing up the way we did."

"Wrong. You and I had each other. He has no children in his life, and you won't even let him have a pet."

"He went to school, and they made fun of him. I love him, Erika. Do you think this is easy for me?"

"No, but I think it's indicative."

"Of what?"

"Of your wanting to protect everyone."

David said, "This is a bad time for this conversation, Erika." As he spoke he saw Jean hanging back in the unlit galley. Instead of answering Erika, he glared down the companionway at his new contract labor. Her pale green eyes were so wide she reminded him of a kitten ready to bolt. She'd probably heard plenty, and the possibility embarrassed him. He growled, "Are you ready?"

"Oh, David," said Erika, plainly exasperated.

"I'm ready." Jean tossed her dive bag up onto the sole of the salon and scrambled up the stairs. "I hear Baby outside making a racket."

Smiling, Erika pushed her wheelchair forward. "Baby? Is that the dolphin? She's so beautiful."

David pulled on the sleeves of his wet suit, his eyes flashing away from Jean's. Next Erika was going to want to get Chris a dolphin for Christmas.

"I'm Erika, by the way. David's sister."

Jean grinned. "Jean Young. Slime warrior."

Erika laughed, more heartily than David had heard her laugh in weeks. "I don't envy you. No, scratch that—I do." Before Jean could respond, she said, "I love watching you and that dolphin. They are the most spiritual animals."

"Sensual, anyhow," interjected David.

Erika laughed. "David says I think brine shrimp are spiritual."

"You do."

Still smiling, Erika sat back in her chair and said, "Jean, I have to confess, you're even prettier up close than you are from a distance. Frankly, for months now I've been dying to paint you. Say you'll sit for me. I'll pay you."

David cast his eyes away in disgust, then back. Clenching his teeth, he watched Jean's gaze gravitate toward the watercolor over the stairwell.

She didn't speak, and he didn't plan to. Damn Erika. He hoped she did move out, the sooner the better.

At last Jean said, "Thank you, Erika. That's very flattering." She glanced at David, then indicated the painting. "I'm sorry about your loss." Hastily she added, "I mean, I know it was a long time ago...."

"Not long enough." He looked away. "Shall we dive?"

Jean turned to take leave of Erika. "I'm glad to have met you."

Erika said, "Me, too. I meant that about painting you, Jean. And I probably pay better than the slave driver here."

David threw them a last glare of impatience, and Jean hurriedly claimed her dive bag and followed him up to the diving alcove.

CHRISTIAN WAS still sitting on the aft cushions watching the dolphin, and Jean would have smiled when she saw him, but her rush of pleasure was too short-lived. She couldn't enjoy the child's interest in the animal without thinking of what she had overheard inside. No school, no friends, no pets, no life. No wonder he was so withdrawn.

David frowned at Baby. "We're going to have company, I see."

David Blade wasn't going to win any maritime congeniality awards, Jean decided. But there were things he should know about Baby. Fins and mask in hand, she said, "I'm glad you're able to dive with me today. But I want to warn you that Baby can be possessive."

He looked at her.

Unintimidated, Jean explained, "She's careful of breathing apparatus—"

"As careful as a possessive four-hundred-pound female can be."

Straightening, Jean said, "I didn't invite Baby into my life, but I feel privileged to know her. We made friends when I was surfing, and now she finds me whenever I'm in the water. Wherever I'm in the water."

"You encouraged this relationship, then."

Jean met his eyes and was unprepared for their impact. Her voice trembled. "I've had some concerns, but yes. And now it's too late." She paused. "You're not the way I thought you'd be."

Spoken aloud, the words sounded childish, and Jean wished she'd kept them to herself. The silence that followed seemed huge.

David selected a mask from the locker. "And just how did you think I would be?"

*All right. You asked, I'll answer.* "I thought you'd appreciate the beauty of this kind of kinship with a marine mammal—with any creature of the sea. And I thought you'd have more respect for a dolphin who's been used by humans for their war games and to entertain them in public aquariums."

"And now, apparently, to accompany them on solo dives." David spared her a cool glance. "Your naiveté is truly remarkable. Believe me, I have enough respect for Baby to know her limitations. As a diving partner, she's criminally inadequate." He nodded toward Jean's regulator, the weakest part of her diving ensemble. "And I wouldn't stake my life on your equipment, either. I hope you don't dive anywhere else with that thing." Pushing open the door of the diving alcove, he walked out into the afternoon sun. "Let's get on with this, unless there's anything helpful you can tell me about your possessive friend."

There wasn't. Gritting her teeth, Jean trailed after him and joined him in the sun.

Lifting the aft railing, David stepped down to the diving platform and crouched by the water. Watching Baby peer up at him with one liquid eye, Jean said, "Hi, you pretty thing."

If David had a drop of humanity, his hand would itch to touch the animal, Jean thought. Dolphins were irresistibly tactile, seductive to touch; surely David Blade knew that. But instead, he stood up. "Let's get to work."

As he and Jean put on their fins, he smiled at Christian. "What are you going to do with yourself, Chris?"

His son shrugged, eyeing Jean distrustfully. He turned

away from both of them, effectively erasing David's smile, and concentrated on the dolphin.

Seeing David's reaction to his son's withdrawal, Jean felt sympathy for him. It wasn't easy to be responsible for another person, for needs emotional and spiritual, as well as physical. And with Chris's mother gone, the emotional part had to be tough—for father *and* son.

While she and David donned the rest of their equipment, Jean tried to remember if Christian had been on the *Skye* at the time of the accident. It was possible and could account for a lot. From the corner of her eye, she watched Chris crane his head over the railing to get a better look at Baby.

*Good. Maybe he can keep her busy.* Jean knew she'd rather not see David's reaction to Baby's more vexatious behaviors. She doubted patience was his strong suit.

Fortunately Baby did seem happily preoccupied. As Jean and David entered the water and cleared their masks, the dolphin stayed near the surface with Chris. Only when the divers had grabbed scrapers and brushes and dropped down along the hull did Baby join them, nosing against Jean for a caress. *Good girl,* thought Jean. *Be good. Please.* Knowing how Baby craved touch, she stroked her smooth, soft belly before setting to work with the dolphin swimming peacefully nearby.

The water was tepid, thanks to El Niño, the warm-water current flowing through the channel, and before long Jean was sweating in her wet suit. Never stopping her work, she glanced over at David scrubbing the slime that clung to the black hull. Beneath the close-cropped beard his jaw looked intractable, and Jean reflected that already she'd seen evidence of a temperament to match.

Why didn't he want his son in school? Why no pets? Why had the children made fun of Chris? He was a handsome child and apparently quite intelligent. None of it made sense. Certainly none of it agreed with the man Jean had always believed David Blade to be.

Jean's scraper paused momentarily on the hull. David had already made clear that he wasn't what she'd once perceived. He had called her naive. Thinking of the way he had spoken to her—chewed her out, really—about her diving habits and her equipment, Jean flushed behind her mask and resumed scraping. No wonder she hadn't been able to get a decent job. But even without the things David had criticized, that incident in Baja four summers earlier was a strike against her. And so, probably, was Baby.

Feeling her nearby, Jean glanced over to find the dolphin turning mischievous. Helpless, she watched Baby push between David and the ship, sliding her body against his. But Jean's annoyance gave way to mystification.

This wasn't Baby's usual behavior around strangers. It was more like the way she treated Jean, and Jean was stunned. Baby had accepted David.

He was oblivious to the compliment. Dumbfounded, Jean watched him continue scrubbing the hull, indifferent to Baby's show of affection. Sorry for her friend, Jean reached out to touch the dolphin's back as she swam by, but Baby had found a new curiosity and gamely rubbed David's legs, then lingered beside him blowing bubbles, a certain attempt at communication. She was ignored.

A little hurt by Baby's desertion, Jean returned her attention to the boat. She and David worked side by side, only the sounds of their regulators, the occasional shift of the dock overhead, and their brushes against the hull breaking the stillness.

Baby was not discouraged.

Still receiving no response, she made another pass along David's side and shoved him against Jean. Arms and shoulders bumped, then hips and legs. Jean almost dropped her mouthpiece and was annoyed when Baby pushed her into

David again. It was a bad situation, but safety soon became a secondary concern.

She chanced a look at David to see how he was handling Baby's antics.

He'd been watching Jean, waiting for her to meet his gaze. Now, eyes flashing behind his scuba mask, he pointed toward the surface.

Jean's exasperation took a turn toward resentment. *Darn it, Baby. You're about to cost me a job.*

WHEN THEY SURFACED, David dropped his mouthpiece and pushed back his mask. "That's possessive?"

Jean grabbed a rung of the swimming ladder. "That's not what she usually does." Pulling off her mask, she saw that Christian had deserted the deck. She and David were just inches apart in the water, and his hand was against hers on the ladder.

Conscious of the contact, Jean moved her hand so they weren't touching, and he drew back, as well.

Emerging beside them, Baby touched Jean's cheek with her tongue, as if to say, *Hi, Mom. Here I am. Did you miss me?*

It took all Jean's willpower not to respond. Hopeful because he hadn't fired her yet, she asked David, "Shall we try again?"

"In a minute."

Holding her breath, Jean saw him search her face.

"This is why you dive alone."

"Not exactly this." Jean wished she could stop the heat rushing through her. "Baby doesn't usually do this. She does...other things. I think she likes you."

Baby nudged David's arm with her flipper as though agreeing, and rubbed against his side. David tensed.

Jean caught the reaction. Uncertain what to make of it, she ventured, "Maybe if you just touched her, she'd be satisfied and let us be. She probably thinks you need some affection.'' Jean bit her lip. What imp had inspired that remark?

"I don't.'' He pulled his mask over his eyes and cleared it. ''We're wasting time. I'll touch your dolphin if you think it'll make her go away.''

Jean cleared her own mask. "Oh, she won't go away.''

Eyes dark, David took his mouthpiece. They went down without another word.

ENFOLDED IN THE COMFORT of the water, the sounds around him familiar and soothing, David watched the big dolphin approach and braced himself to touch her as she glided by.

His mind was reeling with a dozen thoughts, a dozen excellent reasons he wanted nothing to do with Baby and less still with Jean Young. Yet, here he was, giving this warm, sensual being a long fluid caress, feeling her slide against his chest in response. He traced her dorsal side with his hand, and Baby nuzzled his jaw with her beak. He thought, *Go away, Baby*.

She didn't. She hung beside him like a shadow, like another shadow in his life, and he kept feeling an urge to turn and find the silver shape in the misty green. When she swam near him with a swish of her tail, it stole his attention and broke the rhythm of his work. But he found her more than a profound annoyance. She was incalculable, and tolerating her presence jeopardized the tenets by which he lived—and by which he sheltered his son. For Chris he wanted to build a world of certainty, and befriending a dolphin was a bad risk.

But he had to put up with Jean's example or find a new bottom-cleaner, of which there was none.

He focused on the hull, but the turbid harbor water was perilous in its own right just for the memories it brought. His body tight with tension, David felt the cold seeping into his wet suit—a December cold, a cold of the mind that was impervious to the effects of El Niño. The recollections began to close on him, and he swiftly redirected his thoughts, knowing the remedy was to concentrate deliberately on something else, something clean and whole and sane.

Jean was convenient. Working peacefully and competently beside him, she seemed interested in nothing but the hull and Baby, blowing bubbles beside her. The long rope of her braid swung behind her in the water as she worked, and David made himself imagine what it would look like unbound. The best hint was in the tendrils escaping near her hairline. Soft, springy waves in the water.

He began to relax.

Idly he let his gaze continue its remote assessment, taking in her whole body. Her breasts weren't centerfold material, but they filled that purple wet suit. The legs he'd seen earlier beneath the hem of her denim skirt were all muscle and length, as far up as he'd been able to see. David realized he'd like to see farther, all the way to the top.

Unwillingly he had a vision of his hands sliding her panties down over those narrow hips. Pink cotton panties. French cut.

His own wet suit was growing uncomfortable now. As a handpicked distraction, Jean had been a poor choice and he tried to change channels, but all that came to mind was his own concern for her safety. She ought to lose her scuba certification for diving solo. She could lose her life.

Again David tried to redirect his thoughts, telling himself Jean Young was far down on his list of pressing concerns.

Christmas shopping was higher.

And Erika's moving out.

The realization that she was leaving came over him again as it had a dozen times in the past twenty-four hours. What was he going to do?

The question was a welcome diversion. He took refuge in thoughts of keeping order in the wake of his sister's desertion, and his only other thought of Jean was a swift calculation of how fast they could finish the keel so he could get her and that dolphin out of his way.

## CHAPTER THREE

THE SUN WAS TOUCHING the horizon later that hour as Jean dragged herself up the ladder and onto the platform. As David followed, she removed her mask and tank and reached over the stern to pet Baby.

Unzipping his wet suit, David said, "I'm glad Christian isn't hanging around to see your friend."

Squeezing water from her braid, Jean looked up at him.

David said, "Since he's gone, this is as good a time as any to tell you I'll discourage an attachment between him and that creature any way I have to. Dolphins who seek the company of humans have one thing in common—short lives." With a directness Jean was learning to expect from him, he added, "You seem to know something about my wife's death, so I'm sure you're aware of what Chris has already been through. I'd appreciate your cooperation in not adding more tragedy to his life."

Recalling the conversation she'd interrupted in the salon, Jean suspected the present tragedy in Christian Blade's life was an overprotective parent. She asked, "Is that why you took away the wreath? So he wouldn't play with Baby?"

David couldn't have looked more affronted if she'd asked the balance in his checking account. He said, "I did not *take away* the wreath. Chris gave it to Baby and lost it. However, it has been returned, with the hope it will soon reach its natural end. Ephemeral as the season."

*And we're a lover of Christmas, are we?* thought Jean. Glad to know he wasn't a man who went around sticking pins in inflatable toys, she watched the water drip from David's beard and the dark hair on his chest. As her eyes faltered to his scar, he grabbed a beach towel, wrapped it around his shoulders and folded his arms across his chest.

It was all Jean could do to mask her interest. Though disfiguring, the scar made him more intriguing, more a warrior. More a pirate. She asked, "How did that happen?"

"The usual way. Recklessness and stupidity." Setting his tank and fins on the deck, he tossed over his shoulder, "Keep track of your share of the keel, and I'll see you back here in the morning. You can leave your gear in the alcove."

Jean decided she was going to have to get used to abrupt leave-takings. "What time in the morning?"

"Nine." As though reading her mind, he murmured with the most forced courtesy Jean had ever heard, "I have dinner plans, so I hope you'll excuse me." From the deck, he dropped the aft railing into place and pointed to it. "Don't forget this. There's a child on board."

After he had taken his tank and disappeared into the alcove, Jean spent a few minutes more at the water's edge with Baby, murmuring inanities to the dolphin in a hushed voice. "Doesn't he have a nice dockside manner? Yes, from now on we charge *three* dollars a foot to people with personality disorders. Also to pirates. What do you think, Baby, is that Jolly Roger for real?"

Baby reared up in the water, clicking agreeably.

Jean grew thoughtful. Despite her jesting, she knew David's behavior must be the result of the loss he'd suffered three years ago. Running over his wife in an eighty-foot ship was bound to make anybody cranky.

Remembering, Jean winced. The books he had written, books that had affected her deeply, showed a man of sensitivity and depth. It was hard to believe that one incident, however horrifying and tragic, could completely change a person. Somewhere under that barbwire exterior was the real David Blade.

Maybe, thought Jean. And maybe I'm naive, like he said.

In any event, she couldn't help wondering about the nature of his dinner plans. There had to be a woman on the agenda. For a moment she entertained a vision of David Blade scowling through a dinner interspersed with caustic remarks. It was difficult to imagine him as a charming dinner companion. A rock would be more engaging—and more sensitive.

*But what if he's not like that with everyone?* she wondered. Suppose there was a woman with whom he relaxed—someone who understood. Someone who rubbed his shoulders and massaged his scalp and listened to his troubles.

It seemed distinctly possible. And a little disheartening.

Jean was unaware of any movement behind her, so she jumped when a slender arm reached out beside her, and a small hand touched Baby. Christian had lifted the guardrail and joined her on the diving platform.

As Jean watched him, she recalled his father's clearly expressed wishes concerning Christian and Baby. If David should find his son befriending the dolphin, he might fire her. And Jean wasn't sure she'd blame him. David might be overprotective, but that was better than the reverse. Experience had taught her that. Besides, he must know his own son's vulnerabilities.

Yet Jean couldn't bring herself to tear the solemn little boy from his new pastime. And Chris had remembered to put on a life vest, which meant either he was extremely well trained or one of the other two adults on the ship had sanctioned this adventure. If so, it wasn't David.

Jean asked him, "Have you touched a dolphin before?"

Christian shook his head almost imperceptibly.

"Watch out for her blowhole," Jean cautioned. "It's like

a nostril, so she won't like to be poked there. She likes her tummy rubbed.''

Christian experimented with this technique and was rewarded with more attention from Baby, who turned in the water to look at him.

Nervous that David would reappear, Jean suggested, "I'd better get dressed. We should let Baby go home." Wherever Baby's home was, which Jean wasn't sure.

Standing, she searched for a question that would draw even a single word from the child. He didn't go to school, so that was a bad subject. Same with pets and friends. As Chris gave Baby's head a last pat and climbed up on deck, Jean ventured, "How old are you?"

Six fingers. Erika called his name from below deck, and he turned apologetically and retreated to the cabin.

A nice little boy, she thought. But very quiet.

She undressed in the diving alcove, pulling her clothes on over her swimsuit. David didn't reappear, so she hung her wet suit on a hook in the alcove, stashed her equipment in a locker and departed without saying goodbye.

She left the marina at a slower pace than usual. For four years she'd been on the run to classes or the library or the gym. Tonight she had nowhere to go but home and nothing on her hands but time—and a university degree.

Elation was absent. Completing her studies felt like weight off her shoulders and little more. Even the K. L. Sayles Award had seemed like a minor accomplishment, jumbled in with the other awards given at the ceremony that morning, far less meaningful than her belt rank advancements in tae kwon do, for instance. And Jean was almost past hoping the award would help her secure the kind of work she wanted. She was still scrubbing keels, and every interview she'd wangled for better work had turned out the same. A very, very brief chat, followed by the offer of a lab position in a coastal facility, or of administrative work, or sometimes no offer at all. Never fieldwork.

Though she had graduated with highest honors, she knew she wouldn't attend the commencement ceremonies later in the year. Cecily, if she was in the country, might come to see her graduate in a cap and gown, but the fact that her parents, particularly her father, wouldn't be there made the prospect too painful. She'd rather skip it.

Wandering past the docks and the breakwater, she followed the beach west. One mile down was the property she and her sister had inherited when their parents passed away. The sun had nearly dipped out of sight as Jean reached the stairs that led up to the rambling adobe where she had lived since childhood.

For a moment she paused on the beach, absorbing the familiar smell of tar, the cool sand beneath her bare feet, and the waves rushing to the shore under the orange-and-lavender sky. The swell was good, and several figures in wet suits floated on boards beyond the breakers. Jean waved to them, and someone waved back. Watching one surfer wipe out in a spray of foam, she turned to climb the sandy, tar-spotted stairs to the house on the cliff.

She checked the mail first. A notification from a marine institute in Florida that the job she'd applied for had gone to someone else. And a brief letter, *par avion,* from Cecily in Paris, dashed off in her graceful, feminine hand:

Dear Jean,
Shooting will keep me busy till 23 Dec., I'm afraid. Jean-Claude has asked me to St. Moritz for Christmas (he has the most precious *enfants;* they call me Tante Cecily in the dearest voices), and it makes more sense than trying to come home. Anyhow, where is home? I'm becoming more European daily. I think I was meant to be French.

I've been taking French cooking evenings, creating the most incredible dishes. Monsieur Renault thinks women should not be chefs, but I am changing his

mind. *Bon appétit!* Can't wait to cook for you, but it
may be as late as February. I do miss you. I know this
is bad news, but I hope the holidays have special
things in store for you, *ma chère soeur*. Look for a
huge package in the post.

Love,
Cecily

Jean held off the tears suddenly steaming behind her
eyes. She'd half expected news of this sort, and last year
had been worse, when the Caribbean country where Cecily
had been modeling someone-or-other's summer line had
become politically unstable overnight. Nonetheless, as she
put down Cecily's letter Jean spontaneously leveled a halfhearted kick at some boxes stacked near the kitchen
counter—the artificial tree and Christmas ornaments she'd
brought out of the garage that morning for the first time
since her parents' death. She'd planned to decorate that
night.

Her kick toppled the box on top, and she grabbed it,
rescuing what was precious—Christmas past. Christmases
when people came home.

Feeling a sudden kinship with David Blade in his sen-
timents about the season, Jean hurried to her room and
changed into shorts and T-shirt, then returned to the living
room she had long since adapted to her own needs. All
furniture was pushed to the walls, clearing the hardwood
floor. In her mother's lifetime, practicing martial arts in the
living room would have been unthinkable; winter or summer, Jean and her father were banished to the patio to spar.
Now, seeing her mother's enormous Christmas cactus
blooming near the sliding glass doors, like an embodiment
of the woman who had prized it, Jean felt a familiar guilt
at violating the Sanctuary, as her father had called it.

But tae kwon do was as sacred to her as the room had
been to her mother.

She knelt in the center of the floor, facing the long orange line of the sun's reflection setting on the sea, and sat back on her heels to meditate. But peace did not come. Only hurt and emptiness and anger at her younger sister.

After a workout that left her calmer but lonelier than before, she ate the last two slices of a frozen pizza for dinner, then curled up on the living room couch with a pirate romance she'd bought at the campus bookstore—a graduation present to herself. But she didn't crack the cover. Instead, she stood up and went to the bookcase across the room and selected a book about whales by David Blade. It made sense to bone up—in case he considered her for more serious work than slime removal.

She opened it to a section in the middle on gray whales, but time after time, her eyes strayed from the page. Listening to the waves hitting the beach, she stared at the black-and-white photo on the back of the book jacket. In this picture David had no beard, instead sporting a gorgeous, incredibly rugged chin and jaw that, for the sake of her sensibilities, Jean was glad he disguised. She turned the book faceup. David Blade was a bad choice for an unrequited passion.

Still, her encounter with his family had left her curious. A sister in a wheelchair, a son whose classmates had made fun of him for reasons unknown. And what had Erika said about David? *You want to protect everyone.* Jean could empathize with that. After her parents' death, her own protective instincts had come out, focused on Cecily.

But Ceci, seventeen at the time and already making waves on the international modeling scene, did not appreciate being protected. And the last thing Jean had ever wanted was to hold back her sister. On the contrary. She wanted Cecily to have every opportunity she would have had if their parents were still alive—maybe more. And Cecily had proven time and again that she could take care of herself.

Jean turned her thoughts back to the Blades.

Did David protect Erika, as well as Chris? With mixed emotions, Jean recalled Erika's offer to paint her, and David's displeasure, and her mind's eye conjured up the portrait of Skye. The watercolor was well executed, the style familiar. It seemed possible Erika was a professional and Jean had seen other pieces of her work without knowing who she was.

What had happened to Erika that she couldn't walk? Illness? Accident? Something stirred in her memory, and she reopened the whale book, leafing through the pages until she found what she was looking for.

A photo of a suntanned brunette standing on the fly bridge of the *Skye*, pointing at a humpback whale spouting in the distance. The tails of the work shirt she wore over her swimsuit were whipping away from her, blown by the breeze, revealing a tall, strong body. The caption did not identify the woman, but Jean knew her. It was Erika Blade.

Swiftly she paged to the front of the book to check the copyright date. Only four years earlier.

Jean turned back to the photo, noted Erika's muscular legs, her long hair, her laughing expression. Remembering the woman she had met that day, still spirited and beautiful but now confined to a wheelchair, she wondered again, *What happened?*

"AH, FREE AT LAST."

David, completely in agreement, loosened the bow tie at his throat, then removed it, folded it and stuffed it into an outside pocket of his tuxedo jacket. He'd needed to attend the dinner, but the combination of University Center food and black-tie attire was always hard to stomach. Unfastening the top button of his shirt, he paused beside the information desk to glance at a student newspaper abandoned there.

The professor who had left the banquet hall beside him paused, as well. "Any trips planned this winter?"

David picked up the paper. "Baja. Whales." He glanced at the row of four student photographs above the masthead, started to flip the paper to see the lower half of the page, then stopped.

It was her, in a yearbook photo that made her look even younger than usual. *Jean Young. K. L. Sayles Award for outstanding work in marine biology. B.S. Marine Biology. Summa cum laude.*

For a moment he was stunned. She had said her last final was today. Remembering their meeting outside the marina that afternoon—and Jean, obviously fresh from her exam—he thought, *I didn't even ask how it went.*

David glanced at the professor. The man was looking toward the exit but going nowhere, undoubtedly waiting to see if they would walk to the parking lot together. *The Haverford Trust,* David thought. Everyone wanted a grant, and his was always the deciding word. The responsibility was huge, but so were the benefits to the Blade Institute. Skye's will had made those benefits possible, though no easier for him to accept. Once, the institute had stood on its own.

Impulsively he turned to the professor and pointed at Jean's picture. "Do you know her?"

Absently unclipping his tie, the other man nodded. "I recommended her for that award."

David replied with only an expression of vague surprise.

The professor seemed to take his measure. "If this is professional interest, I would recommend her absolutely."

David regarded him coolly, with a direct gaze that tended to freeze speculation in its tracks. "She's doing some work for me," he said. "She's a bottom-cleaner."

"I know." The professor nodded with a slight smile of amusement—and respect for Jean. "Though I didn't know she was working for you."

He paused, reflective, and David sensed he was debating further revelations. What? he wondered. *I would recommend her absolutely* had sounded like unqualified approval.

At last the professor said, "She's a neighbor of mine. Her parents were friends of my wife and myself."

"Were."

"Killed in a car accident. It's just her and her sister now, though her sister spends a lot of time abroad. She's made it big in modeling."

David said nothing, but his conscience was talking plenty, and so was his heart. Both shouted an uncomfortable message—that somewhere along the line he had stopped behaving like the man he wanted to be. His mind said he'd had reasons, but David could no longer accept that excuse. As he listened to the warring parts of himself, all he could think was that today Jean had finished earning her degree and won an academic award, and he had treated her like something they'd scraped off the keel.

THE WATER WAS SO DEEP she couldn't see the top, but Jean wasn't afraid. Her partner's brown eyes watching her from behind his scuba mask made her feel as though she was in the grip of nitrogen narcosis. She wouldn't leave for anything.

Except the toll of the doorbell. It broke into her dreams, and Jean blinked up at the green shade of the reading lamp glowing over the back of the couch. The bell rang again.

She sat up and peered at the digital clock on the VCR. It was 10 p.m.

Groggy, she stood and went to the door, squinted through the peephole and saw a man in a delivery jacket. He held a bouquet.

For Cecily, thought Jean. Someone doesn't know she's out of the country.

She briefly considered not answering—after all, Ceci would never see the flowers. Then, thinking she could at least drop her sister the card, she shrugged and opened the door. The van parked at the curb bore the name of a Montecito florist.

"Jean Young?"

She nodded, still only half-alert.

He smiled and handed her the large vase. It was overflowing with orchids, two or three dozen at a glance, and weighed a ton. She needed both arms. Cecily's beaux were never cheap.

Absently she said, "Thank you," and shut the door with her foot.

She carried the vase into the kitchen, examining it as she walked. The orchids were spilling over the edges of a blued-copper urn in the shape of two dolphins. The vase was exquisite and had to be worth a pretty penny. Possibly a big-name designer was behind the gesture. It had happened before.

As she admired the abundance of color and species in the arrangement and the silver-and-gold holiday bows cascading down the front, her eyes fell on the envelope with the name *Jean* scrawled on the front.

The words of the man who had delivered the bouquet echoed in her mind. *Jean Young?*

Jean, not Cecily.

Her heart pounded as she set the vase on the table. She didn't have to open the envelope. In her heart she knew.

A copper vase. Orchids delivered at 10 p.m., when florists were closed.

She could think of only one man with the wealth to arrange it. Only one man.

Unconscious of doing so, she clasped the envelope briefly to her thundering heart before slipping the card from within. No ordinary floral card, this pictured a watercolor of a girl beachcombing. It was an Erika Blade print. Jean sank into a chair at the table before opening it.

Masculine script, too natural for any florist-written card:

"Congratulations on your academic achievements. David."

FOR DAVID the dawn was bound by ritual. Coffee, brief reflection and an hour of ancient fighting drills steeped in two thousand years of Eastern tradition. When he was done, he ran. Running was a good remedy for the aftermath of bad impulses—like his of the previous night.

But he hadn't counted on running into Jean.

She was standing in the packed sand at the water's edge, peeling off a black wet suit that had seen heavy wear, and her surfboard lay on the beach beside her. Seeing her, David drew to a halt, then wondered if he should have kept running. Against the morning fog and the dark gray-green channel, she seemed as exotic as the orchids he wished he hadn't sent.

Jean looked stunned to see him, so he spoke first, neither warmly nor coldly. "You're an early riser."

Her hair was loose, hanging halfway down her back and front like spiraling tangles of kelp, and her eyes reminded him of the sea. Yesterday, the Mediterranean; today, the channel. Between her hair and her eyes and the fact that she stood before him in only a black swimsuit, David found it impossible to see her as anything but a pretty woman in very little clothing. She was...well arranged.

Hesitantly she said, "Thank you for the flowers. They're beautiful, and so is the vase."

"You're welcome."

She said, "It's been years since I've gotten flowers."

"It's been a long time since I've given any."

They both fell silent, and David was about to excuse himself to continue his run when she said, "I live up there." She nodded at the stairs to the cliff top.

David thought about the address he'd hunted in the phone book the night before. He said, "I know."

Jean blushed, something he noticed she did often.

She said, "It's the house I grew up in. My sister and I own it. Our parents died a few years ago...."

David straightened. She wasn't telling him anything he didn't know, but he was unexpectedly touched that she was telling him. He said, "I'm sorry." A moment passed during which they heard only the waves. At last he said, "Well, you live on my favorite beach."

"Mine, too."

Shivering, Jean dropped her wet suit on top of her surfboard and wrapped her beach towel around herself. Her swimsuit would have said function-not-fashion on another woman, but Jean had assets the cold and wet only more sharply defined. Trying to secure the towel around her body—a good idea, he thought—she said, "How was your date?"

"My date?"

"Dinner. You had to go to dinner. I assumed it was a date."

Lingering when he'd intended to leave, David asked, "Why do women always think it's a date when you have a dinner engagement?"

Jean looked startled—even alarmed. "Not because they're hoping to go on one with you, if that's what you're thinking."

David was surprised to feel the corners of his mouth twitching. "Do you always say what you think?"

"This time I didn't think what I said. I'm sure women do want to date you." She threw him a wary glance. "I'm sharper after coffee. Have you had breakfast?"

David couldn't remember the last time he'd had an urge to tease a woman other than his sister. "Are you asking me on a date?"

Her apprehension turned to dismay. "No. And I wasn't asking you to breakfast. We're going to start on your boat in an hour, and I was just wondering if you'd eaten. You look...hungry," she finished lamely, pulling her eyes away from his body.

Suddenly David found it hard to believe she didn't want to go out with him. Surprising himself for the second or third time that morning, he said, "I am hungry."

An expression of panic crossed her face. She was deliciously easy to tease, much better than Erika. David said nothing, waiting to see what would happen next.

Meeting his eyes in a no-nonsense fashion that seemed completely at odds with the quivering pulse at the base of her throat, she said, "Do you think if you stand there expectantly I'll invite you for breakfast?"

"Would it help if I fainted?"

Jean paled slightly. "I think we've already established that you don't have to grovel for dates."

"And that this isn't one," he added.

"Of course it isn't. I haven't invited you!" She clamped her lips shut, as though determined not to be roped in.

David said, "I think I should taste your cooking. I need a galley slave for my next expedition."

At once he wished he hadn't said it. Jake Doherty had told him Jean's career was her Achilles' heel. David wondered what she'd actually do for it. Granted, there were some things he wouldn't ask, however seductive the prospect, but if she could cook... Or care for a child?

He rejected the idea. Meals were one thing, Chris was another. It was a bracing thought. What was he doing here, anyway? Flirting with the bottom-cleaner, a woman he wanted nothing to do with, that was what. He hadn't had this kind of conversation in years, hadn't wanted to. Possibly hadn't been able to.

As Jean stood biting her lip, David glanced at his watch and started to excuse himself.

Jean blurted out, "What do you like?"

His heart played tug-of-war with his mind. He echoed, "What do I like?"

"For breakfast."

He could leave now. This was his chance. He *had* been joking about tasting her cooking.

But he said, "Oh, anything. Are you sure this isn't an imposition?"

Rolling her eyes good-naturedly, she turned away.

While he waited, stretching in the cool, foggy air, she took her wet suit to the water and rinsed it in the breakers, soaking her towel in the process. The way it clung to her legs and rear end was sexier than if she'd been wearing nothing. Watching her clutch her wet things as she stooped to pick up her surfboard, David decided they'd both be better off once she was dressed.

When she rejoined David, he took her surfboard without asking and accidentally dislodged her towel. It fell off, and she pulled it clumsily back around her body, spreading sand all over herself. The sand was much paler than the bare skin of her legs. Unexpectedly her eyes lifted and met his. Her lips were parted, her nipples erect, and David understood the vulnerability in her eyes. She knew what she did to him and that he knew he did the same to her.

For David, the knowledge was life-affirming. Like flirtation, it hadn't happened in a long time and was vaguely painful, analogous to pushing muscles that had grown slack from disuse.

She was only inches away, and he said softly, "This feels dangerous."

Hugging the towel around her shoulders and breasts, leaving her legs exposed, Jean turned and walked in the direction of the stairs. Her voice shook only slightly as she said, "A perceptive remark from a man who's never tasted my cooking."

The comment distracted him. She had deliberately misunderstood him, and David wondered why. Perhaps the invitation he'd cajoled *was* an imposition.

Or maybe she had a boyfriend.

Falling into step beside her, he offered, "I could make breakfast."

Jean paused, then started toward the stairs—fast. "And miss the opportunity to taste my cooking? Don't think of it." Stopping at the foot of the steps, she pointed out, "I invited you, after all. I'll scare something up. You just sit and relax." She lifted her chin slightly. "I've cooked before."

"How reassuring." David smiled again. "Shall I make out my will?"

Jean laughed, but inside she suddenly felt a little hollow. She couldn't hear David mention death and money without thinking of Skye Haverford Blade.

# CHAPTER FOUR

WHAT WAS SHE GOING to feed him? A man like that could probably really put it away. He was all muscle, but suddenly even his lean build made Jean think of a ravenous lion. And she could barely cook! Was he really looking for a galley slave? Or something else?

*This feels dangerous.* Her heart still hadn't settled from that comment—or from anything else that had happened on the beach. He'd been flirting with her. Unmistakably. Somehow, in the past twenty-four hours, she had won David's acceptance. Had he learned about the K. L. Sayles Award? That could explain the flowers. That and the way they'd been eating each other up with their eyes moments earlier. As she opened the patio door and led him into the living room, Jean felt a stirring of excitement. Months of silent glances on the boardwalk and across the harbor were actually leading to something.

*To making a fool of myself,* she thought. As far as she knew, the Pizza Palace didn't deliver at eight in the morning, and a large, thick-crust Vegetarian Dream probably wasn't David's idea of breakfast.

But at least the house was neat. Receiving his flowers had woken her from her lethargy, and she'd opened the boxes of Christmas ornaments. Because setting up an eight-foot tree had seemed like overkill for a woman living alone, she'd brought inside her mother's only surviving bonsai, a miniature olive tree. Jean had hung some of the smaller, lighter ornaments from the limbs and set the tree on the coffee table, then taken the rest of the boxes outside. Now, she was glad she'd made at least that concession to the season. It was good to see some of her family's ornaments again. Together the bonsai and the flowering Christmas cactus made the house more cheerful.

So did the presence of another human being.

Leaving David in the living room, Jean went to her bedroom to change into a sweatshirt and shorts. When she returned, he was sitting on the edge of the couch staring at the bonsai Christmas tree. Jean was relieved; perhaps he wouldn't wonder why his book was lying on the table beside the pot—next to her pirate romance with its no-holds-barred cover.

David said, "You must be good with these. This tree looks old."

"It's older than me," said Jean, "but only by luck and the care my mother gave it. After she died, it took me less than a month to kill a Japanese boxwood and a scrub oak. And that little monster—" she indicated the olive tree "—has had every kind of professional help but psychotherapy."

David laughed. Their eyes met for a moment, and Jean thought of the two plants in the room, the ancient bonsai and the gargantuan cactus, and all they represented. Little of it was good.

*Take care of children? Jean, I wouldn't trust you with my houseplants for the summer. You're never home for more than a few minutes at a time—*

The memory of her mother's words stopped abruptly as she realized David's attention had turned to the books on the table. She felt compelled to explain why his was there. Stepping around the bar to the kitchen, she said, "I was reading up." *Reading up and gazing at your face on the cover.* "What would you like to drink?"

"Whatever you have." Bypassing his own book, he picked up her pirate romance.

Watching over the bar, Jean wished she'd had the presence of mind to stuff that particular volume under a cushion.

David perused the back cover. "Reading up on what?"

"Mating habits." *Bad, Jean,* she thought. *Any old lie would have done.* She opened the refrigerator door, prepared for the worst. There were eggs, a few vegetables and a pitcher of water.

"Mating habits?" Setting down the romance, David trailed after her into the kitchen. The flowers were still on the table, and he glanced at them disinterestedly.

Jean slammed the refrigerator door, not wanting him to see what wasn't inside. "Mating habits of gray whales. The book is about whales. You know that. You wrote it." *An omelet,* she thought. Omelets were made from eggs.

She paged through three cookbooks while he wandered around the kitchen, examining prints on the walls and photos of her and Cecily, most of which had hung in the same places when her parents were alive. David paused beside one framed picture. "'Mean Jean and Ceci-la-belle,'" he read.

Jean swallowed. "My dad called me that. It was affectionate." The nickname had been part and parcel of the bonds between them—diving, surfing, tae kwon do. Still, Mean Jean struck a deep and sometimes stinging contrast to Ceci-la-belle, particularly when Jean remembered the different inflections her mother had put on the two names. She'd never needed to spell it out. Cecily was Ceci the sought-after, universally desired for her womanly qualities, while Mean Jean was the self-absorbed, pleasure-seeking tomboy. It was a perception Jean was still trying to live down.

As she leafed through the cookbook, she felt David's silence behind her and imagined he was looking at Cecily's modeling shots.

"You're a black belt." He sounded shocked, and Jean

glanced over to see him staring at a five-by-seven her father had taken of her executing a flying side kick. "In?"

"Tae kwon do. Popularly known as Korean karate."

David stared at the photo for a moment more, his expression neutral. Then, unexpectedly, he turned and gave her a very slight, circumspect bow.

Eyes on his, Jean returned it reflexively, then looked away, discomposed. It wasn't a gesture she was used to seeing from anyone but other tae kwon doists. Why had David done it?

Embarrassed, she said, "We only do that in the gym." But when her father was alive, the two of them had followed the same formal courtesies whenever they practiced together at home. She told David, "I've gotten away from it lately."

"Why?"

"School, mainly. And Baby." She could imagine what David thought of that and wished she'd kept it to herself. He'd probably have more empathy with her strongest reason—avoiding memories of her father.

But he said nothing.

Jean found an omelet recipe, retrieved the vegetables from the hydrator and set to work at the cutting board with the cookbook open in front of her.

Behind her, David asked, "What are you attempting?"

"An omelet. Vegetarian." She looked at him.

"Sounds wonderful."

He was brave, Jean decided. It was bad news when someone needed a cookbook to make an omelet. Sloppily she broke an egg over a cast-iron skillet. "So who watches Chris while you run?" She fished an eggshell from the pan.

"Erika. I should probably give them a call, now that you mention it."

"Go ahead." Jean nodded to the phone.

David went to the wall phone, lifted the receiver and

punched in a number. "Hi. It's me. I stopped for break-fast."

Jean noticed he didn't say where. She heard the soft tones of Erika's voice at the other end.

David said, "That's bad. Can you manage for an hour?"

Erika's reassurance was audible.

"Good. And yes, I'll buy more Christmas bulbs." A pause was filled with more words from Erika. "Not the kind that blink. Not the kind that make the others blink. Not too many red ones. I understand."

Jean looked up as he replaced the receiver.

"They turned off the dock power this morning to repair a line. Now our generator's down." In a tone of resignation, he added, "Erika likes to do the whole Christmas thing. With lots of lights."

It sounded unsafe. But then so was this meal. And David would be home soon to help with the lights, if he didn't die from her cooking.

She picked up another egg to break it.

"Jean."

She turned to find him inches away, so close she could see his skin through a tiny, worn hole in the arm of his T-shirt. He smelled like the ocean and very male. Jean thought it nearly unnatural for a man to smell that good in the morning—and after a run.

Oblivious to the overwork he was causing her circulatory system, he stepped past her to the sink and turned on the water to wash his hands. He grimaced. "I can't watch this any longer. Go sit down."

Jean slowly met his eyes.

"I mean it. Sit down. I'll cook."

Jean wasn't sure whether she should be mortified or overjoyed, but one thing was clear—she wasn't in the running for galley slave. Retreating to the counter, she sat down on a bar stool. Unhappily she thought of her mother forever saying, *The way to a man's heart is through his stomach.* To Jean, it had always sounded like an arduous way to win a man's love. But as David diced an onion in record time, she asked, "Can I do anything to help?"

"Talk to me. Did Baby join you surfing today, or were you out there alone?"

*Here we go,* thought Jean. That sounded like the David Blade who had hired her to scrub his ship. She told him, "Baby was with me this morning, but there were people, too, if that's what you're getting at. I know lots of surfers, and we look out for each other."

"Isn't there anyone you can dive with?"

*You.* Especially since Baby had actually allowed them to work the previous day.... "Baby's made nothing but enemies among my diving buddies, I'm afraid. She swims into them, knocks brushes out of their hands, pins them against whatever keel we're cleaning. And, of course, lately she likes to steal Christmas trimmings." Jean paused and decided to chance it. One thing she could depend on from David was candor. Trying to keep her tone even, she said, "I've sometimes wondered if Baby is why I can't get decent diving jobs. You must have been amused to see me leap at the idea of being your galley slave."

Was that guilt in his expression? He said nothing.

Jean told him, "The fact is, I'd settle for nearly any kind of work on an expedition. I'm happy to start at the bottom—no pun intended—but I can't even get out of the harbor. I'm a deep-water diver, and I've been a lab assistant at school, but I can't get even an internship on a research vessel. And none of the salvage companies will take me. I've applied to places on both coasts, but nobody seems to think I'm fit for more than scrubbing boats in the harbor."

David shook his head. "Wrong."

"Then what is it?" Her mind stirred uneasily. Did he know? The Baja story had certainly made the rounds at the university, but that was years earlier. And she'd never heard it mentioned on the waterfront, not even by Jake Doherty, who knew everyone's business better than his own.

David set a green pepper on the cutting board and sliced it expertly. "No, I'm sure they just think you're a little too young—"

Choking down her relief, Jean pointed out, "I'm twenty-three."

"—and a lot too pretty," he finished, "to be at sea for months on a ship full of men." His eyes drifted to hers. "Twenty-three?"

He had called her pretty. Heart hammering, she asked, "How old are you?"

"Thirty-one. Look, to address your problem, I know how I'd feel if I got an application from a twenty-three-year-old woman straight out of school."

Jean remarked, "We make great slime warriors."

David glanced at her, then back to the stove. After a moment he took a breath and said, "I'll make you a deal."

Jean looked at him.

"Ever handled a camera in the water?"

"Some." Her heart started pounding again—hard.

"What else can you do?" He adjusted the heat under the skillet. "Typing? Computers?"

Jean nodded without expression. Office work would take her away from Baby. But if the job was with the Blade Institute, wouldn't it be worth it?

"How would you like to work on my ship?"

Gripping the edge of her stool, she attempted poise. "Very much."

He smiled. "There's a catch. A few catches."

Jean wondered if the catches would make a lifetime of slime removal look attractive.

"I don't need a full-time diver, but I could use a secretary—and someone to help look after my son occasionally. Erika's going into rehab this Christmas, and she doesn't plan to return to the *Skye*."

Jean was surprised by the news. The transition had to be harder than he was making it sound. As far as she knew, his sister had lived with him since his wife's death.

David said, "I'm booked on a trip to Baja over Christmas, a whale project in Scammon's Bay. We're trying to observe mating, actually. The trip's been in the works for almost a year, but I wouldn't dream of being apart from Chris over the holidays. Needless to say, I can't look after him while I'm working." He reached for the pepper shaker. "Do you have plans?"

Jean's thoughts spun. David Blade wanted her to look after his son? Over Christmas? Light shone ahead onto the bleak holiday she'd been anticipating. Instead of spending Christmas alone in Santa Barbara with only memories of her family for company, she would be in Baja with David Blade.

And his son. Jean drew a long, shallow breath.

She couldn't let this offer slip by! She'd studied cetaceans for four years but had never been to Scammon's Bay to see the birthing and mating place of the gray whales. She couldn't imagine a finer way to spend Christmas.

But looking after his son—

*Take care of children? Jean, I wouldn't trust you with my houseplants....*

David said, "I know it's a family time. I suppose, if you like, your sister could come. There's room, and then you'd be together."

Jean said, "She's out of the country."

"For Christmas?" He seemed surprised, but Jean's thoughts were elsewhere—on the offer he'd made. And the fact that she couldn't lie to him about her past.

But on the other hand, if he didn't ask, she wouldn't *have* to tell him about Baja. Hadn't her own career counselor at school cautioned her, *If I were you, I just wouldn't mention any of that, Jean. It's unrelated.*

To marine biology, yes, thought Jean. But not to caring

for Christian Blade. And she doubted David would care that what had happened in Baja wasn't her fault.

She noticed he was starting to look irritated that she hadn't leapt at his offer. And Jean saw it slipping away, the *Skye* sailing without her.

Her acceptance escaped her lips in an unexpectedly throaty question. "Sure I'm not too young?"

David made a sound that might have been a laugh. Or he might have been choking. "No."

Too pretty? wondered Jean. Apparently she wasn't. He was hiring her.

And she was letting him.

*Courtesy, integrity, perseverance, self-control, indomitable spirit.* The tenets of tae kwon do, drilled into her since she was a child, came to her now. *Courtesy. Integrity...*

David left the stove and came to her, meeting her eyes.

"Here's the bargain, Jean. If you work for me, you must promise you will never under any circumstances dive alone. Ever. And Baby doesn't count."

Jean held his gaze, telling herself discretion was not deceit. In this case it was self-preservation. She told David, "That's fine. I don't like to dive alone."

"I'll be with you." He returned to the stove and fell silent, watching the skillet. Finally he said, "There's something else I don't know if you've picked up on. Sometimes people don't." He paused as though the next words were hard for him. "Chris doesn't talk."

Jean listened to the sputtering of the frying pan. *Doesn't talk?*

"Not since his mother died."

In a flash, Jean glimpsed the sore, still open and unhealed, of Skye Haverford Blade's death.

"He knows sign language, but he doesn't use it much. He's just damned...quiet."

The revelation shook Jean. She wanted the job, but knew she shouldn't take it. The incident in Baja aside, she was lousy with children. She told David, "You should find someone else."

David lifted his eyebrows and stirred the onions in the skillet. "Why is that?"

Jean tried to center herself. If she let this chance escape, she might never have another. At last she said, "I mean there are people trained to be nannies, and you could certainly afford to hire one." Her face felt hot as she said this. "I like kids and I like your son, but I'm not sure I'm cut out to be a nanny." She *knew* she wasn't. She told David, "Even my mom said I'd probably never be a very good mother."

David's expression was well masked. After a moment he remarked dryly, "No one's asked you to be a mother."

Jean's face burned. "That isn't what I meant."

"Or a nanny," David added. "As it stands, this is a temporary arrangement. After the Baja trip, we'll see. If you want the job."

"I want the job."

Switching off the burner, David stepped back and leaned against the counter. After reflecting for a moment he looked at her. "I'll take you provisionally, but I'd like references. Five. At least one academic, two employers, no relatives."

*Five?* It seemed extreme for a temporary job, but she was prepared for extremes. There were five references on her résumé, and she would give them to David immediately after breakfast. *He's giving me a chance,* she thought in astonishment. *He's actually giving me a chance.*

Silently she vowed he wouldn't be sorry he had.

AFTER BREAKFAST, as they walked back along the beach toward the *Skye,* she said, "Perhaps it would be best if you tell me exactly what you expect of me with Christian. I understand he doesn't go to school." She said the last cautiously, remembering the subject was touchy.

"No," David answered. "And you're not responsible for

his schooling. As for what I expect—I don't expect you to hover over him. There are rules on the *Skye,* and he knows them. He shouldn't be on the diving platform without a life vest and an adult present. The same goes for the foredeck while we're under way."

Jean guessed the reason for that. Nonetheless, the ship had a bow rail, and it was a mystery to her how Skye Haverford could have managed to fall off. No wonder the police had doubted David's story. But Jean never had.

David said, "Just be yourself with Chris. Keep him company. Play with him a few hours a day, and let him have some time alone."

"Sounds like a nanny." When David looked at her sharply, Jean said, "David, your son is important, and a ship can be a hazardous place for a child, as you pointed out yesterday. I think we need clear communication on this. When is he my responsibility, and when is he yours?"

The question both jarred and impressed him. He paused on the beach and found her eyes directly on his, clear and focused with a sobriety he admired.

"As I said before, looking after him is only part of your job," David answered. "I'll tell you whenever he becomes your responsibility. Otherwise he's mine." Noting the tension in her shoulders and wondering again at her mother's influence on her self-confidence, he added, "The words will be, 'Jean, watch Chris.' Clear enough?"

She had wrapped her arms around herself as though she was cold—even though the sun had come out. She told him, "Perfectly."

THOUGH ELECTRICITY from the dock hookup was restored by the time they returned to the *Skye,* the generator needed to be repaired before the ship sailed for Baja. Because that project and Erika's holiday decorating plans promised to keep David busy most of the morning, bottom-cleaning was out of the question, and he assigned Jean another task.

"You may as well clean the office."

Sliding open a door in the galley, he led her down a spiral companionway to a dark, dusty cabin. David flicked the wall switch, and a single tracklight overhead illuminated the chamber.

It was an office, but not of the utilitarian variety Jean had anticipated. The work space had once been lavish. Now cobwebs and dust dulled everything, and the place had an eerie, stagnant feeling.

There was a cherry-and-leather executive chair, a large desk of cherry burl, its top littered with dust-covered papers, and a wall crammed with photographs. File folders, photos and more documents lay strewn on the floor beside the desk, as though they had slid there when the ship was at sea and no one had bothered to pick them up. Sheets of paper lay half-torn and crumpled in balls as if savaged by someone in a rage. Even the blotter on the desk had slid far to one side.

Two filing cabinets stood against the wall, and they, like everything else, were shrouded in dust. The handles shone where fingers had opened the drawers, and footprints tracked through the dust on the sole.

The disorder was in complete contrast to the rest of the ship, and as she joined David at the foot of the stairs Jean endeavored to hide her shock.

He admitted, "Out of sight, out of mind. The washer and dryer are behind those folding doors." He indicated the koa doors beside another spiral stairway. "I come down here to wash clothes, and that's about it."

Nodding toward an elegant floor lamp mounted to the wooden sole near the desk, he told her, "I'll get you a bulb for that. Just…do what you need to. The mops and brooms are by the dryer. Make yourself comfortable, and throw out anything that doesn't relate to the business or have obvious legal significance. There's nothing else down here I want."

Jean nodded, her throat dry.

David waited a moment for a reply, then mounted the stairs and ducked through the door, leaving her staring helplessly at what she knew had been Skye Haverford Blade's office.

HE DIDN'T WANT to make the calls from the ship, not with her on board. The obvious choice was his office at the marine supply, where he could pick up Christmas bulbs and parts for the generator and telephone Jean's references.

Four of them, anyway. The other was Jake Doherty.

As he left the marina and hurried down the boardwalk toward the wharf, he studied the names she'd given him. He knew four of the people on her list: Jake; the professor who had recommended her for the Sayles Award; the owner of a local dive shop; and Frank Smith, who ran the martial-arts center.

The last was a neighbor.

The professor had already given a recommendation. David knew what Jake thought of her. And sooner or later he'd run into Frank and could quiz him about his student.

Spontaneously David crumpled the list and tossed it into a nearby trash can. For form's sake he would ask Jake a couple of questions, but the bottom line was he trusted her.

"JUST THROW EVERYTHING out, eh?" Jean murmured aloud, guardedly approaching the desk. Lying on the floor beside it was a framed photograph of David and Skye. The glass was cracked, a long, jagged line dividing the two subjects, but Jean couldn't stop herself from bending to pick up the frame.

The couple must have been on their honeymoon. They stood against a blue sky, and the light in their eyes as they smiled at each other, embracing, was that reserved for lovers. David looked young.

Swiftly Jean calculated the years. Christian was six, so David and Skye must have been married at least four years.

A good foundation, she thought. They would have lived out their days together, perhaps had more children.

How David had changed. In the photo, he looked as though he held everything he'd ever wanted right in his arms. His wife was beautiful. Not pretty or cute or attractive, but exquisite, with skin like buffed porcelain and eyes the color of her name. High cheekbones gave way to dimples and a nearly impertinent grin. Reflecting that Skye could have made a second fortune as a model, Jean lay the photo on the desk. Definitely David didn't mean to get rid of that. The broken glass could be replaced.

Finally she crossed the room and opened the folding doors. Besides a washer, dryer and ironing board, she found cleaning supplies, heavy-duty garbage bags and two empty cardboard boxes. The last two would come in handy.

Assessing the task ahead of her, Jean allowed herself a small groan. Regardless of David's instructions, she was not about to discard his wife's personal effects. Probably he found it painful to see her things, but someday he would want them. Taking the boxes and a rag, she went to the desk and set to work, first dusting the chair, then sitting.

On the blotter lay an engagement calendar turned to December 6, and Jean wondered, *Is it the sixth already?* But it wasn't. She stared, immobilized, realizing the calendar was three years old.

And Skye Haverford Blade had died on St. Nicholas Day.

It came back to her. The eerie gray weather. The holiday decorations on the docks fighting the wind and losing. The huge Christmas wreaths swaying from cables over State Street and the wharf.

Had nothing in the office been touched since Skye's death?

*Oh, David,* Jean thought. *Is it that bad?*

But it would be, she decided, remembering the healing she had gained from dressing her parents for burial. A friend had made the suggestion, pointing out that caring for the dead had once been women's work. Jean had gone through with it, though Cecily had declined, and now she knew that helping the funeral director care for her parents' bodies had helped her with her own grief.

But David had never even seen his wife's body.

Reassessing the chaos of the office, Jean wondered, Had there been no one to help with these details when Skye died? Erika couldn't have made it down the stairs, but surely there was some friend, someone David trusted. On the other hand, if there was, why had he waited three years and assigned the task to a virtual stranger?

Involuntarily she recalled sitting at her father's and mother's desks, going through their papers, their address books, everything marked with their familiar scripts. All the details came back. The funeral director, their bodies, the settling of the estate—and the sense of life on hold, of unfinished business. The argument with her mother over the catastrophe in Baja was responsible for that.

Jean shook off her memories. This wasn't her parents' office, and she could spare David some pain.

She began separating the paper and other odds and ends into personal and business categories, discarding trash. There were opened letters she glanced at to determine their nature, then filed in their rightful stack. She came across a few letters from David to Skye, probably written while he was at sea and she at home in Santa Barbara, because many bore foreign postmarks. Love letters, concluded Jean, biting her lip as she tossed the envelopes into the box of personal items.

After clearing the desktop, she tried to pull open the drawers, only to find them locked. She located the keys in the bottom of the letter caddy, unlocked the top middle drawer and slid it open. Inside lay more cards and letters and photos, packed so tightly it was a wonder the drawer had opened at all.

Sighing at the sorting ahead of her, Jean reached for a photo on top. It showed Skye in a bikini, embracing a mustached blond man whose lips were dragging sensuously over her hair. Puzzled, Jean turned over the photo and found bold, masculine writing on the back.

*In love in the Bahamas—with you. Homeless Shelter Fashion Shoot with my favorite model.* It was dated four years earlier, during Skye and David's marriage. So Skye had modeled—for charity. The blond man must have been her photographer.

Doubting David would want it, Jean tossed the snapshot into the trash and continued working. Beneath a jumble of postcards, she unearthed vials of pills and examined the labels with interest, but she knew too little about medicine to determine what Skye had been taking or for what. Only that they were Skye's pills, from a variety of doctors, mostly marked No Refill.

More letters then, from David and other people. Leafing through a stack of postcards, Jean was surprised to find one showing a stone relief she recognized from one of her tae kwon do books. The photograph showed two giant figures poised in tae kwon do stance carved in the tower wall of a Buddhist temple in the ancient city of Kyongju. Two thousand years old, the carvings were considered evidence of the antiquity of the martial art.

Until that point Jean had refrained from reading Skye's mail, but when she turned over the postcard and saw it was from David, she could resist no longer.

Dear Skye,
I used to visit this place often when I lived here. It feels the same now, as though the deepest part of me were born here. The other parts came from the sea. Where did you come from? I need to know, and so do you. I love you deeply.

David

Jean felt as though someone had stuffed a rock in her windpipe. For a moment she sat frozen, holding the postcard. Skye had been so young, and they were in love. They had a child, the ultimate symbol of their love for each other.

Trying not to puzzle over his words, which led her nowhere but to the final message of love, Jean, instead, pondered the news that David had lived in Korea. It made her think of his bow to her in her kitchen that morning. Knowing he had lived in the Far East, she found the gesture less surprising. What did surprise her was that he used to visit the temple at Kyongju, a place Jean would never have heard of but for her study of tae kwon do.

Long seconds passed before she at last put the postcard with his other letters and reached for the keys to unlock one of the bigger, lower drawers.

The drawer opened slowly, and her efforts were met with the clinking of glass. She had discovered Skye's private liquor stash. Grasping two nearly empty bottles by the necks, Jean pulled them out. Grand Marnier and Irish cream. Next came a half-empty gin bottle, another mostly gone cognac and a glass containing a decomposed olive. In the back of the drawer were two broken bottles, a half-drunk fifth of tequila and one decayed lime. The inside of the drawer was sticky with spilled alcohol.

Wondering how much Skye had drunk and why she hadn't used the bar in the salon, Jean debated over the bottles. She wasn't sure three-year-old liquor was still good or if there was enough in the bottles to merit saving.

At last she placed the bottles in the garbage bag, then began picking the broken glass out of the drawer. A sound at the top of the stairs startled her, and she jumped, slicing her hand on a jagged piece of glass. Wincing, she saw Christian looking down the companionway.

Her hand was bleeding, and she grabbed the dust rag to put over the cut, but she could feel glass in the wound. Hurriedly she stood up. ''Chris, your dad asked me to clean this office and I cut myself. Can you show me where the first-aid kit is?"

He nodded, and when she got to the top of the stairs, Jean showed him her wound. The cut was more than an inch long, and she couldn't tell how deep. Taking charge, Chris reached for her other hand and led her into the galley.

The galley steps had been raised and latched overhead, revealing the open door of the engine room. Leaving Jean in the galley, Chris went into the engine room and emerged a moment later. He was opening a locker beneath the sink when David appeared, his hair tumbled across his forehead, his slacks stained with engine grease.

"Chris said you cut yourself."

"It's nothing." She clasped the dusty rag to her hand. "I'll just clean it out."

David ducked into the galley. "Show me."

Jean lifted the rag. "See? Nothing." Her heart was hammering.

"Chris, thanks for getting me. I'll take care of Jean." David stepped to the sink and took the first-aid box from his son. "You did just the right thing."

As though reading something unspoken in David's eyes, Chris hurried up the steps that led to his father's cabin and went inside, closing the door behind him.

Jean asked, "Is he okay?"

"Shouldn't he be?" David's glance was incisive.

Jean reflected that she'd been sitting at Skye's desk when Chris appeared at the top of the stairs. Had the sight stirred up memories of his mother? She said, "He left quickly."

Without reply David led her to the sink and held her hand under a cold stream of water. "There's glass in that cut. What from?"

His jaw was taut, and Jean trembled. She could feel the heat from his body.

"Just...some broken bottles." Jean tried to sound nonchalant, but the admission discomfited her. She'd never known anyone who kept a bar in a desk. Did David even know which bottles she meant?

Apparently, because he was silent as he washed his own hands and shut off the water. Leading her back to the dining booth, he gestured for her to sit down. He sat beside her, his thigh against hers, and with tweezers from the first-aid kit began to remove the glass from her hand.

"I can do this," said Jean.

"With your left hand? I don't think so."

They sat in silence for nearly a minute, and Jean stared absently at the advent calendar on the wall. Another door had been opened to show a stocking hanging by a hearth. The fifth, she thought as a glass sliver pricked her wound.

She shuddered, and David's arm slid around her shoulders over her braid. "Sorry. Just another minute." His hand squeezed her shoulder through the cotton of her sweatshirt as he extracted the sliver, then set to work on another. "Bottles," he remarked. "I'm sorry I asked you to do that. If there's broken glass, leave it for me, all right?"

"I didn't mind." Jean could think only of his arm around her. She could feel his heart beating against her side.

Again a sliver dug into the cut, and she gasped involuntarily.

David pressed her shoulder gently.

Recklessly Jean looked up, and her pulse lodged in her throat. "Sorry I'm such a baby."

David shook his head. "It's nice to— Speaking of babies, where is she?"

Nice to what? Hold her? It took all Jean's concentration to think of Baby. The dolphin had appeared soon after she and David reached the *Skye*, but Jean could no longer hear her outside. She shrugged. "I guess she knows we're not diving today. Baby doesn't hang around begging for attention." She said this guiltily, because Baby would do exactly that if given the slightest encouragement.

"That's good," said David. "At times I've suspected she's very emotionally dependent on you."

"At least you see she has emotions," Jean answered, sidestepping the remark. "Most scientists won't admit to that."

"As a scientist I won't, either. As a human—" he plucked the last sliver from her hand "—I can't believe anything else. And that kind of emotional attachment with a wild animal is a mistake." He inspected her hand under the light. "Did I get it all?"

"I think so." Jean studied his face, pondering his remarks about Baby. How could loving her be wrong?

But David seemed finished with the subject—and her hand. He doused the wound in betadine and closed it with a butterfly bandage. "Good as new," he said, holding her finger slightly. "Leave the glass for me, now, okay?"

The touch was too much. To Jean, it felt hot and sexy and forbidden, yet she knew it couldn't be affecting him that way or he couldn't sit there so calmly. Good grief, he was her boss.

Abruptly he dropped her hand and stood up, and Jean felt a shaft of disappointment run through her as he murmured a dismissal she couldn't make out and disappeared into the engine room.

Left behind at the table, she gazed at the closed doors of the calendar, all the unknown days until Christmas. Imagining the anticipation Chris must feel before opening each door, Jean realized she was looking ahead to the coming days with similar excitement, for what each might reveal about David. Yet she was apprehensive, too. This morning he had begun to thaw, and she, without meaning to, had begun to care—and to understand.

David was a man with grave responsibilities, including a disabled sister and a mute son. Thinking of his shifts in mood, the shell of coldness replaced by warmth, Jean knew he was scarred, badly, by the death of the woman he'd loved.

IN THE ENGINE ROOM David rested his chin in his hands and stared sightlessly at the generator.

He'd touched her.

Quite a bit, for him. Keeping his hands off was going to be a problem, and unfortunately not the only one.

Over breakfast and since, he had begun to perceive that Jean was both uniquely independent and highly unpredictable, qualities that attracted him but made her a dubious choice for a shipmate. A crew member could be either part of a ship's operation, a cog in the wheel or a separate force, disrupting established patterns, shaking things up. Like Skye.

Like Jean.

Big mistake, hiring her. The offer had been impulse, and he was rarely impulsive. But Jean continued to surprise him, and part of him could not resist surprises. For instance, the knowledge that she studied tae kwon do. He'd dived headfirst into hot water with a black belt who read romance novels and was a klutz in the kitchen and thought she was bad with kids. And he'd forgotten what a ship's close quarters could accomplish unasked.

David heard her tread on the companionway, then a thud from the galley and the clanking sound of bottles hitting each other.

He made his way out of the engine room and into the galley.

Jean had set a cardboard box on the table. On top was a photo of him and Skye. Letters and open papers lay underneath.

David said, "What's that?"

"I thought you might want these things."

"I don't." And he had told her so. "Throw it out."

Jean looked up at him. Now her eyes were the same color

as her sweatshirt—sage. From her expression, David knew he was going to get an argument.

She said, "Her family might want these things. Or Chris might. There are diplomas, letters—"

"Thank you for going to that trouble, but this ship's not big enough to keep everything. You can throw those out." He said the last in a voice he hoped would convey how little he liked repeating himself.

Jean toyed with the tail of her braid and regarded him with a frown. In the manner of someone uncomfortable offering unsolicited advice, she suggested, "You must have a safety-deposit box or something. Why don't you just…take a few of your letters—for Chris."

Giving her a brief, icy stare, David washed his hands at the sink and returned to the box at the table. He reached for the stack of letters, flipped through them and selected a few of the older ones, stuffing them into the pocket of his canvas shirt. He tossed the rest in the box and told Jean, "To the Dumpster."

She said, "You're making a mistake."

He had to hand it to her—she had nerve. David clenched his teeth and enunciated with cool precision, "Throw out the box." He pulled the letters from his pocket and tossed them on top of the rest. "And take those too."

Jean took a step back, and David realized in disbelief that she had no intention of following his orders. She said quietly, "If you want to throw those things out, you can carry them to the Dumpster yourself. You couldn't even bring yourself to tell me it was your wife's office."

"You figured it out."

She moved toward the sink as though she was avoiding him. If so, she had good instincts. He wanted to throttle her.

But when there was more distance between them, she turned to meet his eyes. "You have no right to be angry at me. You should have looked through those things yourself. That's the only way to deal with death—to look it in the face."

David felt momentarily light-headed. She'd called him a coward. He said, "How dare you. You don't have a clue what I've seen."

She looked as though he'd hit her. Her features were white, stricken, her eyes huge with an expression of self-blame and sorrow David found infuriating. "My God, I'm sorry," she whispered.

He didn't reply. She was shaking things up all right. David did not like to be shaken.

Jean turned her back on him and leaned against the counter, overwhelmed by the realization of what David actually might have seen, not just when his wife died but also when the *Siren* went down. And she'd self-righteously accused him of refusing to face death—as though he'd had a choice.

Watching her back, David locked his arms across his chest, primarily so he wouldn't touch her. The thought that he might made him treat her coldly. "Pull yourself together. I didn't hire you to come apart at the seams when I give you a simple order."

Jean wheeled where she stood, fighting for control as she thought of his "simple" order—to throw out his wife's belongings. She glanced at the box, then at him. "I am not coming apart at the seams, and that order was not simple or reasonable. You have a son to consider. Those things belonged to his mother."

*"Don't tell me about my family."* Face tense, eyes mad with emotion, he stepped toward her.

Jean drew back, her hands flat, facing him. Two palms that could easily curl into fists. She said, "Stay back!"

Her voice was strong enough, her stance sure enough, to give him pause. But the look in her eye charged him, and a small knot somewhere inside him unraveled. He said, "No."

Watching her back, David ...

# CHAPTER FIVE

SHE DIDN'T WANT to hurt him, only keep him away. Without time to think it through, to think more than that he was
nearly upon her, she delivered a glancing side kick, pulled
so as not to hurt him. Faster than she could blink, David
blocked the blow and counterattacked.

Jean hit the sole of the galley like a sack of laundry, for
a moment uncertain what he had done. Belatedly she realized she had met one of her own.

She said, "You bastard."

"We're not done." As she began to spring up, he easily
shoved her the rest of the way down, slipping a hand beneath her head so it didn't hit the teak sole and at the same
time covering her body, pinning her ankles to the floor.
Then, he kissed her.

Jean froze. Because she didn't want to fight, she closed
her eyes. In a kind of quiet trance, she absorbed the brush
of his beard, the feel of his muscles, of his mouth, of his
hand on her braid. He was tense, but gentle. And for a
fraction of an instant, in a dark corner of her mind where
wild concepts roamed, Jean wondered if he was frightened.

Abruptly David moved off her and sat up. Pulse erratic,
body still, Jean stared up at him.

He drew a long breath and leaned back on his hands as
though signaling that if she wanted to hit him he would
allow it. He said, "That was inexcusable. I'm very sorry."
He met her eyes. "I know you pulled that kick. Are you
hurt?"

Sitting up, Jean shook her head. "Not how you mean."

He looked interested. "How do *you* mean?"

Jean said, "It's just not how I dream of being kissed."

David shut his eyes, and she knew the words had cut, primarily because they were deserved.

After a few seconds, he opened his eyes and met hers. "May I try again?"

Jean's breath quickened. In the past minutes she had wondered many things about him, but never if he would physically hurt her. Her attempt to keep him from touching her had been only that. They had both been wildly upset.

With a slight tilt of her chin, she nodded.

David moved closer to her on the floor. His eyes flickered over her, and then he touched the corner of her mouth.

Jean's lungs squeezed closed. It was hard to look into his eyes, and yet she wanted to and sensed he wanted her to. They were dark and full of so much. She had seen him rude and cool and remote and now angry, but she knew that ultimately he was deep. So deep, she wondered if she could even scratch the surface.

Jean held her breath as he stroked back a lock of her hair loosened in their tussle and searched her face. Then he fitted his mouth to hers.

Jean was unprepared for her own response. Her throat tightened, and her heart felt as though it were going to jump out of her body. The artery in her neck pulsed so violently she knew David must feel it. He did, because he put his hand there as he kissed her.

It was a simple kiss and an incredibly complicated one. When he drew her closer, Jean acquiesced without struggle. She pushed nearer, feeling the muscles in his arm and the wall of his chest. His thigh pressed against hers. She felt his breath and discovered it was as uneven as her own.

Her lips parted and she felt, as she'd hoped she would, the touch of his tongue, tasting, experimenting. He clasped her more tightly to his body, and Jean wondered if he wanted to lie down as badly as she did.

When he finally pulled away, she felt mildly disoriented. He unwound her arms from his neck and set her hands in her lap—away from him. Then he stood and offered her his own hand. Jean took it and rose, as well, wondering if he would embrace her.

He didn't. He let go of her and bowed.

Meeting his eyes, Jean returned the courtesy and offered her hands.

He took them. *"Kamsa hamnida."* Thank you. "Let's not do that again."

Kissing? Jean wondered as they released hands. Or spontaneous sparring?

She thought of the postcard of the Kyongju temple and his bow to her that morning. She wanted to ask him why he hadn't told her he'd studied tae kwon do, but David spoke first. Directing her attention to the box on the table, the catalyst that had set off their argument—and everything else—he said, "Please get rid of that. It's the last time I'm asking. And believe me, I won't be so patient again."

Jean recognized a warning. She said nothing.

"You can take it to her lawyer's office. It's at 51 Coast Village Road. Peter Barnes. Tell him I'll call him about what to do with it."

As Jean chewed on the realization that this particular order was a compromise, he took some keys from his pants pocket and dropped them in her hand. "Take my car. It's in space three beside the café."

Jean stared at the key ring.

David said, "Can you drive a stick?"

She nodded.

"Go get some lunch, but be careful. It's a fast car." He ducked into the engine room. "You can take the top down."

Her eyes followed him. "Do you want anything?"

He turned and looked at her, his own eyes like two sentinels guarding a dungeon that might hold monsters—or treasure. "I want you to go."

Nodding toward his cabin, the exit she should take, he disappeared into the engine room.

Jean looked down at the letters he'd tossed on the box and wondered if he planned to call the lawyer and tell *him* to throw them out. Impulsively she removed his letters, placed them on the table, then picked up the box and the garbage sack. David might have looked death in the face, but love was harder.

AS SHE CARRIED the bulging garbage bag and the box to the parking lot, Jean played back everything that had occurred in the galley—argument, anger, takedown, kisses.

She was far from blameless. When he'd stepped toward her, she'd overreacted—almost as though for a moment a part of her had wondered if he *had* killed his wife.

But that wasn't it at all. The thought had never crossed her mind. The simple fact was he affected her as no man ever had, and she'd lost all semblance of composure and forgotten the basis of her tae kwon do training—self-control.

Apparently so had David.

Jean didn't know what to make of him or of what he had done. She'd seen a gamut of responses in him, all unrestrained as though something inside had snapped.

Which was possible. Their dispute had been intense and, for him, highly personal. Part of her wished she could take back things she'd said. It was mentioning Chris that had sent him over the edge. Or maybe Skye.

*Don't tell me about my family.*

As she neared the boardwalk, a sight on the other side of the marina gate jerked her from her thoughts. Jake Doherty, who ran the marine supply, sat outside the espresso shop.

*Bad timing*, thought Jean. For her, not Jake.

Six foot six, with a waist-length mane of auburn hair, Jake lived in the harbor on his Chinese junk, the *Lien Hua*. Jean knew vaguely that his past included college basketball, an engineering degree and time spent doing practically nothing in places like Jamaica and Thailand. But for the past six years he'd been in business on the wharf, and now he was a harbor institution, respected for his mechanical savvy and his omniscience. He knew everything that had happened on the Santa Barbara waterfront in the past decade and much before that, and he lived to learn new things daily.

Before Jean reached the marina gate she saw his eyes light up, more with curiosity than pleasure. He stood to help her with the gate, glancing with apparent disinterest at her box and the heavy-duty garbage bag.

Jean wasn't fooled. Like Santa Claus, Jake missed nothing. Right now, he was as welcome as the bad fairy at a christening.

She said, "Hi, Jake," and walked past him through the gate.

"Hi yourself, stranger. Let me give you a hand with that." Before she could protest, both items had been lifted from her arms and Jake was striding down the boardwalk beside her, peering into the box he was hefting. "Where to, gorgeous?"

"The Dumpster for the garbage. I'll take the box," she said, reaching for it.

He held it out of the way. "I wouldn't hear of it." He eyed the photo of Skye and David at the top of the box. "So David let you clean the shrine?"

Jean felt a new respect for Jake's powers of deduction. It was hard to fathom how he had known exactly where the contents of the box had originated. She said, "The shrine?"

Jake grinned at her. They had reached the nearest

Dumpster, and he handed her the box and tossed the garbage bag inside. It landed with a loud shatter of glass, and he chuckled at her expression. "Skye's medicine chest?" He winked. "The babe had some great parties."

Jean thought of the tequila and cognac and unmarked vials of pills. Jake sounded as though he'd had personal experience with Skye's parties—and her "medicine chest." Briefly she imagined him and Skye sitting together in the office, laughing and enjoying drinks. It was a strange picture, two unlikely people linked by a common thread— David. At a loss for a suitable reply, she said, a little ironically, "Thanks for carrying the trash."

"No problem." Jake started to take the box, but Jean moved away.

She said, "I'll carry it." She wasn't sure why she felt as she did about the box. A glance inside could tell nothing, yet Jean felt compelled to protect the contents, almost as though she was protecting David and Chris and even Erika, the people Skye's death had touched.

Jake didn't quibble over the box, in which he now seemed genuinely uninterested. He said, "I hear you've been promoted."

With a start Jean remembered she had listed Jake among the references she'd given to David that morning. David must have spoken with him, and Jean wondered what he had asked—and how Jake had replied.

"He wanted to know if you have any secrets."

Jean almost dropped the box, and Jake rescued it. When she didn't object, he assumed the burden, remarking, "A royal flush, eh?"

Jean said nothing. His words were as good as an admission that he knew nothing about Baja, but that didn't stop her heart's frantic knocking. The last thing she wanted was for David to hear that story. If even her own mother had doubted her, how would he react? David, who was so protective of his family.

Jake shrugged. "Like I told him, everyone has secrets. Including David, by the way." He jostled the box. "Where does this go?"

"David's car." Jean's breathing had almost returned to normal, but her mind was racing. What were David's secrets?

Jake eyed the car keys in her hand. "The 'Vette." He smiled sideways at Jean as they walked around the espresso shop. "Don't feel too special. I think he secretly hopes someone will total it and he'll be relieved of the responsibility."

Jean's eyes darted toward his. "What do you mean?"

They had reached space three, and Jake set down the box and began stripping the cover from a long, low sports car. "See for yourself. A 'sixty-five roadster. Low miles, totally cherry. The thing's priceless. Rich people—people richer than David—buy cars like these and park them in their garages and drive them on Sundays. David parks his here. At the waterfront. Nothing's ever happened to it, but like I said, I think he's hoping."

Jean hurried to the side of the car to help with the cover. She was of a mind to march back to the *Skye* and tell David Blade she wouldn't drive his car as far as the next parking space. Priceless? What if she wrecked it? She asked, "Why does he have the car if he doesn't like it?"

"Skye," said Jake, rolling back the cover to reveal a sleek black hood.

Jean looked at him.

Catching her glance, Jake said, "The woman was a mindblower, wanted to control everyone she met. She couldn't control David, so she married him. Some people are like that. The big challenge in life is to crack the whip. If Skye had ever figured out how to control David she would've left him. Hell," Jake added, "she's working on it even now. Voilà. The will. The car."

Jean blinked at him, not understanding.

Jake took the car cover and folded it neatly, his eyes on hers. "She left him a seven-digit life-insurance plan—and more—provided he'd take the car. She'd been trying to buy him a fast car the whole time they were married. He used to drive this VW squareback with the roof torn off. It was a classic in its own realm, but Skye hated it so much she finally totaled it. *Whammo*. Then, she leaves David a vintage Corvette of untold value in her will. He's got to take it—or else." Jake pantomimed cracking a whip. "The state the Blade Institute was in, he didn't have a choice. He would have lost his ship—everything."

Jean tried to look as though she knew just what he was talking about. The Blade Institute in trouble?

"Note the vanity plates. They came with."

Jean looked. The California license read PRESENT.

"I mean, you're a woman, Jean. What do you think when you see a guy who looks like David driving a car like this with plates like that? You think he's the favorite toy of some rich babe, and she bought him a hot car to show her appreciation."

Jean reddened. "I—I don't—"

"Of course not. You're still an innocent. But trust me, Skye knew what she was doing. You know what I think those plates mean?" He tucked the car cover under his arm. "I think they mean she's present, even now. She's here. You're on that ship sometime at night, you'll know what I mean. You can feel her, teasing him. They say the soul of a drowned person never rests." Jake shrugged. "But what do you care? It's just a job, right? And better than slime war, eh, babe? By the way your check for the *Lien Hua* is at the marine supply. You were so gaga over David's offer you forgot to collect." He gave her a teasing smile, then looked at the car. "You want the top down on this monster?"

Jean nodded, relieved to see the conversation change

course. Together, she and Jake lowered the top of the convertible.

WHEN JEAN RETURNED to the *Skye* after her errand and a quick lunch, Chris was lying on the aft deck, his arms stretched out under the railing, trying vainly to touch Baby. The deck was much too high.

Jean longed to take him out onto the diving platform, but it would violate one of her own Baby policies and result in a host of undesirable behavior from the dolphin, all stemming from a need for attention.

Besides, David had been clear about Chris and Baby, and what he'd said about the life spans of lone dolphins was true. More than once, Jean had been kept awake by fears that Baby would be hit by a speedboat in the harbor. If Christian became as attached as she was to Baby, the dolphin's death could devastate him.

She paused on the aft deck. "Hi, Chris."

He looked up, but did not smile.

Embarrassed by his ambivalence toward her, Jean moved toward the cabin, wondering if Chris was safe lying on the deck that way. It was easy to see him reaching farther and farther to touch Baby—

She turned around. "Chris, that's not safe. Sit up on the cushions or stand against the railing."

He glanced at her but didn't move.

Again Jean felt a sense of her own failure with children. How could she take care of Chris if he wouldn't obey her?

A circle of fear tightened her throat, and she pushed it away. He *would* obey her.

She walked over and crouched on the deck beside Chris, meeting his eyes. It was a nerve-racking experience. His eyes were so like David's.

Swallowing, Jean said, "I guess your dad didn't tell you this, but he hired me to help look after you. I'm going to make the same decisions for you I would for a child of my own, and I hope you can help with the decision-making."

Chris shifted his eyes, watching Baby, but she kept talking, feeling her way. "Right now you have a choice. You can get up and sit on the cushions, or I can go get your dad. He's not crazy about you playing with Baby, anyhow."

Chris didn't move. It wasn't working.

Jean stood up and turned away, but when she looked back from the diving alcove, Chris had moved to the cushions.

She released a breath she hadn't known she'd been holding.

DAVID AND ERIKA were in the salon, surrounded by strings of Christmas lights. An artificial tree stood in one corner of the room, and David lay sideways beneath it, bolting the stand to the sole of the cabin.

Seeing him again, Jean stiffened slightly, both anticipating and dreading the moment he would turn and see her.

Erika said, "Jean! I'm so glad you're here. We need another pair of hands."

"We need to get rid of some lights is what we need." David did not look up as he spoke. He'd hoped to be gone when Jean returned, but Erika had waylaid him.

"Scrooge," accused his sister. "I'm glad Jean's going along to Baja with you, to make sure you don't ruin everyone's Christmas with your whining."

David stood up. "I never whine. I make practical suggestions." Bracing himself, he turned to Jean. "I finished the office for you. There's a new bulb in the floor lamp."

"Thanks." She didn't quite meet his gaze.

"I left a W-2 form on the desk for you."

That got her attention.

He said, "You passed."

He meant the references, Jean thought dimly. She was

hired. With confusion she remembered what had happened before lunch, and as she caught David's expression she wondered if he was remembering the same thing.

"Can you two do business later?" Erika asked. She told Jean, "If I let David get away from this now he won't come back."

"That's true," he agreed.

Erika wheeled through a path between the lights and picked up a bunch of mistletoe from the floor. She handed it to Jean, instructing, "You find a place for this, and David can tack it up. I have to go find the star." She sped down the aft ramp.

Jean looked down at the mistletoe in her hand, then scouted the salon for somewhere to hang it. David scooped up a couple of thumbtacks from a box beneath the tree.

She asked, "Where does this usually go?"

"Usually?" He glanced indifferently at the mistletoe. "We haven't had the stuff around for years. I'm surprised Erika bought some." Catching Jean's inquisitive glance, he explained, "Let's just say she and I are both a little cynical."

"Cynical?" said Jean. "Erika?"

"You'll understand when you know her better." He eyed Jean distantly. "I notice you didn't question *my* cynicism."

Jean smiled faintly. "You must have hung the mistletoe somewhere before you turned cynical."

There followed an uncomfortable silence in which his eyes spoke volumes. B.C.—before cynicism—must have been before Skye's death. David wouldn't want to hang the mistletoe where he had kissed his wife and lover many times.

Jean hastily suggested, "Let's put it in the galley, so the cook and the dishwasher get lots of kisses."

At David's look of speculation, she remembered that was where they had kissed, and her face flamed to her hairline. "Or maybe…over the stairwell."

His eyes slanted toward hers. "Maybe we should just hang it in my cabin and be done with it."

Jean stammered, "Let's put it over the stairwell. The aft stairwell." The one farthest from his cabin.

David took the bough from her hands, his fingers grazing hers. "I like the idea of putting it in the galley. Come on." He gave her a gentle push toward the galley stairs. "You can help me hang it straight."

She didn't move. David looked at her for a moment, then stepped around her to descend the companionway. After a moment Jean followed.

When she entered the galley she saw the table was clear. The letters she had left were nowhere in sight, and she wondered what David had done with them—and if he would mention this violation of his orders.

Not immediately at any rate. He was tacking up the mistletoe. His expression did not invite company, and Jean hung back by the table.

Finishing, he looked at her and said rather remotely, "Go ahead and help Erika for now. Then suit up so we can tackle the hull again. I'll meet you topside in—" he glanced at his watch "—one hour."

His change of mood baffled her. Chewing on her lip, Jean wondered if it was because she had hesitated in the salon. Tentatively she moved toward him.

David shook his head at her. "You were right." Without another word he started up the stairs to his cabin and disappeared inside, shutting the door behind him.

Jean wasn't sure what to feel. Did this mean he intended to keep their relationship strictly business? That was wise, but disappointing. Casting a last glance at his closed door, Jean started up the other companionway to the salon.

Erika's voice called to her from aft. "Where'd you put the mistletoe?"

"In the galley near the sink."

Erika wheeled up the ramp, a stack of ornament boxes in her lap. "Where's David?"

"In his cabin." Hoping her inner turbulence didn't show, Jean focused her attention to the lights on the carpet. "Have these been tested? Should we string them yet?"

"Sure. I'm a little concerned about Chris," admitted Erika. "I haven't seen him for a while."

Jean climbed to the salon door and looked through the windowpane and the windows of the diving alcove to the aft deck. David was there. He must have gone out through the wheelhouse. Jean watched him hoist his son on his shoulders.

The comfortable display of affection tore at her somehow, and her voice was less than even as she told Erika, "I think David's taking him to town."

"Good." Erika frowned at the lights. "Yes, I think these are ready to go up. Let's plug them in one more time."

Jean fitted the plug into the nearest socket, and the bulbs sprang to light.

"Hooray!" said Erika. "Always a happy sight."

Jean smiled. "It's fun to do this in a family environment. My sister—" She stopped, but Erika looked interested, and Jean found herself confessing what her last Christmas had been like.

Erika nodded understandingly. "David and I spent the holidays apart, too, for a couple of years after our parents died. Money was the problem. I was studying in Australia when the ship went down, and David insisted we use the life insurance to continue paying for my education. He was living in Korea, fishing, and airfare seemed like an extravagance."

Korea again. Had David studied martial arts in the Orient?

Erika said, "And then, the year Skye died was another story. David just forgot about Christmas. No tree. No Santa Claus. It just didn't happen." She told Jean, "I meant that about being glad you're going to Baja with him. He tries to make the holidays nice for Chris, but he gets pretty black, too. Those two really need a woman around.''

Jean liked the sound of the words. They seemed to imply that she, a woman who had killed two out of three bonsai trees and couldn't cook breakfast, possessed the nurturing qualities to bring out the Christmas spirit in an unhappy widower and his somber little boy.

But if Erika knew how much David and Chris needed a woman, why was she moving out? It seemed sad that she would spend Christmas alone at the rehab center.

As Jean unplugged the lights and gathered up the string, Erika asked, ''Do you mind if I get my book and sketch you while you do that?''

Shaking her head, Jean began clipping lights to the tree branches as Erika retrieved a sketchbook and pencils from a drawer in the end table. Arranging the lights, Jean peered across the room to the painting over the stairwell. Skye's silvery turquoise eyes and bewitching smile seemed to follow her every move.

Seeing Erika watching her, Jean said, ''It's a beautiful painting. Can you make me look that good?''

Erika laughed. ''Skye would've hated that. Sort of like the queen in *Snow White*.'' Her humor faded. ''I shouldn't have said that. It sounded terrible.'' Brow creased, she said, ''Skye truly was 'the fairest of them all.''''

Jean longed to ask questions. Erika was clearly a remarkable person. She handled her disability with courageous optimism and always seemed full of kind words for others. What had she thought of David's wife? Jean said, ''I saw Skye's photograph. Her eyes really were as blue as you painted them.''

Erika nodded, subdued, and Jean wondered what she had felt toward her sister-in-law. She said, ''I'm sorry, Erika. That was insensitive of me.''

Erika cut her short. ''Don't apologize, Jean. Just because

things are unpleasant doesn't mean we should never speak of them.''

Jean relaxed, reassured. She liked David's sister more than ever.

Erika drew a line on the paper. ''I was just thinking of a conversation we had—David and Jake and me. You know Jake, don't you? He's served as our first mate on many shorter expeditions, even before he and David opened the marine supply. I think he's going to Baja.''

This was all news to Jean, and she asked herself why Jake had never mentioned that David was his partner. *Probably a silent partner,* she reflected.

''Anyhow,'' said Erika, ''Skye had been dead just a month or so. We were sitting around here when Jake started telling this absolutely beautiful Chumash myth about souls going to Šimilaqša.''

Jean listened with interest. The Chumash were the Native Americans who had inhabited the south coast before the Spanish settlement. Their rock art was painted on the walls of many caves in the area, but the tribe was nearly extinct, destroyed by the scourges that came with the settlers.

''Jake said some Chumash believed that after death souls traveled west toward the sun, where they were born again. Others thought they went to Šimilaqša, the place where they never grew old, like a Christian heaven. On the way the soul encountered many dangers—a woman who could sting with her tail and ravens who plucked out the eyes. But then the soul picked poppies from the ground and placed them in his eye sockets and could see again. When he reached Similaqša, the soul was given eyes of blue abalone.''

Erika shut her eyes briefly, then reopened them. ''But David interrupted Jake and said the Chumash also believed the soul of a drowned person wandered the sea forever and never reached the land to the west to be born again. I'll never forget how David looked just then. He said, 'Skye's eyes were like blue abalone when she was alive. And I don't care if her soul rests or not. You think mine does?'" Erika looked down at her drawing paper. "I don't know why I'm telling you this. The whole thing was awful." She gave a shake of her head like a shudder. "I've just never forgotten the way he talked about her eyes."

He had talked like a lover, thought Jean. She wondered exactly what Erika meant by awful. What had happened out in the channel? Jean wished David would talk about it, but she imagined it was something he discussed rarely— and only with those closest to him.

Still, unable to stop herself, she nodded out the window toward the islands and asked Erika, "What really happened out there?"

Erika lifted her shoulders in an exaggerated shrug. "Ask my brother. You might get further than I ever did." Releasing a long breath, she said, "I suppose it's only fair to warn you that tomorrow's the anniversary of her death."

Jean straightened. December sixth. Of course.

Erika said, "Don't worry. He probably won't ask you to work. He usually takes Chris out to the islands. There's a marker on one of them, and they leave some flowers." She explained, "I just wanted you to know that if he seems touchy, that may be why."

Jean thought of their skirmish in the galley. As she rearranged a section of light cord, her eyes again caught the painting of Skye. Bending an uncooperative tree bough, she asked, "Erika, don't answer if this is too painful, but...what was she like?"

Unexpectedly Erika laughed. When Jean looked over at her, she said, "That's a big question, and I'm probably not the person to answer it." She glanced at Jean. "Why did you ask? Do you like David?"

Jean was sure her face gave her away. Squeezing behind the tree and taking the light string with her, she said, "I probably don't have to answer that."

Erika smiled but said only, "Let's see. What can I tell you about Skye?" Thoughtfully she remarked, "She went to two different European universities. I'm not up on that sort of thing, but David has said they're famous schools. I think he envied her that—he's never been to school at all, and he reads like a fiend." Erika looked faraway, as though recollecting her sister-in-law. "God, sometimes she used to make me laugh, Jean. Her sense of humor was hilarious. She was so mean and so funny all at once. And creative. She made that beautiful quilt on David's bed."

Jean noticed Erika had managed to make meanness sound like a positive attribute. Like being clever.

David's sister fell silent, then shrugged gracefully. "As for the rest, I guess it would suffice to say she was no angel. But she didn't marry one, either."

Jean peered at her through the branches of the tree. "That sounded like a warning."

"I'm not sure I meant it that way. David's a complicated man. I think he could be a lot to handle."

*No kidding,* Jean thought.

Erika smiled. "And shut up so I can sketch your mouth, all right?"

Jean answered with a grin, knowing the instruction was Erika's playful way of saying the discussion was over.

Under Erika's guidance, she decorated the salon and the tree, tying the ornaments to the branches so they wouldn't shake off at sea. It was a disturbing task. She was charmed by the gold sand-dollar ornaments and other slightly damaged treasures Erika said dated back to her father's life and had been salvaged from the *Siren.* There was even an aluminum ornament David had made as a child. But also, nestled in protective layers of tissue, were the inevitable personalized trinkets: *David and Skye—Our First Christmas Together; Skye's Silver Skate; Christian's First Christmas.* There was even a photo of Skye nestled in a pearly ball.

Jean asked, "Does this go up?"

"Oh, no." Erika wheeled forward to take it. "And don't put up any of the ones with her name on them."

Jean reflected that the ship still had her name on it. And her portrait hung on the aft stairwell.

Perplexed, Jean watched Erika grab a shoe box from the floor and hastily stuff the Skye ornaments into it, then shut the lid as though she were locking up a shameful secret— or something dangerous, like a loaded gun.

# CHAPTER SIX

WHEN DAVID SAW HER an hour later, she was leaving the aft head in a teal swimsuit, her clothing tucked under one arm, a coffee cup in her other hand. The mug had been Skye's and bore a cartoon of a chatty-looking woman and the quip, *If you don't have anything nice to say about anyone, sit right here by me.*

David had never been able to bring himself to get rid of it.

Seeing her just feet away in the narrow hall, he slipped back into the doorway of the darkroom, which he had been restocking.

Jean didn't see him at first. The hall was in shadow, and when she made out the tall figure in the doorframe, her heart stopped.

He said, "You need to wear more clothes around here."

Unconsciously she clutched her stack of clothing and the coffee cup against her front. She said, "My wet suit's in the diving alcove. I'm sorry."

"It wasn't a criticism." In the dimness, he let his eyes take swift inventory of her figure, then made a decision. Inclining his head toward the bow, he said, "Your cabin will be the crew's quarters—since you're my crew. You can get there from the foredeck or my cabin or the office. And please use the forward head and showers." After a pause, he added, "You and I share."

Jean nodded, picturing walking in on him in the shower some morning. Then the reverse.

David said, "Soon there'll be half a dozen men on this ship. And you. So this is the best arrangement." He asked, "Do you get seasick?"

She'd never been out in rough weather. "I don't think so."

"The bow's the worst for that, but it can't be helped. That's where I want you."

Accessible to him and no one else, Jean thought. But it made her feel protected and cared for as she hadn't been for years. She said, "Okay."

He was looking at her coffee cup, the one Erika had said was fine to use—"None of our cups are important." The one Jean knew had been Skye's.

Now it was empty, and David reached for it. "I'll take that to the galley for you. It's on my way. I'll see you on deck."

Their hands did not touch as she handed him the mug.

JEAN WAS ZIPPING her wet suit when he stepped out of the salon. He was wearing a pair of blue trunks and nothing else. He was sinew and suntanned skin, hard and scarred, a man who'd been shark-bit.

He made Jean's heart thunder, and as he took his wet suit from where it was hanging, she said, "You need to wear more clothes."

David cast her a look that was both amused and grudgingly respectful. "Touché. And thank you. I will." His eyes lingered on hers for a moment, as though silently measuring her. Then he began pulling on his wet suit. Nodding toward the diving platform, he said, "Let's see if we can finish the keel in the next few days. We have a lot of other work before we leave for Baja."

Jean thought of the next day, the anniversary of Skye's death. So far, David hadn't mentioned a break in their schedule.

They readied for the dive in silence and emerged on deck

to find Christian kneeling on the aft cushions, holding the end of a cotton rope. On the other end was the inflatable wreath in which he had interested Baby. Recalling David's hopes for the wreath's demise, Jean glanced his way. But he was watching his son.

When Jean and David reached the stern, Chris looked up and signed something to his father—his first use of sign language in Jean's presence.

David's face showed little expression as he turned to her and said, "Chris would like to go swimming with Baby."

The look in his eye made Jean think of a stick of dynamite with the fuse lit. She said nothing, and Chris watched his father hopefully.

With a dark look at Jean that said, *This is your fault,* David told Chris, "You may swim. Wear your wet suit. And bring your snorkel, so you can help us."

As Chris leapt off the cushions and raced toward the cabin, David said, "Walk."

When the child had disappeared inside, he turned to Jean. His voice and features were even and uninvolved, but his eyes told her a different story. "I don't appreciate any of this."

Suspecting she heard a veiled reference to the letters she'd left on the galley table, Jean tugged nervously at the rubber strap on her mask but made no reply.

David went aft and lifted the railing. "Go away, Baby."

The dolphin nestled up to the platform, lifting her head for a stroke.

David stepped down to the platform and looked back at Jean. He said, "I told you to take everything in that box to Skye's lawyer. You need to follow instructions. Consider yourself warned."

WITHIN AN HOUR Chris was enjoying "rides" through the water as he clung to Baby's dorsal fin. Jean and David watched him with help from Erika, and Jean wondered what David felt when he saw his son's delight in the animal. How could he feel negative about something so obviously healthy for Chris?

Whatever his feelings, he didn't confide them. Whenever they were topside he said little, and Jean realized he was still angry. Justifiably. But his demands had opposed the instincts of her heart. And the boundary between personal and professional now seemed blurred and indistinct, as though part of it had been erased.

Which it was, Jean thought, earlier today. *Whether he likes it or not.*

The water had begun to darken when her scrub brush uncovered something engraved in the black hull near the propellers. Serial number, Jean assumed. But as she continued scrubbing, she realized she was wrong. With rigid muscles, she cleaned away the grime, her eyes watching each letter grow clear.

*For all at last returns to the sea. SKYE HAVERFORD BLADE. December 6—*

Jean stopped scrubbing and stared at the words, forcing herself to breathe evenly. She had known David loved his wife, but for some reason the cenotaph, like the postcard she'd read and the incident with Skye's coffee cup, brought the fact to vivid life. She felt illogically as though she had just walked into a room and found him in bed with another woman.

Silly. Not only was this woman his wife, she was dead. Gone forever.

*And he's your employer, Jean,* she reminded herself, but the thought rang hollow. Right or not, David was more to her than an employer. On a strictly private plane, she felt involved with him and his family. She liked his sister and was concerned for his son. Christian's feelings for Baby matched her own, and Jean longed to find other common ground with the silent boy.

Moreover, somewhere so deep inside she barely acknowledged it, lurked the desire to help Chris heal so he would speak again. Yet that seemed a laughable goal for a woman with her history with children.

Baby nosed against her, and Jean turned in the water. David was behind the dolphin, and he pointed topside. But his eyes were on the cenotaph, and even the soupy harbor water could not veil the emotion exposed in his face. In a blink of time Jean glimpsed how vulnerable he really was.

WHEN THEY REACHED the surface, Chris was sitting on the diving platform holding the inflatable wreath, which seemed to have lost some air. As Baby surfaced, he leaned over the water to touch her head. Ignoring the action, David pushed back his mask and nodded at Jean's regulator. "That piece concerns me. You should have something better."

"It was my dad's," Jean explained, then wished she hadn't. She could guess David's feelings about sentimental attachment to inferior diving equipment. "I'm used to it, so it's hard to part with."

"Like Baby." His eyes were cool with irony. "That's it for today. Take tomorrow off, and I'll see you the next day at nine."

There it was, the locked door to his past. He was excluding her from the family ritual. As was appropriate, Jean knew.

Fighting a sense of hurt and sudden loneliness, she grabbed the rails of the dive ladder and started up, removing her tank once she was on the platform.

David did not follow. He remained in the water with Baby and began explaining the dolphin's physiology to Chris. Listening while she removed her fins and mask, Jean suspected he was trying to reduce his son's emotional involvement with Baby by treating her like an object of scientific interest.

She watched as he answered a question Chris had signed to him.

Seeing her eyes on him, David translated, "Chris wants to know if Baby's in danger from sharks." He shook his head at his son. "A big shark maybe, but I don't think so. Dolphins are more dangerous to sharks than the reverse. Of course, Baby would be much safer with her own kind. Dolphins protect each other from predators like sharks. But here in the harbor she's at greater risk from fishing lines and nets, boats with propellers, and polluted water. Of course, for an orca Baby would be easy prey, loner that she is. I can't picture any orcas swimming into the harbor, but if Baby continues to follow Jean up and down the coast, anything could happen."

Jean said, "I think you're slanting things a bit. No shark is going to bother Baby, and no orcas, either. Killer whales are unusual here, and the ones who come are only passing through." She'd told herself so repeatedly.

Giving her a look that said he wished she'd shut up, David answered, "You may be right. I was just pointing out to Chris that he shouldn't be surprised if Baby washes up dead on the beach someday."

Jean was tempted to retort that the same thing could happen to any of them. In deference to Chris, she said only, "Well, Baby has been a victim of circumstances, but we're all lucky to know her." She crouched beside Chris to stroke Baby's skin, enjoying the sweetness of the eye that watched her from the water. "She really likes you, Chris, or she wouldn't have stayed so close to you today and let you ride on her fin."

Chris looked doubtful—and slightly distrustful.

"She shies away from most people," Jean explained, "and to others she's downright mean."

"Let's not attribute our own feelings to her, Jean," said David. "As scientists."

"As scientists?" Jean bent over the water and exchanged

kisses with Baby, then forced a smile as she stood up. "I thought we agreed to be human, instead."

David's eyes followed her as she lifted her tank and gear to the deck and swung herself after them. "As humans we'd be doing her a favor to return her to her own kind."

Jean toyed with the zipper toggle on her wet suit. "She's free, David. I don't think she'd go to her own kind, and I doubt they'd have her—even if this were a part of the ocean where her species abounds."

David rested his arms on the top step of the diving ladder. "We could take her there."

Chris began signing at his father with great urgency. His face was worried, and David gave Jean a look clearer than language. *See what you've done?*

JEAN'S THOUGHTS were still on David's inexplicable attitude toward Baby when Cecily called from Paris that evening. Her sister asked, "Is the connection good at your end?"

"Yes." Jean bent along her outstretched legs to hook her hands over her feet. Ceci had caught her readying to go to the first tae kwon do class she'd attended in weeks, and Jean had grabbed the receiver from the floor. "Can you hear me?"

"Basically. It's a little scratchy," said Cecily. "I just wanted to talk to you and find out if you'd like to come here for Christmas?"

Jean was surprised by the offer—and pleased. Sometimes she wondered if Cecily cared as much as she did about their relationship. She felt genuine regret as she said, "I'd love to, but I've made plans, and they're important."

"Tell," said Ceci.

"Do you know who David Blade is?" Jean didn't want to wait for an answer. "Anyhow, he's a pretty big-time marine explorer, and first he hired me for bottom-cleaning, then he asked me to work on his ship. It's not a real diving job, but it's getting closer." Jean hesitated. "He wants me to watch his son."

"*Ee*," said Cecily expressively. "Did you tell him—"

"No," answered Jean.

"David Blade," said Cecily. "That name's familiar." She gasped. "*Click.* I just made the connection. The Blade Institute, right? He killed his wife." The last was uttered in a tone of bewilderment. "You're working for *him?*"

"He didn't kill his wife," said Jean.

"So he says. I remember that story, and it sure looked like the perfect crime to me. Don't take any boat rides, Jean."

Jean heard the warning, incredulous. Whatever David's problems, she couldn't believe him capable of murder. In her heart she believed he really hadn't recovered from Skye's death. Painfully she remembered how he had taken the coffee cup from her hand that afternoon, as though it was something precious to him. She told her sister, "Well, I am going on a boat ride. I'm going to Baja with him."

"With other people," said Cecily. "Say yes."

"Yes. And I don't think he killed her."

Cecily said, "Just do your Korean karate thing if he gets too close. *Hi-yah!*"

Jean bit her tongue. That method had already failed.

Suspiciously Cecily asked, "Are you falling for him or something?"

"Yes."

Cecily said, "Tell me more. You never fall for anyone. This is interesting."

Jean told Ceci about Chris and Erika and about David's ambivalence toward Baby. She didn't tell her sister he had kissed her. Or that Chris couldn't talk.

"Well, does he like you?" Cecily asked.

Jean wondered what "like" meant. Want to sleep with? Or want to love? Was throwing a woman to the galley floor and kissing her as an encore to anger a sign of affection?

Hesitantly she revealed, "He sent me flowers for graduation." *Orchids*. She bent her left knee, tucking her leg to the side, and stretched forward again.

Cecily gasped. "Oh, God, graduation! Jean, I blew it, didn't I?"

"It's no big deal." She stretched, thinking what a difference those flowers had made.

"It is too a big deal. *Damn,*" said Cecily. "Well, I don't feel as bad as if no one had sent you anything. Tell Monsieur Blade *merci beaucoup* from *moi.*"

Jean tried to imagine herself saying, *My sister says to tell you thank you for doing her the favor of sending me flowers, David, because if you hadn't no one would have.*

She asked Cecily, "Isn't this phone call costing you a fortune?"

"It's been worth it. Did my box come?"

"No." Jean reminded herself to send Cecily's presents the following day.

"Well, if you have a hot date, open the one from the London shop early. It'll keep you warm so you won't have to rely on the arms of a suspected murderer."

Jean wondered if her sister guessed how appealing was the image stirred by her flippant comment. David keeping her warm. She knew he could be gentle from the way he'd held her when he kissed her. She knew he wasn't a murderer.

And she was glad to get off the phone and turn her attention to her martial art. Spending the evening at Frank's class would clear her mind.

"MR. BLADE."

"Mr. Smith."

Jean's head was touching the floor of the gym when she heard David's name. When she heard his voice she nearly lost her balance. What was he doing here at Frank Smith's tae kwon do class? She stared between her spread legs at him, upside down. He looked easy and relaxed as he bowed to Frank.

Without moving Jean watched in fascination as David rose first from the bow, a sign he was the senior black belt. Then she noticed his belt itself.

Jean knew a well-used black belt was the hallmark of a dedicated warrior of the *do,* the way. David's belt looked as if it had seen years of practice and many launderings. Considering its condition—tattered and faded to charcoal, the ragged cotton showing white in places—she felt less chagrined by her own loss of control that morning.

And more astonished by his. Using martial arts to steal a kiss was *not* exemplary black belt behavior.

Jean straightened up from her stretch, and a teenage girl working on her black belt came over and asked her a question about pattern Choong-Moo. Jean showed her, deliberately not looking at David. She wished he would leave, but he was dressed for tae kwon do, so it seemed unlikely.

Frank clapped his hands, calling the class to order. Because she wasn't officially a member of the class, Jean moved to the back of the room with David. He nodded to her. She didn't feel like bowing, but she did, in case Frank was watching. The instructor was half-Korean and ran a traditional martial-arts class, steeped in formality. Nonetheless, as she took her place beside David, Jean couldn't help murmuring, "It *was* inexcusable, sir."

David smiled slightly, and Jean realized with shock that he was embarrassed.

The senior student said, *"Cha-ryot!"*

AS THEY SALUTED the flag, then dropped to the floor for meditation, David remained aware of Jean. She was gorgeous, and he regretted coming. He hadn't expected to see her there, and he'd wanted to talk to Frank about her. The two men had known each other more than ten years, long enough for David to be able to count on Frank's candor—

and discretion. Though the questions would be professional, his reasons for asking them were personal.

Unfortunately his showing up at the gym when she was there was awkward. He could imagine a host of uncomfortable scenarios.

Frank nodded to him across the room, and David moved to the front, reluctantly.

"For those of you who do not know him, this is Mr. David Blade. He is a fifth-degree black belt and a master instructor. You may address him as *'Sabumnim'* or 'Mr. Blade, *sir.*'"

Everyone bowed. Jean had never met a fifth-degree black belt before David.

Frank said, "Mr. Blade practices tae kwon do on his ship. A martial-arts historian would tell you this is not as unusual as it sounds. During the Ch'ing dynasty, students of the *hung gar* style of kung fu were forced to train in secrecy to avoid persecution, and many of them practiced in junks and sampans in the ports of southern China. Confined spaces and low ceilings forced them to make adaptations in their style." Frank smiled. "Tonight we may have the opportunity to observe Mr. Blade's unique and formidable fighting style."

As Frank spoke, Jean watched David. His manner was quietly dignified and he exuded the presence of a warrior, but Jean suspected he would have preferred less attention.

She would have preferred to be absent. Whenever she recalled how she'd kicked David that morning—and been felled like a tree for her efforts—she wished the floor of the gym would open and swallow her. Now, when she longed to redeem herself and prove her competence, she felt, instead, the impact of her erratic class attendance since her parents' death. And the reality that nearly five years had passed since she'd advanced to second *dan*.

Toward the end of the evening, the black belts took turns free-sparring, and her partner was a high school senior she had never fought before. He was well focused, while Jean was nervous and conscious of David's presence. She took a painful blow to the ribs before Frank stopped them and looked at David, as though inviting his comment.

Sure that his presence was at least partially to blame, David said nothing. He was glad when Jean and her partner bowed, shook hands and sat down on the other side of the room. Then, by prearrangement, he stepped forward and invited Frank to spar.

Watching, Jean understood the subtleties of the proposition. For Frank to extend the challenge would have meant that Frank must spar at David's level. She sat back, silent.

They began.

As Frank and David exchanged kicks, punches and blocks, Jean's sparring partner muttered, "That guy has *ki* in spades."

True, when he moved David appeared to be wielding not only his own strength but an additional unseen energy operating beyond the laws of physics—and in concert with them. Jean remembered what Frank had told her long ago. Ki *is everywhere. Everyone has it. The trick is learning to use it.*

Nonetheless, observing David's skill, she was both mesmerized and dispirited. Before she'd known him, he'd seemed unattainable, miles above her realm. Writer, explorer, pirate of the seas with his own vessel to command. Now she was beginning to know him, yet he seemed further out of reach than ever.

She felt like crying, and the minute everyone stood up and clapped at the end of class, she bowed to Frank and to David and to her sparring partner, and headed for the wall where her sweatshirt lay. In a minute, she was out the door.

"JEAN."

David's voice reached her in the night, and her heart started hammering. *I'm going to have a cardiac condition when this job is over,* she thought. Did workman's comp cover emotional duress? She turned to look at him.

Standing over her, the security light in the parking lot shining behind him, he asked, "Where's your car?"

Jean said, "I walked. On the bike path."

David could imagine which one. It was isolated, and the waning moon shed just enough light to make her visible to someone who might hurt her. He said, "I'll drive you home."

"Okay. Thanks."

Deciding to take up the topic of basic safety at another time, David asked, "Don't you have a car?"

"I still have my dad's car, but I don't drive it often." Hastily she said, "I'm a good driver. Don't think I was dangerous in your car."

She was going to be in his car again, this time with him, and David smiled at her choice of words. As she glanced toward the parking lot where the Corvette was parked, he said, "Give me a minute. My clothes are inside."

He looked her over as she followed him back toward the gym, and Jean wondered if he was thinking about her uniform and the fact that she was still wearing it. Ceci's call was to blame in part for her lack of street clothes. Dressing at home was always faster than getting a locker at the gym. But she was breaking a philosophical code by wearing her uniform in transit. Seeing her black belt, potential adversaries would be alerted to her skills—and might even view them as a challenge.

David said nothing about it. As they reentered the lobby, he told her, "I'll be right back."

Soon he was, dressed in a pair of toffee-colored canvas pants and a thick, black rugby shirt that had faded to dark gray. His uniform was folded in his hands, his belt with it, and he told Jean, "Let's go."

In the parking lot, he unlocked the passenger door of his car, his body brushing her shoulder briefly. At the contact,

Jean couldn't stop herself from looking up at him, and for a moment their eyes met in the dim glow of the parking lamps.

From the walkway that led to the street, Frank Smith called, "Don't go home with that man."

David looked up and replied, "She's taking *me* home." He winked at Jean and opened the door for her.

Seconds later, when he had slid behind the wheel and closed his own door, Jean asked, "How do you know Frank? And why have I never seen you here?"

David fastened his seat belt and started the car. "I train at a place in Ventura. It's—" he searched for the right word "—low profile." A converted storeroom on a back alley. The master was a seventh-degree black belt with whom David had never exchanged a word of English. David told Jean, "I met Frank in Korea. He was visiting family. I used to live there."

"Is that where you learned tae kwon do?" Even as she asked, Jean knew it couldn't be the whole answer. David must have a good twenty years of training.

He said, "I've had many teachers. Actually my father was the first. He was very good." He backed out of the parking space.

Jean said, "My father was my sparring partner."

David heard the sadness in her voice and understood it better than she would ever know. They had been about the same age when they lost their parents. Another parallel, like their interest in tae kwon do. If he'd believed in such things, he would have wondered if she was his soul mate, come to him at last.

He didn't believe in such things.

He said, "Have you eaten?" It was nine-thirty.

She'd had only a peanut-butter-and-jelly sandwich, which she didn't care to confide. She said, "I eat light before class."

"Want some dinner?" They were at the exit to the parking lot, and he waited for her answer.

Jean couldn't believe her ears. "That would be great." Then she remembered she didn't have any money with her. She told him so.

David looked at her and shook his head, as though at a charming but appallingly ignorant child. "I'll pay," he said. "Always."

HE TOOK HER to Sulphur Springs Tavern in the Santa Inez Mountains. It was a tavern in the truest sense, with a bar next door that was the haunt of college students and bikers alike; yet the restaurant itself, located in a separate building, was considered one of the finest in the area, with a reputation for superb food, from seafood to wild game to a natural California cuisine. Pricey but informal.

The drive took nearly half an hour, and Jean loved every minute of it. It was too cold to have the top down, but riding in the Corvette on the highway was like being in a rocket. Pulling the elastic band from the end of her braid, she loosened her hair and leaned back in the seat, shifting to ease the pain from the kick she'd taken.

David caught the motion and remembered the blow. He said, "Go ahead and take off your belt. This place can be rough, and drunks sometimes see a black belt as an invitation to fight. Better to look like a pastry chef."

Jean laughed at the image. She had two *doboks*—one all white, symbolizing purity, and another trimmed in black, symbolizing the dignity of a black belt. Without a belt, the all-white uniform she was wearing did resemble a chef's outfit. Appreciating the way David had cautioned without criticizing, she untied her belt. "You haven't been in a fight here?"

He shook his head. "I run fast. I've never been in a fight anywhere." His eyes hit hers briefly. "Except with you."

Dropping her belt on top of David's uniform between

the seats, Jean smiled, unsurprised. Avoiding unnecessary violence was part of the martial way. Yet she knew if David's family was threatened he would stand his ground.

David fell silent, suddenly wondering what he was doing. He should have driven her straight home. Or taken her somewhere in town. This impulse to feed her at the best restaurant in Santa Barbara County was stupid. Now she was practically lying down in the passenger seat, her hair all around her, like a woman who'd just gotten out of bed— or was on her way there. She looked happy and relaxed and as though she'd love to be ravished. By him.

And he wasn't looking forward to sitting through dinner with a hard-on. He didn't even have anything to say to her.

She said, "Is Erika with Chris?"

"Yes."

She said, "I'd better learn some sign language so I can understand him."

David nodded, relieved she had chosen a simple topic. "He writes, too. Extremely well. But I'll teach you a couple of signs at the restaurant."

When they pulled up in front, there were rows of motorcycles parked on both sides of the mountain road in front of the log tavern, and university students in fraternity sweatshirts were spilling outside. Rock and roll blared from inside the building, where neon beer signs blinked in the windows, offering holiday slogans.

Before getting out of the car, David tugged a heavy, navy blue sweater on over his head. Jean pulled on her sweatshirt, opened her door and stepped out into the night. She locked the door before she shut it, then shivered. It was a pristine night. The white Christmas lights on the roof eaves of the tavern buildings seemed a pale imitation of the stars winking through the towering evergreens.

David said, "Come on." He didn't move toward her or touch her as they crossed the road to the restaurant.

When they were seated in the rustic dining room at a

table ornamented with a spray of holly and a single red candle, David ordered a bottle of wine, then proceeded to show Jean some sign language as promised.

"This is Hank the Cowdog. Do you know about Hank?" he asked.

Jean shook her head.

"Chris will tell you," David told her. "I think I'll leave it to him." His hands moved. "This is SR-71 Blackbird. That's his favorite plane. And Corvette. His favorite car." Then he showed her some practical signs, but when Jean tried to copy them, he stopped her. "Don't. You talk. Let him sign to you. I want him to talk."

Abruptly David fell silent. That was something he never said to anyone, never uttered aloud. To cover the revelation he showed Jean some other words. "Bow. Stern. Fore. Aft. Locker. Stateroom." He moved faster, teasing her until she laughed.

She said, "I can't remember all that."

"You'll catch on. And there's this one, of course."

Jean watched the movements. He didn't say anything afterward, just lowered his hands and gazed toward the kitchen.

Jean said, "What's that one?"

His eyes shifted to hers. "I love you." Then, he reached for his water glass and looked at his watch, as though wondering where the waitress was so they could order and eat and leave.

SHE WAS ASLEEP when he pulled up to the curb in front of her house and killed the engine. The wine, thought David. It was excellent, but he should have ordered a couple of glasses of the house, instead. He and Jean were both pretty loose by the end of the meal, and he'd put his hand on her shoulder on the way to the car. Three or four times she'd given him a look that said plain as words, *I want you to kiss me.*

He wasn't going to do that again.

But he thought about it as he watched her sleeping in his car, his sweater over her legs. He thought of kissing her. He considered starting the car again and taking her to the ship. He briefly envisioned making love to her in the car, at the curb. Finally he clapped his hands, the sound she would have heard at the beginning of every tae kwon do class.

She blinked and looked at him, momentarily disoriented.

He said, *"Cha-ryot."*

Attention. Jean winced, then rubbed her eyes.

"You're home." David scooped up a black belt and dropped it into her lap. "I'll see you to the door." The lawn was dark and tree-shaded, the moon now shrouded in fog. Not liking the fact that Jean came and went from this place alone at night, he opened his door and got out.

Groggy, she opened the passenger door and stood up, clutching the belt and David's sweater. She set his sweater back on the seat, then looked up to realize he was holding the door for her. When she stepped away from the car, he shut it.

Jean led the way through the side gate and across the lawn to the patio and the back door. The house towered over them like a monster of the night. She had left the back light on but was glad for David's presence. Had she actually fallen asleep in the car? Yes. She could still feel the effects of the wine.

Watching her fit the key into the lock, David reflected that he should come in and check the house for her. But if he did he would never leave. He kept quiet.

When the door was open, Jean snapped on a light, then turned to him with a smile. She gave him a small, sweet bow.

It was too much for him.

Instead of returning it, he reached for her. She seemed momentarily stunned, then came near, holding his arms. He rearranged her, wrapping her arms around him. She hugged tightly.

*Good,* thought David. It was what he wanted.

His mouth started out against her hair, then hungrily worked its way to her face and her lips. Already he was as hard as could be and had to pull her close to him, closer, had to take everything he could from the mouth he'd been watching all night. His hand found her breast, small and high and taut. She pressed nearer to him, plainly returning his desire.

David relaxed some, continuing to draw her near, fit her against his body, learn the feel of her mouth. If a kiss was all that was going to happen—and it was—he planned to enjoy it and extend it. But he wanted so much more. He wanted her hands on him, places no one else touched. He wanted to touch her, undress her, put his mouth on her everywhere, taste her, come inside her. But he only kissed her and wrapped her hair around and around his hand.

The hair was the mistake. Holding her hair.

The colors came back to him, the fluid red, the shape in the sea, and he backed away so fast that Jean lost her balance and nearly fell. He caught her and set her toward the door.

His desire was gone, snuffed out. A heartbeat earlier she had been the source of his need, the whole of his focus, but now he couldn't even touch her. The life force inside him had died and rotted. Images still swam at the edges of his consciousness, threatening, and he wanted to be alone to deal with them, banish them if he could. He said, "Good night."

She said, "Thank you, David."

He nodded and waited until she went in and closed the door. Then he went back to his car and waited there, listening, because he hadn't checked her house and knew he should have.

And because he couldn't bring himself to return to the ship.

AFTER LOCKING UP, Jean went into the living room and hurled herself onto the couch, tossing down the black belt she held. Her emotions were a tumult, her body still hot from holding him.

David had ended the kiss abruptly, but Jean thought she understood. She'd felt his excitement, and he was being decent to her, which she appreciated. She wasn't sure she was ready for much more than he'd given, but she knew if he had tried to take her to bed she would have gone.

*He's nice,* she thought in wonder as she had so many times that evening. He'd been a good date. Attentive. Not especially talkative, but never rude, either. Not tonight, anyhow.

Her mind flashed back to the sign language he'd shown her, to his eyes on hers when he said, *I love you.* He was just translating, but for a moment it had felt almost as though he wasn't, as though he had found a way to tell her something he didn't feel ready to say more plainly.

Jean squelched the notion. It had been a beautiful one— she and David knowing immediately they were right for each other and being unable to help falling in love.

But then she remembered Skye Haverford Blade and that the following day was the anniversary of her death. The thought upset her. She didn't want David to still be mourning his wife.

*He's not for you, Jean. You're a good student and a diver and a black belt, but his wife was sophisticated and apparently brilliant. Two European universities.*

Which schools? Oxford? Cambridge? It hardly mattered. Undoubtedly the heiress had been a match for David. If someone asked him, he would probably say in an understated way, *Yes, Skye was smart.* And behind the words would be a backlog of memories.

Jean cut off the thought. She was torturing herself, and she knew it. He had kissed her tonight with dizzying thoroughness, and that should be enough.

Idly she reached for the black belt at her feet, preparing to roll it, and felt with shock the texture of frayed edges beneath her fingertips. It was his.

CHAPTER SEVEN

WHEN SHE ARRIVED at the *Skye* two mornings later he was
already on deck in his wet suit. Jean asked, "Am I late?"

She was uneasy.

David looked wary. He shook his head and nodded to a
coffee mug sitting on a locker beside him. "I'm just waiting for the fog to lift."

The twofold reply encompassed the weather and the
early hour. It was a chilly morning with a smell of salt
rather than tar in the air.

Jean wondered how the previous day had gone. She had
thought of little but David and Chris as she went about her
own chores, Christmas shopping and gift wrapping. What
were they thinking about? What did the marker for Skye
look like? Did Chris remember his mother?

Did David cry?

His belt, still on her couch, was a constant reminder of
their dinner together and the kiss at her back door. Although she knew he had handed it to her accidentally, the
belt reminded her of a man leaving a hat in a woman's
closet so he'd have an excuse to see her again.

But of course David didn't need an excuse. He was her
boss.

As she joined him on the aft deck, Jean told him, "I
forgot your belt."

David shrugged. "You can keep it for a while. I've been
using yours." He didn't add that Erika had noticed, not just
the belt switch but Jean's initials. *J. Y. Do I know someone*

*whose initials are J. Y.?* David had thought he'd never hear the end of it, but he liked the idea of Jean having his belt. For a while.

Pleased that he was in no hurry to have his belt back, Jean remembered an idea she'd mulled over the day before. She didn't know how to ask. David was staring out over the stern at a spot in the water, and she tried to imagine what his reaction might be.

When he looked up she bowed. "Would you please teach me?"

*Teach you what?* He hoped she didn't ask other men that question with those trusting green eyes. She must mean tae kwon do. For a moment he studied her. Then, unsure of his voice, he said, "If you like. We can work out together, and I'm sure we'll both benefit. I start at five-thirty every morning." Hearing himself, he wanted to wince. What was he getting into?

Jean Young. Ready-made diving buddy and sparring partner, albeit light and small for the latter. They'd both have to be careful.

He nodded at her jeans and sweatshirt, pointing out that she wasn't suited up. "Let's get to work."

OVER THE NEXT FEW DAYS they fell into a routine. Jean arrived at 5:25 each morning, after walking from her house in the dark. David usually seemed restless when she arrived. He was always stretching on the deck, eyes alert as though he'd been watching for her arrival. Jean changed in the crew's quarters, and then joined him on the aft deck or in the salon.

Only the first day was different. Jean had worn her uniform to the harbor, carrying a change of clothes in a day pack, and David met her as she boarded the ship. In the gray-blue light before dawn, he drew her aft, and in the dimness under the canopy he stepped close to her and began untying his black belt from around her waist. Meeting her eyes, he said, "I think we'd better trade back."

Jean didn't move, only watched his hands as he took the belt. A moment later he reached for hers, which had been lying on a chair nearby where she hadn't even noticed it. He tied it around her waist, his eyes on hers as he knotted the ends. Jean felt like a pirate's captive who'd just been tenderly bound to be enjoyed later. She couldn't talk and was both relieved and crushed when David stepped back and bowed to her.

Moments later Baby started calling to them from the water, and David said, "She's a distraction. Let's go below."

It was a new relationship, different from diving with him and taking his orders, different from the times they'd kissed. Tae kwon do was mental, physical and spiritual. It was combat and honor and integrity. Jean had not sparred so regularly with any one man since her father's death, and sometimes she felt almost as though she had been passed from her father's hands to David's.

And David was a master.

But he didn't kiss her again.

He seemed to have neatly compartmentalized his treatment of her, following different rules in different situations. For work, it was cool professionalism; for tae kwon do, formal courtesy. She was "ma'am." He was "sir." *Sabumnim.* Master instructor.

Whenever he touched her during sparring or teaching, the courtesy was a wall between them, but Jean knew it was also a channel. The silence of meditation, the challenge of drill and the intensity of fighting all reinforced a common philosophy and mutual respect. When they met each other's eyes, bowed to each other and clasped hands after sparring, Jean was always reminded of a favorite saying of her father's. *Respect is love in plain clothes.*

She loved David.

It was useless to tell herself she barely knew him. It was also increasingly untrue. His character permeated his life and his actions. He was a good father and brother, a hard worker, a shrewd businessman, and a gentleman. And he intrigued her endlessly. Jean could not imagine wanting a different man—or ever having this one. When days passed and he made no mention of kissing her or eating dinner with her, she realized they were operating in a professional mode and likely to remain that way. Tae kwon do, "the way of punching and kicking," became intimacy. Work became a means of knowing David better.

As the days passed, she helped him with maintenance and cleaning and began to assume the role of personal secretary. Trying to focus on furthering her career, Jean tirelessly swabbed the decks, filled the water and composed business letters, and she sensed she was winning David's approval. When she took the time to recoil a disarranged line on the deck, she could feel him watching her, and she knew it was what he would have done.

And then there was Chris. Jean had never believed a child could really like her, and it shocked and thrilled her to learn she was wrong. After her first morning workout with David, she was on her way to change clothes in the crew's quarters when she came upon Chris in the galley, opening the eighth door on his advent calendar. When he saw her black belt, his eyes grew huge—which surprised Jean, because his father was a black belt, too. A master.

But his reaction provided an opportunity for communication, and she asked him about the calendar. Was it his? One nod. Did Erika give it to him? A shake of his head. His dad? Big, emphatic nod. Stunned by that, Jean asked what was in the eighth door, and he showed her. An angel. Then a game began. What did he think was in the next door? Shrug. An elephant? He shook his head, and Jean tried to think of something more ridiculous. A squashed peanut-butter sandwich? For a moment, she thought he would giggle, but instead, she saw only a silent expression of merriment, laughter without sound. But every morning thereafter, when she and David finished their workout, Chris was waiting for her to play the calendar game and count the days until Christmas.

Three days after the anniversary of Skye's death—the ninth on the calendar, marked by a candy cane—David asked her to watch Chris for the afternoon. Eager to prove herself, Jean took him to the park and to the library, where she found a book on Christmas crafts to make with children. They spent the rest of the day making ornaments from macaroni, yarn and bottle caps and cutting out paper snowflakes, which Erika hung all over the ship until David said it felt like Ellesmere Island.

But he seemed quietly pleased, and later that same day he suggested Jean teach Chris some beginning tae kwon do techniques. So every afternoon she took Chris to the East Beach lawn for a lesson. He clearly loved it. Jean caught him in moments alone practicing elementary kicks and punches, and she knew he longed for the uniform David said he *might* get for Christmas.

On their third day of lessons, Jean glanced up from teaching and saw David sitting on a boardwalk bench watching. She told Chris, "There's your dad."

Chris looked at him and waved, then returned his attention to her, waiting for his next instructions.

Jean said, "Shall we show him the Very Best Method of Self-Defense?"

Chris nodded.

With a mock roar, she leapt toward him to tickle him.

Grinning, Chris darted away and ran to the bench where his father sat. David smiled in approval, complimented him on his escape, and sent him back.

Because they'd been at it for forty-five minutes, Jean told Chris, "Time to call it quits, sir. *Cha-ryot.*"

After a brief meditation, they walked over to the boardwalk, and David stood up from the bench. He touched Christian's hair, but his eyes were on Jean.

She sensed he wanted to talk and was glad when he took fifty cents from his pocket and handed it to his son. "Salt-water taffy. We're right behind you."

Giving a small leap in the air, an unusual show of exuberance, Chris skipped ahead of them down the boardwalk toward the wharf. David and Jean followed at a slower pace.

David said, "I like what you're doing with him."

Jean let herself feel the sun on her face, the light breeze in her hair, the pleasure of walking beside David and hearing him—or anyone—tell her she was doing the right thing with a child. But a concern had come to her more than once when she was working with Chris, and though she knew the problem couldn't be helped she felt a need to share it. Her only hesitation was in giving David pain—and in knowing he must already be aware of the obstacle. But she spoke.

"David, he can't *ki-hop*. I know that's obvious, but the loud yell is such an important part of self-defense, of tae kwon do." She didn't add what David knew, that besides adding force to blows, the *ki-hop* gave the practitioner a powerful physical and psychological advantage. She glanced at David's face and wished she'd said nothing. His features were quiet, but she sensed a storm in his heart. She said, "I'm sorry. I know you can't do anything about it."

He stared ahead on the boardwalk, watching his son turn onto the wharf and pause to investigate something on the planks. He found himself admitting, "A few months ago, after a series of speech therapists failed, I tried to teach him to *ki-hop* as a means to get him to speak." When she glanced up at him, he avoided her eyes but said, "Christian ended up in tears, and so did Erika." And so had he, though not until later. Taking a small breath, he said, "But if you want to try, be my guest."

Jean realized he was giving her permission to do whatever she could to help his son speak, even at the price of Chris's eerie, silent tears. It was a tremendous sign of trust. But Jean said, "I think the problem's out of my league."

"Join the club." They had reached the wharf, and David watched Chris, still ahead of them, pause for a long look at a pelican sitting on a piling. Then he glanced at Jean, whose eyes were also on Chris. She was watchful, as though she half expected him to slide beneath the wooden railings that edged the pier. He said quietly, "I think you'd make a very good mother."

Jean drew in her breath, tasting the salt and tar in the air. Her chest felt full, swelling, and she remembered telling him her mother had said she'd make a bad mom. She knew David had said what he had because he, too, remembered. Waves of emotion scattered through her, and it was a moment before she could formulate a reply. She said, "That's the nicest thing anyone's ever said to me."

David looked at her and put his hand on her back over her braid as they walked. A moment later he dropped his hand to his side and shoved it into the pocket of his pants as though to keep from touching her any more.

AFTER THAT DAY, he asked her more frequently to watch Chris, and Jean loved it. The only drawback was Baby. The more time she spent on shore, the less Jean saw of the dolphin. Often, when she'd been working on deck and had to go below to complete a different job, Baby cried to her from the water. Every evening Jean swam with her in the ocean, but she sensed the dolphin's sadness, and she couldn't forget David's saying he suspected Baby was dependent on her. Now, whenever work absorbed her, Baby was lonesome.

To make amends, Jean began to spend her breaks and lunch hour with Baby. On the afternoon of the sixteenth, three days before they were scheduled to depart for Baja,

Jean was playing with Baby when David came to the aft deck with a thick manila envelope and asked her if she'd look at a grant proposal someone had sent him for the Haverford Trust.

Jean threw the deflated Christmas wreath to Baby one last time and stood up on the diving platform to climb back on deck. Erika was there sketching her, and Jean wondered whether David would have offered her a hand if his sister hadn't been present. When they were alone or with Chris, he sometimes did.

But now he stood holding the envelope and watching Baby retrieve the wreath. Scrambling onto the aft deck, Jean said, "I don't know anything about grants."

David stepped behind her, directing her toward the salon. "You're going to learn. I read a lot of them, and so will you."

It was a promising remark, the first hint Jean had heard from him that her position on his ship might be leading to something permanent. It wasn't diving, but Jean felt confident that would come.

David told Erika, "Sorry for taking your model."

"I'll do Baby," said Erika. "She'll appreciate the attention since you're keeping Jean so busy. If I didn't know better, David, I'd think you were hoping Baby would go find a different friend." Her tone was ironic—and challenging.

Jean paused, struck by the words. She hoped David would answer his sister, but instead, he put his hand on her own shoulder, urging her toward the cabin.

Compliantly Jean went below. Only when David had followed her into the salon did she speak. "Is what Erika said true? Are you trying to keep me from Baby?"

"I'm trying to keep Baby away from my ship. Yesterday she showed up with a tinsel garland she'd taken off someone's boat. She's mischievous, noisy and demanding, and none of us have time for her."

Jean took a step back. "We could have time for her. Instead, you send me into town and over to the park with Chris to keep us from being near her."

David heard the "us." He found it threatening. "That's my prerogative. Where Chris is concerned at any rate. Where you work and for whom is your choice, of course. We have no contract, *ma'am*," he added.

Jean heard that as a subtle reminder that she could be dismissed with a word. And that the coaching he gave her in tae kwon do was a gift. That was the "ma'am" part.

Jean thought it graceless of him to mention it. Graceless, but clever. Carefully concealing all sarcasm, she said, "Your point, sir."

"Thank you." Shifting the manila envelope, he said, "Let's look at this in my cabin. The light's better."

His cabin. Thoughts of Baby evaporated as she followed him down through the galley and up to his room. But when they went inside, David left the door open.

The top of his desk was rolled up, and stacks of paper, manila folders, account books and correspondence covered the writing surface. Until that moment, Jean had never appreciated how much paperwork he must have to do. What he sent her way was the light stuff.

Indicating that she should sit in the chair, he took the edge of the berth, the only other seat, and briefly explained his obligation to the Haverford Trust. Each year he had to select a number of scientific and academic grants to award.

Jean's curiosity simmered like a pot on a stove, and as soon as he had said that much, she asked, "The Haverford Trust? Is that...yours?"

David looked at her, first startled, then amused. "I didn't know that my holdings interested you."

Jean reddened. "I didn't mean it that way."

David was sure she did. "The answer is, no, the trust is not *mine*, as you put it. I am one of several trustees, and the Blade Institute is one of several beneficiaries. The other trustees take care of many tasks I dislike.'' He met her eyes for a moment. He wanted to tease her more and wondered if it would be a mistake. With Jean, the verbal sparring was trickier than anything they did during their morning workouts. He was more likely to lose his balance.

But she was still blushing.

He said, ''There's a copy of last year's income-tax receipt almost right under your nose.''

Jean looked deliberately away from the desk, her color deepening. He must know how nearly irresistible an invitation that was. Her feelings for him had nothing to do with his financial worth, but that didn't mean she wasn't curious. Lifting her eyes to his for a moment, she said, ''You're very mean.''

''Very rich, too,'' said David, eyes warm on hers. ''More than rich enough to keep a woman in wet suits and diving equipment for the rest of her life.''

Jean swallowed hard.

Seeing her throbbing pulse and the wide green eyes that could never hide anything, David cursed himself. What in God's name had prompted him to say something so insane? Realizing he now had little choice but to add something that might hurt her, he no longer felt playful. He felt only self-disgust. He muttered, ''I shouldn't have said that. Please don't read anything into it.''

''Of course not.'' She folded her arms across her chest and blinked at the manila envelope, which lay against his knee. ''Tell me about the proposal.''

David watched her reaction. It was on the tip of his tongue to say something that would soften his comment, but he held back. He'd been honest, and that was what he had to be.

Trying to put the indiscretion out of his mind, he reached for the envelope, removed the bulk of paper from inside and set the proposal on his desk. ''The applicant is a man you probably know. He's a professor of marine biology at the university. Michael Avery.''

Jean felt faint.

David said, ''He wants to go to Antarctica to study krill.''

*Krill*, thought Jean stupidly, trying to focus. The tiny shrimplike krill were a major food source for many arctic animals. She asked David, ''What do you want me to do?''

He nodded at the proposal. ''Read that and tell me if you think we should award the grant. I have my own ideas, but I'd like a second opinion.''

Jean considered suggesting Erika provide it. She wasn't sure she could be objective.

But David had stood up. ''That will take you some time. Look for me if you want to talk about it. I have to meet with some board members this afternoon, and I'd like to tell them something.''

For several minutes after he'd gone, Jean sat motionless at his desk. Was this fate, come to collect payment? Did David *know* Michael Avery?

She rested her elbows on David's desk and buried her face in her hands. She had to tell him what had happened in Baja.

If she could.

WHEN JEAN EMERGED FROM his cabin more than an hour later, David was nowhere in sight, but Erika was in the salon inspecting the matting and frames on some of her paintings, which were going into an exhibit that weekend. There were pictures on the couch and on all the chairs and leaning against two walls.

Erika said, ''There you are. I was beginning to wonder if my brother had locked you in the cargo hold.'' With a quick glance at Jean, she said, ''Don't read anything into that.''

*I shouldn't have said that. Please don't read anything*

*into it.* David's words echoed through her, and Jean shut them from her mind. Seeing Erika reminded her of her dispute with David over Baby. Perhaps Erika would have some insight into her brother's attitude. Postponing her search for David, Jean asked, "What do you think he has against Baby?"

Erika looked at her, eyes direct. "What do *you* think, Jean?"

Jean gave a helpless shrug. "I know he doesn't want Chris becoming attached to her."

Erika nodded. "In David's experience, loving something that can die is a hazard. I think he would prefer for Chris—and himself—to love only the more permanent things in this world. The ocean. The sun. Ideas. The things he thinks can never be taken from him."

Jean found Erika's choice of words telling. The ocean had been taken from her. She said, "But, Erika, a person can't go through life like that. David loves Chris—and you. He can't help that."

"But he can help loving Baby. And he thinks he can stop Chris from loving her."

Jean said, "I suppose that explains it. I'd wondered if maybe he just doesn't care for animals—or if that shark attack affected him."

Erika shook her head. "No. David likes animals, but he keeps an emotional distance. They can die, you see."

"Like Skye," murmured Jean, hardly knowing she spoke.

"Not just that," said Erika. "Our parents' death was awful for him. Apparently, when the *Siren* started sinking, Dad ordered him to ready the life raft. Mother went below to get something. And that was the last David saw of either of them."

Jean was shocked. It was easy to imagine the scene. David inflating a life raft on the icy deck, waiting for his parents to come, then searching for them. And finally realizing he would lose his own life if he didn't leave the ship.

Erika changed the subject. "Are you interested in David's shark bite? You must be," she said without waiting for an answer. "You're a diver. You need to watch some unedited Blade-family home videos." Wheeling across the salon, she opened a locker containing rows of videotapes. She found the right one in moments and closed the locker. "You won't want to watch this whole thing. It's uncut footage from our series on sharks," Erika explained, turning on the monitor and popping the tape into the VCR. "David was seventeen and very playful with the sharks."

Jean badly wanted to watch, but she remembered the proposal on David's desk. And what she must tell him. Her stomach pitched at the thought. She told Erika, "I'm supposed to talk to David."

"He went to the marine supply."

To see Jake? Jean reminded herself again that Jake didn't know about the Averys; he had as much as told her so.

Erika gestured to the floor. "Take a load off, woman. David would want you to. He might not want you to see this," she admitted, laughing as she pushed the play button, "but he would want you to have a break."

Christian slipped up the companionway into the salon and joined Jean on the carpet in front of the screen.

Erika laughed. "Chris likes to watch his dad pull the shark by the tail."

Jean remembered how David had said the bite had happened: *recklessness and stupidity.*

As the tape reeled, she rapidly became engrossed, her attention glued to the first test shots on the deck of the *Siren*, Christopher Blade's famous research vessel. Jean had seen the Blade shark series on public television years earlier, but it was entirely different to see the footage as a "family home video." These were people she knew: Erika walking the deck in a wet suit, her hair bound in a jaunty ponytail. A much-younger David, his brown eyes untouched by years and experience. Most intriguing, however, was the patriarch and captain, Christopher Blade, his hair salt-and-pepper gray, his body young and fit.

Watching her father help toss a shark cage overboard, Erika remarked, "David was very close to Dad, which I think is why resurrecting the Institute was so important to him. Unfortunately the bad publicity around Skye's death almost destroyed us. The Institute's just me and David now. We have an office in Washington that handles mailings and book and video sales, but we'll never have the reputation we once had. Some blows are just too devastating."

Remembering that Jake had mentioned David was in danger of losing his ship at the time of Skye's death, Jean wondered what blows she meant. But her attention was drawn back to the screen as Christopher Blade explained that Erika would film the sequence from a separate cage while he and David manned the larger one and chummed the water to attract sharks.

"Where is this?" Jean asked.

"Hawaii." Erika smiled. "When the paramedics came, one of them said David had received a great blessing from Kama-Hoa-Lii, the shark king, and would be reincarnated as a shark in his next life. David was losing lots of blood at the time, and Dad was just furious at the remark. The next-life bit, especially."

Jean watched David and his father descend in the shark cage and begin to chum the water with fish.

"We were trying to provoke a feeding frenzy," Erika explained. "The blood in the water drew them, but they just fed calmly, and we all got impatient. We'd picked Hawaii rather than another locale because we were short on funding just then, but the sharks had been disappointing."

David opened the cage door, and he and his father swam out.

"See that device in David's hand? It produces a beating sound that attracts the sharks."

Jean glanced at Chris, and he smiled at her. He had lost a tooth just the previous day and had been left a silver dollar by the tooth fairy. Unable to stop herself, Jean reached an arm around him and hugged his shoulders, and Chris settled comfortably against her.

Jean watched David approach a shark twice his size and latch onto its tail. Flabbergasted, she asked, "What species is—"

The animal turned and bit David's side around his chest and shoulder. Jean watched David push back the shark's snout with the sound-maker while Christopher Blade came wielding a big camera.

"The cameras were our best protection," Erika explained as another shark narrowed on them and attempted to bite David.

Jean was frozen in place, her heart racing. *He lived,* she reminded herself. *You know he's safe.*

Yet David and his father were yards from the cage, and sharks surrounded them, swimming faster as streams of David's blood clouded the water. Barely breathing, Jean followed the Blades' long journey back to the cage and the fight to keep the big sharks from joining them while smaller ones slipped between the bars. Then the camera cut to the deck and David's young body, bleeding. A man his father's age pressed a blood-soaked towel hard on the wound, stemming the flow, and said, "That'll be two inches deep, and you're lucky he didn't take a piece of you with him."

David, white, looked at the camera and said, "Erika, do you have to take movies? I might be dying."

Laughing, Erika shut off the VCR. "My favorite line. He went into shock a few minutes later. There's more—mainly family stuff with his wound and his stitches—but it's not that interesting."

*For you.* Jean was hungry to know more about David,

even the smallest things. Feeling wan, she smiled down at Christian. "Do you think your Dad's brave?"

Chris nodded earnestly.

Jean wondered what else lay in the Blades' home-video collection. Seeing a younger Erika reminded her that David's sister hadn't always been disabled. What had happened? No one ever talked about it.

When Chris had gone to play with Baby, Jean asked, "Erika, do you swim?"

"Sometimes," Erika admitted. "And I swim vicariously, watching you dive every day. There are so few women divers courageous enough to find employment in diving. I know cleaning boats is dirty work, but when I see you out there with Baby— Suffice it to say I'm envious."

Jean wanted to ask the details of her disability but felt her questions wouldn't be welcome. She'd observed that Erika never walked and seldom put weight on her legs. Yet her legs appeared to be intact.

Jean suggested, "Why don't you come swimming with Chris and Baby and me this afternoon? It's sunny, and the water's warm."

With some persuasion, Erika joined them. Jean helped her from the deck to the diving platform, and the three spent an hour in the water, Baby befriending Erika as she had the other Blades.

Erika's eyes shone as she hung on to the swimming ladder and tossed the flattened Christmas wreath to the dolphin. Jean felt a strong empathy for David's sister. Erika had been a diver, too, and it was easy for Jean to imagine herself in the other woman's shoes, deprived of the undersea world she loved. Jean admired David for making it possible for Erika to enjoy a life on the ocean, however altered from the one she had known. Surely it had been costly and difficult to make the *Skye* even partially accessible to a wheelchair.

They were still swimming when David returned from his

errands. He reacted with pleasure seeing Erika in the water, and his good mood spread over the ship like the warmth of a Santa Ana wind. From the water, Jean watched Chris, still dripping, run to his father and embrace him.

David said, "What's this running on deck? Down, Hank."

Chris performed a frolicsome cowdog imitation, based on the hero of his favorite series of books, then proceeded to challenge David to a wrestling match. Clutching the edge of the diving platform, Jean laughed as David succumbed dramatically on the aft deck, pinned. A minute later, he flopped his son over and returned the favor.

There was love shining in his eyes, and Jean realized again, more potently than ever, that Christian was the center of his world, the thing most important to him, most carefully guarded. Soberly she watched them as they lay on the deck together, Chris signing at his father and David looking as though he had all the time in the world, which Jean knew he didn't. He had a board meeting to attend.

And she had something to tell him.

SHE WAS DRYING HERSELF in the diving alcove fifteen minutes later when David finally approached her. He'd just helped his sister out of the water and seen her inside, and he told Jean, "Swimming's good for Erika. Thanks."

"Thank Baby." Jean unzipped her wet suit.

Glimpsing her swimsuit and the curve of her breast, David reached for her zipper toggle and pulled it back up, hiding her body from his own eyes. "In your cabin."

She stared down at his hand. David withdrew it and turned to leave the alcove before he could touch her again.

She asked, "David, what happened to Erika?"

"Car accident." He opened the door.

"What, exactly, is wrong?"

David paused. She had a right to an answer. He said, "I don't know. It's been three years, and the doctors say it's all in her head. Psychological. Any physical problems are healed, but when she tries to make her legs work she's only frustrated. She says she has no sensation."

Jean studied him for a moment. "Three years. Was that before or after——" She stopped, looked away.

David knew how the question ended. Before or after Skye's death. "Before." He watched her eyes dart up. Holding the doorframe, reminding himself he needed to leave, he asked, "Did you finish your reading?"

Jean nodded, her face pale, and he waited for her to say what she'd thought of the proposal. At last she did. "It seems expensive, but it might be worth it."

Just what David had thought. It didn't help, except as flimsy proof that Jean's mind worked somewhat like his own. He said, "Thanks." His eyes lingered on her body, and he remembered what had happened the night they'd met at the gym. Right now she seemed as desirable as she had when he'd kissed her that night—until the colors came. The horror locked inside him.

Would the nightmare ever stop?

He watched Jean thoughtfully as she shivered in her wet suit. She seemed preoccupied, as he was, and he wondered what was on her mind.

Deliberately David called up the darkness inside him. For a moment the ghastly images and sensations filled his mind, and then he choked them down and let himself see Jean. She was blameless, unconnected with his pain. Neither of them could help it that he wanted her.

He knew he shouldn't be afraid.

He told himself he wasn't.

As she shivered again, he touched her. His hand fell to her hair, then slid against her neck to cup the underside of her jaw.

She shuddered faintly at the touch and moved nearer.

Lightly, he let the length of his body meet hers, then wrapped his arms around her and hugged her close. How had she ever come to him, this woman who lived in a wet suit and sparred in a black belt? Like a cat burglar, she had penetrated the outer barriers, eluded the guards.

A part of him wanted to let her in deeper.

The larger, more combative part wanted to snarl at her for how close she had already come.

But now his mouth was beside her hair. He said, "Jean, how would you like it if I were to begin to feel seriously about you?"

## CHAPTER EIGHT

JEAN DIDN'T TRUST her voice, but she answered, "Very much."

He moved back a little, enough to see her eyes. Then he kissed her.

The heat and gentleness of the action disconcerted her, highlighting her own deception. But Jean knew she could no longer risk the truth. The stakes had suddenly become much too high.

Was it possible David could love her?

Panic raced through her. His question had suggested he could turn serious feelings on and off like tap water, which seemed possible. He'd probably had practice. Jean hadn't. If she could have stopped loving him, she would have already. Emotionally the man was as accessible as a shredded document.

Except when they kissed. His mouth conveyed more as it touched hers than it ever did through speech. She felt the ever-present tension in him, but also something else, something deeper than desire. Need. And darkness. And some quaking emotion she couldn't quite make out. It reminded her that he could hurt her.

Against his lips Jean whispered almost inaudibly, "I haven't had a lot of relationships, David."

David stiffened almost imperceptibly, but he didn't pull away. He said, "Neither have I. And let's not call this one."

Jean looked up, and David felt himself relax slightly at

her expression. He said softly, "I think, in this context, a relationship implies something that doesn't work out."

Jean felt as though she were dreaming. He *was* serious.

Her heart thudded against him, and David, feeling it, experienced a mixture of pleasure and apprehension. He said, he hoped gently, "It also implies something I'm not ready for."

She met his eyes. "I'm in no hurry, either. I've only had one lover, David. It was a long time ago."

He couldn't help his reaction. Everything inside him recoiled—not from what she said but because the admission was intimate. His desire to be close to her warred with three years of survival instincts—and lost.

David released her and stepped back, and Jean's heart plunged.

He saw her expression, and he wished he could reassure her. But he already felt as though he was coming apart just at the uninvited glimpse into her sexuality. He responded the only way he could. "That's not my business."

He turned and left the diving alcove, shutting the door hard behind him as though locking an ungovernable animal inside.

LEAVING THE SHIP and the marina, David crossed the breakwater and climbed down the tar-coated rocks to the sand. He had an appointment in forty-five minutes, but for now he needed to be away from the ship, away from Jean, away from everyone.

No one was on the beach, so he tore off his clothes and went into the water. The cold was bracing, but even swimming felt like madness. He had somewhere to be, and he'd have to return to the ship to shower and wash the tar off his body.

He didn't care. He swam out far past the breakers, hoping it would make him tired. The afternoon sun was setting, and he seemed to have the stretch of water to himself. With every stroke he heard her repeat that whispered confession. And he heard his own brutal reply.

Why had she told him? He hadn't asked her to sleep with him, and he wasn't sure he ever would. Naked and inside her, where could he hide? If the colors came— If she was to look in his eyes and really see— And what if he—

As his throat closed on the thought he couldn't finish, the water parted beside him, and a glistening silver shape appeared and took a breath through a blowhole. Baby's eyes cleared the surface, and she looked at him.

David stopped swimming. "Go!"

Baby pushed against his chest, and the heat, the strange contact from one of another world and yet his world, set his nerves tingling. He did not pet her. He turned back toward shore and started swimming.

Baby followed, sliding against his side like a woman trying to seduce a man. Treading water and attempting to dodge her attentions, David said in a tone that had shades of affection he hadn't intended, "You little tramp, get out of here."

She clicked at him and touched him on the arm with one of her flippers.

David said, "Go find Jean. I don't want to be friends. Go!" He pointed toward the islands.

She cried at him softly.

David swam away from her. She didn't follow him, but her sorrowful cries did as he rode the waves to the shore.

He had never in his life felt so cruel.

THE SANTA ANA WINDS came in that night. They were a gift from the mountains, a breath of summer in the midst of December, and they made Jean wish she was doing something more exciting than going to the library to research the death of Skye Haverford Blade. But she honored the warm weather and the approach of Christmas, now only nine days off, by dressing in an outfit Ceci had given her for her birthday, a multicolored ribbon-weave tank top and gauzy, tricolor, wraparound column skirt. The outfit, which Ceci had modeled in Paris, made her feel feminine, freed from the image of the androgynous athlete whose biggest fashion decision was which wet suit to wear.

Nonetheless, Jean felt conspicuous as she approached the reference desk at the library and filled out request slips for several issues of the *South Coast Sun* from just after the heiress's death. No one could guess her purpose, yet she couldn't stop thinking of David and what he might feel if he knew what she was doing. As she went to the microfiche viewers and set to work with the first film sheet, she was filled with shame. But she couldn't stop.

She had to know, not just to satisfy her own curiosity but to try to understand what had made David so...

*Terminally repressed,* thought Jean, flushing again as she recalled his telling her that how many lovers she'd had was none of his business. As this was none of hers.

The first paper she examined featured a photo of David taken at the harbor the day of Skye's death. Jean stared at his image, the face she now knew well, and tried to discern his emotions from his expression. She couldn't. He looked handsome and unapproachable. For a moment she reached out to touch his face on the screen, then hastily withdrew her hand, glancing behind her to see if anyone had noticed. The area was deserted.

Scrolling down to the article, Jean began to read. The most apparent fact was that David's story was the only one anyone had—and would ever have, unless Chris, three at the time, came to remember the accident. The more Jean thought about it, the more unlikely that seemed. Three was very young to recollect much of anything.

What interested Jean was the doubt the police had shed on David's version of the accident. An officer called it "improbable"; another said "hard to swallow." According to

the paper, David claimed Skye had fallen from the bow
while the ship was cruising full throttle in the middle of
the channel. He'd been making a small repair to the fly-
bridge railing, and it took him a few seconds to reach the
helm and kill the engine. When he did, he saw blood in the
water behind the ship. After taking his distraught son below
deck, he put on a mask and dove beneath the hull looking
for Skye. Finding nothing, he returned to the deck and ra-
dioed the Coast Guard, who arrived in minutes. The wind
and the seas had begun to rise, impeding their investigation
under the ship, and they were forced to return to the harbor.

Jean knew what had happened there.

Finishing the article, she wondered why the police found
his story incredible. Did they doubt that a twenty-seven-
year-old woman could have fallen from the bow of a ship?
Something in the article didn't ring true, and Jean suspected
that certain important details had been omitted from the
story. But if so, what? The *Sun* had the sensibilities of a
local paper, but usually it gave the facts.

Dissatisfied, Jean shifted the position of the microfiche
until she found a glowing editorial obituary praising Skye's
education, beauty and generosity, and naming a number of
charity events she had organized and hosted. The final
words were, "The South Coast will miss this great lady."

A pair of hands closed on her bare shoulders, and Jean
tipped her head back, half expecting to see someone from
school or an old diving partner.

"Hi." David smiled down at her, and Jean saw the progress of his eyes from the ribbon-weave curving over her
breasts to the tullelike film clinging to her legs. When their
eyes met, Jean decided his repression probably wasn't ter-
minal, after all. He said, "You look like an ad for somewhere I'd like to go."

Heart racing, Jean fumbled for the switch to turn off the
viewer. While she was still trying, David's hands slid from
her shoulders and he stepped back.

Jean stood up, jerked the microfiche from the viewer and clumsily returned it to its envelope while David watched aloofly. She said, "What brings you to the library?"

"Returning books." His gaze drifted to the microfiche in her hands, then back to her face. "Are you done?"

Jean nodded, sick inside. Judging by the look in his eye, he knew what she'd been doing. Did he feel betrayed?

He said, "Let's go somewhere."

Jean felt a confusing mixture of misery, misgiving and anticipation. She wanted to be with him more than anything, yet it occurred to her that he was going to fire her. Subdued, she said, "Okay. Let me take these back to the desk."

Minutes later, as they walked outside into the warm, caressing breeze, David asked quietly, "What were you researching?"

*Damn,* Jean thought. Trust David to waste no time. Holding her skirt down to keep it from flying open in the breeze, she said, "I wanted to know what happened to your wife."

He didn't answer, and Jean thought of the blood in the water. He had seen Skye's blood. She wondered if her curiosity pained him.

The wind rustled palm fronds in the trees above and pushed on a large tinsel wreath hanging from a guy wire over the street. David nodded toward the far curb, where his car was parked. As they crossed the street he asked, "Want to come home with me?"

With David, that could mean anything. There'd never yet been any reason for her to spend the night on the ship, but Jean wondered if that was what he was suggesting now. She thought of her cabin on the *Skye*—and his.

What *had* he meant? Wasn't he angry? He didn't seem so.

And the warm, heady magic of the Santa Ana night was seeping into her veins, intensifying all her feelings for him. She said, "I'll come."

Without reply, David led her to the bare-topped Corvette and opened her door.

The *Skye* was dark, but David offered no steadying hand as he led her through the salon to the galley, where a night-light burned over the sink. Jean knew that Erika was home and that Chris was asleep in his stateroom, but the ship seemed deathly quiet. Even the things most familiar and comforting, the snowflakes she and Chris had cut out and the advent calendar with its sixteen open doors, looked different at night.

David said, "Let's go in my cabin. Would you like a drink before we go up? Or coffee?"

"Sure. Anything." Jean began to relax. David's mood was serious but not ominous. Perhaps he would tell her, at last, about his wife's death.

He said, "What do you drink?"

Jean shrugged. "I hardly ever drink." She remembered the bottle of wine they'd shared at the restaurant.

David seemed to be remembering it, too. With the first smile she'd seen since his initial appearance at the library, he said, "I can believe that."

He fixed two café mochas with Irish cream and carried them up the companionway. In his cabin he turned on a banker's lamp on his desk, then raised the hatch overhead, letting in the warm winds. The lamp lit the room with only the most mellow glow, and the dimness was inviting. David pulled out his desk chair and held it for Jean. He sat on the bed, and Jean thought of the last time they had sat like this, before she'd read Michael Avery's proposal.

Now his eyes were warm but distant. Careful. He asked, "Did you try your coffee?"

Jean sipped at it, remembering the bottle of Irish cream in Skye's desk drawer. Undoubtedly David had done this before. "Delicious," she said.

"Good."

They sat in silence, seeming to have nothing to say to

each other, and as the pause extended, Jean began to wonder why he had asked her there. She said, "Are you mad?"

David didn't ask about what. He said, "No. You were curious, and I'm grateful you didn't ask me."

Jean wondered if he knew that answer would hurt. Trying to tell herself that his experience probably became no easier to relate upon repetition, she nonetheless felt shut out. They were close enough for honesty.

*But you haven't been honest with him,* an inner voice pointed out.

David took a drink of his coffee, his eyes on hers. He said, "I can see the wheels spinning. What are you thinking?"

Jean cloaked her feelings. "That I wish I knew you better."

"It takes time. You know me better than you think you do." He paused. "Better than I know you."

Jean thought of the Averys. He might be right.

David said, "I'll tell you what. We'll trade personal questions. You ask one, I ask one. Then we're done, for now. Sound fair?"

It sounded like Russian roulette, but Jean nodded.

He said, "Go ahead."

Wanting to ask him about Skye, she shook her head. "You."

David took another drink of his coffee, wishing it contained something stronger. All he could think was what she had told him that day—one lover, a long time ago.

Questions knotted inside him. How was it? Who was it? Did she love him? He didn't know which to ask. So he said, "Why only one lover?"

She choked on her coffee. He didn't blame her, but he didn't withdraw the question. It was some time before she answered, and when she did she didn't quite meet his eyes. She said, "It ended badly and…and I haven't met anyone else I want to be that close to."

David imagined sliding his hand under her clingy skirt to test her words. He said, "Really?"

Jean flushed. "Is it my turn now?"

He gave her a long look, then began to laugh. "I guess it is. Ask away."

Jean was soothed by the warmth in his eyes, a guarded fire. Now it was her question, but before she could decide what to ask, an unholy scream erupted in the night. David rose at once and moved toward the door.

Jean was momentarily paralyzed. She opened her mouth to ask what it was, but David said, "Chris. He makes all his sounds at night." He pulled open the door and went below to the galley.

Jean stood up and followed, but he was already out of sight, and she had to find her own way back up the companionway and across the salon in the dark. Under Skye Haverford Blade's icy blue gaze and secretive smile, she slipped past the unlit Christmas tree and navigated the aft stairs, following the screams to a starboard stateroom near the stern. When she reached the door David was sitting on a narrow bunk holding the crying child. Seeing Chris's crumpled face, hearing his tearful sobs, Jean felt her heart shake in her chest.

There was a sound from across the hall, and David called, "Don't get up, Erika. I'm here."

Erika's voice murmured, "So am I if you need anything."

Jean stayed against the wall as David held his son and attempted, unsuccessfully, to quiet the screaming rage. Standing in the shadows, she realized she had seen only the tip of the iceberg when it came to the impact of Skye's death on the lives of her family. As Chris screamed in the dark, it seemed unbearably cruel. Aching inside, Jean watched David bury his head against Chris's, clutching the small body against his chest.

The episode lasted only a couple of minutes, but when

Chris at last quieted and dropped back onto his pillow, Jean's heart was racing, her breath short. Tae kwon do had made her used to loud yells, but not of this kind.

David pulled the blankets over his son and tucked them around him, then stood. He ushered Jean out the door and back up to the salon, saying, "We've driven neighbors out of their berths before, but the harbor master's very understanding. Now we have no neighbors—just boats."

As David bent over to plug in the Christmas-tree lights, Jean asked, "Has this been going on long?"

"Three years." The room sprang to light. "Do you play chess?"

Jean nodded. "I used to—with my dad."

David opened one of the lockers to retrieve a chess set from inside. "Will you play?"

"Sure." She settled on the carpet across from him and helped arrange the pieces. "Has Chris seen a doctor? A psychiatrist?"

"Psychologists, psychiatrists, neurologists, hypnotists. He's seen them all. They agree he's having night terrors, though they're unusual in a child his age. It happens about once a week, sometimes more."

Jean asked, "Did he see her fall?"

"Yes."

Jean knew if she wanted details she would have to ask for them. She remembered the one personal question she was allowed but found herself unable to ask. David had as much as said he didn't want to discuss his wife's death.

They played a long chess game, which he finally won, and by then it was nearly midnight.

As he put away the set, he said, "You're staying, aren't you?"

Jean nodded, sorry to see the night end. In a moment, she would go to her own cabin and David to his.

He interrupted her thoughts. "Want to walk off some of

that coffee before we turn in? Chris won't be up again tonight."

THEY LEFT the *Skye* and walked up the dock to the marina gate. Sailboat rigging chimed in the wind. Together with the splash of the water and soft creaking of the docks, it made a quiet music, the song of a harbor night. Lights burned on several boats, all on other marinas, and from across the water Jean heard the faint sound of a carol playing:

Sleep, my love, and peace attend thee
All through the night....

It made her think of Chris and of what David had said about their lack of neighbors. Now, the waterfront seemed deserted except for a homeless person drinking from a thermos on the bench outside the espresso shop. Holding the gate for Jean, David greeted him by name and remarked, "Nice night."

"Beautiful," the man answered. "I've been watching the stars. Can't bring myself to move. Scorpio was spectacular earlier." He said, "Hey, David, thanks for those sleeping bags. We really needed them a few nights ago. That was a great St. Nicholas Day gift."

As the gate clanged shut behind Jean, David said, "Forget it." Nodding to the man, he led Jean down the boardwalk toward the breakwater.

Thinking of what she'd just learned, Jean remarked, "You know everyone."

Casting her a glance, David said, "Street people were one of Skye's big causes. She raised a lot of money for them nationally."

It occurred to Jean that giving sleeping bags to homeless people on the anniversary of her death might be something he had done in her memory. As they crossed the breakwater and paused to take off their shoes and socks, she remembered the photo she'd found in Skye's desk of her and the blond man—Homeless Shelter Fashion Shoot. In her mind, she pictured the man's lips caressing Skye's hair and wondered if David had ever seen the photo and how he would have felt if he had. The more she knew him, the less she believed he would like it.

Her conversation with Jake days earlier had made her curious about the kind of woman Skye Haverford had been; so did this new thought.

Under the stars, David set his running shoes and socks beside a rock and gestured toward her sandals. "We can leave these here."

In the dark, his eyes looked black, and Jean felt the intimacy of being alone with him on such a warm, beautiful night. As they trudged across the beach toward the white breakers and followed the wet sand at the water's edge, Jean tried to think of a way to draw him out.

David asked, "Want to swim?"

Jean surveyed the dark cliff and the empty beach, noting the absence of moonlight. David was little more than a tall black shape beside her, but she glimpsed his even white teeth as he spoke.

They hadn't brought swimsuits. Thinking of this, she said, "I always thought that wasn't safe. Because of sharks."

Not responding, David stripped off his shirt. His pants followed, and he kicked them into a pile with his shirt. As Jean wondered if he was going to remove anything else, he said, "Don't let me drown," and started toward the sea.

Watching his tall, muscular form in the black night, Jean said, "I won't be able to see you."

"Then you'd better come."

Recklessly she took off her skirt and top and dropped them to the sand. Shivering slightly in her pale blue panties and bra, she followed David into the velvety darkness.

The water was cold, but the breakers were old friends. David was a couple of yards away, and Jean felt him glance over at her. Ignoring him, she held on to her underwear as she fell into the tossing foam, the current ripping beneath her. Ignoring the cold, she swam under a wave and emerged beyond the first set of breakers, feeling the freedom of her loose hair sweeping around her shoulders in the water. It had been months since she'd been in the ocean without a wet suit. The adrenaline sent her blood rushing fast, and she was glad when David emerged near her. Another wave was coming, and they both stroked toward it, watching it rise over their heads.

Jean gasped, "This is crazy," and dove under the wave, trying not to think about sharks as she swam through the dark, cold sea, feeling the force of the swell over her. When she came up, she was beyond the breakers. David was swimming toward her. Jean had warmed up, and for a moment she floated, enjoying the buoyancy of the salt water. Her cotton underwear clung to her loosely, and she hoped it wouldn't come off.

She stopped floating and tread water, letting the ocean hide her body when he neared. David seemed so much more *male* than anyone she'd ever known. Her eyes fell on the dark hairs curling wet on his chest and the scar tracing over his shoulder.

David said, "Not so bad, is it? No sharks, just me."

He looked a lot more threatening and unpredictable than a shark, but Jean nodded, enjoying their closeness. "It's fun." Her leg brushed his under the water, and she moved back. "Sorry."

He smiled at that.

"What?"

"Nothing."

He was near enough to touch and seemed much bigger than she was, a dark, wild stranger of the sea. But now, in the night and the water, she could feel his affection for her and his desire.

He came closer.

Jean gasped as the water moved beneath her and something rose between them, a warm, gray body. She cried out, afraid, and then released a breath that sounded like a sob and a laugh. "Baby."

As the dolphin slid against her chest, hugging Jean with her flippers, David said, "I suppose she has no context for the expression 'fifth wheel.'"

Jean laughed. Stroking the dolphin's side, she said, "Baby, you're nice and warm." She hugged her and laid her cheek against Baby's soft skin. Jean's senses had never felt so alive. She wanted to share her bliss with David, but when she slid away from the dolphin to turn to him he was watching her with a look she recognized. A look like a storm bulletin.

Baby came over to nuzzle him and he ran a casual hand down from her beak. "Hi, Baby." He told Jean, "Let's go in."

"But Baby just got here. We'll hurt her feelings." Jean touched her, but Baby was more interested in David. She brushed along his front, and he backed away, starting for the shore.

With regret Jean gave the dolphin a final stroke and followed.

Baby swam with them, calling in the night, pleading for them to stay, and Jean ached for her. Baby was alone out there, without friends, tragically solitary and desperate for love. Why didn't David understand that?

Jean caught a wave and rode it into shore, then spent a moment rinsing the sand from herself as best she could. Standing up in the shallow breakers, she forgot about Baby as she realized how much her underwear and bra revealed in their dripping state. After readjusting both, she folded her arms across her chest and walked to where she and David had left their clothes.

David was zipping up his pants, and he reached for his shirt when he saw her. Keeping her back to him, Jean scooped up her clothes. When she stood David stepped near her and slid his shirt over her head. The thick cotton tumbled around her body, dropping to midthigh, and Jean gratefully slipped her arms into the long sleeves. "Thank you," she whispered, looking up. "You're not cold?"

"No. Put on your skirt and we'll walk back." He wondered if she wanted to take off her wet underwear. Then he wondered if she'd like help. Cooling the thought, he turned away as she finished dressing. Together they walked back toward the breakwater to retrieve their shoes.

As Jean bent to pick up hers, she said, "Thanks, David."

"For what?" The chance to see her in transparent underwear, her breasts slick with water and swaying ever so slightly when she moved? He should thank her—or curse her.

Jean said, "For the swim."

"Sure," he made himself say. "It was nice."

The words sounded heartbreakingly casual, and Jean couldn't escape the feeling she'd made some mistake. She wanted to undo it, but since she didn't know what she'd done, that seemed impossible. His mood had changed when Baby joined them.

In tune with her thoughts, David said, "Look, Baby belongs with other dolphins. Perhaps if you left her alone, she'd find her own kind."

Jean didn't believe that, but she was glad he felt empathy for Baby's plight. As they crossed the breakwater, she said, "Baby would never be accepted by a school. Their social order just doesn't work that way. To the best of my knowledge, they don't take strangers."

"No one knows that for sure."

Jean fell in step beside him on the boardwalk. "I can't

believe you really think Baby would choose the company of any person over that of other dolphins."

"I don't see why not. You prefer her to humans."

Jean stared up at him, suddenly remembering the moment in the water when Baby had come between them. She said, "You sound jealous."

She half expected withdrawal, but instead, he smiled—almost. "Your point, ma'am."

Once they'd returned to the *Skye,* David led her through the wheelhouse and his cabin and slid open the door to the landing that separated their quarters. Then he walked her to the crew's quarters, and when Jean switched on the light he idled in the doorway, looking at the walls.

Jean loved her cabin, had from the first time she'd seen it. A high, double-wide berth of Hawaiian koa was nestled against the forward hold, and the space beneath contained drawers and cupboards with footholds for climbing to the bunk. David had suggested she bring from home whatever she felt would brighten the place, and Jean had chosen three photos and a net strung with shells she'd collected with her father.

Now the net hung against the bulkhead like a tapestry, and David smiled when he saw it. Jean watched his silent examination of the three pictures—she and her father sparring, Ceci mugging, and an underwater shot of Baby. Of the last, David asked, "Yours?"

Jean nodded, her eyes clandestinely tracing the lines of his shoulders and the ropes of muscle on his stomach, with its dark hair tracing downward in a seductive line.

"You've got a steady hand." He turned to meet her eyes, only inches below his. "Sleep tight." Briefly he let his mouth touch hers, then stepped carefully back.

Jean recalled her question. If she didn't ask now, she might never have the chance. As he began to leave she said, "David, don't I get to ask you something?"

He turned toward her again, his eyes clear and cool, a wall hiding his soul. "Ask."

She said, "I want to know what happened to your wife."

David paused. There were a number of replies that would be equally correct. He chose the most succinct.

"Skye killed herself."

# CHAPTER NINE

*SKYE KILLED HERSELF.*

Jean whispered, "How?"

"One question, remember?" He looked at her, and now Jean saw emotions she couldn't identify. He said softly, "What you read in the papers was close enough. Please don't ask me again."

Jean said, "It's better to talk about it."

David felt as though there were an earthquake in his chest. "Not for me."

That could be true. Nonetheless, she hurt for him.

Seeing what looked like indecision in her eyes, David told her, "You might not know there's a tae kwon do philosophy suggesting that one should honor the requests of one who is five or more years older than oneself."

David was eight years older. *How convenient for you,* thought Jean.

David's eyes smiled faintly, as though he knew what she was thinking. Then he turned and left, shutting the door behind him.

A moment later Jean heard the door of his cabin shut, as well.

SHE AWAKENED in the darkness to the sound of the shower running. Seeing the portholes beside her bunk, she recognized her surroundings and recalled what had happened the night before.

It must be David in the shower.

Sleepy, she reached for her diving watch hanging on a hook and pressed the button that would illuminate the dial. Three twenty-three. Hanging the watch back in place, Jean reclined against her pillow, listening to the shower shut off. What was he doing up? Had her questions about Skye interfered with his sleep?

The idea was painful, and it started a carousel of questions in her brain.

Had Skye really killed herself?

Jean could hardly believe it, yet it made an unlikely lie. All the information at her hands, everything she had read and heard, came rushing back at her. They were the same questions she'd asked herself when David had left her in her cabin earlier, and Jean wished she had some answers. The one he'd given her had only raised more doubts.

Why had the paper never mentioned suicide? And what of the "seven-digit" life-insurance policy Jake said David had received—by accepting the Corvette? Had David told anyone else that Skye had killed herself? He must have told Erika, and he should have told the authorities. To withhold that and then collect Skye's life insurance was fraud. Jean could not picture David compromising his integrity that way.

But hadn't Erika and Jake both said the Blade Institute was floundering at the time of Skye's death?

Lying in her berth, Jean listened to David leave the shower room as she played through her mind what she could be reasonably sure was true.

Skye must have jumped from the bow. David had implied as much by saying that the story in the papers was "close enough." But what kind of woman jumped from the bow of a cruising ship—with her husband and son looking on? Jean had asked if Chris had seen her fall, and David had said yes. *Fall,* Jean thought. He hadn't said anything about her jumping then.

Had Skye shot herself first? Jean disliked herself for even

trying to guess. Whatever Skye's manner of death, David must blame himself—whether or not he would ever admit it. His wife had killed herself and his son had witnessed it. Little Chris, whose child's mind had mercifully locked away the memory where it couldn't plague him.

Chris, who no longer spoke.

Added to the fact that David had been unable to stop the ship in time, the tragedy was enough to keep a man awake all the nights of his life.

Jean listened to the silence of the ship. She was wide-awake now and thirsty. She got down from the bunk.

She'd slept in David's shirt, and before sliding open the door to her quarters she took a pair of faded gym shorts from her locker and pulled them on. Then she stepped out onto the landing.

No light shone under David's door. Was he back in bed? Restless and walking the deck? Concluding that he must have gone out, she slipped soundlessly down the companionway into the office, black in the night.

Skye's place. How could a woman with so much have killed herself?

But anyone could be unhappy. Remembering the pills she'd found in the desk drawer, Jean wondered if Skye had been depressed. Scars from childhood? Abuse could happen in the best of homes, and its consequences were sometimes far-reaching.

Hurrying through the office, Jean felt for the stair railing in the dark and crept up the companionway to the galley. As she slid open the door, she sensed motion near the sink, and David snapped on the small light over the stove and looked at her. He was wearing a pair of well-worn blue jeans and nothing else, and his hair was wet and uncombed. He ran his hand through it as he saw her.

Jean said, "Sorry. I wanted a glass of water."

"Don't be sorry. You live here—basically." He lifted a

glass from the shelf and filled it from the cold-water tap in the freezer door.

Stepping into the galley, Jean took it from his hand. She drew it to her mouth, wondering if he expected her to leave.

He said, "I hope I didn't wake you."

She shook her head, eyes on the muscles in his upper arms, sleek and tanned. She wanted to touch him.

David said, "You slept in my shirt."

He didn't sound bothered, just interested, but Jean wished she hadn't done it. Her reason was that she hadn't been prepared to sleep on the ship; she had only one change of clothes in her locker. And—her secret reason—she'd wanted to absorb David's scent as she slept. She said, "I didn't think you'd mind."

"I don't. Just don't let my sister see you or she'll be wishing us joy. You look like I've made you mine."

Jean's legs felt unsteady. Hesitantly she asked, "Are you going back to bed?"

He seemed restive at the question. "No. I don't need a lot of sleep."

Jean silently calculated. He'd had two hours at the most and didn't appear remotely rested.

David turned away and opened the freezer to take out a bag of coffee. From the corner of his eye, he saw her lift the water glass to her mouth again. She didn't appear to be leaving. He said, "What I told you last night is confidential."

"Naturally." But it wasn't natural at all, she thought. Why the secrecy? It reeked of shame and darkness. She thought of the life-insurance policy and knew she wouldn't ask. Some lines should not be crossed, and on the *Skye* those lines surrounded her.

David was a time bomb. She didn't want to be the detonator.

Her eyes fell on the calendar on the wall, and she counted the closed doors. Chris would open the seventeenth when he awoke in a few hours. On the nineteenth they would leave for Baja. Then, just a few days until Christmas. Somehow it was hard to believe it would ever really feel like Christmas on the *Skye*. For David and Chris, the season could only mark the passing of the years.

Growing impatient with her presence and yet also somehow glad of it, David asked, "Are you up now? I'll make you breakfast if you are."

"I never refuse a meal," said Jean.

David smiled, remembering their breakfast at her house. Leaving the coffee bag on the counter, he opened the freezer door again, removed a can of frozen orange juice and handed it to her. "Read the directions if you're confused."

Knowing she was being teased, Jean pressed her heel lightly on his instep.

He murmured, "So you want to spar at my level now." With two quick moves he took the can from her hand, deposited it on the counter and pulled her where he wanted her—under the mistletoe.

Jean's hand and arm were twisted behind her, and with her free hand she slapped her leg, a silent request that he let her go.

He released her arm and drew her against him. He didn't kiss her immediately but murmured, "What have we got on under here?" and lifted the hem of the shirt she wore to slide his hand beneath. As he felt the silk of her skin he told her, "Say no if you want me to stop."

She closed her eyes and let her forehead rest against his throat as his hand moved up to caress her breast.

David could feel her heart keeping time with his own. Fast and hard. He pressed his hips lightly against her, acquainting her with the need she'd awakened. He touched her nipple, thinking of the galley stairs and wanting to latch them overhead so no one could come upon them. There was only Chris and Erika, but he wanted utter privacy. And he didn't want her in his cabin.

His mouth fell on her hair, tracing her hairline, and Jean put her lips to his throat. When she whispered his name there was a plea in it.

He said, "Okay?"

"I'm fine."

He could barely hear her. He kissed her mouth and touched her other breast. He couldn't remember ever wanting a woman so badly, not even Skye.

Skye.

He tried to forget the thought, but it was too late. He drew his hand out from under her shirt—his shirt—and hugged her close with both arms, vowing he wouldn't back away till he was ready. The images were there, but he was prepared this time. He could accept their presence with hers—at least like this. Holding her.

Jean's arms stretched around him, feeling the muscles in his back. She respected his strength and his tenderness. There was a power in size that made a man's gentleness toward a woman a quality by which she could most esteem him.

David was gentle.

But why had he stopped touching her breasts?

Closing her eyes, Jean let her cheek and nose sink against the base of his throat, nuzzling his skin. She wished it were so easy to touch his heart and mind. When he'd told her of Skye's suicide, David had made a chink in the wall that divided them. His kissing her tonight was another chink. Perhaps in time the crack would widen and she could see inside. Yet she feared the smallest misstep on her part could threaten their newfound closeness. *Trust me, David,* she thought silently. Her heart cried that she loved him.

His hand beneath her hair, he tilted her head back again and kissed her once more. Kissing him back, Jean knew the caress was extending longer than he'd intended. She sensed he didn't want to release her.

But eventually he did. He stepped back against the counter and let his eyes rest on her. They conceded nothing.

Jean said, "If that's sparring at your level, I think I could get used to it."

David picked up the can of orange concentrate and handed it to her. As it slid into her hand, ice cold and wet, he nodded to a locker overhead. "There's a pitcher up there."

LATER THAT DAY David suggested she take the Corvette home and pack what she needed for Baja. He planned to take Erika to her rehab center in Los Angeles early the next morning, leaving Chris with Jean, so it made sense for her to spend the night on the ship again. And the day after that they would leave for Baja.

Jean and Chris had made exhaustive plans for their day together—a visit to the natural history museum, then Christmas shopping. Jean was looking forward to it, but she felt the weight of responsibility. David would be leaving his son with her for more than twelve hours while he went out of town, and as she packed for the trip and closed up her house she could think of nothing else. Nothing else except the fact that she'd never told him about working for Michael and Jennifer Avery in Baja.

Most of the time Jean could forget the fiasco—or convince herself David would understand. But at home, in her own house, she heard the echo of her mother's voice and saw her skeptical stare, and she knew she could expect no better of David.

Even the houseplants accused her—or at least the Christmas cactus did. The bonsai olive tree was too needy to accuse. It seemed to cry to her, *Don't leave me for two weeks. The neighbors might not water me.*

But the cactus played tapes from the past.

*Ceci's our nurturer. Jean's a little too self-involved. I don't know what kind of mother she'd make. For one thing, she's never home.*

Small wonder, thought Jean. She looked at the flourishing olive tree, and another tape began to play.

*You must be good with these. This tree looks old.*

*I think you'd make a very good mother.*

Tears stung her eyes. Quickly she went to the kitchen table where paper and gift tags lay. She scrawled a card to the professor who'd recommended her for the Sayles Award and his wife, then collected a gift bow to stick on the cactus planter. She opened the front door, then returned to the cactus and hefted it into her arms to carry across the street.

Briefly she wondered what Ceci would think of her giving their mother's Christmas cactus to the neighbors. But then it occurred to her that her sister was seldom home and never noticed the plant when she was.

And later, as she carried the bonsai to the Corvette to take with her on the *Skye,* Jean remembered the olive branch was a symbol of peace. She knew she would never look at the little tree again without hearing David say she was good with plants and would make a very good mother. And without seeing Chris waiting in his pajamas for her to watch him open the next door of the advent calendar.

That was peace—unbroken but for the shadow of her lie to David.

WHEN SHE AWOKE the next morning to a heavy knock on the door of her cabin she was momentarily confused. David had said she and Chris should sleep in. He and Erika would be gone when they awoke.

But it wasn't Chris's small hand on her door. It was David's, and David's voice saying, "Sorry, Jean. Chris is up. Just throw something on and come out."

She was wearing her turquoise flannel pajamas, another

of Ceci's selections, and she climbed out of bed and opened
the door at once. David was on the landing, waiting. He
was alone.

Seeing her, David remembered the feel of her skin two
nights earlier. He hadn't touched her since. But now her
hair was down and uncombed, and her pajamas looked
loose and soft and easy to remove. He wanted to feel the
curves beneath them so badly it took him a moment to
remember why he was there.

He said, "Chris is pretty upset about Erika. Would you
like me to take him with us?"

Jean was surprised by the question. It wasn't like David
to give in to his son's tears. But Erika's departure must be
traumatic for both of them.

She said, "If you think that's the best thing." As David
frowned at her answer she asked, "Where is he?"

"Out in the salon with Erika." Jean nodded and started
to turn down the companionway, but he said, "Wait a minute," and touched her sleeve.

Jean paused, looking up.

David felt something give inside his chest, another tie
coming unbound. He said, "A day seems like a long time
not to see you." He meant only to touch her shoulder, but
somehow, instead, she was in his arms. He pressed his
mouth against hers, kissing first her bottom lip, then the
top, then both, for much longer. Against her he said,
"Jean," and felt her stir, trying to get closer. David knew
how close he wanted to be—naked and inside her.

He envisioned it for a moment, sliding inside her, melting any resistance, hearing her whimper and cry out.
Though she might not.

It ought to be simple, but it never would be. It would be
complicated and intense—or a nightmare.

For a moment he saw blood.

Jean sensed his tension and wondered what he was thinking. "Are you all right?"

"Sure." With a hand on her back, he guided her down the companionway ahead of him, and as they descended into the darkness of the office he asked, "Do you have enough money?"

Jean couldn't help laughing. The night before, he had given her a hundred dollars, a major credit card and the keys to the Corvette. He was taking the Blade Institute van. She said, "What do you think we're going to do?"

David smiled in the darkness. "Order pizza."

Apparently he'd given up the idea of taking Chris with him. Jean was glad. Erika's leaving was going to be a hard adjustment for Chris, and she wanted to help ease it—if she could.

When she and David came up from the galley they found Chris sitting in Erika's lap in her wheelchair, his arms around her neck. He was still wearing his pajamas and was crying hard, but without sound.

Jean felt a hollow cracking sensation inside her, like a glacier breaking off a cascade and falling a thousand feet.

Erika looked up at Jean and shook her head, pain in her eyes.

Chris followed her gaze.

Jean said, "Hi, there. Calendar time?"

Chris sniffed and rested his head back against Erika's chest. He stared at Jean but made no reply.

Jean's heart fell. Giving Christian, Erika and David a compassionate glance, she said, "I think I'll have some coffee." She felt stupid. Chris's whole life was changing. Why would he care about his calendar now?

As she hurried down into the galley she heard David say, "Come on, Chris. Erika can't sit like that too long."

"Oh, let him stay, David."

Jean ached inside. She wanted to be able to comfort Chris. His tears always seemed more pitiful for being unaccompanied by any sound but sniffling and gasping breaths. If he had come to her, she would have held him as long as he wanted, till the sobs stopped.

She took the lid off the espresso maker and turned to fill the pot at the sink, only to bump into Chris. Jean hadn't heard him come down to the galley, and when she said his name in surprise, he signed something to her. He was still drying his eyes and his expression was serious, but he looked apologetic.

Jean knew David or Erika must have made him come down.

She crouched on the sole beside him and put her arms around him. "You don't have to be nice, Chris. I know you feel rotten."

He pressed his cheek, still wet, against hers, and held on to her hair.

FIVE MINUTES LATER David called down from the salon to tell them he and Erika were going out to the car. Jean and Chris stood in the center of the galley floor, where she was rearranging his walking stance and low block. She said, "Okay, now this arm comes up like this, and this one comes up this way, so you can step and *punch*." She demonstrated.

Chris copied—almost.

"Your fist and your wrist twist here. Relax, then… *punch*."

Chris tried again.

David smiled, admiring the techniques of both—Chris's athletic, her interpersonal. Unable to stop himself, he came partway down the stairs and leaned around the door to see Chris's calendar. The eighteenth door was open, revealing a dove.

Jean looked up.

David said, "We're leaving."

Chris waved disinterestedly and returned to starting position again.

Jean told him, "Let me say goodbye to Erika, and we'll do it again."

Chris signed something at his father.

David said, "That's fine." As Jean climbed the stairs he told her, "Chris already said goodbye."

And so had they to each other, but during the second they were alone in the salon, David put his lips against hers again, felt her hair brush his skin. Then, not wanting to speak, he went ahead of her onto the deck.

A HUNDRED DOLLARS and the fact that it was a "special occasion" justified breakfast downtown before embarking on the day's missions. With Chris beside her in the Corvette, Jean drove to one of her favorite breakfast spots, a natural-foods café on a downtown side street. As they ate baked goods and drank fresh-squeezed orange juice, they finalized plans for the day. Museum, then shopping.

For Jean, Christmas gifts for the Blades presented a dilemma. Erika had been the easiest. The previous night, Jean had given Erika her gift, an artist's smock batiked with dolphins. David's sister had been delighted, and Jean felt certain she could please Chris just as easily.

For him, she had bought stickers, colored glue, a hacky sack, a collection of plastic bugs from the natural history museum, a simple balsa airplane model, the newest adventures of *Hank the Cowdog* and a children's tae kwon do book. It was a lot. When she realized how much she'd chosen for the six-year-old, Jean wondered how she would find the courage to give him the presents under David's eye. One gift should have been enough, and Jean was afraid David would think she was assuming something that wasn't there. Family ties. She wasn't Santa Claus, after all.

But Jean had put the problem out of her mind to confront later. The purpose of this day's shopping trip was to choose gifts for David, a complicated task. Jean wanted to give him something, and she wanted to make sure Chris found something to give his father that would be satisfying to both.

As they wandered downtown together, looking in shop windows, Chris seemed as much at a loss for ideas as she was. Things were complicated by the ever-present language barrier. Jean had spent some evenings studying sign-language books, but her understanding of Chris was clumsy at best. Sometimes he signed at her almost frantically, and she couldn't read a word. When they went downtown, she prepared herself, taking a pen and notepad. As David had assured her, Chris could write well for his age, a skill that helped them over many hurdles.

They had been window-shopping without result for nearly a half hour when Chris tugged on her arm and pointed at the store they were passing. It was a photography studio.

Jean said, "A photo of you? Chris, that's a good idea. I bet there's nothing he'd like better."

Chris was shaking his head and pointing to both of them.

"No," said Jean. "You're his son. I just work for him."

Chris signed at her. Jean didn't understand him, but she wondered if he'd seen David kiss her that morning.

He frowned.

She told him, "My camera's on the ship." She'd packed it to take to Baja. "Let's go home and get it. We can shoot a roll of film and take it down to the one-hour photo shop. Maybe they'll do an enlargement for us today."

Chris nodded agreeably, and they hurried back toward the Corvette.

Jean said, "We'll do the photos, and you can make him something, too."

Chris looked at her as though she'd suddenly grown antlers. *What?*

"Whatever you think he'd like," said Jean.

Balancing on one foot on the curb, Chris frowned in dissatisfaction.

"I have a really good idea," Jean told him. "Something I did for an art class in high school. Do you mind getting your face gunky?"

Chris shook his head and pointed at her.

"I have a gunky face?" Jean guessed.

Chris shook his head.

"You want my face to get gunky, too."

He nodded enthusiastically.

Jean said, "Deal."

A voice broke into their exchange. "Squiring around the prettiest girl in Santa Barbara? Gimme five, Chris." Jake Doherty, just emerged from a sandwich shop, crouched to exchange high fives with David's son. Eventually he stood and turned to Jean. "Where's David?"

Jean explained that he'd taken Erika to rehab.

Jake said, "Erika's got it tough. David will do penance on that one for the rest of his life."

For Erika's accident? He made it sound as though David had been driving. Jean longed to ask for details, but not with Chris standing near. It was too tempting to rely on the fact that he couldn't talk.

Her eyes drifted to Chris, and Jake's followed. He shrugged at Jean. "I'll see you tomorrow. Bringing party clothes?"

Party clothes? Jean said, "I'll be working."

Jake snorted lightly and made a dismissive motion with his hand. "You'll be playing, too. Didn't David tell you?" Shaking his head at his own question, Jake said, "He wouldn't think about clothes. He owns four or five tuxes, and Skye had evening gowns in every locker."

"Evening gowns?" said Jean. She didn't own one, and it seemed both presumptuous and highly inappropriate to pack such a garment for a scientific expedition.

Jake said, "There's an annual holiday party at Cabo San Anselmo. We do it every year."

*Cabo San Anselmo.* On Baja. Jean carefully did not react,

nor ask precisely where on the cape the party was. She said, "I'm sure David plans for me to take care of Chris." At Cabo San Anselmo.

"Ah." Jake smiled. "I forgot. You're the nanny." He winked at her, and Jean told herself his choice of words was coincidental. He reached down and ruffled Chris's hair. "See you tomorrow, cowboy. Gonna help steer the ship?"

Chris nodded eagerly, and Jean knew it must be something they had done before. She began to relax, but in the back of her mind lingered the unsettling knowledge that the *Skye* would be making a stop at Cabo San Anselmo.

AFTER LEAVING JAKE, Jean and Chris stopped at a drugstore to get supplies they needed for their art project, then returned to the *Skye*. Because the light would be better later in the day, they postponed the photo session and, instead, set to work on their art project for David. In the late afternoon, refusing Baby's pleas for a swim, they left the harbor and went to the beach.

Jean took pictures of Chris standing in the breakers and building sand castles, and when he showed interest in using the camera she allowed him to take some of her. Then, carefully placing the camera on a rock, she set the timer to shoot a few pictures of both of them to have for her own. She wanted the physical memento of the time she spent with Chris.

When they had shot an entire roll, they hurried the film to the All-Night Developers, and Jean asked them to make prints and select the two best of Chris for a five-by-seven and an eight-by-ten.

After eating pizza they'd had delivered to the *Skye*, they returned downtown to collect their photos. The developer had taken the liberty of making three from which to choose, one including Jean. At Chris's insistence she bought them all, and they hurried back to the ship, eager to be there before David returned from L.A. He wasn't home yet, so

Jean read Chris a chapter of *Treasure Island,* his most recent interest, then hugged him good-night.

As she straightened up from his bed, Chris signed a phrase Jean recognized and had seen before in the Sulphur Springs Tavern.

*I love you.*

Immeasurably grateful and pleased, she hugged him again and whispered, "I love you, too."

And then he asked something else. It took her a moment, but at last she understood. *Will you sing to me?*

Without thinking she asked, "Did your mom used to sing to you?"

But Chris only looked at her blankly, and she knew he didn't remember.

She said, "A Christmas carol?"

He nodded.

She chose the carol she'd heard nights earlier, when she was out with David.

Sleep my love, and peace attend thee
All through the night.
Guardian angels I will lend thee
All through the night....

ON THE DOCK beside the ship David heard her voice. There was a husky, boyish quality to it that always seemed sexy to him. Now, hearing her singing in Chris's cabin, he remembered something long ago on the *Siren.* Christmas. His mother singing to him, holding his hand. How could he remember that when Chris couldn't remember three years past?

Because what Chris had forgotten was too horrible to remember.

Love alone my watch is keeping
All through the night....

He pictured Jean sitting beside Chris's bunk. Her braid would be loose now. It always was at night, like the night before when he'd found her on the aft deck watering that bonsai tree. Thinking of the bonsai, of her bringing a plant onto his ship, he tensed inside. He knew he should go inside and get it over with. Everything.

But her voice moved the memories inside him. The *Siren*'s silhouette plunging down in the icy sea. And a much older warmth.

He looked across the misty night at the Christmas lights glowing pastel in the fog. The other boats seemed faraway, their shrouds gossamer spiderwebs. Everything seemed distant but the silence he now heard from the cabin.

He realized it felt like Christmas.

And he turned and left the ship to go walk on the beach.

AFRAID TO RETIRE to her cabin for fear Chris would have a night terror and she wouldn't hear, Jean settled in the salon with her sign-language book, but it was hard to focus on the page. Repeatedly her attention wandered to the watercolor of Skye. Words and images jumbled in her mind. The photo of the newly wed David and Skye that she'd found in the office. The postcard from the Kyongju temple.

*Where did you come from?*

*The big challenge in life is to crack the whip.*

*She was so mean and funny all at once.*

*Skye,* carved on the windowsill in David's cabin.

*Skye's eyes were like blue abalone when she was alive. And I don't care if her soul rests or not. You think mine does?*

*I love you deeply...deeply....*

Suicide, thought Jean. What kind of pain had she been in?

Even with her eyes closed, she felt Skye's eyes of abalone blue watching her in the dark, and an echo of Jake's words came to her.

*You're on that ship sometime at night, you'll know what I mean. You can feel her....*

DAVID TUCKED the quilt from his bed around her body. He wasn't sure why he had chosen it to cover her, except that it was warm and beautiful, like her, the woman who could sleep in a chair.

Jean stirred beneath his hands and opened her eyes.

He said, "It's me. Sorry for waking you. I didn't want you to be cold."

Jean looked down at the quilt, and David saw her start. Erika must have told her Skye had made it.

Breaking the silence, he said, "Did Chris run you ragged?"

She shook her head sleepily. "He was wonderful." Recalling how they had spent the day, Jean almost jumped out of the chair before she remembered that the things they had made for David were safely stowed in Chris's cabin.

She met David's eyes. "He says he loves me."

David stared at her for a moment. "And you understood him."

Sign language. Jean wondered if he, too, was thinking of the night they'd gone to the tavern. She said, "Yes. I remember that one."

Their eyes held for what seemed like a very long time. At last David suggested, "Let's go up on deck for a while. No Santa Ana winds, but it's not too cold, either."

"Okay." Standing, Jean folded the quilt and set it on the chair.

Watching her sit down on the carpet beside the tree to put on her sneakers, David asked, "Like a nightcap?"

She shook her head, tied her last shoe and stood up.

They went up to the deck, and in the diving alcove he

silently helped her into a foul-weather jacket, sizes too large for her, to break the wind, then drew her outside into the night.

Jean paused under the canopy. "Where shall we sit?"

The cushions on the foredeck would be wet from the fog. David grabbed a towel from a hook inside the door of the alcove and said, "This way."

They went out on the forward deck under the starless sky. A filmy gray murk hung in the air, socking in the harbor. Damp wisps of fog swirled round the masts of the nearby sailboats, and the dock lights shone through a haze. David dried off the forward seat and they sat down a couple of feet apart.

"Cold?" he asked.

If she said yes, would he put his arm around her? She hesitated, but he didn't move. Jean said, "I'm fine."

"Good."

Silence fell between them, and Jean hurried to fill it. "How was your trip? I hated to say goodbye to Erika, knowing she'd be alone for Christmas."

David shared her feeling, but he said, "The research trips are hard for her. She wants to dive."

"Could she?" Jean asked.

"It's not safe. As divers we deal with certain limitations, anyhow. Without the use of her legs, Erika is doubly vulnerable." He gazed absently down at the zipper on his hooded shell, then looked up at her. "I want to ask you something. A couple of things, actually. Would you like to start with the difficult or the shocking?"

The question terrified her. Concluding that there was no point in postponing it, she asked, "Are you going to fire me?"

"God, no." He laughed, his eyes finding hers.

Jean wasn't sure she'd ever seen him so handsome.

He said, "Don't think it for a minute." Watching her,

he ran his teeth over his lower lip as though making a hard decision.

Jean said, "Then I suppose we should start with the difficult and move to the shocking."

"Okay." David appeared relieved. Stuffing his hands in the pockets of his jacket, he sat back against the cushions. "In L.A. I talked to a few people who think Baby might be accepted by other dolphins if we give her a chance. I'd like to try to get her down to Mexico with us, if she'll follow the ship. We'll probably see some dolphins of her species, and there's a possibility she'd join them."

Jean felt as though she might be crushed by the weight of his words. Baby join a school? Of course it would be best for her, but it would never work. The trip would only endanger her.

When she could trust her voice, she said, "I've read that orcas wait at the mouth of Scammon's Bay to ambush mother whales and their calves, but they'd just as soon attack a dolphin. I'd hate to expose Baby to that risk." Her voice was casual, but her feelings were not. Orcas were savage, and the thought of Baby coming to harm made her sick.

David said, "I may as well point out that I think she'll follow the ship, anyway—to be near you."

Jean had never considered that possibility. Baby's home was Santa Barbara. To lead her away from it was to lead her into risk. But the alternative—abandoning the Baja trip and Chris and David—she wouldn't consider.

David said, "Let's drop this for now. Baby will do what she wants, and I need to talk to you about something else." He paused and said very quietly, "You and me."

Jean's head snapped up. It was the last thing she'd expected, and his tone made her instantly fearful. Was he going to push her away again?

David turned his head and looked at her. "I gave our situation a great deal of thought today. An expedition can be a very intense professional situation, and obviously you and I have something personal going on.''

From David, it was a huge admission. Jean thought, *Don't say you want to end it.*

He told her, ''You should also be aware that on a ship, when two people feel a strong attraction for each other, it becomes glaringly apparent to everyone else.''

He must be thinking of Skye. Though Jean tried to ignore it, the thought pricked her like the point of a dagger. It was impossible not to imagine the lovers slipping away to their cabin in the middle of the afternoon to make love.

Sitting back, David stared aimlessly over the bow at the boats in the next marina. ''I know this job means a lot to your career. If you want to be taken seriously, it won't help for anyone involved with this expedition to suspect you're sleeping with me.''

Jean hadn't given a thought to what anyone would think. She was stunned, but at the same time she understood the message that she wouldn't be working for him forever, that at some point she would need to apply to someone else for employment.

*Temporary,* she thought. *All of this is temporary.* Dizzy with the implication of his words, she thought of the fact that it was David who had chosen to put her in the crew's quarters, in the one berth on the ship with easy access to his. She said, ''Perhaps I should move to an aft stateroom.'' It was the last thing she wanted.

David said, ''That's a solution and not one I'm fond of.''

Jean drew a silent breath of relief. ''What do you suggest?''

His brown eyes turned to hers in the darkness. ''I'd like to marry you.''

## CHAPTER TEN

FOR A MOMENT Jean couldn't speak. When she could, she said in a fragile voice, "Marry me, as in…marriage of convenience?"

David thought of the pirate romance he'd seen in her house. If not for the gravity of the topic, he would have laughed. Instead, he shook his head. "Inconvenience. Life on a ship doesn't agree with most people. Which is why an engagement of reasonable length would be a good idea first." He added, "If you're interested."

Jean could hardly think. Of course she was interested, but what on earth could be his motive? He didn't love her. At least she didn't think so. She turned in her seat and saw him stand, clearly restless.

Jean's voice shook madly. "Why are you doing this? I don't understand. Are you talking about a real engagement? A real marriage?" Before he could answer she said, "It seems like an extreme way to protect my career."

In the fog David looked down at her. "This isn't about your career. I was wrong to start that way."

In the faded glow from the distant dock lights, Jean peered up at him, probing his eyes, wishing she knew his thoughts.

Moving away, David stared out across the water. "We have so much in common it's uncanny."

Jean wasn't sure he was going to say any more, but eventually he turned back. Despite the absence of light, Jean had the impression his eyes were as clear and candid as she'd ever seen them.

He told her, "I don't think there are two of you out there, Jean."

Jean pondered that, understanding what he meant—that he believed she was unique and somehow right for him.

He sat down again, closer to her this time. "And my son loves you. Isn't that what you said?"

*You're* supposed to love me, she thought, wondering how large a factor Christian's affection for her really was. Huddling in the yellow sailing slicker, she replied, "I'm not sure Chris loves me so much he wants you to marry me."

David smiled. "He probably wants to marry you himself." He put his hand on her back and touched her hair. It was loose, so thick he could drown in it in bed. He wanted to.

*Why am I hesitating?* Jean asked herself. *This is David sitting out here in the fog asking me to marry him.* So what if she'd known him only two weeks? In her soul she'd known him forever.

She loved him. She said, "Okay."

Because she sat beside him, David had to move his head forward to meet her eyes. "Yes?"

"Yes." Her heart was rushing. She was afraid she was going to cry. This was exactly what she wanted and yet it wasn't. She huddled deeper into the foul-weather jacket.

David said, "Sure?"

Was he hoping she'd change her mind? She said, "If you are."

"I'm not, but for grown men that goes with the territory. I think we'll do fine together." David couldn't take his hand out of her hair. It was a relief to know he didn't have to, but he wished he could see her face.

Jean said, "So we're engaged?"

Her voice sounded strange, thought David. Very emotional. He stroked her back. "Yes." Thinking of it, he said,

"Tomorrow's busy, but we can take an hour in the morning and look for a ring, if you like. Not that it's something we should rush."

Jean's throat closed. *So we won't have to return it?*

"We want something special," David said. "You'll be wearing it a long time."

Jean couldn't help it then. She turned her face against his shoulder, buried it against the yielding folds of his jacket and cried. *Don't be lying to me,* she thought. *Please don't.*

WHEN DAVID RETIRED to his cabin, two hours after he'd seen Jean to hers, he took her bonsai olive tree and his bottle of tequila with him. The tree was a surprisingly pleasant symbol of the season—and of her. The tequila was a necessity. Since he'd left her, he'd already drunk more than was good for him but not enough to make him unconscious, which was what he wanted.

He had not expected her to cry. Or to say yes.

He'd handled the moment by kissing her and touching her as long as he could, but then the strain had become too intense. He'd seen her to the crew's quarters and given her a brief kiss outside the door. It was easy to leave her in her own room, much easier than it would ever be to lead her into his. That was an eventuality he was happy to postpone.

Lying in the dark, he stared at the bonsai and nursed the bottle comfortingly, no longer minding the fire. It was making him drowsy. Good.

*Oh, Jean, why did you have to say yes? Why did I ask?*

Because it seemed obvious that he should. It was more than tae kwon do or diving or that she was young and beautiful, though those were the things that had swayed him where he thought he would never be swayed. When he'd thought about her on the drive back from Los Angeles, he'd realized she met and exceeded his own stringent criteria for what was acceptable in a mate. She was sober, assertive, honest and complex.

And what she had said about Chris had clinched it. *He says he loves me.*

Chris needed a mother—one who would sing Christmas carols at his bedside.

That was a huge factor, that and a casual remark from Erika, who had said, *Chris fell in love with her right away, didn't he, David? It's wonderful for him to have someone like that.*

David had seen the corollary—that it would be heart-breaking for Chris to lose her.

Which, as he'd told Jean, wouldn't have been enough by itself. She had provided the rest, with her individuality and her integrity.

David thought of her tears that night, her incredible explanation. *I never thought this would happen, David.*

Neither had he.

He drained the tequila and shoved the empty bottle onto the nightstand. Then he lay down in the darkness. Listening to the water and the docks, he remembered how her hair and her mouth felt.

He thought how different she was from Skye in every way.

He slept.

THE ALARM ON HER WATCH beeped at five-thirty, and Jean sat straight up in her bunk, remembering she was engaged to David. Hugging herself, she thought, *Yes, Jean, there is a Santa Claus.* Not only was she engaged to the man she loved, but they were leaving for Baja that afternoon to see whales. She would spend Christmas in David's arms, in Scammon's Bay, the place of her dreams.

Unfortunately Baja was also the land of her worst night-mares, but she tried to forget that. Jake had to be wrong about their going to Cabo San Anselmo, if only because everything else was so perfectly right.

Unable to sleep when David left her in her cabin the night before, Jean had used pages from her notebook to write a long letter of explanation to Ceci, which, through careful editing, had become shorter and shorter. Now, she wondered if she would even send it. What if David changed his mind?

The thought was terrifying to her, the more so because it seemed possible, even likely. Two weeks' acquaintance was enough for her, but she could hardly believe it was enough for David. Considering that the first time around he'd married a woman who had killed herself.

Jean shivered in the morning air. There would still be fog outside, and she didn't bother to lean close to the porthole and check. Instead, she climbed out of the berth, took her *dobok* and belt from her locker, laid them on the bed and looked under the door that led into the shower room. No light.

She knocked, then went in and switched on the light herself.

It was a space she liked. The showers were separated from the forward head by a door made of woven wood, bamboo and beads. David had remarked once that he was going to replace the door because it was a magnet for mold, but Jean loved the look, just as she loved the shower room's one mahogany-framed, stained-glass window. Giant sea turtles. There were two shower heads and a large sunken bath with whirlpool jets. Jean wanted to try the bath sometime, but it seemed wasteful of the ship's water reserves.

She stepped into the shower stall closest to her cabin and turned on the spray.

In the next cabin, the sound of the water roused David, though he neither noticed nor identified it. All he noticed was the way he felt.

It wasn't the worst hangover of his life or even in the

top five, but it was sufficiently unpleasant to fog the world and distract him from thoughts of the previous evening and the fact that he was now engaged. He remembered the last almost immediately, but at the moment it seemed less overwhelming than the hangover.

He hadn't done this to himself since the weeks after Skye's death, and as he kicked himself out of bed and rose naked to his feet, he wondered if asking a woman to marry him was sufficient justification for having done it again.

Yes.

He pushed open the door to the forward head and a few moments later opened the door and went into the shower room.

David realized his mistake at once. The room was full of steam and the scent of her shampoo. She was there outside the starboard shower stall, paused in the midst of drying off as she stared at him with wide eyes.

Frightened? Flustered? He didn't analyze it. He left, taking the sight of her small, long-legged muscular body and pink-tipped nipples with him.

As he paused at the sink and washed his face, she called through the door, "I'm done, David."

Which meant she'd taken her hair out of the drain, too, thought David. Conscientious. Again, exceeding the criteria.

He didn't answer. He was thinking of the glimpse of her slender hips, the triangle of hair at the top, the way she looked bent over just slightly as she dried herself.

*"Mine,"* he murmured. His hangover seemed to ease.

JEAN DRESSED for tae kwon do and waited for him on the aft deck in the darkness. She hadn't seen him since he'd come in when she was getting out of the shower, and his silence when she'd called to him through the door was unnerving. Jean half expected that when he joined her on deck it would be with bad news—that he'd acted hastily the night before, perhaps spurred into a proposal by her announcement that Chris had said he loved her.

When David at last emerged from the cabin, dressed not in his *dobok* but in a pair of khaki canvas pants and a thick Blade Institute sweatshirt, her fears buoyed to the surface. He was going to call it off.

Jean watched him, trying to keep from showing her insecurity. He was carrying a cup of coffee and a bran muffin.

Eyes hooded with what looked like regret, he said, "Hi."

Jean stood up from a stretch but didn't move toward him.

Crossing the deck, he took a seat on a steel locker near the stern. In his condition, sparring was out of the question. He'd end up with cracked ribs or worse. He suggested, "Why don't you work on patterns this morning? I'll…coach."

Jean bowed to him and began to move the deck furniture to make room. Then, suddenly, she stopped and glanced all over the deck.

David knew she was looking for the olive tree. He said, "It's in my cabin."

Jean looked at him. "Was it in the way?"

He shook his head. "I like it. It seems like…Christmas. In a good way."

For a moment he thought she was going to cry again, but instead, she knelt to meditate. David watched her posture, her closed eyes, her tranquil expression, her even breathing, and felt his heart stir.

Again, he thought, *Mine*.

DAVID DID NOT MENTION going downtown to look for a ring. Instead, he seemed wholly focused on preparations for the trip. Even less talkative than usual, he gave concise directions, which Jean followed to the letter. But her disappointment was keen. Though he had commandeered her bonsai tree, his "forgetting" their date to look for a ring was inauspicious. Again she wondered if he wanted to spare himself the trouble of returning it. Hiding her anguish, she played the calendar game with Chris and helped ready the ship for departure. If they finished early, perhaps David would take her downtown. There was no one to watch Chris, but they could take him along.

On the other hand, perhaps David didn't want his son to know about the engagement.

Or maybe he was waiting for an opportunity to break it.

When Jake Doherty arrived at nine, her last hopes were dashed. Jake came bearing provisions for the expedition and bad news. The cook they had hired for the trip had bailed out at the last minute and no other was to be found.

As Jean stowed the groceries in the galley, she thought how ironic it was that David needed a cook. Jean remembered her father telling her, *Look, Jean, don't worry about what your mother says. Anyone can read a cookbook. You don't need to be Julia Child.*

Jean imagined that at this point David would settle for less than a chef. She thought of the engagement ring he was avoiding, and when the cabin door opened and she saw him coming down into the salon, she leaned up the companionway from the galley and said, "David, I could cook."

David reminded himself that she was going to be his wife, and witticisms about her culinary skills should probably be kept to a minimum for the time being.

Jean saw the reservation he was striving to hide. It made her want to persuade him. Coming up the companionway to meet him in the salon, she said, "I'm a biologist. The kitchen's not that different from the lab."

She had a point, although it only underlined her unsuitability for the job. But her offer to do something he knew she disliked was endearing. He nodded at her. "Okay." Watching her eyes widen at the realization that he'd agreed, David said, "Jake's going to watch Chris for a while. Ready to go downtown?"

Jean heard his words with joyful amazement. He had remembered the ring. Her palpable fear at the thought of cooking for a half-dozen men receded.

David saw her emotions flit over her face. Her vulnerability—and her inability to hide it—touched him and made him want to take her to bed and prove his gentleness. It made him want to see the symbol of his promise on her finger.

He said, "Let's go."

AS THE CORVETTE IDLED at a traffic light, Jean asked, "Have you said anything to Chris?"

He shook his head. "We'll tell him when we get home."

*We.* The word was a promise. She was part of his life.

The Christmas shoppers were out in force, and the first store they entered was busy with a mother looking for "something special" for her daughter, three ladies shopping for a gift for a co-worker, and a husband choosing for his wife. But the jeweler knew an engaged couple when he saw one. When he offered to show them rings, David looked at Jean, then said, "We'll browse for now."

Peering silently into cases lined with red velvet, Jean felt almost as though she were doing something forbidden. Was she really engaged to David? Were they really choosing rings together? Large diamonds winked at her from the cases. Simple settings. Ornate settings.

They left the store and stepped out into the sunshine on State Street. David asked, "Did you see anything you liked?"

Jean had seen a lot, but she wasn't even sure what she liked. She wished David would choose something.

He told her, "I'll say first that money is no object, second that you should like the ring. Those are the rules." His hand slid into hers. "Good enough?"

Jean nodded, smiling up at him. She said, "I think a ring from a gum machine would satisfy me."

David looked down at her. "Today it might. Wait till we're married, though. Everything changes then."

Jean noticed that after he spoke he looked somber, as though lost in a saddening memory.

Hand in hand they continued down the street, at home with the Spanish-style architecture, red-tile roofs under shading palms. Near the outdoor shopping plaza, a costumed madrigal group was singing renaissance carols, and as they paused to listen, David put his arm around Jean's shoulders and brushed a kiss across her temple. He bought hot apple cider from a street vender and kissed the spice from her lips. Jean felt as though she were in some other woman's body, living a dream that belonged to someone else. But it was *her* dream, the man *she* loved.

When at last they moved on to another jewelry store, David opened the door and held it for her. Jean stepped in ahead of him, wishing, not for the first time that morning, she was wearing something more stylish than faded jeans and a sweatshirt. Or at least more feminine and Christmassy.

But the elegantly dressed young woman behind the counter did not frown at her attire. Like the first jeweler, she seemed to sense they were a couple scouting for rings. Jean watched her smile broaden as she hurried toward them. Then, abruptly, the smile vanished and shock took over. For a moment Jean thought the woman was going to faint. She actually seemed to pale before regaining even a semblance of her former expression.

"David. What a surprise."

David nodded, wishing he'd chosen a different store. "Hi, Jill. I didn't know you were working."

Jean was interested that he did not add "here."

"I come in and help Daddy once in a while. Usually in the Montecito shop." The woman had recovered admirably, and now her carefully lashed eyes were busy taking in Jean.

"Today I just got lucky." She remembered to look at David. "What can I help you find? A Christmas gift?"

"A wedding set."

Jean noticed that Jill looked like a woman who had just received enough news to last her a lifetime. She turned to Jean, brown eyes wide. "Well, my goodness. Congratulations, my dear."

David studied Jean's face and doubted she recognized the cut. She was blushing. Before she could reply and give Jill further opening for ridicule, David said, "Thank you, Jill. I don't think we see anything in here today."

Jill looked momentarily taken aback. Then she said smoothly, "I'm so sorry. You used to have such luck coming here with Skye. She liked everything. I'll never forget those freshwater pearls you bought that one Christmas."

David turned Jean around and guided her to the door, then opened it.

Sensitive to David's pain, Jean hurried out, but she felt as though her own heart were breaking. She was aware of him behind her, his face a cool mask, showing nothing. For a moment he paused on the sidewalk, watching the cars pass, as though in the grip of indecision.

Waiting in the shade of the shop awning, Jean stared in the window at a display of rings lying beside some artfully arranged red glass Christmas balls.

*You used to have such luck coming here with Skye.*

Had he only remembered what store it was once he was inside? Or was that when the memories had suddenly become too much?

She thought of Jill's sleek style. The jeweler's daughter must have been a friend of Skye's. Jill's French twist looked unmussed, her makeup as though it had been applied by a professional and wouldn't fade by the end of the day. Despite Ceci's coaching, Jean's own experiments with makeup were always unsatisfactory. She preferred to go without, but inside the store, beside Jill, she had felt messy and unpolished.

She was certain Skye had been of Jill's ilk. Glossy and immaculate.

Jean saw David in the glass behind her. He was watching her reflection, and he put both hands on her shoulders. He said, "Would you trust me to have something made for us?"

The rings. Jean turned and looked up at him, her throat suddenly huge. She nodded.

It seemed natural that he would embrace her, but he did not. He said, "Then let's go home."

WHEN THEY PULLED into space number three in the marina parking lot, a uniformed mechanic from a nearby garage was waiting for them.

As he got out of the car, David said, "Hi, Jim. Thanks for coming to get it." He handed the mechanic the keys as he walked around the hood to let Jean out. She had already opened the door, so he shut it after her.

Jim said, "No problem to come and get this beast. I love to work on her."

David wished him a happy holiday and turned with Jean to lead her toward the marina.

She asked, "Is he going to take care of your car while you're gone?"

David nodded. "Leaving it here while I'm home is risky enough."

So Jake had been mistaken when he said David wanted the Corvette to come to harm. That seemed to debunk his insinuations about problems in David's marriage. Perhaps he was wrong about the party at Cabo San Anselmo, too.

If they were going David would have mentioned it, unless he expected her to stay home with Chris. That would have been natural at first—the job she was hired for—but she was his fiancée now. If there was a party he would take her.

Jean hoped there was no party. And she hoped they would not stop at Cabo San Anselmo.

As they reached marina D and David used his key card in the gate, he said, "Jean, I think perhaps I should be alone when I tell Chris." He didn't say what he was going to tell him; they both knew.

Jean glanced up at him as she moved through the gate, wondering what had prompted the change of course. Did he think Chris would be upset? And what if Chris *was* upset, was worried or hurt or angry? Jean closed off the thoughts. "If you think that's best."

David shut the gate behind them. "I do."

Jean spent the next half hour making the office shipshape for departure. It was the perfect task because it kept her hands busy and her mind free, and it kept her out of the way of Jake and any arriving expedition members. Below, in the security of the lower cabin, there was no need to hide the worry on her face as she thought of David talking to Chris—and no need to hide her preoccupation as she replayed her brief date with David.

The final scene in the jewelry store became more painful upon mental repetition. Jill's congratulating her, as though she were the big winner. She, about to blunder her thanks while David chivalrously accepted the courtesy. How different it must have been for him with Skye.

Numbly she imagined him choosing those freshwater pearls, a Christmas surprise. Or had Skye gone with him? Had they lingered over the cases together? Had he shaken his head at her choices or she at his? Had they found together what they liked and David said, *Those, please?* What a contrast to today. He had asked to see nothing, not even to have her sized, and Jean doubted now it was because nothing had pleased him.

She was distracted from her musings and her work when

the door at the top of the stairs opened, letting light shine in from the galley. She saw Chris's small silhouette and David's larger one behind him. They stepped onto the landing, and David closed the door as Chris started down the companionway.

His progress was laggard, and Jean was reminded of the withdrawn child she had met two weeks earlier. His behavior had changed so much since then, and the reversion was worrisome. Was learning of his father's engagement to her the cause? If Jean had doubted it, she would have seen the answer in David's eyes. He seemed lost in thought, absently focused on Chris and almost unaware of her.

Chris came to stand near the desk where she was working and signed a phrase at her. Jean recognized "family."

After a moment, David said, "He's glad you're going to be part of our family."

Chris glanced at his father as though to ask, *Is that good enough?*

David nodded at him, a cue for the next step.

Looking at David again, Chris moved forward and hugged Jean around the neck.

*A charade,* she thought. *At David's insistence?* Courtesy was important, but how did Chris really feel?

She hugged him back—an abbreviated hug—and looked into his eyes.

He turned away.

David, who had come down to the foot of the stairs, seemed dissatisfied but tolerant. He told Chris, "You may go."

Chris gave them both a final, opaque look and trudged back up the steps. David stood silently at the bottom of the companionway until his son had gone out and closed the door.

Jean said, "David, if he's unhappy about it, we don't need to—"

"He doesn't necessarily know what's good for him."

Jean swallowed that answer. It wasn't what she'd been hoping for. First, he had not denied Chris's unhappiness. Second, why hadn't David said *he* cared for her and that was the bottom line?

Because it wasn't. He was acquiring a mother for Chris.

Setting that aside to ponder later, she asked, "What did he say?"

David hesitated. "Not everything. I'm sure of that." With obvious reluctance he admitted, "He has an idea his mother is coming back—that I go out on the channel looking for her." Before Jean could feel more than one hard, pounding heartbeat, he said, "I should say, he *had* that idea. I think I dispossessed him of it."

Jean recalled her own parents' death. Morning after morning she had awoken with the feeling that everything was as usual. Then, each day, when she'd realized they were dead, the world had fallen around her. She had wanted to go back to sleep, to wake up from the nightmare.

If somewhere in his subconscious Chris still held the recollection of his mother falling off the ship and never surfacing, his idea made a kind of sense. Hardly knowing she spoke, she whispered, "Poor Chris." And poor David, who had seen his wife's blood and would never lose the memory of it.

David watched her, his thoughts divided between the emotion on her face, the unseen feelings in her heart and his own conversation with Chris—his effort to convince a child who did not even remember his mother or her death that the woman was in fact dead. And all the while trying to preserve something of a six-year-old's innocence.

He told Jean, "Truthfully, I think he was focusing on that to avoid other fears. Being sent away. My no longer loving him or loving you more."

It was the first time he had mentioned loving her at all and now only as a possibility to be denied to his son. Jean said, "You reassured him?"

"Of course." Apparently eager to close the subject, he glanced at the office. "When you're done here, come on up. Some people have arrived, and it's time for introductions."

As JEAN LOCKED the desk drawers and made sure nothing could be dislodged at sea, she heard the loud hum of the engines warming up. It sent a faint vibration through the ship, the sound of a vessel preparing to move. It excited her, helping to erase the gloom of a morning whose bright buds of hope had been blown away by the winds of reality.

Still, the gravity of her situation immersed her. She was engaged to a man who didn't love her and whose son might or might not accept her as a stepmother. David was marrying her for Chris's sake, and yet Chris wanted his own mother, whose picture still hung in the salon.

As she passed through the salon, Jean noticed the watercolor again. How long did David intend to keep the portrait there? Forever, as permanent tribute to his first wife?

Jean wondered if she could stand it—and if she could stand always being second. But David came with a past.

As she opened the salon door, she found him coming through the diving alcove accompanied by a tall, white-haired man. He said, "There you are. Jean, this is Dr. Grant Geary, our expedition doctor. Dr. Geary was a friend of my father's. Besides being an MD, he's also a qualified veterinarian and a cetacean specialist. Grant, this is my fiancée, Jean Young."

*Fiancée*. Even hearing him utter the word didn't make it seem real.

For a moment she and Dr. Geary assessed each other. Studying the doctor's face, Jean recognized him from the shark video as the man who had tended David's wound. Now, as he returned her appraisal, she saw something behind his eyes that disconcerted her. Reservation. But the look was well concealed as he held out his hand and said,

"I'm pleased to make your acquaintance, Miss Young. I've already met Baby."

Jean smiled and shook his hand. She could hear Baby outside, whistling from the side of the ship. She said, "It's nice to meet you, Dr. Geary."

They exchanged pleasantries for a few moments more, and Jean began to relax. Then Dr. Geary went below to his cabin, and David invited her outside to meet the other members of the expedition—biologist Ken Lightman and Australian cinematographer Robin Frost. Jake had gone into town for last-minute supplies.

Jean spent the time until departure on the diving platform with Baby and the inflatable Christmas wreath, now patched with duct tape. Part of her worried that it was a mistake to show the dolphin attention at this time. If Baby followed the ship away from Santa Barbara, she might become separated from them and never find her way back. What was more, the unknown southern waters seemed to offer infinitely more peril to the lone dolphin. But surely Baby had the sense to remain behind in a place familiar to her.

At one in the afternoon they cast off and the *Skye* churned slowly out of the harbor. Seeing Chris occupied in the salon with an aircraft carrier and fleet of die-cast metal planes Dr. Geary had given him as an early Christmas gift, Jean went to the wheelhouse to find out if there was anything she could do for David.

The channel was calm, with only the wind disturbing the water. Jean discovered she liked the motion of the ship; the ocean was in her blood. She liked feeling the sun on her skin and the salt spray in her hair as she made her way along the railing toward the bridge.

Nearing the wheelhouse, Jean realized Jake must be inside with David, smoking a cigarette. The starboard window of the cockpit was open, and his voice drifted out with the smoke.

"Your first marriage made more sense to me, and I have to say, that one never made a lot. Marrying a woman you've known two weeks makes *none*."

Jean froze, listening for David's response, but Jake drowned him out. "Oh, Jean's got secrets, all right." He paused. "I know because I know, David. Say the word to her sometime. Watch what happens. What word? *Secrets.* That word."

Jean's heart clenched and unclenched a hundred times. Wondering whether to go into the wheelhouse or try to hear more, she hesitated outside the cabin. She heard the murmur of David's voice beneath the engine but couldn't make out the words.

Jake said, "Okay, okay. I like her, David. You know that. I wish you joy."

Bracing herself, Jean pulled open the door of the wheelhouse and stepped inside.

Jake's back was to her, but David's was not. Eyes dark on hers he said, "Hi, Jean."

Jake shrugged at David. Reaching for his pack of cigarettes, he echoed, "Hi, Jean." Then he slipped out of the wheelhouse, leaving the helm to David.

As the door shut behind him, Jean recalled why she had come. "Chris is playing with airplanes. Do you have something for me to do?"

David looked thoughtful. Watching his profile, Jean wondered if he knew what she had overheard. Did he want to uncover her secrets?

He nodded toward the bow. "I think Baby's up there, playing off the prow. If you go down in the observation chamber, you can see her."

A number of reactions went through her. Worry that Baby was swimming with the ship. Excitement at seeing the inside of the underwater observation chamber, which David had never shown her. And worry over what suspicions Jake might have awakened. She'd sensed David had defended her, but that was what she would have expected of him. It would be a violation of his personal code to let anyone criticize his family or choice of fiancée.

Jean decided to test the waters. "I guess Jake doesn't approve."

David glanced at her. "I wondered if you'd heard that." He turned his eyes to the channel and said, "Don't think about it. You and I have known each other a short time. People will have their say."

Jean thought of Jake. He would say plenty if he knew the truth.

Unexpectedly David put his hand on her back, over her braid. Coming out from in front of the captain's seat, he guided her into his place and set her hands on the ship's wheel. Jean gripped the glossy hardwood of the helm and realized she was steering. Gesturing to the distant islands, David said, "Point the nose under that southernmost mountain. I'm going to see what Chris is up to."

Then he left.

For a moment, Jean felt overwhelmed. There was tremendous power in her hands, and she could feel the other power, the sea, beneath the vessel. Yet the sensation of being at the helm was intoxicating. Other concerns crept away, and after a minute or so she moved and sat upon the leather-covered captain's seat, moving the wheel slightly to keep the bow pointed toward the island mountain David had indicated.

A moment later, the door of the wheelhouse opened again and Jake came in, smelling of cigarettes. She started to move from the seat, and he said, "You're fine," then increased the throttle.

Jean was uneasy, not because she felt Jake might try to ferret out her past, but because he was bound to stumble upon it. Both Jake and David had connections in Baja, and now they were going there. With her. Possibly to Cabo San

Anselmo. She didn't dare ask if the cape was really on the itinerary.

Feeling almost as though Jake might read her thoughts, Jean shifted them to the other part of his conversation with David. Why had Jake said David's first marriage hadn't made sense to him? Jean longed to quiz him, not only about that enigmatic statement but about Erika's accident and the puzzling comment he had made to her earlier about David "doing penance." Jake was a well of information begging to be tapped with questions Jean couldn't bring herself to ask. David would be her husband; if she wanted to know something she should ask him. Except that he wouldn't talk about what she wanted to know.

She was watching the channel through the windshield, but she felt Jake studying her. He lit another cigarette and said, "Sorry about what you heard, Jean, but David's my friend, and I had to say it. Strangers shouldn't marry."

Jean said, "Please consider the possibility that we know each other better than you think."

Jake said, "Please consider the possibility that you don't know David *at all.*"

Jean's palms grew damp on the steering wheel. She told herself it was just Jake, Jake with his way of turning life into gothic intrigue. But there was enough truth in his remark to set her on edge.

And, as though he couldn't keep quiet, he said, "David wouldn't thank me for this, but I've got to say it, Jean. You marry him, you marry his past. And you're sitting on it. *Skye.*"

Because he had said the name, Jean couldn't stop herself. She looked at him and asked, "Did you like her, Jake?"

"Skye?" Jake spread his hands wide, drawing a plume of smoke across the cockpit. "I loved her. I hated her. Everyone did, David most of all. They were screaming one minute and screwing the next. Skye was a bitch and a lush, but she was great. Funniest woman you ever met. Sweetest, too, when she wasn't the meanest. But, baby, Skye made trouble like a baker makes bread, and she made David a lifetime supply. *His* lifetime, not hers. You want to live with that?''

Paralyzed by his speech, Jean hardly saw Jake's eyes drift toward the channel.

He said, "Watch your course."

Blinking, stunned, Jean faced the sea. The ship had veered sharply, and she concentrated on regaining her heading as Jake's words spun through her mind. *Bitch? Lush?* Jean couldn't focus on that, only on David and Skye, together. In one breath, she saw them in moments of passionate rage; in the next, making love in every cabin and on every deck of the ship, from engine room to fly bridge, from bow to stern. She saw David buying pearls for Christmas, and she remembered, with horror, that Skye had killed herself. Did Jake know that?

Jean didn't have long to ponder it. The door of the wheelhouse opened, and David came in.

He did not look at her but gazed off the bow, checking her course. Then he stole one of her hands from the helm and said, "Come on. I want to show you something."

NOT RELEASING HER HAND, he led her out onto the bow and opened the forwardmost hatch, which Jean knew led down into the underwater observation chamber. Nodding below into the darkness, a darkness shining with faint aquamarine light, he said, "You first."

Jean noticed he held her hand until she had crouched on the deck to lower herself down the hatch. The bow, she thought. He's nervous because we're near the bow.

His concern made her heart ache. *David, what did she do, this incomprehensible woman you loved? How did she go over that bow rail? Drunk?*

But there were no answers, could be none until he decided to give them. Which might be never. Watching David's running shoes, inches from her eyes, Jean continued below, into the hull.

Portholes followed the ladder down the ship's nose. Through the layers of glass she saw sunlight rippling in the foam produced by the prow. As she descended the ladder, her eyes caught a sleek, silver shape in the blue and she gasped. Baby, swimming fast and strong in the wake.

David said, "Go on."

At his urging, Jean continued down the ladder, and David followed, shutting the hatch over their heads. The space was small, with barely room for the two of them to stand comfortably. But the chamber curved aft, creating a low-ceilinged nook where the floor was covered by an old mattress. A quilt lay on top, shielding the mattress, and Jean knew in a glance it must be another of Skye's. The colorful, intricate style was like that of the spread on David's bed.

David drew her eyes away from the quilt with the touch of his hands. They were on her waist, and Jean looked at him in surprise.

He said, "Hi." And he kissed her.

# CHAPTER ELEVEN

HE HAD KISSED HER on the street that morning, but this was a real kiss, a private kiss, and there was a moment of adjusting mouths, of finding each other again, of remembering.

As the ship hit a wave and the bow bounced, David locked his arm around her, simultaneously holding the ladder. He said, "We'll do better on the floor."

Her heart racing, Jean let him steady her as they slipped down onto the mattress, not sitting but lying, facing each other. Her blood rushed down through her stomach, pooling heat and desire, and she let her legs press against David's as he kissed her again and began unbuttoning her work shirt. Jean did not stop him, but she was shocked. Weren't they supposed to be working? What was happening on deck? Would they be missed?

David's single-mindedness left no room for questions. He made short work of the front closure of her bra, pushing aside the cups to expose her breasts to the cool air and the soft aqua light.

And to his eyes.

Aside from the time they had glimpsed each other through the fog of the steamy shower room, he had never seen her naked. And Jean had never felt so revealed. Years ago, she had joined her body with someone she knew as well as she knew herself. But she felt more now in simply allowing David to look at her. More intimate, more excited, more vulnerable. More right.

As she trembled David kissed her and dragged his lips down her throat to her collarbone and breastbone. He said, "I've wanted to do this for a week."

*Here?* wondered Jean irrationally. *In this chamber? Or was he simply talking about taking off her clothes, caressing her?* Again came the echo of Skye, a taunting mystery. Had he and Skye lain together on this spot? Had they made love while the foam broke away from the prow?

David touched her, drawing her mind from the thoughts. His hand on her bare side, he let his lips graze her breasts, then one nipple. He tasted the pink skin with his tongue, then closed his mouth over her.

Jean's breath folded inside her, and her fingers caught his hair. His mouth and hands tasted and explored, kissed and stroked. It was not the way he'd touched her the night before—with restraint, as though he had somewhere to be and must leave shortly. No. Now, he kissed and caressed her as though he might continue for hours.

His mouth wandered to hers again, and they kissed with their tongues. Jean's breasts pressed against his shirt, and with wonder she felt his hand between her legs, cupping her over her jeans. She jerked against him, hard, unrestrained.

David murmured something she didn't understand, and she drew closer to him, one of her legs slipping between his. He released the buttons on her jeans. The denim was worn, and the fly parted with one movement of his hand. He said, "Are you all right?"

She nodded, her eyes holding his for one flustered moment. As he'd known she would be, she was a mass of feverish confusion and want. When he slipped his hand under her clothes, into the tangled silken down beneath the cotton scrap of her panties, he found no surprises. Only her, wet and clinging to him, reaching for his pants.

He moved her hand away. "Let's keep things simple." As though anything about it was simple.

He stroked her, and she cried softly, "David."

He felt as though no one had ever said his name before.

But she hadn't surrendered. David felt part of her fighting—herself, not him—as though she didn't picture herself finding sexual fulfillment in his arms in a hollow chamber beneath the sea while others walked overhead. He felt sorry for doing it, but not sorry enough to stop. He wanted to make her come.

It was very easy, the work of quiet minutes.

Jean felt her whole body rushing, burning, floating against him. His name came from her mouth three times, like a spell, and she felt a swift rush of realization, then embarrassment. What had she done?

He wasn't letting her think about it. He was kissing her, touching her hair that had fallen from her disheveled braid, then hugging her against him tightly, as though she were a dear friend he hadn't seen for a very long time.

Her words muffled by the barrier of his body, she said, "No one else has ever done that to me."

Liking the information, that whoever had shared her body had never succeeded in awakening her and that he had, David said, "No one else ever will."

Jean could hear a trace of a smile in his voice but something else, too. A warning? Or a vow. The possessive words filled her like nourishment, and she rested her head against his heart.

After a moment, David moved her onto the mattress, onto her back, then fitted his mouth to hers again, kissing her at leisure.

Jean said, "You're like a dream come true."

Against her cheek and her hair, David murmured, "It's fair to warn you I have total recall of statements like that. Those words may come back to haunt you."

A moment passed before Jean understood the allusion to the long road of marriage. David's comment promised something lasting—the ordinary fights and reconciliations of a lifetime together. But it also reminded her of what Jake had said about him and Skye.

David seemed in no hurry to go, but spent long moments with his lips against her bare skin, his hands caressing her as though he required them to memorize the curves of her form. He cared for her in every way she could imagine before he at last buttoned her jeans, then fitted her bra around her and fastened it.

Dreamlike and wanting to stay in the dream, Jean asked softly, "Where did you learn all this, *Sabumnim?*"

"Books."

He met her eyes, and Jean knew it was a lie, but one that for the space of a moment she could believe. With the sea moving around them like an ever-changing cocoon, in the cool depths of the dark chamber with only his body to warm her, she could almost believe it had always been only her for him. That Skye had been unimportant, a trivial mistake.

As David finished buttoning her shirt, he glanced through the glass of one of the deadlights and remarked, "Baby has company."

Jean had forgotten about the dolphin. She sat up and saw Baby leap out of the way to allow another dolphin to play in the waves. Realizing David's thoughts beyond his words, she said, "It doesn't mean she'll be accepted by a school."

"True."

Jean wished Baby wasn't following the ship. The last thing she wanted at this beautiful, perfect moment was a disagreement with David, so she changed the subject, asking a question that had crossed her mind earlier in the day. "When are you going to tell Erika?"

"I already did." On the phone that morning. Erika had said, *I knew you were in love with her.* He wasn't, but he hadn't disagreed with his sister. Erika wouldn't understand. Being in love was nothing he wanted, and it wasn't what he felt with Jean.

No. Jean was the ominous approach of a hurricane. When she'd shuddered against him, calling his name, he'd felt things inside him coming unglued. The pieces were breaking apart and mixing up. He couldn't find the dark places anymore, and he had the uneasy feeling they had made a run toward the exit and were lurking near the top.

The thought scared him very much.

JEAN SPENT THE REST of the day in the salon with Chris, playing airplanes. Except for being more subdued, the interaction between them seemed unchanged from any other day, but Jean could not ignore the difference in their relationship. She was going to be Chris's stepmother, and everything they said and did together took on greater significance. But over her head still hung the memory of a long-ago error she had made, a failure less mistake than misfortune. If David ever found out, would he still think her good mother material? Would he find her to be a fit guardian for his son?

Jean wasn't sure.

In any case one thing she could never be was Chris's biological mother. He would always feel the emptiness of missing Skye, whoever she had been.

As she made a P-51 Mustang take off from the deck of the carrier, Jean watched Chris's plane bomb an enemy base made from an encyclopedia volume. The bomb exploded without sound. The engines of his planes were silent.

In a way she never had, Jean felt frustration at his speechlessness. Now she was going to be part of David's family, and the anomalies seemed more glaring, their sting sharper. She began to think of Chris as the boy who would be her son, and she understood more than ever the agony David must face daily in witnessing his child's endless silence. More than ever, she wished Chris's speech restored—and doubted she could in any way effect such a change. Worse, it was a change she now feared, because she sensed it might come with the return of a memory too monstrous for a child to bear.

She wondered how a man could bear it.

LATE THAT AFTERNOON the *Skye* anchored in a cove on one of the southernmost islands, and Robin Frost asked Jean if she'd get in the water with Baby so he could get some footage of them swimming together. Jean agreed, and when Chris asked to join her, David allowed it.

Nor did he raise any objection to Robin's filming Chris with Baby. Taking advantage of David's tolerance, Jean asked to use one of his underwater cameras and took some shots of Chris snorkeling with the dolphin. Then she climbed into the Zodiac, the inflatable motorized pontoon boat, with the others for an excursion to a nearby coral reef, where Robin wanted to film her diving with Baby.

David joined her on the dive, and Jean was acutely conscious of what they had shared earlier in the afternoon. She had never felt so close to anyone, and as they dove together near the reef, she reminded herself that their love of the sea united them, too. There was an easy chemistry between them in the water, a silent communication of spirits, as though they were meant to share the deep.

Robin wanted footage under a variety of conditions that took the whole party—Jean and David, Robin, Dr. Geary and Ken—to more than a hundred feet below the surface. It had been months since Jean had dived at such a depth. She welcomed the world of blue and was spellbound by the slow, graceful movements of large sharks below. Jean had learned in many ocean dives that sharks, while unpredictable, seldom bothered divers. Still, when Baby skirted away, a wave of uneasiness washed over her, and she remembered, as in a trance, the film of David's attack.

*David,* she thought, meeting his eyes and finding them absorbed with her. He seemed aware of the sharks but uninterested in them—only in her. He was so close Jean felt as though they were children in the same womb, or lovers, naked to each other as she had been naked to him that day.

We *are* lovers now, she thought. He must care.

Then, another truth came to her, subtle and sure. Though she couldn't be certain if Jake's impression of David's and Skye's marital interaction was accurate, she knew this: the David she loved would not relish the kind of constant emotional turmoil Jake had described. David craved tranquillity and clarity of mind. She saw that daily.

And as her eyes met his, Jean knew what she wanted— to bring peace to his soul.

Dr. Geary and the others swam upward, but a powerful allure begged Jean to remain below. She could stay at these depths with David forever, watching his eyes behind his mask. But as she watched, those eyes grew resolute—and regretful. David firmly took her hand and drew her up with him.

Forcing herself to heed the threat of nitrogen narcosis, Jean followed, grateful for his hand in hers. The rapturous high she'd felt gave way to emotional exhaustion, and each time they paused for decompression David stayed close, as though sensing her need for him. He was at her elbow when her regulator went out and her airflow stopped.

David grasped the problem immediately. His gaze locked with hers, and the expression in his eyes calmed her as he passed her his secondary regulator. Frightened, Jean glanced uneasily at his dive computer, doubting he had adequate air, but David thrust the mouthpiece into her hand with a gesture that defied argument. Aware the only alternative was a rapid ascent that would leave her bent and in peril of an embolism, Jean exchanged mouthpieces. David held her, his arm half-around her, as they alternated breaths. Using her buoyancy compensator, he regulated their ascent so they wouldn't have to swim and use precious air.

As they paused for a last decompression stop, Jean

wished she could tell him she loved him. She loved everything about him. His intelligence, his competence, his spirit. In two weeks, he had become the person closest to her, the man she would marry. The dearest gift of the season and of her life.

She *could* tell him she loved him. Freeing her hand from his, Jean faced him in the water and signed the phrase she had learned from him.

*I love you.*

In response David stared at her for a moment, then drew his hand across his throat.

They were out of air.

JEAN GASPED as they broke the surface. The air at the top was sweet, and the setting sun cast a brilliant glow over the water, momentarily blinding her. Trembling, she pushed her mask up on her forehead, buoyed by her vest.

Beside her, David inflated his vest, and as Jean squinted at him through her dripping lashes he would not meet her eyes. When he looked up it was to wave at the Zodiac, some distance away. Chris was leaning over one pontoon, petting Baby, but Jake returned the wave. Pushing back his mask, David ducked under the water then shook his hair, blinking the salt from his eyes. He still wouldn't look at her, and Jean thought of what had passed between them before they'd swum for the surface.

She had told him she loved him.

Seeing she wasn't going to get a response to that, she said, "Thank you, David."

"You're welcome."

The answer was cool, and Jean realized his mood had nothing to do with her silent underwater confession of love. He was angry about her regulator. Unquestionably and with good reason. He'd criticized her equipment the first day they dived together and had warned her about it since.

Jean told him, "You have every right to be mad."

Mad didn't touch it, and his maelstrom of emotions wasn't all for her. David's dark eyes met hers with icy brevity, and when Baby swam near them, lifting her head from the water to kiss Jean, he said, "A good thing you weren't alone with your old diving partner, isn't it?"

"I wouldn't have come out here with just Baby." Jean touched the dolphin, stroking her skin in long, soothing motions.

David watched, irrationally wishing she was touching him, instead. He had never before had the impulse to kick an animal. Or to yell at a woman, *And by the way, I don't love you.*

But as she rested her cheek against the curve of Baby's back, David couldn't stop his eyes from tracing the contours of her face, and he thought, *I can't afford to love you.*

DAVID CAME into the galley as she was rummaging in the cupboards. He'd said nothing to her during the ride back to the ship in the Zodiac nor since, but as Jean started turning the pages of a cookbook on the counter he said, "Make spaghetti. Lots."

Jean looked up at him. Her hair, still wet from a shower, tumbled down her back in an indifferent ponytail, and she was wearing a white T-shirt and a pair of faded Levi's that hung loosely from her small hips. She made him think of raw sex, and without wanting to David remembered her in his arms that afternoon. The vision had come and gone all day, pleasant but teasing, like the recollection of her taste and scent and the feel of her skin. Unfortunately, equally strong was the memory of her air stopping at eighty-five feet. It had been a reminder, not that she was heedless but that she was mortal.

David hadn't planned to care, but he did.

Seeing her gaze still upon him, he said, "Don't cook the noodles too long, and you'll be fine."

Jean was glad he'd decided to speak to her. Recognizing

good advice, she put water on the stove to boil, then took a bulk jar of whole-grain noodles from the shelf and unscrewed the lid. She glanced at him. "How much?"

"More." He watched her, his eyes drawn to the curve beneath her small breasts. "More."

Jean held out two huge handfuls. "Enough?"

"One more," said David.

She bowed, eyes flirtatious. "Thank you, *Sabumnim*."

David felt himself getting hard and made a mental note to speak to her later about calling him that. Someone would ask what it meant and never stop laughing over her addressing him by his title as a master instructor, no matter of what.

But they were alone, and she was making him smile. He answered in Korean—at some length.

Jean stared up at him, her mouth round. "What does that mean?"

"I was just putting you in your place."

But he had looked as though he was promising carnal delights. Eyes flickering like candle flames, Jean answered, "That's something I'd like to hear in English—if you can say it."

*Sassy wench*, thought David. He could say it. Turning his back to the door, blocking her body from view to anyone who might interrupt them, he drew her close to him and put his hand on her breast, stroking her nipple through her bra. Meeting her eyes, he translated roughly, in a low voice. "You have beautiful hair. I've tasted your breasts and your lips and your tongue. I want to put my mouth between your legs. All parts of you belong to me, and someday I will spill my seed inside you." Watching the flush in her cheeks and knowing it was flamed by desire as much as his frank words, he said, "You did ask," and kissed her mouth lightly, then released her.

Watching him leave the galley and go up to his cabin, Jean decided being put in her place by David was the best thing associated with cooking that had ever happened to her.

The next best thing was that the meal worked, garlic bread and all. She even made brownies from a mix and didn't burn them. Over dinner with Chris and the members of the expedition, David remarked, "You'd hardly know it was amateur hour in the galley tonight." But as the others laughed, his hand clasped hers beneath the table. It didn't hurt her feelings when later that night she heard him tell Jake they would stop in L.A. the next day to hire a cook.

THE FOLLOWING DAY the *Skye* tied up at a large industrial port near Los Angeles. Jean was playing chess with Chris in his stateroom, and when the game was over she went up on deck and found Jake smoking a cigarette and reading a sci-fi novel. No one else was in sight.

Jean asked, "Where is everyone?"

"David's looking for a cook. The other guys went to get lunch."

Jean surveyed her surroundings. The air was laden with smog and factory smoke and tar, and the sky had a yellow-ish cast. The neighboring ships ranged from a barge to large commercial vessels to luxury yachts. On shore, Jean could see a metropolitan area to the north and industry to the south. Thinking of the letter to Ceci she had never mailed, she asked, "How long will we be here?"

Jake shrugged. "Two hours."

Time enough for an overseas phone call if she wanted. This would be a chance to talk to Cecily in privacy, away from the ship—and the ears of Jake Doherty. Jean thought of other things she would like to do on shore, such as look for a gift for David. There were only five days till Christmas, and what she'd made for him with Chris seemed too little to give a fiancé.

Mentally Jean made a list. Phone call. Christmas gift. Clothes.

If David planned to take her to a party, she was unprepared. She hadn't packed even a skirt for the simple reason that she couldn't go to a party on Cabo San Anselmo. She would be crazy to try.

What she ought to try was telling David the truth.

Deciding that more than anything she wanted to reach Ceci and get her sister's advice, Jean told Jake, "I'd like to call my sister."

Jake said, "I'll watch Chris."

AFTER GOING BELOW to tell Chris what she was doing, Jean tucked her sister's number, a credit card and some cash into a pocket of her jeans and left the ship and the docks. The port had a completely different feel from Santa Barbara, but she welcomed the change. It was a symbol of what she had wanted for years. To be on the move, seeing different places, different people, different waters.

The street outside the marina's chain link fence was alive with activity, but it was the impersonal hubbub of an urban transitional zone. A businessman hurrying to catch a cab. A bicycle courier racing through a light. Dock and factory workers in grease-coated coveralls. Panhandlers. As Jean scanned the sidewalk, then prepared to cross a busy avenue, no one met her eyes. The only signs of the Christmas season were impersonal civic banners hanging high over the boulevard and a billboard inviting drivers to take advantage of holiday bargains at a nearby factory-outlet mall.

Crossing a grassy park shaded by palm trees, Jean saw a sign for a pay phone and rushed toward it to make her call, but when she reached it she found the receiver had been torn out. Dodging cars across another street, she headed for a row of three pay phones on the sidewalk. All were in use.

She hurried farther up the street, two blocks, with a close eye to her surroundings. There was less traffic here and fewer pedestrians. Nearly all were men, and though it was a weekday only a few looked as if they were on their way to or from work—unless they sold drugs or bartered in prostitutes for a living. They all noticed her, and it occurred to Jean that she was in an unfamiliar area and not a safe one. She was about to turn back toward the commercial district when she saw a deserted phone.

Rushing across another street on a yellow light, she dashed down the side street. The phone hutch was attached to the stone wall of a fire-damaged factory building with a realty sign hanging from an upper floor. No phone book, but the phone was intact, and when she lifted the receiver she heard a dial tone.

She got the long-distance operator and charged the call to her home phone, but when the number finally rang in Cecily's apartment an answering machine came on with her sister's voice, speaking in French. Jean bit her lip. She wanted Ceci to know she was engaged, but she couldn't leave her a message to that effect. Ceci would want the details.

The machine beeped, demanding an answer.

She said, "Hi. This is Jean. I'm on my way to Baja. I love you. I'll, um, talk to you when I get back. Merry Christmas." She hung up the phone and turned to go back to the waterfront.

She saw she was in danger.

DAVID FOUND A COOK in twenty minutes.

He asked first at the waterfront diner, wasting more time than he wanted with acquaintances there, and was on his way to check the boards outside the harbor master's office when a meaty hand grabbed his shoulder.

"David Blade! I'll be damned."

Jack "Jolly" Holly, 250 pounds of professional diver and ship's cook. They had dived and fished together in the South Pacific, and David recognized the hand of fate. Five minutes later Holly had signed on, then gone off to throw together his possessions. David jogged back to the ship, thinking of taking Chris and Jean to look at a mine sweeper farther along the waterfront. More than once he'd thought of buying one and converting it to a research vessel. The *Skye* was small and laden with ghosts and memories.

But a pretty ship.

Jake and Chris were sword-fighting on the foredeck with cardboard wrapping-paper tubes, and David smiled as he watched his son land a blow to Jake's knees.

Jake said, "Avast you, matey!" and attempted to take off his head in return.

Chris raised his left arm in a tae kwon do high block and warded off the blow.

Not bad, thought David. He wondered where Jean was, and the words came out of his mouth while he was still standing on the dock. "Where's Jean?"

Jake dropped his sword to his side. "Now, don't get riled at the nanny. I told her I'd watch Chris. She's making a phone call."

"Why didn't you go with her?"

The question sounded like an accusation, and Jake lifted an eyebrow but did not respond.

David tried to quiet the alarm tolling through him. A woman should be able to walk a few blocks alone to a phone booth without coming to harm. But he remembered the night he'd taken her home from the gym. She'd been headed for a lonely bike path, a bad choice. She might make another one, and in this neighborhood there was opportunity. Only yards from the waterfront were streets crawling with junkies, dealers and pimps. Drive-by shootings over drug territory were weekly fare.

He felt panic inside him—less for her safety than at the knowledge that suddenly he cared a little too much, that suddenly she was first and last in his mind, that suddenly a small worry for a woman he'd known a few weeks had become the sort of fear a man felt only for those he cherished. He asked Jake, "How long has she been gone?"

The first mate shrugged. "Ten, fifteen minutes. She's calling her sister."

In Europe. Jean was probably telling her sister-model who didn't come home for Christmas about their engagement.

He never moved toward the gangway. Conscious that Jake was tuned in to his every move, he tried to sound casual. "I think I'll go look for her."

But as he headed up the dock, he realized he was hurrying, mapping in his mind all the nearby phones whose locations he knew. Driven by a force he neither named nor analyzed, he jogged across the thoroughfare toward the park. When he saw the phone with the receiver torn off, he started to run.

*THE VERY BEST METHOD of self-defense*, Frank always said, *is run.*

It was what she'd taught Chris, but it wouldn't work now. Her only avenue of escape would take her farther from help, and any of the men in front of her could outrun her in two strides. Three were nearly as tall as David, and one was as big. Another, a man with bleached blond hair and a skull dangling from one ear, had a knife and had already detailed how he would use it. Altogether there were four—long-legged young men with feral eyes.

She knew they would hurt her with relish.

Laughing and talking obscenely about her, they moved closer, and Jean watched the knife, mentally processing the comparatively little she recalled about fighting armed assailants. Knowing she should get her back to a wall to protect herself from the blade, Jean focused on the man who held it and saw his eyes quivering in their sockets—a new reason for fear. If they were strung out, they would be harder to take down.

She had no doubt they would do everything they promised. If they could.

She glanced behind her down the side street and saw it ended at another narrow passageway, edged by a tall, windowless building. Was that a street or an alley? Where were the cars? Where were the people?

Jean looked at her opponents again and wondered if she could make a run for it to the main street. As she started to, she saw a car passing and waved at it, yelling at the top of her lungs, "Help! Rape!"

The driver never noticed, like a bad dream. This couldn't be happening to her now, in broad daylight, on a city street.

But it happened every day.

Jean told herself she would not be overcome by fear—that was what the black of her belt symbolized. The thought steadied her, but it did not make her unafraid. As they came toward her, she began yelling at them, using words she hoped would attract passersby. She no longer hoped to scare them. She hoped to distract them and find a path of escape between them.

Remembering the essence of her training, she summoned confidence the only way she knew—by focusing utterly on the task before her.

She ran.

The one with the knife stood in front of her, and another grabbed her arm. She pulled free, but the knife lunged toward her. Blocking instinctively, her arm perilously close to the blade, she grabbed the wrist of her attacker and twisted it as she drove a side kick into his knee. It was weak, and she panicked, abandoning years of advice to keep her kicks low during an assault. She slammed her foot hard into his solar plexus, then up toward his chin. Miraculously she hit his temple, instead.

Someone tackled her, a human shape falling on her like a demolition ball, and she hit the curb with the side of her head. For the space of a few seconds, her eyes closed.

When she opened them with a sick, searing pain, it was to a face of pimples and savage eyes. The pain of his weight was full on her knees, and her nose was filled with his rank, alien scent. Reflexively Jean stabbed at his eyes, but the blow to her head had set the world in slow motion. She was late.

*Your timing is off, ma'am.*

Someone else grasped her arms, pulled them back, and she was being dragged. As she rolled to free her arms, her head hit the walk. Her right arm was seized again, squeezed hard enough to bruise, bent hard enough to break. It was locked behind her head, and then wrenched. Her shoulder slid from its socket, and she moaned at the unfamiliar pain. She tried to shut out the voices.

"She's not so scary. She's just a bitch. We're going to have fun with you, bitch."

"Sledge ain't gettin' up. Get up, Sledge!"

She remembered kicking that one and wasn't sure he would get up. She wanted to beg them not to move her. She was going to be sick. The viselike grip on her arm was released, sending another slough of pain pouring through her. She felt faint, and the bile rose in her throat again. Someone was ripping at the buttons on her jeans, uttering profanities and spitting on her with each obscene promise. She tried to raise her legs but she knew it was useless. She felt fear, numbed by semiconsciousness.

They were going to kill her.

"No." The word fell from her mouth, and she knew it would become a mantra. "No. No."

# CHAPTER TWELVE

WHEN HE SAW THEM David felt only numb shock that his intuition had been correct, that Jean was coming to harm. But as he drew close, horror crawled his throat and squeezed his heart, revulsion he transformed immediately to something more useful—total awareness and focus. He half expected someone to step from that slot between the building with an automatic weapon, but he saw none, and the decision was easy. He ran, his mind clear and centered on his targets and what would take them down.

Number one on top of Jean. Number two behind her.

Number three would run—if no one had a gun.

His body felt swift and solid as a well-tuned machine, but faster and finer. He did not doubt its capabilities for a moment, because he knew that hesitation could cost him his life and Jean's.

He was prepared to kill.

SHE THOUGHT of David and imagined she heard the sound of running feet, of a warrior answering a call to arms. But it was not imagination. A dark, killing cry rang in her ears, the first *ki-hop* of its kind she had ever heard, a deep, ultimately frightening, *"Hi-yah!"* that seemed to come from another land and time. It was accompanied by the flight of a black shadow, a body shooting over her like a missile, and the sound of hard, certain contact.

Someone stepped on her left arm, escaping, and feet

pounded the pavement, running fast, then fading away. Jean forced her eyes open.

She thought she must be dead or dreaming, because he was there, staring up the street after the fleeing thugs. Then he looked at her.

She said, *"Sabumnim."*

He seemed dark and eerie. A shadow in the shadows of the concrete buildings. Vaguely Jean realized she'd been dragged into an alley or niche between two of the structures. Feeling tears in her eyes, of relief and misery, she said, "David?"

He crouched over her, not touching her at all, just looking. Her jeans were unfastened, and he resisted the urge to turn and kick the head of the still body behind him. The restraint he'd already shown would keep things cleaner for everyone. The man was alive and would walk away—eventually.

Closing his mind to his own decision of mercy and his private reason for it, David focused on Jean. "Tell me where you're hurt. I see your shoulder. What else? Can you move?"

Jean started to sit up, but the dislocation of her shoulder sent a primal warning through her system. She said, "I don't want to."

"Is your back or neck hurt?"

"No. Shoulder."

David nodded soberly and reached for her. Jean cried, "Don't!" at the same moment she realized his hands were on her arm and his foot against her side. As he pulled on her arm and the joint realigned itself, she felt as though she'd had the wind knocked out of her.

David gave her a few seconds' rest and watched her breathe shallowly, her face contorted. Then her breaths grew deeper. He hadn't wanted to touch her and would have let her shoulder be if he had met more resistance, but everything about the situation made him nervous, and the street still felt like a place where violence could explode without warning. The squeal of tires and a burst of gunfire. He had to get Jean away to a safer place, preferably the ship.

He said, "Can you walk?"

Jean nodded, eyes half-shut, and began to sit up. She was white, and he put his arm around her.

"Easy. Take it slow."

She nodded and leaned on him as she stood.

David watched her knees fold, then straighten. He picked her up and saw her wince as he jostled her shoulder. With a last glance at the body he'd left behind, he strode toward the main street, his eye marking the spot where he'd launched the flying kick. As he carried Jean toward the traffic, he saw the other figure lying in the gutter, showing faint signs of motion. Jean's work.

David looked down at her.

Her eyes were closed, but they flickered at him for a moment, two flashes of the sea, and she said, "I can walk."

*Indomitable spirit,* thought David. He hoped she really possessed it, because she would need it. He said, "I know you can."

DR. GEARY STEPPED OUT onto the landing over the galley, and David followed, shutting the door to his cabin all but a crack.

Grant gave him a reproving glance. "You were lucky with that shoulder."

David knew. He thought of Jean in his own bed, going without painkillers because of the lump on her head. "Is she all right?"

"Seems to be, but she needs X rays." Grant's eyes met David's. "And some counseling might be in order. Where's her sister?"

"Europe."

The doctor nodded. After a moment he said, "The police are done?"

"Yes." David could still hear one radio outside, but he knew they'd leave soon. The thugs had escaped, which was just as well. Jean didn't want to press charges, and he hadn't argued. Her spending months tied up in the courts with people she should never have to see again hadn't sounded like justice to him.

Thinking of her, he looked at his door, not even knowing he did. Grant touched his arm and went down the companionway, and David went back into his cabin and shut the door.

Catching sight of him, Jean closed her eyes. She didn't want to see anyone, least of all David. Even less herself. The endless pain in her shoulder was good. It matched what her mind felt.

Everything was still foggy, but clear enough that she could begin to remember details. Clothing. Hair. Teeth. Scent. The feeling of a body lunging against her and taking her down like a bowling pin, just when she'd landed some solid blows. Just when she'd thought she could make a space in which to flee. Instead, she'd been beaten. If not for David, she would have been raped. She might be dead.

And he had found her lying there like a broken doll, a woman who should have known better than to go alone down the side street. A woman with the awareness of a black belt.

David folded his arms across his chest and watched her, wondering why she'd closed her eyes when he walked through the door. What was she thinking? Was she angry he hadn't come sooner? Was she imagining what would have happened if he hadn't come at all?

Again he thought of the moment in the street, the split second in the air after he'd yelled, when he'd seen his target paralyzed by the sound and had known he could kill him—and probably should. And had decided not to.

He lived by the *do,* the way of tae kwon. *Never take life unjustly.* Staring at the dark ink of Jean's eyelashes against her pale cheeks, he knew it would have been justice to kill to save her. The warrior inside him wished he had. But in that moment in the air he'd seen blood and remembered its taste, and he'd seen Skye's face in the petrified eyes watching him, empty eyes waiting for death. And he'd pulled his kick.

Jean's eyes were still closed, and again David wondered why. What had they done to her before he arrived? What had they said? Where had they put their hands? Everything about her said, *Don't touch me. Don't come any closer.*

And all he wanted was to lie down and hold her for a thousand and one days and nights. He wanted to undo the damage he hadn't been able to stop.

Feeling choked him. What he'd told himself about the two of them was a lie. What he felt for her was too frightening to think or utter.

Jean held her eyes tightly shut, wishing he would leave yet feeling him all around her. She leaned back against the pillows, which, like the faded T-shirt she wore, carried the faint scent of David. A sling bound and supported her arm, and ice was packed around her shoulder, her only relief from the steady throbbing that seemed to increase with each breath she took. Her head, like her shoulder, ached with intensity, and so did her heart. She wished David would leave.

He didn't.

He came to the side of the bed and sat down on the edge with the grace of a cat, never jostling her shoulder. Avoiding his eyes, Jean stared dully across the room at her bonsai tree. David had made a nest for it in a top-opening locker in a corner of the cabin. It seemed like a symbol of his faith in her—and of the hope of Christmas that had seemed so bright hours earlier.

David still watched her, but she wouldn't meet his gaze.

At last he reached for her hair and gently pulled the end of her tangled braid over her shoulder, then removed the elastic band. Her eyes dropped lifelessly, emotionlessly, to his hand. Struck by the flatness of her expression, David carefully stroked a lock of hair away from her face and withdrew. He said, "This isn't how I've dreamed of getting you in my bed."

He saw her swallow and thought she was going to cry.

She didn't. When his arms went around her, her eyes were squeezed shut, frozen against everything. The unending ache in her shoulder seemed less, but the reality of what had happened hurt more. And David was holding her, David who was both stranger and lover, David who she'd thought would no longer care for her. His fingers were in her hair, combing free the remnants of her braid, while his other hand rubbed her back in a soothing motion that was as rhythmic as the tide.

She wanted to jerk her head up, to cry at him, *Do you love me?*

Waves of shame washed over her, and she wished he would speak to her.

He didn't. He pulled back, and Jean felt him looking at her face, but she didn't want to look at his.

David backed away and stood up, then went into the bathroom and opened the cabinet where he had seen her hairbrush. It lay on the top shelf, a simple, wooden hairbrush. She had never used it in front of him.

When he glanced back into the cabin she was lying on her side, turned toward the port windows. He went in and climbed onto the bed beside her, at her back. First he checked her ice packs and balanced them over her injury. Then, not touching her scalp, he dragged the brush gently through her hair.

She shivered.

He held a lock and brushed a snarl from the end in small, gentle strokes. "If you want me to go, you should say so."

She was silent, and David realized she was thinking about it. He closed his eyes, glad she couldn't see his face.

Jean lay in agony, fighting down the only words that came to her lips. *I love you.* If she could have, she would have grabbed his hand, held it against her cheek, against her lips. Finally she whispered, "Thanks for staying." But as she spoke, she discovered what she really wanted, even more than his hands in her hair and the weight of his body next to hers.

She wanted to be away from the smoggy, smoky smell of the port.

She wanted to be at sea.

Safe.

David was surprised by her sudden movement, more surprised when she rolled slowly onto her back, knocking two bags of ice into his lap. Moving them, he eased his leg out of the way and let his hand fall to her side. *Look at me,* he thought.

She did. With eyes not her own, eyes that seemed pained to meet his. She asked, "Can we please leave this place?"

He felt relief, huge relief, that there was something he could do. He said, "Yes." And he stood and went up the stairs to the door to the wheelhouse.

A moment later, the engines started.

JEAN FELT SOMETHING soft on her cheek. Delicate. Small. Then on her arm. Her eyes fluttered open, and she saw Chris looking at her. He held a muffin on a plate in one hand and a notepad in the other. In the late-afternoon light that shone through the stained-glass windows of the cabin, Jean squinted at the words Chris had written in his child's printing. "Jolly made you this. It is a banana-bread muffin. I love you."

Conscious of the forward motion of the ship through the sea, Jean sat up, wincing at her shoulder. It had not improved with time. Her voice husky from disuse, she told

Chris, "Thank you, sweetie. I love you, too." She bent over to kiss him, and the pain streaked forward in her head. Chris raised his face for her kiss. Then he started signing at her, something about Hank the Cowdog.

Jean said, "Slow down. I'm not as fast as you." When he complied, she saw he was offering to read to her.

Jean realized the magnitude of the gift, how difficult it would be for him to translate a whole chapter of a book into sign language. She wouldn't be able to follow him, either, certainly not in her present state. She watched him, unsure what to say. Her head felt as though it had been hit with a brick.

She reached for the muffin with little appetite and told Chris, "I'd like that. Unless you'd rather I read to you."

She could tell from his response that the latter was his preference. He scampered to the door of the cabin, slid it open and went out onto the galley landing, then closed the door. Slowly Jean set down the muffin and used her good arm to prop pillows behind her. Who was Jolly? The new cook?

She bit into the muffin, which was moist and warm from the oven and smelled heavenly. Then she set it on the plate again and turned carefully to switch on the reading lamp over the bed. David's bed. There was a glass-encased bookshelf built into the wall behind the headboard containing titles ranging from Pulitzer Prize winners to bestsellers to Eastern philosophy and world history. Jean saw a well-worn copy of *Don Quixote* in Spanish. As she spotted a tae kwon do manual written in characters she assumed were Korean, a long, sick pain flowed through her head, and she sank against the pillows once more.

Chris came back into the cabin with a book and crawled onto the bed beside her. Jean opened to the place where he'd left the bookmark and forced herself to read. The chapter was particularly amusing, and soon she was trying not to laugh over the cowdog's adventures, because laughter hurt her body. She did not hear footsteps on the companionway.

Dr. Geary said, "And I was going to offer you something for pain."

Jean said, "I'll take it."

"I thought so." He came inside and looked sternly at Chris. "You told us you were going to read to *her*, young man."

Chris smiled sheepishly and shrugged, then snuggled closer to Jean, against her injured shoulder.

Jean said, "Whoa, Chris. Move over to the other side."

But Dr. Geary shooed him out of the room so he could examine her shoulder and shine a flashlight in her eyes. As he was finishing up, the door to the wheelhouse opened, and David entered the cabin. Grant handed him a small pill bottle and said, "One every four to six hours as needed." Then he turned and nodded to Jean with a kindly smile. "No more laughing."

When he had gone, David glanced down the companionway, slid shut the door behind him and said, "If you were laughing over Hank, you're out of luck. Jolly's put Chris to work in the galley."

Jean said, "Oh," but she wasn't thinking of Chris. She was looking at David, who seemed so solid and strong and familiar—and very kind. It was easier to be near him now than it had been earlier. Everything seemed easier since she had awakened to Christian's small face watching her, waiting for her attention. Since she had felt the motion of the ship and realized they must be far from the port city where she had been assaulted. Remembering what David had said, she asked, "Jolly who makes great muffins?"

"Yes." David was conscious of the beat of his heart, faster and harder than usual. He knew it was because she was meeting his eyes. Not as she once had, but even the way they skirted away now was an improvement over what he'd seen when he'd brought her back to the ship. Con-

scious of her hold on his heart—and his blindness in not
seeing it earlier—he climbed onto the bed beside her and
kissed her temple very lightly. He said, "How do you like
my bed?"

Looking down at the covers over her lap, she answered,
"I like it best with you in it."

David felt a tightening in his chest, yearning and reluctance exerting their separate strengths. This was it. Jean was
here, in his bed; she couldn't climb in and out of her own
berth with an injured shoulder. He knew she didn't want
to. She wanted him.

Jean felt the long silence. The sound of the engines
seemed eternal, like the pulse of time, counting how long
it could take a man to find a way to tell a woman he didn't
want to sleep with her.

David leaned back against the headboard beside her and
examined the bottle of pills in his hand. Narcotics. They
seemed both a symbol and an easy excuse. He took off the
cap and handed her one. He said, "I want you to be conscious and healed."

He didn't say, *when we make love*. Jean heard the omission even more than she heard his words. Inside, all along
her throat, she felt as though she was strangling. She remembered lying on her back in the street, strange hands
tearing at her jeans, a strange person breathing on her.

Her jeans were gone now. When he'd brought her back,
David had taken them off, along with her sweatshirt and
everything else she'd been wearing. Then he'd dressed her
in a T-shirt of his and a pair of clean underwear from her
locker. Jean was glad. She never again wanted to see the
clothes in which she'd been dragged on the pavement, the
clothes another man had tried to tear from her body.

David climbed off the bed and went into the bathroom.
Jean heard him fill a water glass, and in a moment he
brought it out to her. She swallowed the pill, then gulped

down the water, wishing it could ease the pain in her heart. But only David could.

Staring out the starboard window, she saw nothing but ocean with the sun setting upon it. She asked, "Where are we?"

David met her eyes for a moment, then said, "Let me get the chart, and I'll show you." He went into the wheel-house, returning with a couple of charts, then sat down on the bed beside her and began explaining how to read them. After pinpointing the ship's bearing, still off the California coast in U.S. waters, he showed her the port where they would stop that night.

Her voice was little more than a whisper. "Can't we anchor?"

David sensed the fear and anguish behind the question. It was all he could do to control his own features, to grip his own heart. He said, "You need X rays. This is a different kind of port, a different kind of town." He spoke as steadily as he could and tried to smile. "Ritzier than Santa Barbara."

She was quivering like an animal, and David wished they dared forego the X rays. He said, "I'm sorry."

Anyone could see that he was. Jean wondered if he knew he had grabbed her hand and was hurting it. He seemed to realize it and released her.

He looked down at the chart as though it was a foreign object. After a moment he said, "I'll show you our itinerary." He did, starting with the chart on top, then switching to the one beneath, which showed the Baja coast. Jean listened almost indifferently until he pointed to a big cape on the Mexican shoreline. He was saying, "Cabo San Anselmo on Christmas Eve. Then Scammon's Bay the next day."

Jean's stomach plunged. Until David had said it aloud, even the possibility had seemed unreal. But what had happened during the afternoon was a reminder that nightmares, like dreams, could come true.

David studied her face, noted her pallor. A crash course in navigation wasn't the kind of distraction she needed. Setting the charts on the far corner of the bed, he knelt over her so that his legs straddled her body. Then he kissed her mouth and, when he felt her response, slipped his tongue inside.

She made a soft sound in her throat, involuntary and needy.

He said, "It's an hour till we're in port. Would you like me to take your mind off your shoulder?"

"Yes." The word was faint, altered by the kiss they'd just shared.

Lips still near hers, David said, "Thank you." Trailing kisses along her jaw and her neck, he drew the covers away from her body.

... he was glad she couldn't see his race. He said,
"Sure." Then he ... ... ... ... looking at her. That how
much ... ... ... ... to get back to work.

... for a moment he assumed discipline on the ... of
the body, feeling like an ... ashed prudery, aware why he
just never said ... ... ... ... ... ... ... ... ... He had of
pledging with his ... ... ... ... ... ... ... into for being a
chance that fell ... ... into that.

# CHAPTER THIRTEEN

SHE TOSSED in hot, shivering confusion, surrendering to a
rapture she had only imagined. What he had said the evening before was the only hint she'd ever had that David
would want to know her this way, to taste her and venerate
her so intimately. She had to draw the knuckles of her hand
against her mouth to silence her lips.

Most of the time, their hands were clasped, but David
had felt hers stray to his hair more than once as he let his
tongue roam inside her, tasting her. He could feel the
smooth skin of her slim, taut legs around him. Those legs
were shaking, and she was shuddering. He heard her muffled, almost tearful gasp, and a sob that was his name.

There was a heat high in his own throat, emotion riding
a river of rushing blood and breath. He continued to tease
her and caress her till her quaking ceased, and then longer,
because he didn't want to stop. And then his mouth rested
on the inside of her thigh, and he couldn't speak.

But she was pulling at him, calling him, like a voice from
the sunlight dragging him up from a very deep dive, saving
him from a fatal high, from rapture of the depths. He
wanted to tear off his clothes and become one with her.

And it felt good to want it so badly.

He sat up and moved over her body to her left side, then
lay down beside her and buried his face in the cascade of
her hair. *Someday,* he thought. *Someday, Jean.*

She said, "Can I do that to you?"

David almost inhaled her hair. For the second time that

day, he was glad she couldn't see his face. He said, "Sure." Then he sat up, not looking at her. "Not now, though. I need to get back to work."

But for a moment he remained immobile on the edge of the bed, feeling like an indebted property owner who has just received the final extension on his taxes. His hour of reckoning was near. David groped behind him for Jean's hand and felt it slide into his.

And when he turned to kiss her it was he who could not meet her eyes.

HE TOOK HER to an exclusive facility where he knew there would be no questions, and when Jean had received a clean bill of health they drove back to the ship in the rental car he'd had delivered to the marina. No cabs. No strangers. Only the two of them, much closer than before. He held her hand while he drove.

When they reached the ship, Baby was there, chattering under the dock lights. David saw she had drawn the attention of people on the decks of yachts nearby—and entertained them by pulling a string of large plastic candy canes off the side of a nearby cabin cruiser. The owner had retrieved the decoration and was trying to hang it back up.

Jean stooped by the edge of the dock to pet the dolphin and lower her face to Baby's for a kiss, and the cocktail-sipping spectators across the way oohed and aahed over Baby's friendliness to her.

David barely noticed the reactions of the audience. He saw only the effect of Baby's closeness on Jean. He found himself saying, "If you feel well enough, we could go out on the diving platform." The stern was out of view of the other boats. It lay in shadow. Private.

Jean heard David's suggestion and felt her heart stir. He must be worried about her to propose they spend time with Baby. Straightening up, she managed a smile. "Thanks."

He put his arm around her and guided her toward the

ship. As he helped her aboard and led her past the lights
of the salon to the darkness of the aft deck, he tried to catch
her eye, but she wouldn't look at him.

Thinking of her attack, he felt the same constriction in
his chest he had felt periodically all afternoon as he imagined them touching her. They'd never gotten her clothes
off and she hadn't been raped, but other than that he wasn't
sure what had happened.

As he debated asking her, Jake stepped out of the diving
alcove, and a lighter flared, illuminating his face. David
nodded to him. Jake returned the nod and edged around the
cabin toward the bow, giving them privacy.

David lifted Jean down to the diving platform by her
waist and saw Baby waiting for them there. He said, "Let
me find a toy for her," and scouted the deck in the darkness
until he found the inflatable wreath, pathetically deflated.
He blew it up, then joined Jean on the diving platform. She
was sitting down.

He tossed the ring to Baby, hoping to keep her occupied,
and asked Jean, "Did they touch you?"

"No." She watched Baby swim the ring back to them.
David leaned forward to retrieve it and hurled it farther this
time. Jean said, "You're playing with her."

*In other words,* David thought, *let's talk about something
else.* He didn't answer her. She couldn't know how inadequate he felt. There was not a single woman on his ship
with whom she could share her feelings. He would do anything to ease her trauma, even lie beside her in his bed that
night. Without touching her. He'd already made that decision. And though the solstice was still two days off, he
knew this would be the longest night of the year.

When Baby came to the platform, he petted her, feeling
her heart. She was a sweet animal. He had never thought
anything else. Not facing Jean, he said, "I spent some time
with a lone beluga whale many years ago, when I was

fishing. I had a Japanese trawler, a sailboat. She used to come feed near my nets.''

Jean sat silent in the darkness, listening as though the water might tell David's secrets. It was hard to believe he was telling her one himself.

"Then, some fishermen killed her. I…sort of…came upon it.'' Baby rolled for a caress on her belly. David gave it, then reached for the ring and threw it as far as it would fly. She took off like a missile.

Jean didn't say anything. But she finally understood the thing about him that had puzzled her most—his trouble with Baby. His revelation threw her off base. She was unready when he said, "I want you to tell me everything that happened today. Every word, every touch, every ugly threat.''

She did. And when she cried against him he felt outrage for her but also relief that she wouldn't hold it inside. That she wasn't like him. For a moment he wanted to call her his master instructor. Instead, because it seemed years too late for him to learn the lesson, he carried her inside through the wheelhouse to his cabin and his bed.

HE COULDN'T WORK without sleep, and lying beside Jean's dozing body was a recipe for insomnia. The only relief would be inside her, but she was in no condition to bear his weight or lie on top of him. And their first time together should be very, very good.

Right now David wasn't sure he could be even mediocre. Sleepless and horny as hell, he lay staring at the ceiling and weighing the odds. Bad. How could the life force, the *him* inside him, be simultaneously so urgent and demanding, yet fickle? It was the worst of both worlds.

He heard the echo of a woman's laughter in his mind. Skye's. He could see her with ease. He could imagine what she would say. But he didn't believe she was saying it now.

He didn't believe in ghosts, except those that lived in the human psyche. He had a roomful, and they were all her.

Jean made a quiet sleeping sound, not of pain, but when she rolled toward him David saw the flicker of discomfort on her face, and her eyes opened. Shut. Opened and stared at him. She didn't say, *Why are you awake?* but he felt it from her.

He glanced at the glowing red dials on the alarm clock and asked, "Want another pill?"

He heard Skye saying, *Good idea, David. Keep her drugged as long as you can. Then she won't find out.*

Jean was shaking her head against the pillow.

Thinking of Skye taunting him—and wondering why she still could—he moved closer to Jean. Why did he war with a woman who no longer existed except as a memory?

Because the havoc she'd left was everywhere. In Chris, in Erika, in him. In those shapes and colors in his mind, in that horrible sensation surrounding his whole body. He could feel it now. He wanted a shower.

Jean watched him in the glow from the dock lights that shone through the window. Didn't he ever sleep? A number of possibilities, reasons he wasn't sleeping, occurred to her. The most likely seemed desire, and if that was David's problem she'd like to ease it. Didn't he know that?

Yes. She'd offered that afternoon—plainly and more than once. He hadn't been able to meet her eyes, and Jean thought she knew why.

Since Skye's death David had never had another woman in his bed. She was nearly certain of that. And now her own presence must be keeping him awake. Was that why he wouldn't share himself with her? Because she wasn't Skye?

Or because, like Jake, he believed she had secrets?

Jean felt a chill pass over her.

David saw. His hand went at once to her cheek.

She said, "I'm fine."

He reflected that she hadn't bathed since that scene in the street. He still caught the scent of the place on her. Without asking her preference he got out of bed and went into the shower room.

Jean watched his tall shape, clad in only a pair of dark sweatpants that hugged the muscles in his legs, pass out of her field of vision. The water went on. Tub water.

A moment later, he came back into the cabin. Returning to the bed, he pulled the covers from her, exposing her small, long-legged body clad only in another of his T-shirts and a pair of pale pink panties. He said, "Say something if I hurt your shoulder." And he picked her up.

THE SHOWER ROOM was lit by sconces, two of them, flickering high on the wall over the big sunken tub. David set her down and dipped a toe in the water. Hot, but not, he hoped, too hot for her.

They were inches apart. With the precise perception of a martial artist, David knew exactly how close they stood, how little he would need to move to touch her. He knew when she was going to touch him and where.

On his scar.

A tremor passed through him as her fingers found his chest, and when Jean dropped her eyes she saw and felt he was aroused, stemmed hard against her body. She wanted his sweatpants off. She wanted him to love her.

Eyeing the tub, still filling, she said, "Are you getting in?"

Eyes on her face, David reached for the hand on his chest and guided it downward. "Yes, ma'am."

THEIR BODIES were entwined, slick with soap, their tongues in each other's mouths. David felt her hand sliding over the length of him again and again, bringing him higher than he had ever thought he would go. At first his fingers had played inside her, too, but now he could only draw her closer, so she was sliding along his leg. She was slippery, but not from the soap.

He said again, "Jean." It was all he could say anymore, and he said it a lot. Didn't her shoulder hurt? They'd taken off her good sling and replaced it with one made from the T-shirt she'd been wearing. Now it was wet.

Everything was wet. Clean hair and bodies. Mouths. Everything.

Jean watched his face, his half-closed eyes. Giving to him was the deepest pleasure she'd ever known. He'd entrusted himself to her at last, as she had long ago to him. And now, as she touched him, he was incoherent, his head back, his mouth relaxed, then moving with reaction to the feel of her hand. She sank harder against the muscles of his thigh, hardly knowing what she did, only that he was guiding her, holding her, dragging her nearer to him. She could feel his longing for her, and she could see it in his face, now so altered by emotions and passion. Not lust, but a need of the heart. And maybe something more.

She said, "Make love to me."

David's mind was foggy as the room, floating on scent and sensation. Her words changed none of that. They were what he wanted to hear.

He reached for Jean, slick and wet, and lifted her to the edge of the tub, then lowered her back to the floor. Wanting her to feel what he felt, a hunger so intense he could hardly stand it, he caressed her—first with his hands and then with his mouth until she cried. Then he rose up in the tub, his eyes on hers, coming closer. Their bodies touched, more intimate than ever before, poised for the greatest intimacy of all. David's voice shook, rough, as he said, "Put your legs around me, Jean."

She did, never knowing that her head was already tossing, not knowing her eyes were flickering open and shut and she was making a small animal sound of want, the same sound over and over again.

He said, "I love you," and he drove himself inside her.

IT WASN'T A NIGHTMARE, but it was intense and complicated. And sweet.

Afterward, empty and sated, he lay against her on the wet floor and the towels, knowing he must be hurting her and yet needing to stay a minute longer. On top of her. Inside her.

She said, "David," and he made himself move, slipping away from her and then joining her on the cold floor. He neither spoke nor looked at her, only closed his eyes and placed a hand on her breast, on the body that belonged to him.

She told him, "David, that was perfect."

*Thank God,* he thought. If he'd done anything right, she was responsible. She gave him a power purer than desire and stronger than death.

He was in love with her.

He couldn't speak, so he moved closer to her and rested his face in the curve beside her breast. *Jean.* He touched her skin with his mouth, feeling her heat, knowing her scent. His mouth against her skin, he hugged her close, like a drowning man clinging to a life raft.

Jean felt the emotion in him as she had ever since they'd begun making love. When they were joined it had escalated, and she'd met a David she hadn't known before. Vividly she remembered her own panic as he filled her, then his drawing her into his arms and back into the tub, holding her against his heart and kissing her long and deep as he let her know what it was to have all of him. She had pictures of him in her mind, pictures she would treasure of his eyes on hers, his mouth drinking her wet skin, of water beading in the hair on his chest and on his scar, of his head back against the edge of the tub and his eyes closed as he brought her down on him. Of how he looked before he kissed her and when he came.

She belonged to him.

She loved him madly.

And she had seen his darkness. A communion of minds, perhaps, spurred by the union of bodies, but now she knew with a certainty beyond intuition where his pain must lie. Only the details remained unknown.

Feeling the air on her damp body, she shivered, and David stood up to get more towels from an overhead locker.

Her shoulder aching, Jean sat up. He toweled her hair and body, then untied her wet sling. Working quickly and carefully, he secured her dry sling, wrapped fluffy towels around her, and dried her hair with her hair dryer.

Last, he blew out the candles in the sconces and led her back into the cabin.

THE ROOM SEEMED cold as a tomb, which surprised David. It had always been his cabin, never Skye's, and he had always liked it. Now, he noticed the quilt on the bed. And without seeing them, he was aware of the scars she had left on his windowsill. Four letters.

His eyes flickered to the corners of the room. A faint light from outside flickered on the Christmas ornaments on the bonsai. The tree of life and renewal, a promise of Christmas and the cyclical return of the solstice, of longer days and shorter nights.

Jean was beside him, clutching the arm that must be aching now. Thinking of her, of the seeming impossibility of meshing past and present, he drew out his desk chair and said, "Can you sit here for a minute?"

She nodded with a small movement and sat down. David brought her a pill for pain and a glass of water, then efficiently stripped the bed and changed the sheets and pillowcases, thinking that they, too, must carry the scent of the street, of what had hurt her. Thinking also that he could get the quilt out of his sight.

Jean watched him, contemplating his silence. Not even

love made him talkative, but what he had said and done was perfect. Even the soreness between her legs was welcome, an ancient earthy symbol that he had bound her to him, that she was his. She had believed lovemaking could be so perfect, and David had proved it.

Briefly it occurred to her that they had made love with nothing between them, that he had come inside her, that they'd been reckless. She had no regrets. In her mind he was already her husband. He was hers forever.

Seeing he had finished with the bed, Jean stood up. David helped her into his bed and covered her with the sheet and blanket. He kissed her, and Jean remembered the feel of him inside her. She reached for him, but he was gone, gathering up the laundry and taking it down into the office where the washer and dryer were.

With effort Jean sat up, looked around the cabin, then fell back against the pillow. The quilt was gone. He had taken it, the quilt made by Skye, the wife who had killed herself.

*David,* she thought, *how can you ever forget?*

Remembering the way he had made love to her, the gentle intensity, the unstoppable overflow, she wondered if a man could live a healthy life and raise a family without ever talking about the things that had hurt him most. She wondered if David would ever talk or if he could.

And she thought of the irony that his son, too, was silent.

She was drowsy when at last he returned and slid shut the door. Jean's eyes wavered upon him as he came to the berth and threw a thick, plaid wool blanket over the bed and over her.

He got into bed with her and lay his body alongside hers, then kissed her. No words, just the intimacy of touch, of skin against skin. Glad for his heat to chase away her dark thoughts, Jean rested her head on his shoulder for long minutes, feeling his skin and the solid length of his muscles. He stirred only once, turning and resting his hand on the inside of her thigh, as though to make sure she was still there and couldn't leave.

Moments later he slept.

DAVID LIKED MORNINGS. He liked the alarm on his watch, he liked swimming before the sun rose, he liked meditating and working tae kwon do forms on the deck of his ship before anyone else was awake. Jean in his bed was a perfect addition to mornings.

Her hair spilled over the pillows, and the sheets were half-off her, exposing her breasts and shoulders and arms— and the sling that was a reminder of violence. As David debated touching her, the alarm on his watch beeped, and her eyes opened, reminding him of a waking kitten. Asleep one moment, alert the next.

David didn't bother apologizing for the alarm. Seeing the sea green of her eyes made him unsorry for waking her, and he asked the only thing that seemed essential. "How's your shoulder?"

"Stiff. Okay."

David was glad she wasn't in agony, because of what he wanted to do. As he reached for her and felt her respond, moving closer, seeking him, he thought of responsibility and what they'd risked the previous night. Now he would take more care. And someday later, he very much hoped, she would be the mother of his children.

As her fingers slid down his stomach, she said, "You can always wake me up, David. Even in the middle of the night."

That meant more to him than she could know. Thinking of the progress of her hand, he said, "I will." A moment later he choked out her name and pulled her close, all the other words lost against her skin. But when he was inside her, what she had said came back to him. And it occurred to him that that was what she had done to him. She had woken him in the middle of an endless night—and from a horrible dream.

He sank deeper inside her.

OVER THE NEXT THREE DAYS the *Skye* followed a leisurely, zigzagging course to Baja. Whales appeared every day, and David slowed the ship to follow them, changed course to see them better.

Jean assisted the scientists. She took copious notes on the activity of the cetaceans, as well as that of other marine life in the vicinity. Ken Lightman put her to work sketching slide samples of seawater and recording related information for him. Robin made her his favorite photographic subject, next to Baby. And Dr. Geary asked her to research past observations from texts and journals in David's collection.

Yet it felt more like Christmas than any season of her memory. Playing the calendar game in the morning with Chris. Making construction-paper ornaments together in the afternoon. Singing carols to him at night.

And lying in the dark of David's cabin with the olive tree a silent witness to their passion. Hearing him say again and again that he loved her.

It was a love without censure or criticism, and Jean could almost believe it wouldn't be altered if at some point he learned about what had happened when she'd worked for Michael and Jennifer Avery in Cabo San Anselmo. She could almost believe that in his eyes she could do no wrong, that if he ever heard the story he would see her side and take her part. After all, he'd even accepted Baby now. He seemed resigned to the dolphin's attachment to his ship and to his son, and early Christmas Eve morning Jean found him alone in the water with Baby, playing with her.

In the predawn light, Jean climbed down onto the diving platform in time to see Baby kiss his cheek and hear David say, "We can't, Baby. Jean would never forgive us. Her fiancé and her best friend. And you're a dolphin, don't you know that?" As Jean watched Baby attempt to hug him with her flippers, David glanced toward the ship and saw her. He told Baby, "See? Caught."

Baby maneuvered around his body, four hundred pounds of possessive female, impeding his progress back to the ship.

Jean laughed, wishing she had a camera.

Finally David climbed onto the diving platform, dripping, and Jean grabbed a towel to throw over his bare shoulders. He kissed her mouth, glanced briefly at the sky and asked, "Want to go ashore this morning? I have to pick up mail."

Baby cried at him from the water, and he leaned forward to touch her beak.

Jean stared across the water at the shoreline, the coast of Baja California. Condos lined the beach, reminding her of Cabo San Anselmo. She shook her head.

David thought of the last time he had gone ashore—two days earlier with Chris, to one of the towns south of the border where junk was beautiful and treasures could be found if one knew where to look. He had asked Jean to come with them then, and she had declined. It had bothered him then, and it bothered him now. He said, "You can't stay on the water forever."

Jean swallowed an attack of conscience. He thought she didn't want to go ashore because of what had happened in L.A. when the problem was her being in Baja. And the fact that they would anchor at Cabo San Anselmo that night.

She looked at his eyes, sable in the morning light. The red dawn turned his skin to rosewood. She said, "I'm all right, David. Really."

He let it go, mainly because he didn't have time for anything else. The sky was red, and storm bulletins the previous night had played out the sailor's verse. Sensing the sea brewing, he said, "If you're not going, watch Chris, will you? I won't be long."

He went inside to dress, and Jean went below to the galley to suggest to Chris that there might be a cowdog named Hank behind the twenty-fourth door of the advent calendar. There wasn't.

There was a wreath.

IT WAS STORMING when David returned with the mail. Conditions were so bad that he, Jake and Ken were all needed to manage the Zodiac as the hoist lifted it back onto the canopy beside the dinghy. They weighed anchor immediately afterward, and everyone but David promptly became seasick.

For the first couple of hours Jean could do nothing but care for Chris and deal with her own nausea, but then her symptoms subsided. Seeing Chris asleep in his stateroom, she went up through David's cabin to the wheelhouse.

He was alone, the only one able to tolerate the onslaught of twenty-foot waves, and he smiled when he saw Jean.

She said, "You look lonely."

"You look better."

Jean smiled weakly. They'd met an hour earlier at the railing.

David nodded to the navigator's seat and a small stack of letters tucked into a well in the cockpit. "Read me Erika's letter. It's to both of us."

Jean held the back of the captain's seat for balance as she made her way to the navigator's station. Climbing up on the stool, she reached for the stack of mail and leafed through until she found Erika's letter, addressed to Miss Jean Young and Mr. David Blade. She opened the envelope and withdrew a single sheet. The loose, even writing was like Erika, relaxed and approachable. Her greeting went straight to Jean's heart.

David said, "I'm waiting." With a glance at the sky, he said, "Better start before the lightning comes."

"Lightning?"

"Read."

Jean eyed the dark horizon and saw a distant flash, faint in the gray. She turned to the page in her hand. "'Dear Brother and Sister-To-Be, I have very good news for you. I have sensation in my legs.'" Jean looked at David.

He was watching the sea, but when she stopped he said, "Keep reading. She's right. It's good news. Great news."

Jean lifted the sheet again. "'Hard to believe, yes? And the fault of my Swiss miracle doctor. He's put me in AN-GER therapy.' That's in caps, David."

"I'm sure."

The bland reply struck Jean, but she forced herself to keep reading. "'It's incredible. We throw things and say every horrible thing we ever wanted to say about anyone. I strongly recommend it, *David.*' That's underlined."

This time he said nothing. Looking up, Jean watched waves come over the bow and saw the first slivers of electricity in the sky. A low roll of thunder mingled with the sounds of the sea and the wind and the engines.

Returning to the letter, she resumed reading Erika's words. "'I was never willing to express my real feelings about the accident before, but I can now.'"

Abruptly the letter was taken from her hands.

Jean said, "David," in protest as he held the page against the steering wheel and read it, glancing intermittently toward the sea.

Jean thought, *He's worried about what she's going to say about that accident. Why?*

David flipped the page over, scanned the other side and handed it back to her without apology.

Cool, Jean said, "Do you want me to read it to you anymore?"

"No."

He seemed irritated, and Jean recalled what Erika had said about anger therapy. David had plenty to be angry about, but his sister's letter? Jean turned it over and read silently.

...I was never willing to express my real feelings about the accident before, but I can now. For one thing, I no longer call it an accident. The only thing accidental was that you weren't in the driver's seat, David.

Enough already, I know. In thirty minutes, I get to give an earful to my therapy group, so I'll save some for them.

I mostly wanted you to know about my legs and that I like the Swiss Marvel, and I wanted to tell Jean how happy I am you're going to be my sister, dear. Crazy me, when I feel my legs, I wonder if we might dive together someday.

Squeeze Chris for me, but don't tell him anything about me that might get his hopes up. I love you all, and I want you to know that my heart is with you on Christmas. We're all together in spirit.

Tidings of comfort and joy,

E.

Jean could hardly contain her feelings. Erika's news was wonderful, confirmation that the problem with her legs was at least partially psychological and might be overcome. The thought of diving with David's sister someday thrilled her, and she held the image in her mind, as hope for Erika.

But everything Erika had said about the accident was puzzling, an invitation for questions. David *hadn't* been driving.

Jean looked up in time to see a flash of lightning illuminate the cockpit. She asked, "Who was driving the car?"

"Erika." A clap of thunder followed his words.

Jean had to raise her voice over the sound of the storm. "Why did she say it wasn't an accident?"

His reply was louder than it needed to be. "Probably so you'd ask me that question."

She'd never have a better chance. "Was it an accident?"

David didn't answer at once. His eyes traced a lightning bolt in the sky, and at last he said, "No."

The reply was drowned out in the thunder, but Jean understood it. She said, "Please tell me what happened."

David seemed not to hear her, but Jean was sure he had. A bright flash exploded the sky near the ship, a huge crack of thunder following. He peered uneasily out the edge of the windshield, as though awaiting the next bolt. Then he looked at the Global Positioning System.

Jean realized he wasn't going to say a word.

Maddened, she stuffed Erika's letter into the well with the others and climbed off the navigator's stool. Grabbing the back of the captain's seat for balance as she prepared to go below, she said, "No wonder Chris can't talk, with you for a role model."

As she spoke, the ship hit a big well, and a blinding light, accompanied by an earsplitting boom, seemed to shake the world. Jean saw sizzling blue.

David, voice tight, said, "Call Jake on the intercom."

Shaking, holding on to anything she could find, Jean reached for the intercom and punched a button. "Jake to the wheelhouse." She asked David, "Are we going to sink?"

"No. That hit the lightning protection." As Jean started to slip past him to the cabin, he grabbed her wrist, his eyes never leaving the sea. He said, "First rule of sparring, Jean. Never hit below the belt. That's for street fighting with the people who want to hurt you."

Feeling him bruising her arm, she said, "*You're* hurting me."

He released her, and she swayed against the side of the wheelhouse.

Grabbing the edge of the cockpit, she added, "And it hurts when you don't talk."

David took his eyes from the sea and met hers. "Skye hit her. All right? She was leaving a party at her parents' house, she was angry at me, and she pulled out of the driveway and saw my car. Erika was driving. If you read the rest of that letter, you can figure out the rest. Now don't ask me about my wife again. *Ever.*"

Jean took a step back.

He was still gazing out at the sea and the storm. He said under his breath, "I won't malign her."

The door from the cabin opened, and Jake came up. He looked at Jean, then at David. "Any sign of Baby?"

Jean's mouth fell open, her thoughts changing direction, and she watched David shake his head, his mouth a tight line. He glanced once at Jean and said, "Sorry."

She knew he was.

Baby was gone.

# Get 2 Books FREE!

## MIRA® BOOKS, The Brightest Stars in Fiction, presents

### The Best of the Best™

**Superb collector's editions of the very best novels by the world's best-known authors!**

### FREE BOOKS!
To introduce you to "The Best of the Best" we'll send you 2 books ABSOLUTELY FREE!"

### FREE GIFT!
Get an exciting mystery gift absolutely free!

### BEST BOOKS!
"The Best of the Best" brings you the best books by the world's hottest authors!

▲ To get your 2 free books, affix this peel-off sticker to the reply card and mail it today!

# Get 2

## HOW TO GET YOUR
## 2 FREE BOOKS AND FREE GIFT

1. Peel off the 2 FREE BOOKS seal from the front cover. Place it in the space provided at right. This automatically entitles you to receive two free books and an exciting mystery gift.

2. Send back this card and you'll get 2 "The Best of the Best™" novels. These books have a combined cover price of $11.00 or more in the U.S. and $13.00 or more in Canada, but they are yours to keep absolutely FREE!

3. There's <u>no</u> catch. You're under <u>no</u> obligation to buy anything. We charge nothing – ZERO – for your first shipment. And you don't have to make any minimum number of purchases – not even one!

4. We call this line "The Best of the Best" because each month you'll receive the best books by the world's hottest authors. These authors show up time and time again on all the major bestseller lists and their books sell out as soon as they hit the stores. You'll like the convenience of getting them delivered to your home at our discount prices…and you'll love your subscriber newsletter featuring author news, horoscopes, recipes, book reviews and much more!

5. We hope that after receiving your free books you'll want to remain a subscriber. But the choice is yours – to continue or cancel, anytime at all! So why not take us up on our invitation, with no risk of any kind. You'll be glad you did!

6. And remember…we'll send you a mystery gift ABSOLUTELY FREE just for giving "The Best of the Best" a try!

MIRA ®

Visit us at
www.mirabooks.com

## SPECIAL FREE GIFT!

We'll send you a fabulous mystery gift, absolutely FREE, simply for accepting our no-risk offer!

# Books **FREE!**

**DETACH AND MAIL CARD TODAY!**

**HURRY! Return this card promptly to get 2 FREE Books and a FREE Gift!**

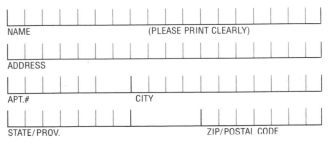

*The Best of the Best*™

**YES!** Please send me the 2 FREE "The Best of the Best" novels and FREE gift for which I qualify. I understand that I am under no obligation to purchase anything further, as explained on the opposite page.

Affix
peel-off
**2 FREE BOOKS**
sticker here.

P-BB1-00
**385 MDL CY2W**

**185 MDL CY2X**

|  |  |  |  |  |  |  |  |  |  |  |  |  |  |  |  |  |  |
|--|--|--|--|--|--|--|--|--|--|--|--|--|--|--|--|--|--|

NAME                    (PLEASE PRINT CLEARLY)

|  |  |  |  |  |  |  |  |  |  |  |  |  |  |  |  |  |  |
|--|--|--|--|--|--|--|--|--|--|--|--|--|--|--|--|--|--|

ADDRESS

|  |  |  |  |  |  |  |  |  |  |  |  |  |  |  |  |  |  |  |
|--|--|--|--|--|--|--|--|--|--|--|--|--|--|--|--|--|--|

APT.#              CITY

|  |  |  |  |  |  |  |  |  |  |  |
|--|--|--|--|--|--|--|--|--|--|

STATE/PROV.                    ZIP/POSTAL CODE

# The Best of the Best™—Here's How it Works

Accepting your 2 free books and gift places you under no obligation to buy anything. You may keep the books and gift and return the shipping statement marked "cancel." If you do not cancel, about a month later we will send you 4 additional novels and bill you just $4.24 each in the U.S., or $4.74 each in Canada, plus 25¢ delivery per book and applicable sales tax, if any.* That's the complete price, and — compared to cover prices of $5.50 or more each in the U.S. and $6.50 or more each in Canada — it's quite a bargain! You may cancel at any time, but if you choose to continue, every month we'll send you 4 more books, which you may either purchase at the discount price…or return to us and cancel your subscription.

*Terms and prices subject to change without notice. Sales tax applicable in N.Y. Canadian residents will be charged applicable provincial taxes and GST.

# CHAPTER FOURTEEN

THEY ANCHORED in a cove on Cabo San Anselmo that night, and it seemed to Jean like a good place for gloom. The ingredients were readily available.

One, Jake and the other members of the expedition were going ashore that night to a party on the cape where she was notorious.

Two, Baby was still gone, and Chris was heartbroken about her disappearance.

And three, the conversation with David in the wheelhouse felt like a mistake. He had broken his silence, but at whose expense? Jean felt as though she had degraded their relationship by prying such an ugly truth from him. He hadn't told her everything about Erika's accident, but she could assemble the pieces. Jake's story about David's old car that Skye had hated and totaled. David's doing "penance." Jake's description of Skye as "a lush and a bitch." Probably alcohol was one of the factors David had omitted from his account. Another would be Erika's statement that the only accident was that David hadn't been driving.

The question that remained unanswered was what could have made Skye so angry.

Obviously David returned the feeling. His remark that he wouldn't malign his wife seemed to indicate that he couldn't talk about her without doing so, which was both telling and curious. Jean wondered how much of that was the result of Skye's suicide, how much Erika's accident, how much other things.

The puzzle came and went from her mind. More urgent was what the evening might bring down on her own head. Although David, as far as she knew, would stay home with her and Chris, Jake's going ashore to the party seemed a one-step plan for disaster. Jean could picture it easily, a casual comment to the wrong person. *No, David stayed on his ship tonight with his fiancée, Jean Young.*

Every time she thought of it, she wanted to moan aloud. Yet she felt helpless, as though she was in the grip of events spiraling out of her control.

And Chris's reaction to Baby's disappearance had the same flavor.

That night, after Jolly's four-course Christmas Eve dinner, Jean waited on the steps of the aft companionway with David while Chris changed into his pajamas for bed. In the salon, the others were drinking rum-and-eggnog, warming up for the party at nine. Behind her on the steps, David was taking out her braid. His impatience to be alone with her made the threat of exposure seem even more dire, and Jean was glad when Chris emerged from his stateroom.

But he did not look like a boy waiting for the sound of sleigh bells.

David nudged Jean to her feet and stood up. He told Chris, "Better set out one of Jolly's cinnamon rolls for Santa Claus."

Chris hardly looked at him but squeezed past them both and up the companionway to the salon. Jean closed her eyes, feeling culpable. David had tried to keep Chris from loving Baby. Only she had swayed him.

As though he knew what she was feeling, David told her, "He'll get over it. And so will you."

Jean wanted to sink into the hold of the ship. Now David thought her moodiness was the result of Baby's absence.

She had to tell him the truth. Tonight, before the others came home. As she watched him follow Chris across the salon, she wished she'd found the courage to tell him sooner.

IN THE GALLEY Chris climbed onto a stool to take down a plate and a glass for Santa Claus, then set out a cinnamon roll and a napkin. Watching him fill the glass with milk, David asked, "Going to write a note for him?"

Feeling superfluous, Jean said, "I'll get the paper."

Minutes later she sat at the galley table beside David as Chris wrote a note to Santa Claus, but her mind was elsewhere, on the evening ahead. It was going to be very hard to tell David the truth and hard for him to hear it. He would be angry, but at some point that anger would fade, wouldn't it?

Maybe she should wait until after Christmas.

But after Christmas might be too late.

David's voice, stressed, called her away from her musings. "Chris, Santa Claus is not going to bring Baby back. That's not part of his job."

Chris signed something at him, and Jean followed the words. *He knows where Baby is. He'll find her. You wouldn't go back to look for her today. You wouldn't even find my mother.*

Jean tried to draw an even breath.

David's face went still. Evenly, quietly, he told Chris, "Please go to your room."

Chris's face collapsed in tears, and he scooted out of the booth and ran up the companionway. The sound of his door sliding shut with a bang rang through the ship like a gunshot.

Jean looked down at the note he had written. "Dear Santa Claus, Please bring Baby back."

David slid out of the booth. "I'm going to say goodnight to him."

Jean sat behind at the galley table, thinking of what Chris had said and of what she had read in the *South Coast Sun*, that David had dived beneath the ship looking for Skye's body. A chill passed over her. What had he told Chris? What could he tell him?

David was gone so long that at last Jean went up to his cabin, intent on taking a shower. After the stormy day, her hair and skin were caked with salt spray. But she had shed only her sweatshirt when David came in, closing the door. Catching a glimpse of his face, an expressionless mask, Jean asked, "Shall I go say good-night to him?"

"He's asleep." David stepped toward her, ran his eyes over her body and asked, "Taking a shower?"

"Yes."

"Good." He drew off his shirt and threw it indifferently in the corner. "So am I. Saves water." He smiled at her—almost—and Jean saw he was exhausted.

Her courage evaporated.

HE MADE LOVE TO HER against the tile wall of the shower, her legs wrapped around him as he moved inside her. After the turmoil of the day, Jean wondered how they could still want each other. Yet the pleasure filled her, overwhelming her, while she clutched his shoulders, feeling the ripple of muscle in his arms and back.

He said, "I love you." The words came out again and again, more than he'd ever said them before, and Jean held him tightly, needing him and feeling at the same time that their lovemaking was a travesty, that she was unworthy of what he was giving her.

David sensed it without knowing what he was sensing, only a sadness in her. Baby? Chris? He didn't analyze it. He made her forget it. Under the water of the shower, he spoke to her softly. The intimacy of words was magic, and soon he felt her clinging more tightly, heard her crying for him low in her throat, an animal with her mate.

Then the hot shivers raked through her, shattering around her, shuddering over him. David drove harder inside her and hardly knew he was saying her name over and over while he came. It was a long time before he let her slide to the floor, rinsed the water over her many more times and turned off the tap.

When he looked at her she was crying. He said, "Are you hurt?"

She shook her head. "I just love you."

"Good." He handed her a towel. "Wait here."

JEAN STARED at the dress on the bed. Waltz-length skirt, draping tiers of gauzy black cotton and a scooped neck embroidered with every color in the rainbow. Birds and flowers in exquisite detail, the work of weeks or months. From the blanket hem dangled six inches of fringe like uncombed hair, woven with trade beads and scraps of silver—silver like the ornate coin belt that must have cost the earth. David had also thought to find her some beaded rope sandals, beautiful and perfect. Everything reflected and would enhance her style, which seemed to Jean some kind of miracle—and testament to how well he knew her.

But the gift seemed ominous. She asked David, "Are we going somewhere?"

"Carlos's party. Grant and Jolly volunteered to stay with Chris so you and I could have a date." Watching a tremor pass over her, David thought of the industrial port in L.A. and the man who had straddled her, ripped at her jeans, promised her pain a woman would never forget. Blinking the image from his mind, he said, "Chris and I found the dress together."

She said, "It's beautiful." And she made herself meet his eyes. "Thank you." She had many excuses to plead, from a headache to the truth. But David was counting on having her beside him, and letting him down would be cowardice.

By going she could remind herself she was innocent. By going she could show David her innocence. And only by going could she convince him there had never been reason for her to tell him anything.

But she knew in her heart he would never agree with the last.

FOR A WRAP Jean wore the gift from the London shop, which Ceci had said she could open early. When David saw her, he said, "And I thought I'd have to keep you warm."

As he touched the fine wool of the long, woven, hooded shawl, Jean stared at him, mesmerized. She'd never been anywhere with a man in a tuxedo, and she couldn't imagine another looking so perfect in one. Tall, broad-shouldered, sinewy. This was her companion, her lover, the man she would marry.

The man she might lose.

There were five in their party—David and Jean, Jake, Robin and Ken—but they took both of the *Skye*'s auxiliary craft, the Zodiac and the smaller glass-bottomed dinghy, across the cove to the party. Jean rode in the dinghy with Jake while the others went in the Zodiac with David, something she knew David had arranged as a matter of courtesy to the expedition members.

In his tuxedo, the holly berries on his battery-powered bow tie blinking in the night, Jake gave her an abbreviated rundown on Carlos, who owned a fishery in Le Paz. As they motored along the shore under a swelling moon past two other craft glowing with Christmas lights, he told Jean, "This is a big party. We'll see most of the people who own property down here and more from up north. You might run into someone you know from Santa Barbara."

As he spoke Jean understood how foolish she'd been to come. When she had fled Cabo San Anselmo it had been with the conviction that she would never want to return— and the certainty she never could. Now she was going back, plunging into a social situation where she was bound to see people with whom she had bitter, unresolved differences. Worse, she realized belatedly that if she'd leveled with David, given him some warning, he might have protected her. Now he could only be angry.

And this was Christmas Eve, a night for peace and joy.

When Jake steered the dinghy up to the dock, the Zodiac, with its more powerful motor, was already there. David took their bowline and helped Jean from the small craft onto the weathered dock, touching both her hands as he steadied her.

Just that contact in the night quickened her pulse, and Jean knew from his eyes that David felt the same. He said, "Ready, ma'am?"

She would never be ready, but she looked toward the lights of the sprawling hacienda on the hill and accepted the arm he offered her. As he guided her up the dock, Jean peered at a building she realized must be a three-car garage. Colored lights etched a nativity scene on each of the doors. The star, the shepherd, the family, the wise men. Symbols of hope and promise of the morning. Christmas Day.

But the emotional anticipation she should have felt was missing. There was only fear. And a sense that she, by her deceit, had broken something beautiful and fragile. It was only a matter of time till David discovered the damage.

THE SMELLS OF THE CAPE were the same, but Carlos's place added its own. From the moment the black-skirted maid took her wrap at the door, Jean inhaled the fiesta of aromas brewing in the kitchen. Fajitas, flan, mole, cinnamon cookies, hot chocolate, and almond torte. Creamy corn soup and flounder rolls, everything a feast for the senses.

Music from the ballroom drifted out to the palatial red-tile foyer, bringing with it the sound of tinkling glasses and many voices talking at once. As David introduced her to Carlos, a short, wiry man with dancing eyes and a surplus of charm, Jean felt short of breath, faint. What would happen when she walked into the next room? Who would be there? Would anyone recognize her? It was all she could do to concentrate on the introduction and keep her eyes on their host as he spoke in perfect, barely accented English, praising her beauty and congratulating David.

As Carlos turned to the others, greeting Jake with familiarity and Robin and Ken with attentiveness, Jean's gaze drifted to the church-size nativity set at the end of the hall, lit with lights and surrounded by flowers. Its beauty reminded her of David's love. And of her own unworthiness.

She deserved coal in her stocking.

David's touch drew her attention back to Carlos, who was urging them toward the ballroom, saying, "I'm so pleased you're all here, my guests. David, you can take care of your *novia*, yes? My wife is showing the upper level to friends, but when she comes down I'll bring her to see you."

Jake, Ken and Robin went ahead, looking for the punch bowls and tables laden with food, and Jean found herself alone with David, gazing upon a majestic room of high stucco arches and ornate chandeliers, all decked with holiday color. She searched the faces in the crowd, but recognized no one. It gave her no ease. Heat was rising over her in waves, and she could not escape the feeling that her minutes were numbered.

David's hand slipped from hers and touched her back near her waist. "Are you all right?"

"Yes." Jean made herself smile at him. She would not use his concern to her own advantage, to escape. She owed him this night, and she wanted him to have it. She only hoped it wouldn't end in disgrace.

She saw no one she knew, except a few vaguely familiar faces who seemed not to place her at all. David brought her food and drink, introduced her to a few close acquaintances and danced with her on the starlit patio outside, occasionally trading her into other hands. Ken, Robin, Jake and, once, Carlos, who asked her many questions about herself and how she'd met David. He seemed to know David very well, and by the end of the dance Jean sensed his approval of her. When he handed her back to David, he called her a treasure.

David did not relinquish her again, and Jean felt herself relaxing as the evening wore on and she spent it at his side and in his arms. Though he never voiced it, she sensed his pride in her. No one had ever made her feel so cherished.

When they had been at the party for nearly two hours, he drew her off to the edge of the patio and said, "I think I'm wearing you out, which I'd rather do at home." He met her eyes significantly. "Ready to go?"

Jean nodded, giving silent thanks that they were escaping now, that nothing had happened to mar the evening, that tonight he would hear the truth from her own lips, not distortions from someone else's. She said, "I need to find the ladies' room first."

David said, "I'll get your wrap."

HE WAS WAYLAID by a brunette in a black-and-white dress that reminded him of the clothes Skye had worn so well. On this woman, whose carriage seemed stridently athletic, the style was more forced, and it was the sense of forced fashion that David remembered about her. He didn't know her name.

"Jennifer Avery," she said. "I'm sorry. It has been a while. Two years perhaps."

David started at the name, then said, "Of course. I remember you." He knew she must be aware of her husband's proposal still on his desk, and he wasn't sure he was glad she'd chosen to speak to him. He found himself glancing down at the empty champagne flute in his hand as though it was a burden he was impatient to lay aside. He searched for something to say to Jennifer and recalled where they had met and the substance of their conversation two years earlier, the horrifying story she had told, the story Erika had said must be incomplete.

He said, "Let's see… You and I met at the gallery opening on the wharf. You'd had trouble with your nanny."

"Yes," said Jennifer. "And how surprised I was to hear just now that you're going to marry her!"

Jean was descending the stairs, her hand tight on the wrought-iron railing. She had spotted Jennifer Avery at once and felt her stomach take a kamikaze dive. Now she saw David's startled movement, the stem of the champagne flute break off in his hand, the remaining drops of wine spill onto the tile floor. He stepped back, staring at the spots on the floor, then at Jennifer Avery.

Knowing what must have been said, Jean felt her insides shatter. She should have spared him that moment.

She should have spared herself.

DAVID PULLED HER WRAP around her silently and nudged her toward the door. They had already bade farewell to their host, David with a smile that Jean could hardly believe he had summoned and that fooled her not at all.

As they moved outside under the moon, Jean said, "The others…"

"They'll take the Zodiac." He glanced both ways as they walked onto the flagstone. They were alone but too close to the house to speak. Touching Jean as little as possible, he led her down the stone steps to the water.

Jean said, "I'd like to know what Jennifer Avery said to you."

They stepped onto the dock. David didn't answer until they'd reached the dinghy and he'd handed her inside. Then he climbed in after her and crouched over the outboard. Before pulling the starter, he took a breath and said, "It's been two years since she told me the story, but it stayed in my mind. Two children left alone in a condominium while the nanny went AWOL with her boyfriend. The children set fire to the condo and barely escaped with their lives, one of them with burns.'' He pulled the starter. Once. Twice. It caught.

Jean was kneeling in the bow, untying the line. As she shoved the dinghy away from the dock, she looked into his eyes.

David said what had been building inside him for twenty minutes, ever since Jennifer Avery uttered those words and that champagne flute came apart in his hands. ''You lied to me.''

''No.'' She shook her head, eyes wide and clear.

David turned the throttle and steered the boat away from the dock out into the cove. He headed the dinghy not for the ship but for a stretch of beach farther south from Carlos's hacienda, deserted and out of reach of the ears on other boats in the cove.

On the forward seat, far from him, Jean asked, ''Where are you going?''

''The beach.'' He silently cursed what the sand would do to the outboard, but it couldn't be helped.

At the shore he helped her out, then turned away.

Jean said, ''You should have my side of the story.''

''First you're going to have mine.'' He spun on her tensely, his tuxedo incongruous with their surroundings, the empty, moonlit beach. ''Say what you will, say you never told me a lie, and I'll tell you there are lies of commission and omission. Yours was the latter. Whatever happened down here, and I'm not sure I care what it was, you lied to me a dozen times about it. You lied when you told me about your mother. You lied when I hired you to care for my son.''

''I did *not*.''

''You lied when I asked you to read Michael Avery's proposal. You lied every time I asked you to watch Chris. It was a *lie*, Jean. A living lie. Day in and day out. God, and to think I was worried you didn't want to come to this party because somebody had tried to rape you!''

Jean was glad of the dark so she didn't have to see his face. But she could feel the anger snapping from him—and the betrayal. She could think of nothing to say in her own defense. Except, "I'm sorry."

"So am I," he said tautly. "So am I."

His words plunged through her like a rock, and the sound of the waves on the shore seemed mournful, as though the tide was playing "Taps" over the remains of David's respect for her. Jean said, "You should try to understand."

He had turned partially away from her, but she had his full attention now. "Forgive me for not understanding that you neglected to tell me you'd been a nanny before and that two of your charges almost died from your negligence."

"They did not!"

"Don't shout at me."

"Then listen to me." Her hair waved around her, curling from the dampness of the sea air. She felt wild, out of control. She couldn't lose David's love over this. It would be the final insult.

He said coldly, "I'll listen, but go light on the details about your lover. This is where it happened, isn't it, Jean? Was it your boyfriend? Or your professor? Or both? How many other lies have you told me?"

For a moment Jean couldn't speak. When she could she said, "I don't deserve this. I've never lied to you. I withheld something, and that's my right. I wanted a job, and I knew you wouldn't give me one if I told you this story."

"Then you *lied!*" He was shouting now—because she hadn't answered his question. "That's what it's called, Jean. A lie. You lied because you wanted a job from me! And when I took you into my bed—"

"That's irrelevant, and you know it." He was advancing on her, and she stepped back. "I planned to tell you."

"When? Tonight?" David swore at her. "Every time you shared your body with me, you lied."

"Stop saying that. If my not telling you this was a lie, then you lie to me a hundred times a day!"

"Explain what you mean."

"Do you tell me everything?"

The question made him furious. "Some things are none of your business."

"Wrong. I'm going to be your wife."

And then they both fell silent in the moonlight, hearing only the water.

David said, "Perhaps."

Jean expelled a breath. "You—"

"Dream come true," he supplied. "Remember? Now, tell your story, if you have the nerve."

"You don't deserve to hear it." Hugging herself, Jean turned toward the water. "Just take me home."

Her words inflamed him. Not deserve to hear it? Who did she think she was talking to? David grabbed her arm and wheeled her around. The emotions building inside him had obliterated all thoughts except one, the question that he'd already asked—that she'd never answered. That he knew she shouldn't have to answer. The question that he couldn't ask again. He shoved her down on the sand, mindless of her dress, hating the feel of manhandling a woman's body. It reminded him of Skye, of their screaming, shaking fights. And her constant, unending deceit.

Jean hit the wet sand hard and stared up at him, gasping.

Seeing her eyes begin to tear, David snapped, "Pull yourself together and start talking. I've got more to cry about than you'll ever know."

Jean didn't doubt it. She told him, "Never touch me that way again."

He said, "Talk. Now."

Jean felt the breath steaming like fire through her nostrils, but she knew that if she didn't tell him they would never sort it out. She said, "It was my day off."

"Start before," David said sharply. "How you got the job—you, who said you were no good with children, who said your mother put you down."

"That was why. I wanted to prove to her I could do something useful." Jean swallowed, watching the tiny waves sweep into shore, then crumble to nothingness. "I could talk about this all night, but the bottom line was that she didn't like how I spent my time, except for school. Tae kwon do, surfing, diving—all worthless. All self-gratification, according to her.

"The Averys were friends of my mother's, and they mentioned the job to her, thinking of Ceci, but Ceci was already modeling, getting better assignments all the time. I said I wanted to do it." Jean didn't add her mother's doubts and fateful predictions. They didn't matter. But something else did, something David wouldn't want to hear. She took a long breath and continued.

"Billy Moss was going, too. He had a job at the condos as a sailing instructor, surfing coach, et cetera."

David stepped away from her in the darkness, kicking off the shoes he wished he'd removed earlier, before they'd gotten out of the boat. "Who is Billy Moss?"

"He was my boyfriend. We were high school sweethearts and best friends." Jean looked at David, trying to gauge his reaction. His back was turned. "We dated for three years. Two years of high school and one of college."

David thought of this boy's hand on her breast. He thought of him making love to her, never satisfying. Or had Jean lied about that?

Behind him she said, "David, it was never like what I have with you. The first time—I knew he wasn't the one. It was...rather traumatic." She drew another shaky breath. "That's another reason I came down here. To be alone. He followed. That's why he got the job, to be near me."

David didn't look at her. He moved yards away and sat down on the dry sand above the tide line.

Jean said, "It was strictly platonic by then—on my side, anyhow. We surfed together. On my day off we always went up the coast to San Marcos Island, where the waves are big."

David knew the place. He hadn't known Jean could handle swell of that size. And he didn't care.

"That day—it was about a month after I started the job—we went surfing as usual, and late in the afternoon Billy did a face plant on an easy ride, one of those you think is going to be a piece of cake. I saw him not get up, just lie in the water, and when I went over he wasn't moving. His neck was broken."

David looked at her, and Jean suspected he thought she was lying, but she went on because she didn't know what else to do. "I pulled him out of the water, using everything I knew about lifesaving, and I sat there on the beach holding his head all night."

"All night?" said David. "Wasn't anyone else out?"

"It was cloudy, and the swell was bad. We had talked of going farther up the coast. We'd heard Gila Point was good, but it was too far, because I was supposed to be at the Averys' at seven." She was surprised how calm she sounded now, how calm she felt. "At dawn, some other surfers showed up. People we knew. They went for help, and it took hours. Someone knew someone with a chopper. Finally they came and took him to San Diego."

"And?" said David.

"At the hospital, they drilled holes in his head and put him in traction, if that's what you call it. He had this halo thing around his head. Eventually he walked away."

If it was a lie, it was an ambitious one. David said, "And you?"

"I drove his car back to the condos, and the Averys' was still smoking. They had gone out the night before—'just over to the clubhouse.'" Jean heard the bitterness in her own voice, the mocking of her accuser, Jennifer Avery, who should have been accused herself of criminal negligence. "The boys started a campfire in the TV room." She felt her old ambivalence toward the children, both hellions; toward the parents she felt outrage.

She remembered that David was waiting for her to speak. "The younger boy, Baker, was hurt in the fire. The Averys were threatening lawsuits." She closed her eyes. "I was afraid—being in a foreign country, not knowing the laws. While they were occupied, I took Billy's car and drove home."

David sat still, his reactions mixed. It wasn't what he'd expected to hear. Part of him didn't believe it, was afraid to believe it, afraid it was a lie. He had heard so many from Skye that for a time he'd believed everyone told them habitually.

Jean was still talking. "My parents were shocked to see me, and when they heard the story my mother didn't believe me. She called the hospital in San Diego—not to check on Billy but to see if he was there at all. Even when she found he was, she insisted that I shouldn't have gone up the coast if there was any chance I couldn't get back on time. Maybe she was right." Jean swallowed. "We never had a chance to work things out. A few weeks later she and my father were killed on the interstate, just two miles from home."

David knew how that unresolved argument must have felt—probably still felt. For Jean's sake he wished her mother had retracted her words.

He wished he could believe her himself, but the fact that she had concealed the incident ate at him. He no longer trusted her, and he wasn't sure he ever would again.

He stood up and brushed off his pants, grabbed his socks and shoes, and said, "Let's go home."

# CHAPTER FIFTEEN

JEAN WATCHED HIM remove his jacket and place it on a hanger over the door of his open locker. As he pulled off his bow tie, she said, "I didn't know those things really tied."

Skye had taught him how. He wanted to tell her that, a cruel tidbit about his first marriage. She wanted details. He'd give them.

On a wave of self-disgust David slid open the door to his cabin and went out, up into the wheelhouse, before he could say something he'd regret.

Left behind, Jean was unsure what to do. It was late, time for bed, but he hadn't invited her to his, and the last thing she wanted to do was creep up to him and ask him where she should sleep. She went to her own cabin and retrieved a paper shopping bag from the locker. Christian's Christmas gifts were inside, and she made her way down through the office and aft to his stateroom, where his stocking hung, to leave them for him.

*David and I should be doing this together,* she thought. But there were good reasons why they weren't. His lack of conviction about her story hurt—more, even, than her mother's distrust had at the time.

Tiptoeing into Chris's room, Jean took a moment to reposition the covers he'd kicked off in the night, then turned to set the wrapped packages under and inside his stocking. With thoughts of St. Nicholas, she tucked the hacky sack in one of his small shoes, a pack of stickers in the other.

A shadow hid the glow from a night-light in the hall. It was David, still wearing his white tuxedo shirt and black pants. He had a drink in his hand, and he sipped from the glass as he looked at the gifts she'd tucked into Chris's shoes. He said, "Did you know St. Nicholas was credited with bringing the dead back to life?"

Jean shook her head. She reached for the hacky sack to put it in Chris's stocking instead. She hadn't forgotten about St. Nicholas's Day, but she'd thought the baggage of *that* day wouldn't matter on Christmas morning. Of course she was wrong. It would always matter.

David said, "Don't bother. He'll like it that way." The glass hovered near his lips as he said, "I was just sharing trivia. My mother liked saints, and she used to tell me stories about St. Nicholas. In Greece they say he controls the tempests and the winds. There are churches and shrines all over the coasts dedicated to him, and the icons show him with a dripping beard and brine on his clothes from pulling drowning people out of the sea."

Jean closed her eyes. Erika was right. David did get black at Christmas.

"In other countries they said he could reassemble dismembered bodies."

Jean's heart stilled. She thought of the props on the *Skye*, the blood in the water. On St. Nicholas's Day. She looked at him and said softly, "David?"

But he was looking at his son. "He went to sleep telling me Santa Claus is going to bring Baby back. To you." David swallowed another draft of tequila. He'd poured it into a glass this time—so he would stop. "Your present, not his."

Jean said, "I wouldn't ask that of Santa Claus."

"Good," said David flatly. "I can paint sleigh tracks and hoofprints on the foredeck, but that's the bottom of my bag of tricks."

Jean wondered if he really went to such lengths. She heard no humor in his voice, or warmth.

Chris tossed in his bed, and David watched him dispassionately, as though he were someone else's son. Mirthlessly, bitterly, he said, "Here we go. Time for a little night music."

Chris began to scream. David set down his glass, stepped inside and shut the door. As he moved to the bed to pick up his son, Jean glanced toward the hall. Thinking of the expedition members in the nearby staterooms, she asked, "Should I go out and explain to the others?"

"I already told them." Then, not wanting to see her there in his son's room doing mother things and still less wanting her to witness his family's shame again, he said, "But if you're done you can go."

Jean said, "You're not being fair to me."

Instead of replying, he lifted Chris in his arms and opened the door for her. "Good night."

Jean went out, to her own cabin.

THAT NIGHT the dream was the worst it had ever been but only because it was the most vivid. The details never changed. It always started at the same place, her last words, her strange backward topple over the railing. Then everything else, just as it had been the first time, never getting better. As always David awoke with the feeling that his hair and skin were caked with her blood and worse. He got up to take a shower.

Under the spray, he scrubbed himself with a wood-handled brush, feeling like Lady Macbeth trying to cleanse her hand of the blood of her murder victim. For perfumes of Arabia, substitute white bar soap. Had Jean ever noticed how much of the stuff he went through?

In the midst of his furious scrubbing, she came in and stood on the wet floor looking at him, her legs strong and fine beneath the hem of one of his T-shirts.

David set the scrub brush on the shower caddy and slammed off the water.

Jean handed him a towel and asked, "Why do you do that?"

"Do what?" He dried his face first and shook his hair on her.

"Take showers at three in the morning."

"Because I can't sleep." Feeling his own lies now, he stepped past her to his cabin. Damn her body, she made him hard. He would have banged the door shut behind him if he hadn't wanted her so badly.

Jean saw the invitation and followed him. "Showers help?"

"You help," he said tersely.

Hoping that if she bent, he would, Jean said, "I'm here, David."

He turned so she could see what she did to him. "Then get in bed."

It was better with her arms around him, better still with everything off her. As he felt the heat of her skin, the soft places on her body, relaxation went through him in small shudders. Like a house settling in the ground, he settled against her inch by inch, feeling her hand stroking his hair. He buried his face in hers, wishing he didn't want her. Wishing he didn't love her.

Jean whispered, "Please forgive me, David."

He wondered if she meant, *Please believe me.* And he thought of her boyfriend. He wanted to ask, *Only once?* But he knew it shouldn't matter if it'd been a hundred times—and a hundred men. It was because of Skye that it did. And because he loved Jean so much he could hardly stand it.

He moved against her, anticipating the heat of her around him, hating the thought of the synthetic barrier between them. He longed to forgo it, as he had the first time, but now it seemed more important than ever. He didn't know her as well as he'd thought.

He kissed her, postponing the moment, and as he did it all came to the surface. The same images as the dream, in vivid color. He shut his eyes.

Jean's arms went tight around him almost as though she knew everything inside him, but David knew she couldn't.

He moved her arms away, got out of bed and reached for a pair of sweatpants hanging over a chair. Without a word, he left the room.

HE WAS PULLING on his pants when she opened her eyes the next morning. Without greeting her he said, "There are some whales in a lagoon out there. It's foggy, but Ken was already out and saw them. We're all going now, so watch Chris, will you?"

Jean said, "Merry Christmas?"

David walked to the bed, touched her hair and went up to the wheelhouse.

Thinking of Chris, Jean climbed out of bed, hurried into the crew's quarters and put on an old pair of sweatpants and a sweatshirt. Then she went down through the office and up into the galley. As usual Jolly's domain was ship-shape, except for the note and empty plate and milk glass on the table. Jean paused and read the note again. Beneath Chris's request for Santa to bring back Baby was a reply in David's writing, somewhat disguised:

Dear Chris,
Sorry about Baby. She's celebrating Christmas up north, and I couldn't budge her. But thanks for the cinnamon roll. Ho, ho, ho! People call me jolly, too. Hope you won't mind cleaning off those tracks we left on the deck. Dasher and Dancer just can't seem to get a clean landing on the water.
    You're a good boy.

                                                    Love,
                                                    Santa

In a rush, Jean recalled what had happened before they went to Carlos's party—Chris's *You wouldn't even find my mother.* Poor David. Christmas Eve had been the worst kind of day for him: the storms, Baby's disappearance, Chris's accusation, discovery of her own deceit. And deceit it was, one way or the other. Alone in her berth before she slept, Jean had faced that.

Yet after such a miserable Christmas Eve, David had found the kindness to write a Santa Claus note to his son. And, apparently, leave reindeer and sleigh tracks on the foredeck.

Noticing the last closed door on the advent calendar and thinking that David had left her with a child waking up to Christmas morning, Jean hurried back to Christian's stateroom. But his door was still shut. Sleeping. That wouldn't last long, so Jean took advantage of the time to shower and dress.

As she did she tried to tell herself it was a new day, but her heart wasn't in the thought. David had not kissed her since the night before, when their lovemaking had abruptly ended. Probably he still doubted the story she had told him about working for the Averys.

Everything had turned upside down.

After dressing, Jean hurried back out to the salon. It was fully light now, and Chris's door was still shut. She sat down to wait for him and saw a package with her name on it under the tree. It was from David, she knew. Wondering what it was, she thought again with misgiving of her own presents for him. And when she turned back to look toward Chris's stateroom, Skye's eyes seemed to mock her from the painting over the stairwell.

Before Chris awakened, the Zodiac returned, and Jean went up on deck into the fog-banked, misty morning to greet the men. Jake was saying, "She must have taken him out somewhere. I'll go look for them. Don't sweat it, David."

David was gazing toward the diving platform as though something displeased him, and when at last he glanced up and saw Jean on the deck, his eyes were a portrait in shock. He said, "Where's the dinghy?"

Jean looked toward the diving platform blankly. No dinghy.

David clambered out of the boat, took the aft deck in three strides, then ran into the diving alcove, leaving the door swinging behind him. Jean heard his feet on the companionways, the sliding of a door inside, then his voice shouting through the ship. "Chris!"

The name slammed her in the chest.

A moment later David was back on deck, facing her. "Is he here?"

Jean couldn't answer. She shook her head.

David went to the aft railing and stared out of the cove toward the grayed-over obscurity of the open sea. Jean followed, while behind them Jake said, "I'm on the radio, David."

Never taking his eyes from the water, David said to Jean, "You know where he's gone, don't you?"

She didn't answer, couldn't.

"He's looking for Baby."

THERE WAS NOTHING for her to do but pace the deck and listen to the crackle of the radio. David had taken Grant, Jake and Robin and made her stay behind. He wasn't kind about it, either, just direct, wasting no time on recriminations. They would come later.

It was worse than anything Jean could have imagined, had ever imagined. And it had happened on her watch. A six-year-old boy gone to sea in a seven-foot boat.

Behind her, she heard Jolly talking on the radio. A moment later he stepped out of the wheelhouse and joined her at the rail. He was unshaven, still in his red, long-sleeved undershirt and a pair of olive fatigues held up with dirty, rainbow-striped suspenders. He said, "Nothing yet. You see anything, Jean?"

She shook her head, wishing there was more she could do. Her eyes lingered on the shore, and it occurred to her that if she were a frightened child that was where she'd go. And by now, Chris must be frightened.

She thought of the surfboards in the alcove and her shoulder, still compromised. But the shore was close. She could be there in ten minutes.

She looked up at Jolly. "If I paddled over to the beach on one of the surfboards, would you watch to make sure I don't drown?"

Jolly stepped back uneasily, as though she'd asked a sticky question. "I don't know if David would like that."

All that could matter to David right now was getting his son back. Jean said, "The shore's close. I think that's where Chris might go."

"On the ocean is where he'll get hurt," said Jolly. "If he's on the beach, he'll be fine."

"Not if he's cold and wet." Hypothermia. It was a wet morning, and Chris was a slight child.

Jolly sighed and turned back toward the wheelhouse. "Ah, go look. Yeah, I'll watch you. Just don't get hurt, or David'll have my hide. He probably will, anyhow."

Jean hurried below to put on her wet suit.

JAKE SAID, "I can't believe Chris started that motor."

David wished he hadn't taught him how. Staring off the bow of the Zodiac and into the fog bank, he said, "Keep close to the shore. The tide will sweep him toward those rocks on the point."

Jake pulled a cigarette from the pocket of his slicker, tucked it in a corner of his mouth, then groped for a lighter and lit it, all with the same hand. His other was on the tiller. Drawing on the cigarette, he said, through half-closed lips, "At least the gas was down."

David had refilled it last thing before he turned in. He answered, "No such luck. He's got a full tank."

Robin trained binoculars along the shore, then in the other direction, out into the fog. David wanted to snatch the field glasses from his hands and throw them on the floor of the boat. Visibility was fifty yards, max.

Jake said, "The chopper's coming from north of San Marcos. I'd give it twenty minutes yet. And Carlos took both his boats out."

Twenty minutes. Chris had already been gone forty-five at least, maybe longer. David thought of his son in the dinghy, a boat too small for the open sea. Why had he gone?

But he knew the answer.

Jean.

Baby.

And Skye, the mother he, David, had never tried to find. *She was dead, Chris. I saw her.*

*What if she wasn't? Why did you let her sink?*

That conversation had been a nightmare.

*I couldn't hold her, Chris.*

Jake suddenly pointed at the rocky point where the spray leapt twenty feet in the air. "There he is, David. And there's your girl." He gunned the outboard.

WHEN SHE SAW the dinghy near the rocks, Jean began to run. The boat was going to break apart, and then Chris's small body would be tossed in the foam and smacked hard against the point. He was going to die.

There was no chance of wading or swimming into the swell to the boat. The water would be ten feet deep out there, and as the waves hit the rocks they sprang up in foam to triple that. The only approach was over the black, craggy rocks.

They cut her feet as she climbed them, and her wet suit ripped on a ragged edge. What was worse, her shoulder could support almost no weight. She was reduced to one arm, a hand that could be used only for balance, and her legs. Those legs were her strength, and she stretched them long over the steep side of the point, determined to make faster time.

*Hang on, Chris. Hang on, baby.* Then, desperately, she thought, *Don't die!*

But there was no way she could get him. As she climbed she imagined hanging from the edge of a steep face and letting Chris grab her foot. But one-armed pull-ups were not her specialty.

When she crested the top, she couldn't see the dinghy, but she saw the Zodiac, farther out, headed toward the point. Where was Chris? She scrambled over the rocks until she could peer down to the waves, just in time to see the dinghy wash up on top of a low boulder, the terribly small boy inside. As the waves receded, the boat came to rest, perched on the black rocks.

Jean yelled, "Get out, Chris! Climb!" At the same time, she began climbing down toward him. She saw the next set of waves coming in as he put his leg over the gunwale and stepped out of the boat. "Hurry, Chris! Climb!"

He made for the higher rocks, moving from her view.

Jean saw the waves come in and thought how wet were the rocks down which she was climbing. The tide smashed against the point with a sound like thunder, and the spray showered her. All Jean could think was that Chris was farther below. The waves must have swallowed him. Crushed him.

Drowned him.

The dinghy, still in her view, washed off the boulder and fell down between the rocks on a wave of foam, swamped by the tide. Jean kept moving, sliding down one long ledge after another, feeling a numb certainty that all she would find at the bottom was a small body crushed in the rocks, broken.

Or nothing.

Her feet slipped on the wet surface, and her toes grappled for each fissure in the rocks as she climbed downward. The waves had gone out, and soon they would be back in. As they came she peered down again.

There was Chris, his face crumpled in fear, wet with tears, drenched with water. He clung to the crags below her, his feet on a narrow ledge. Jean knew he must have held on when the last waves came. Now his eyes were on hers. She couldn't get to him before the next breakers came in. She could only make the ledge above him.

She said, "Hold on, honey. You're doing fine. Don't try to go anywhere yet. Here's another wave." It hit, washing over him and drenching her. Jean looked down, drawing a breath when she saw him still there. The next step was too high for him.

She slid down beside him, cutting her palms on the crags and her feet on the knife-blade ledge, the ledge that had saved Christian's life. Knowing that the weakness of her shoulder left her only one option, she braced a foot on the rocks farther down and her knee on the ledge. "Climb up me, Chris. Now."

He did, pulling her hair as he scrambled up on her back, then onto the higher ledge. Jean straightened up just as the next wave hit, knocking away her balance, the onslaught of water suffocating her. She grabbed for rock, anything, as the water threatened to wash her away. Then it was gone, and she fell, a hard drop to the boulder where the dinghy had washed up.

Jean knew the waves were returning and scrambled to her feet on the slick surface; she made it back to the ledge, climbing up to the knife-edge as the water came back. This time she had a firm purchase when the tide came and slammed against her. Feeling her body pressed against the rocks by the force, she thought, *How did little Chris stand it?*

But he had, and he was waiting for her on the rock above. She climbed up to him.

DAVID LIFTED HIS SON down from the rocks and clasped him against his chest, held him tight in his arms. Chris was sniffling and making a humming noise in his throat, and Jean watched him bury his face in his father's neck.

David looked at her once and said, "Thank you." Then, his son against his shoulder, he turned and started across the gray of the beach to where the Zodiac waited on the calm side of the point. Jean was left to climb down the last short pitch by herself, and by the time she reached the Zodiac Chris was bundled inside, his drenched body nestled in the folds of Jake's slicker.

David said, "Jake, see that he gets warm at the ship. I'm getting the dinghy."

Jean said, "You can't. It's down between those rocks."

"I saw where it is." David was scooping spare lines, a bail bucket and a life preserver from the Zodiac.

Jake glanced at David and indicated Jean. "Is she coming with us?"

Jean backed away from the water.

David said, "No."

Robin started to get out of the pontoon boat. "You'll need another hand."

"No, thank you." David didn't want the dinghy as badly as he wanted the privacy in which to tear Jean of Arc limb from limb.

The cinematographer sat down and Jake said, "Give us a shove, Jean."

She did, and then they were gone, leaving her and David alone on the beach without a boat.

David did not even look toward the point. He threw the lines, bail bucket and life vest into the sand and took a desperate step toward Jean, not sure if he was going to shake her like a rag doll or hold her so tight he would drain the life from her.

She saw the wildness in his eyes and remembered the way he had turned away after he'd taken Chris down from the rocks. She said, "I watched his door, David. I took a shower, that's all. I never heard the outboard."

"I'm not blaming you!" David wondered where the yell had come from. She had saved Chris's life—at the risk of her own. For long minutes he had watched the two of them on those rocks fighting for their lives, and him with no way to assist. He had learned the meaning of impotence.

*Again.*

He screamed at Jean, "Don't ever do that again! I'm *done!*" He spread his hands to each side of his body in a swift cutting motion. "No walking bike paths alone at night, no bad diving equipment, no phone calls in crack districts! You want to live like that, you don't live with me!"

Jean didn't ask if she should have left Chris on the rocks. She drew a hand to her face to push a wet lock of hair out of her eyes. Her hand was bleeding.

David saw it, but all he wanted was to keep yelling. He grabbed her shoulders and shook her until her teeth rattled. She looked unafraid, just accepting, a warrior of the way choosing passivity, and her calm drove him wild. Again he saw Chris's small head and shoulders barely clearing the gunwale of the dinghy as it washed up on the point. Again he saw his son climbing out, to certain death David had thought.

Again he felt the grinding in the props of the ship, and he shook Jean again, as though if he shook her hard enough it would somehow help. He saw her hand come up, trembling from what he was doing to her. Yet she touched his face. "Tell me."

"No!"

His body shook against his control, and Jean watched, wanting to hold him.

His hands jerked away from her, pushing her back, and he wheeled, then turned back and yelled at her. "I saw her, Jean!" A pause lingered like a rest in a requiem mass. He whispered hoarsely, "In pieces."

And then there was silence on the beach but for the waves. Jean felt the muscles in her face straining oddly as though they didn't know what expression to form.

"I saw her come at me...." He was barely articulate, and Jean watched him clutch his body like a man whose heart was being ripped out. His hair whipped in the breeze, and tears blurred from his eyes.

She moved toward him cautiously, feeling as though she was approaching a wounded animal. A large, dangerous animal. A weeping moan rose out of him, a long sob from fathomless depths, from the black well she'd known was inside him, and he sank down on the sand and lay face-down, shaking. Jean sat beside him and put her hand on his back, against the salty yellow slicker he wore.

"Her blood was everywhere, and there was... Oh, God. You couldn't see from the surface, but once you were down there..." The cry came again, broken, from his throat. "I tried to go to the screws, and the sea was rough. The water...those colors... It was my wife. It was my *wife!*"

Jean clutched him, feeling his scream expand through his body, hearing it terrify the empty beach. She held her cheek against the back of his hair, clumsily, desperately.

"This *thing* came at me, jarred loose from the screws by the swell, it must have been. It looked like a big dark shape falling through the water, and I knew it must be her, so I grabbed her, and my hands sank into her hair—and I saw her *eyes.*" The anguished, choking cries fell on each other.

Jean combed his hair with her fingers, holding his head, hardly breathing. His voice was so strangled she could barely understand him, but the words were coming out.

"And then, I dropped her—shaking—and I tried to get her again, but she just sank away from me, and I couldn't get her again. The snorkel came out of my mouth, and I swallowed her blood, Jean. Her blood…" He let his face fall to the sand, unable to go on. "In my mouth."

Jean lay against his shaking body and held him, stroking his hair, her heart crooning his name softly with every beat while he cried. Gradually he moved and lay his head against her breasts, against the neoprene of her wet suit, and Jean held him and caressed him, knowing what it was to be a mother and a woman in the comforting of a grown, grieving man. A man who had swallowed death and let it eat away inside him.

His tears were hot and wet against her and as soundless as Christian's. She stroked his cheek and his hair, and without knowing she spoke, she whispered, "I love you."

David pressed tighter against her, fighting the rest, the other things rising in him. It hurt, and he cried, afraid he would never stop. "She said goodbye. 'Goodbye, David.' Like that was all the thought she gave it. 'I'm blasted, and I think I'll tweak my husband by doing a back flip over the bow rail and never coming back.' Chris was right there. Three yards aft."

His voice broke again, and Jean held him hard, hearing his strangled sob. "My son."

*My son who cannot talk.*

"The bitch. I wanted her to die. I used to look her in the eye and think, *Die. Do me a favor and die.*"

Jean drew a shallow breath, put both her hands on his head, in the strands of his hair. She brushed the hot tears from his face.

David tried to stop the escaping words. He didn't want to say them, didn't want to feel them. He wanted to stop.

He wanted peace. He sat up, jerking away from Jean. "I can't say these things."

He sat with his head between his knees, like a man fighting illness, and Jean said, "You can say anything."

"She was my *wife*."

Jean understood him better than she ever had, understood that honor could devour him. She suggested, "Pretend she's a stranger."

David shook his head, making a sound that was a mockery of laughter. "It's so bad, Jean." And the words spilled out. "She was an alcoholic. And drugs. Everything. She took *everything*." Jean knew he was crying again, or still, but she didn't try to move closer to him. "And sex. Completely faithless. She thought fidelity was something stereos had. God!" He yelled the word at the sky. "I wanted a divorce so badly.

"And I wanted Chris. I wanted the bad thing, to take a baby from his mother. But if I didn't stop her, she'd go driving with him when she couldn't focus four feet in front of her. Once she said, 'Who are you?' to me, two minutes before she tried to take him out the door." David looked up at the sky, at the receding fog, the growing brightness heating his face. A cloud-covered sun shining on his shame.

He lay back in the sand, his arm over his face. "I thought I could do it. Divorce her, get Chris. Then she told me what she'd done with the Blade Institute accounts. It amounted to tax fraud in my name, big time. Even when she was sober she was Machiavellian."

And then his features tensed again, and he turned from her, averting his face because he was crying. "That's not true, either. I loved her. She used to... She really loved me. And she had so much brain she didn't know what to do with it. Never even made it through college for sleeping with professors and fixing grades on her computer till she got thrown out."

The two European universities took on new meaning. And so did his asking if she had slept with Michael Avery.

He was shaking his head against his arm. "And then Erika. You want the good part, Jean?" He turned and looked at her. "After she does this senseless thing—gets mad I took her car keys, has the chauffeur hot-wire her car, pulls out of the driveway and tries to take me out, but it's Erika. After all that, when she's lucid enough to know what she did, she wants to make sure none of us thinks she feels guilty. So she sleeps with my sister's fiancé! Comprehend it! I don't." He stood up, pulling off his slicker. "I'm going in the water."

As he stripped off the rest of his clothes, Jean peeled off her wet suit. The Mexican sun was shining through the faint misty remnants of the fog, a light water vapor in the air. It did nothing to warm away the chill in her bones. Goose bumps crept over her skin, and she was glad for the little protection of her purple swimsuit. She'd only taken off her wet suit so David could feel her skin, if he wanted or needed it.

As he walked naked to the shore, she followed, wading into the low breakers a few steps behind him, grateful that a curve in the coastline put them out of sight of the ship and the other boats in the cove.

David waited for her, and then they dove into the sea together and swam out until the water rose to his shoulders and Jean no longer touched bottom. She treaded water and ducked her head back in the salt and watched him do the same, a dozen times, rubbing his skin and his face. And she understood what he had been doing in the shower the night before.

She accepted that he might do it again, for the rest of his life.

At last he moved close to her in the water, reaching for her body, pulling her against him, settling her legs around him. He said, "Jean," and held her close in a tight bear hug while the salt sea washed around them on Christmas morning, trying to make him clean.

## CHAPTER SIXTEEN

THEY DID NOT RECOVER the dinghy. Jake picked them up in the Zodiac, and when they were back on the ship it was only to weigh anchor and set out for Scammon's Bay.

Chris, subdued, stayed with his father in the wheelhouse until David could open presents with him. Jean left them alone and went down into the underwater observation chamber seeking solitude. For hours her stomach had been in knots, not only over what had happened on the beach, but over what had brought them there. Whatever the outcome, Chris had left the ship while he was under her care. David might be able to forgive that, but she couldn't. Not yet. And she doubted either of them would ever forget.

Down in the nose of the ship, she lay on the shark quilt Skye had made and thought of David, everything he had said, words that made the obituary in the *South Coast Sun* a lie. But the answer was easy. Discretion could be bought.

And then she realized it wouldn't have to be. The Haverford family owned the *Sun* and every paper on the south coast, lock, stock and barrel.

She was dense not to see it earlier. That and a few other things.

Her mind returned to the horror David had described, and suddenly the chamber with its motion and its blue light and the waves frothing past seemed suffocating and frightening. She stood up, banging her head on the overhead, and started climbing the ladder as fast as she could, wanting to get out, wanting to be near David.

DAVID OPENED Chris's package and lifted the lid on the box, gazing down at what lay inside. His son's face, in plaster-of-paris relief, painted with bright colors and decorated with feathers and buttons—child things. Jean must have helped him make it.

As he turned to say something to his son, who sat beside him on the stateroom's single berth, David heard a gasp from the hallway and looked up and saw her. Jean's eyes were wide, her hand over her mouth, as she stared at the mask. She said, "Oh, God," and moved out of his sight. He heard her stumble up the companionway, almost as though she were running.

David smiled at Chris, wearing his new tae kwon do uniform, and said, "It's beautiful. I love it. Let me find out what's wrong with Jean. Stay here, okay?" He set the box in Chris's lap and went out of the room, following Jean's course across the empty salon and down into the galley.

He found her in the dark by the sink, making a low moaning sound like a woman in torment. She was clutching the sink and crying, but he sensed the tears were mostly within. He said, "Jean?"

She jumped at the sound of his voice and turned to face him, hardly knowing what she was saying. "I'm sorry, David. I don't know why everything I've tried to do is turning out this way, but it is." Unable to do anything but ridicule her own appalling thoughtlessness, she exclaimed, "What to give the fiancé whose wife was run over by his own ship? plaster-of-paris body parts of his family!"

It took David a moment to follow her. When he did, he realized she must mean the mask. It was a moment when the only safety from tears was mirth, and what she had said struck him as very funny. She was upset, so he tried not to laugh, but without success.

Looking helpless, as though he were coming apart before her eyes, Jean said disconnectedly, "I didn't mean it, David. I love you. I'm just stupid. *Stupid.*"

David shook his head at her, and grabbed her before she could go anywhere. Feeling her shaking in his grasp, he said, "It's beautiful, baby. And I love it that you and Chris made it for me together. I never thought of it for a minute as body parts." Pulling her against him and stroking her hair and her back, he said softly, "Is it too much to hope there's one of you?"

THERE WAS—and also a photo of her and Chris peering around the sides of a hastily built sand castle. Beautiful smiles, Jean's like the one she'd given him that night when she opened her gifts, a new regulator and a silver brush and comb embellished with blue and green tourmaline. The last two he had won for her through lengthy and pleasurable bartering with an enterprising border trader, and after she had opened them he had brushed her hair for a long time.

Now while Jean slept beside him, David stared in the moonlight at the photograph of her and Chris, now on the night table. He thought of all it represented. His silent son, offspring of the marriage from hell. And Jean, who shook him, who never stopped shaking him. She had ridden him hard that night, so hard, as though she loved him more now that she'd seen the worst.

Which David wasn't sure she had.

He felt a numbing awareness of all he had dragged her through, what they had dragged each other through in the past days. With shame, he saw himself shoving her in the sand on Carlos's beach. This morning he had grabbed her and shaken her. He'd never touched Skye that way, ever, nor any other woman. It was beyond apology, and it made him sick.

It also made him wonder if they should be together, because something about it reminded him of Skye. The intensity. And it wasn't Jean, it was him. It was what he had felt in L.A., what he had felt in front of Jennifer Avery, what he had felt when he saw Jean on the rocky promontory with Chris.

He could also hear Erika saying, *Cold feet, David. You're getting cold feet. That's all. Just go on.*

But his feet weren't cold. They were ice.

He looked at Jean and rolled toward her to touch her and wake her in the night, as she'd told him he could, as he often did. And as she moved sleepily against him, reaching her arms around him, he knew he would go on. But only because he couldn't make himself stop.

TAE KWON DO KEPT HIM sane, and he realized neither he nor Jean had practiced for nearly a week. The next morning, before the sun rose on Scammon's Bay, he awakened her and said, "Tae kwon. Let's take the Zodiac over to the beach and get in a workout before the others wake up."

Jean sat up slowly, more slowly than he had expected she would.

He said, "We'll go easy with your shoulder. I know you have some healing to do."

Jean didn't answer but climbed out of bed and went to her cabin.

She was slow dressing, and at last David went to look for her. He found her standing beside her open locker all in white, her black belt in her hand. Her eyes were closed. She couldn't have seen him, but she startled him by saying, "I don't know if I can do this."

David understood. He'd felt something of the same thing when he'd dressed minutes earlier, but he'd moved past it. She needed to do likewise.

He stepped toward her, took the belt from her hands and wrapped it around her waist. Once. Twice. She did not meet his eyes then, or as he knotted it.

Looking at her bowed head, he said, "Ma'am, tae kwon do is a journey toward loss of self. You've lost some. So have I. Now let's get out on that beach and do what we do."

THERE WERE WHALES in the water, all distant but in such numbers that Jean felt as though she was traveling in a world that was theirs and not hers. David used the outboard but kept it low. Nonetheless, the nearest whales dove, disappearing from sight as the first crescent glow of the sun appeared on the horizon.

Jean watched them in reverent silence until the Zodiac reached the beach.

There, her feet feeling the cool of the sand, she knelt opposite David to meditate, realizing that since the last time they had practiced together they had become lovers. Yet here nothing had changed. There was a timelessness to the ritual—and a peace. In it she knew she still possessed the strength and courage to fight.

They practiced for an hour, until David said he needed to get back to the ship and to work. But as he helped Jean into the boat at the shore, her eye caught a commotion in the water about two hundred yards out. She paused, staring, and David followed her gaze.

He said, "Get the paddles. It's a hell of a way to move a boat like this, but it's best. The outboard scares the whales."

As he shoved the boat hard from the shore and climbed on, she did as he asked, found the paddles and gave him one.

They both dug into the water, moving in the direction of the turbulence, and David said, "I hope you're a good observer, because you're all I've got."

At the moment she thought her powers of observation were failing her. She squinted at the sea for long minutes before she discerned whales rolling in the water with great agitation, raising waves from the sea. Her pulse picked up as she realized what was happening before her eyes.

The whales were mating. There were three of them, a female and two males, David said. At first it looked as though the males were taking turns, and then it appeared as though one male was helping the other with the female, attempting to hold the pair in position in the water. It was a scene of incredible confusion.

David rowed as close as was safe, given the excitement of the huge creatures. The wake from the whales' aquatic lovemaking rocked the boat. He took two notebooks from inside an ammo can on the floor of the Zodiac and handed one to Jean, along with a pen.

"I don't want to write. I want to watch," she confessed, enchanted. She had never seen any mammal mating in the wild and in her college years studying whales had never dreamed she would observe them in their most intimate act. Now she was mesmerized, heartstrings pulled tight as she witnessed the noisy, clumsy, yet endearingly erotic endeavors of the gigantic cetaceans.

"You can watch now and write later," David said.

They gazed at the whales in awe, stirred by their awkward dance of love. Observing the whales' bodies struggling for union, David said, "It looks frustrating."

Thinking how easy it was with David, Jean turned to him, but he was staring at the leviathans, and she followed his eyes. Watching the female press her flippers to the sides of the male's body, Jean said, "David, she's hugging him. Oh, David, I love them."

David let his notebook fall to the floor of the boat. Pulling her back against his chest, between his legs, he hugged her tightly. Together they rocked over the water, voyeurs to the primal act of passion of the largest creatures on earth as the sun lifted slowly over the land.

ON NEW YEAR'S DAY on the way home from Scammon's Bay, they spotted the orcas. Jean was on the foredeck with

Chris, Dr. Geary and Robin Frost when Robin saw them and leapt up for his camera, saying, "Killer whales."

Jean felt a flicker of uneasiness, remembering that they were near the spot off the Baja coast where Baby had vanished. Of course Baby was nowhere in sight now, but the tall, black fins broad off the port bow belonged to nomadic orcas. As David identified them over the hailer, Jean lifted her binoculars for a closer look, watching the sleek black-and-white bodies rise and fall in the water. They were her favorite cetaceans, although mortal enemies of others. Ruthless killers, highly intelligent. Jean admired what she'd read of their hunting strategies, but she was glad Baby was nowhere near the ship.

The orcas were swimming toward the *Skye* and abreast of it, but slowly, and watching through the field glasses Jean saw why. They were at the edges of a torn drift net that seemed to extend some distance just beneath the surface of the water. Drowned seabirds and a few other unrecognizable animals floated in the net. Jean flicked past something that moved and went back for a better look. A trapped shark.

She turned to Chris, beside her on the aft cushions, and offered him the binoculars. "Want to see?"

He shook his head. He was playing with plastic horses, making mesas and buttes of the white cushions.

The *Skye* drew closer to the whales, to within a few hundred yards, and slowed to stay clear of the net. Jean continued her observations of the environmental disaster, the untended net, until she found the dorsal-finned animal struggling at its edge. The fin was not triangular but curved, and marked with a black scar.

Jean set the binoculars on her chair and jumped up, rushing to the wheelhouse and throwing open the door. "David, Baby's in that net."

Jake shook loose a cigarette from his pack and glanced toward the net.

David said, "I'm sorry."

Jean stared at him incredulously. "She's alive. Let's get her out."

David said, "Take the wheel, Jake." He moved toward her.

Jean stepped back. "Don't. I don't want to be comforted. I want to get Baby out of that net. We can take the Zodiac. David, the orcas will get her if she doesn't drown." Looking out the windshield, she saw the ship would soon be abreast of the net, but the killer whales were already closing in on the struggling dolphin. Jean could imagine Baby's frightened cries. The thought made her wild. "Think of Chris. Think of me. Dammit, David, stop the ship!"

He didn't touch her, but Jean sensed he would grab her if she moved a muscle. Eyes focused and calm, he said, "I care about you infinitely more than that animal, and I'm not going to let you drown in that net with her—or swim into a killer whales' banquet."

Jean said, "We could take the Zodiac, confuse them, chase them off. We could get her out, David, please. I'll take my tank. You can come with me. The orcas wouldn't hurt a human. You know they never have, ever."

David shook his head. "I've never interfered in the natural order that way, protecting one animal from others. I won't do it."

"David, this isn't just any animal, it's *Baby*. And that net isn't part of the natural order!"

"My ship is in danger from that net, Jean. We don't know how big it is, and those things can drown people. Jean, she's *under* the net. You can't get her out. You can't. Believe me." He looked honestly regretful, heartbroken for her. "All we can do is leave so we don't have to watch."

Turning from him, Jean pushed out the port door of the wheelhouse, going to the railing. The ship still hadn't reached the net, and the orcas hadn't given up. Jean thought of how faithfully Baby had swum with her on dives. There were times she'd been so lonely that the dolphin was her only friend. Because of her, Baby had come to Baja. And now she had to cruise past her and leave her to die? She would never forgive herself.

She spun around to go back in the wheelhouse and landed in David's arms. She looked up into his eyes, pleading. "David, even if she's going to die I want to see her once more. Please. Please stop the ship. Take me in the Zodiac. David, I love her. Even if she's dying, I want to be there. Even if I can't do anything." Laying her head against his throat, she breathed, "Please."

"Okay."

Jean looked up at his face, then back at the net.

"I'll let Jake go farther, and we'll stop. You can help me with the Zodiac."

It would take forever to launch the boat. Jean gazed back across the water at the net and saw an orca rise from beneath it. The others were tearing at the net. Her stomach lurched.

David said, "You couldn't have made it."

Jean did not turn from the sight. She moved from David's arms and faced it, the blood, the devourment. Baby, dying the death of a wild thing. A wild thing caught in a trap of man and left helpless against her natural enemies. Jean's heart felt sick, full and empty, as though she were dying, too. And she remembered the beluga David had known and seen butchered by fishermen.

They were even now.

"Jean! David!" It was Robin Frost on the foredeck, holding his camera in one hand and pointing to starboard with the other.

Four dolphins had joined the *Skye,* catching the wake off the prow.

The photographer said, "It's Baby! She's right here!"

Robin would know. He'd spent a week filming her. The dolphin who'd died in the drift net wasn't Baby! Jean took one look at David and hurried forward to the bow rail, over the sea-sprayed deck.

She was moving fast. Too fast. Watching, David felt a strange presentiment creep over his heart, darker and more certain than anything he had ever felt. He yelled, "Jean!" Then, without waiting for a response, he slammed through the door of the wheelhouse and went for the kill switch.

Skidding on the wet surface of the deck, Jean barely heard his shout. She had gained a momentum the water beneath her feet only increased. Stumbling on the forward hatch, her feet threatening to hydroplane out from under her, she slid across the water-washed bow and crashed against the bow rail. Clutching it as she wavered over the water, Jean stared down at the silver bodies of the dolphins, barely seeing them for fear she would fall.

A child's cry rang through the wind to her ears.

"Mommy, don't!"

Jean realized the engines had stilled. One by one the dolphins looked out of the water as though wondering why the ride had stopped. Baby lifted her head and whistled at Jean, but instead of responding, Jean spun around.

"Daddy, help! Help Mommy. Help, Daddy! Help!" Chris stood in front of the forward cushions, a distant, stunned expression in his eyes. Then, he began to scream.

David had emerged from the wheelhouse, and now he crouched by his son, watching but not touching him. Once, his eyes darted to Jean.

Robin and Dr. Geary peeled away toward the aft deck, Grant saying, "Don't forget I'm here if you need anything, David."

Slowly Jean started across the deck toward David and his son. Chris's screams had turned to sobs, and as David took the boy in his arms Jean knelt beside them.

"Daddy," cried Chris, "where's Mommy? I want Mommy!"

Jean had never felt so helpless, nor such a strange mix-

ture of agony and joy, because she fully understood what
had just happened. Chris's memory had opened, probably
because of seeing a woman fly against the bow rail. And
now he was suffering. What he must be remembering
would be every bit as painful as David's experience.

David said, "Christian, Mommy is dead."

"No!"

Jean realized the child was really hearing it for the first
time, the horrifying words that would bring down the
world. Because now he remembered.

Tormented, she stood. David's eyes followed her and he
nodded, as though he wanted her to leave. Before Jean
could feel the hurt, Chris's face, squished against his dad's
shoulder, turned toward her. His brown eyes solemn, he
reached out one hand, looking dazed.

Jean knelt down, and David gave his son into her arms.
But Jean felt his reluctance. It quivered through her like an
arrow hitting a target.

It scared her.


JEAN LAY in the underwater observation chamber watching
Baby trade places with the other dolphins as they played
in the wake off the prow. Baby had found a group, and
now, seeing what had happened to the lone animal in the
drift net, Jean was glad.

Her nerves were raw. David and Grant were still with
Chris, as she had been for nearly an hour, sitting in David's
desk chair like a bug on the wall while David and Chris
talked about what had happened that day.

*Yes, we were fighting. No, I didn't tell her to jump off
the ship. It was something she decided to do. She wasn't
in her right mind, Chris. She was drunk and on drugs.
We've talked about what that means.*

*But didn't she know she would die?*

Jean had been glad when at last Grant knocked on the
door of the cabin and David suggested she find something

to do. They were the first words he'd spoken to her after he'd brought her to the cabin with them, and since then an eerie sense of disquiet had sunk into her bones. A dread she couldn't pinpoint.

Overhead, the hatch opened, and a square beam of sunlight shone down on her, blotted out as David came down the ladder. Jean watched his long legs in faded blue jeans until he sat beside her on the quilt.

There were shadows under his eyes, and his expression was unlike she had ever seen it. He looked at her once, then eyed Baby through the portholes. But he said nothing about the dolphin. Instead, he told Jean, "We're anchoring in a few minutes. I'd like you to come ashore with me."

Jean studied his profile. "With Chris?"

David shook his head, then stood and started up the ladder again, never touching her.

Jean felt a numb foreboding in her heart, too inconceivable to credit. She didn't credit it. She reminded herself that David's moods were mercurial, that the restoration of his son's power of speech signified a major change in his life, and that Chris's grief must now absorb him totally.

And she told herself that if not for her and the unforgivable thing she had done by accidentally falling against the bow rail, Christian would still be silent.

THEY MOTORED to shore alone in the Zodiac, Jean bringing her wallet and her address book. David was still quiet, his eyes resting on her only occasionally, and the anxiety she had felt earlier returned. As she spotted the dock where he planned to tie up she blurted out the words. "David, is something wrong?"

He looked at her, eyes steady, his lips parted as though he wanted to speak and didn't know what to say. He nodded.

Jean knew. She said, "Will you please stop the boat?"

He tossed his head toward the dock. "We're almost there."

No! Her heart and her head screamed the word, not once but many times. She could hardly think or hear. There was nothing but the blood rushing in her ears. Feeling dizzy, she watched the fishermen on the dock draw near, was aware of David easing back on the throttle and steering carefully around their lines.

Minutes later they were on shore, and he held her hand as they walked up the rocky beach, heading north as the sun came down in the sky.

David was aware of her shaking beside him. He told himself she was going to be all right, they both were. More all right than if they went on this way. Together.

Even before they reached the dock he had seen she knew what was happening. She wouldn't look at him now, and he knew she was gathering herself. He tried to do the same, but it was impossible. He might spend a year finding himself again, maybe the rest of his life, but it wouldn't happen with her. He couldn't afford it. Emotionally he was in the red, had been ever since Skye, and Jean was too expensive.

She'd proved it again today.

Her voice shook him from his thoughts. "I don't want to hear you say the words. I already know what you want. But I want to know why."

David saw a big boulder being licked by the low waves near the shore. He led her toward it because it looked like a good place to talk. As they walked he thought about what she had asked. The answers were ready, because they'd been building in him longer than he'd known. He needed only to arrange them in cohesive order.

He thought of telling her the things that were right and decided it was only hypocrisy to mention what they both already knew. He wanted to keep it simple, yet it wasn't. Struggling, he said, "I don't need to tell you how grateful I am for what happened today with Chris. But I doubt I need to tell you, either, what it was like for me seeing you swaying over the bow rail."

To her credit, the look she gave him was not of contempt. It was disbelieving. *You're breaking our engagement over that?*

David said, "You didn't do anything wrong, Jean. You just did what was natural. You never even ran. I watched. It was just an accident, just something no one could prevent." He drew in a breath, pausing as they reached the boulder he had picked out. "A lot of things happen no one can prevent. Others can be stopped. But I can't keep you in a cage, Jean. You're an independent woman capable of calling your own shots."

Jean stared up at him, dumbfounded. It took her less than a second to conclude he was sparing her feelings. Nobody broke an engagement—a deep love affair—for such a reason. Not even David. She said, "There's more." She could guess what. That she hadn't told him about the Averys. That she had let Chris slip away in a seven-foot dinghy on Christmas morning.

That in bed they were so crazy for each other it was hard to tell love from lust.

That Skye Haverford Blade had killed herself and her husband had come upon her freshly mutilated remains in the sea.

David tried to answer her. "I..." He fell silent, letting the waves talk, instead. He closed his eyes, shook his head. "I can't do it. That's all, Jean. I can't."

Jean knew he was certain. David would not take such a step unless he was. And he would never change his mind. She felt as though she had suddenly run into a wall she hadn't known was there. And there was no way through.

A frightening combination of anger and fear and desperation mounted inside her, a reaction to pain that seemed beyond her, beyond anything she had experienced before. Seeing him standing in front of her, looking like what he was, a man of the sea whose eyes had seen much, she wanted to grab him, shake him, kick him, punch him. Hold him. Scream.

But David would think of her again as he saw her now. In the coming hours and days she might regret showing restraint in this moment, but someday—much, much later—she would be glad.

So she said only what she must. "May I leave now? The ship, I mean."

David nodded, thankful she had suggested it and he hadn't had to. "I can get a car and a driver to take you home. Or to San Diego, if you like." He watched a light sea breeze lift the tendrils of hair that had loosened from her braid. The same strands that always came out. He wanted to tell her that her hair was pretty, that he had always thought so, even before he knew her. Instead, he looked into her eyes, and asked, "Would you like to talk more, or shall we go?"

"Go," said Jean, starting back toward the dock and the road into town. She wanted it to be over.

As they made their way around a private oceanside enclave and out to the road, David said, "I have money for you. I never paid you."

Jean gave him a baleful stare, and he closed his mouth. He knew he could never pay her enough, and she knew it, too. But he said, "I'd like you to take it."

Jean surveyed the flowers in the bed along the path. The sunset was turning them to a crimson sheet. Red sky at night, sailor's delight. She knew the sky was red, but she did not look toward the ocean. It was part of him at the moment. It seemed to belong more to him than to her.

She considered what he had said about paying her, and said, "I'll accept pay for my work up until the night of December eighteenth."

David didn't have to ask what night that was. It was the date he had taken Erika to rehab. The night he had given

Jean his pledge. Now he was breaking it. He drew a crumpled envelope from his pocket and put it in her hand without looking at her.

Jean opened her wallet and stuffed it inside. It was cash, imminently practical. Combined with the money in her checking account, it would take her to Ceci, straight from San Diego. She told David, "Thank you."

There was more to settle. "I'll have someone bring your things to your house." He glanced at the cotton sweater and jeans and denim jacket she wore, which reminded him of the student he had hired weeks earlier. She was a different woman now, and he felt dismally the responsibility of changing her. But marrying her to pay that debt would be no favor to either of them.

He said, "You have enough money to...take care of yourself. If you like, I'll pay plane fare back to Santa Barbara."

They had reached a road, but before David could steer them both toward the next village of condos, where he could find a driver he knew, Jean paused and said, "Please don't insult me again."

He hardly knew what he had said, and he blinked at her.

"The plane fare," said Jean. "You don't have to pay to get rid of me. I'll go."

David winced internally. If she hadn't liked the plane fare, she was really going to hate the next one. So did he. Everything about it. But he made himself say it, because they were standing still and because soon they would be among others and never be alone again.

"There's a chance you could be pregnant."

Jean refrained from asking if this was a biology lesson. She could think of nothing to say on the subject that wasn't ugly, that wouldn't tarnish the preciousness of what they had shared. She remained silent.

He said, as though the words were hard to get out,

"You'll tell me."

She nodded.

THE DRIVER DAVID FOUND was American, a longtime security man for people he knew well. It was a person he could trust.

When the luxury car pulled up to the drive where they waited together, David opened a back door for Jean.

She moved toward the car, then turned and looked at him, her eyes brimming, glossy wet where they hadn't been a moment earlier. She was beautiful and good and didn't deserve what he was doing to her or what he had done.

He bowed to her and reached for her hands.

She gave them with her bow, and a moment of peace passed between them in the touch.

He said, *"Kamsa hamnida."* Thank you.

Jean echoed his words and did not rise from the bow until he did.

David suspected those two displays of courtesy might be the hardest things she had ever done. And the kindest.

As he watched the car pull away, lifting dust in its wake, he put the last memory of her in his mind, and turned back to his ship.

# CHAPTER SEVENTEEN

*The fourth Christmas*

IT DIDN'T FEEL like winter—or like Christmas Eve, although the decorations were out in force. Santa Clauses, Christmas trees and *karavakis,* tiny boats decorated with lights and ornaments, stood in all the shop windows. But on the shores of the Aegean Sea, the real anticipation was reserved for the bigger holiday the following week, New Year's Eve. That was the night for caroling and exchanging gifts, for games of chance and kisses at midnight.

Today was only the twenty-fourth, but the seventy-degree weather felt like summer. Minutes earlier, Giorgio had rolled down the corrugated metal door of his shop and closed up for lunch, and now everyone was home sleeping.

Except her.

As was her routine, weather permitting, Jean raised the sails on Jean-Claude's wooden sloop, *Time-Stealer,* and unwound the line from the dock. Ceci's friend was generous with everything. His house, his boat, his diving equipment. *You go away and spend a year in my little house in Greece, Jean, and you will forget David.* David, said the French way.

Now Jean sent Jean-Claude rent for the house. What Giorgio paid her at his shop was little, but she had money saved from her parents' estate and she used it. She couldn't stand the thought of returning to Santa Barbara, and here she was closer to Cecily. But Ceci had gone to Chamonix for Christmas, and Jean had decided to stay by the sea. This year it seemed easiest to be alone.

Months earlier, after she had left Ceci in Paris and settled into Jean-Claude's vacation home, a package had arrived from Santa Barbara, a huge, well-protected box with the return name Blade. It was from Erika, a watercolor of Jean and Baby swimming underwater. Jean had cried when she saw it, cried more when she read Erika's brief note, written on a card just like the one David had sent with the orchids so long ago.

> Jean—
> I never paid you, and I hope you will accept this. You might want to know David has been working on a book about Baby.
>    I want you to know I can walk and that I'm very sorry about you and my brother.
>
>                                                              E.

Jean put the painting on Jean-Claude's white mantel and tried to remember the days when it was only her and Baby in the harbor. But she could never remember only that, because the harbor was connected with David. Now, Erika's painting still sat on the mantel, but the little *karavaki* Giorgio and his wife had given her was beside it, a reminder of a new season, a new year, a new life.

She'd already spent a year without David.

Now, pushing the tiller so the boom jibed over her head, Jean let Jean-Claude's sailboat take her away from the dock and the marketplace on the Greek waterfront, the oceanside so different from others she had known. Here, the water was turquoise and so clear she could see the bottom. The people were dark and pleasant, and she liked learning their customs. She also liked Jean-Claude's sailboat, with its salt-sprayed icon of St. Nicholas, protector of seamen, mounted in the bow. The icon always made her think of David—and of Skye—but the *Time-Stealer* did exactly as the name implied. It stole the days.

She only wished something could take away the long winter nights.

Studying the sea, the Greek and American naval ships, she thought of an officer on one of the ships who had cooked her a delicious Thanksgiving dinner at Jean-Claude's house weeks before. She hadn't felt able to see him again. The same thing had happened months earlier, with Orion, the sponge diver.

Time had changed nothing. She still loved David.

Her mind flashed unwillingly through thoughts she had tried to obliterate from her consciousness. His face, so many expressions. The sensation of him holding her. His arms around her, her face against his naked chest, her lips on him, touching the scar where the shark had bitten him. His hands on her. His mouth on her. His body pressing down on her and into her.

The pain had not dulled. She could still hear his voice, talking low to her. *I love you.*

He had. Deeply. She knew she would be lucky ever to be loved so much again. But what had happened to that love? Had David just shut it off?

Or had she just imagined it, imagined that a two-week-long engagement really meant something, that a shipboard romance was true love?

Weary of questions she knew she could never answer, she studied the other ships at anchor. A huge yacht. Fishing boats. A barge. And a black-and-white minesweeper flying a Jolly Roger.

Her breath caught at the sight of the pirate flag. The ship

was anchored farther south, straight out from the cobble-
stone street where Jean-Claude's white house perched on a
hill. The vessel wasn't the *Skye;* it was much too large,
completely wrong. But she brought the sailboat about,
wanting to take a closer look. He might have bought a new
ship.

If it was David, his presence in the Aegean would have
nothing to do with her. But part of her was quaking, and
her mind began spinning daydreams, the same as always.
*Take me away, my pirate captain, my warrior, my love.
Come, David, and take me away.*

The breeze flowed through her hair and she felt the sun
on her face and saw the beautiful colors of the jellyfish in
the water, and for a moment she could believe in Christmas
again.

But the dream was short-lived. The name on the stern
was a single Oriental character, and the national flag flying
from the stern was not the Stars and Stripes. It was blue
and green and white, probably from one of the smaller
countries in the Far East.

She wasn't sure what she felt, but she turned the sailboat
again, and lay back under the low winter sun, waiting for
the thief with the sail to steal her afternoon.

At two o'clock the metal doors of the shops rolled up,
and Jean met Giorgio in front of the table of candles. Candles were a big item during the holidays. Candles, nuts and
small boats.

Giorgio said, "You've been out in that sailboat, haven't
you? You're a crazy woman. Do you notice it's winter?
You should sleep at lunch and stay out of the sun. Your
legs are sunburned."

Jean looked down at the skin showing beneath the hem
of the colorful Lapland-style dress Ceci had bought her in

Paris, fresh off the runway, a dress that had cost too much to sail or work in but that Jean had been wearing since November for whatever she wanted. Ceci had promised her another like it for Christmas, and Jean had already guessed which box it was in.

She told Giorgio, "I use sunscreen."

"You've got sun in the brain. I'm going to watch you make change."

Jean laughed as she stepped behind the tables to the counter. It was the fact that Giorgio could speak English that had drawn her to his shop in the waterfront marketplace. His wife was from Canada, so Jean was particularly glad for their friendship in a country where the native language was difficult. And the job in his shop, little as it paid, was a godsend. It was another time-stealer.

She resumed the work she had been doing before lunch, stocking nuts in bulk bins, until a shadow cut out a tall block of afternoon sunlight from the concrete walkway outside.

Giorgio said, "May I help you, sir?"

"Yes, please. I know your shop assistant. May I speak to her?"

Jean froze, knowing the voice, remembering the ship in the Aegean, the minesweeper with the Jolly Roger. Disbelieving, she looked up and saw him, a bearded silhouette against the masts of the boats rocking at the dock behind him. She'd forgotten he was so tall.

Giorgio was regarding him suspiciously.

Jean stepped toward the candle table, uncertain of her legs. "I do know him, Giorgio."

Giorgio eyed her doubtfully. Then, suddenly, he smiled, as though it had just dawned on him what David was to her. As though the appearance of the tall, handsome American explained something that had puzzled him forever. He told Jean, "You want time off? You can have the afternoon off. Just stay out of the sun."

Jean stared at David. He was wearing a long-sleeved shirt with wide, bold stripes, black and red, that made her think of pirates. He looked as he did in her memories, and she wondered why he was there, what he wanted.

If he was her dream come true.

David made a slight motion of his head, a *Please come*.

She said, "Thanks, Giorgio," and squeezed between the bulk bins and the candles.

David watched as she stepped onto the boardwalk. In the black Scandinavian-style dress with its accents of red and blue she looked like a painting, more vivid than reality. Her hair was held back with a red crocheted ribbon in a ponytail so loose it seemed to be slipping out, and David could tell she'd been on the water that day. It was on her skin and her hair. She looked only a little different than before, a year different. It made him uneasy, aware of the chasm he'd put between them. She was beautiful, more beautiful than he remembered, and he was surprised she had chosen to speak with him at all.

But she had always been polite.

She looked up at him expectantly, and he saw that her eyes were the color of the sea they stood beside. The Aegean.

He finally remembered how to talk. "Will you walk on the beach with me?"

She smiled a little. "Sure, David."

Hearing her say his name changed the rhythm of his breath. He said nothing more, just indicated the path at the edge of the waterfront, past the shops and the docks and the shrine to St. Nicholas, the path that led down to the sea.

The beach was rock, and Jean couldn't help saying,

"This really isn't a walking kind of beach. It's a sitting kind of beach." She felt proud of herself for saying something so impersonal, casual and light. She felt none of those things. Her heart was racing.

David glanced behind them toward the marketplace with its Santa Clauses and lights, holiday decorations from the West. He eyed the wooden fishing boats offshore, and the white houses set back on the dry, rocky hill. They were alone. Jean stood before him with a stillness he remembered and admired.

Pained by his own stupidity, by things that couldn't be undone, he asked, "May I hold your hands?"

Jean looked down at his. She nodded and watched him reach for her, hold her fingers and her palms. She thought of his hands touching her, gently and roughly both. She remembered everything, not least what he had done in the end.

David felt the wind of the Aegean blowing over him, mild as the afternoon, and it affected him, made him do the only thing he could. He dropped her hands and fell to his knees on the rocks before her. And bowing his head, he made himself speak, formal words that fell from his mouth unrehearsed, in lieu of others he had planned. "I don't have the right to touch you or to stand holding your hands. When I broke our engagement a year ago, I showed you dishonor—my own. Now I ask your forgiveness, though I don't deserve it."

Jean stared at him, the muscular man at her feet, bowing to her. And she knew that act as no sign of abasement but as the ultimate show of respect. For her.

She couldn't deny his plea, and she whispered with as much honesty as she'd ever felt, "David, I hope you didn't come to Greece to ask me that." He straightened his shoulders but did not move, and she said softly, appreciatively, "You're forgiven, sir."

She sat down on a low rock beside him, and he sat back on his heels looking at her, studying her, possibly wanting her. She wasn't sure. There was respect in his eyes, and as she watched him, her eyes caressing the bones of his face, she realized that whatever happened from this point onward, she was healed. Being apart from him could not feel good, but he had shown her in the most powerful way that she still owned his respect.

And she remembered that respect was love in plain clothes.

She found herself saying, "David, I'm not going to get down on my knees to say this, but I've had time for thinking here, especially about the Averys. After you asked me to marry you, I should have told you." Before he could comment, she said, "As for what happened with Chris on Christmas morning, well, I don't know how I could have stopped it."

"Neither do I, since you and I were both in bed when he left," said David.

Jean blinked at him.

"When we left that morning, Ken, Robin and Grant all noticed the dinghy missing and made up their own explanations in their heads. I didn't know that until you were off the ship. Then each of them told me." And what they'd told him, obliquely, was that he'd done a stupid thing. Chris had been more direct; he had cried. David told Jean, "In any case, that had nothing to do with why…" He drew a quiet breath. "Why I did what I did." After a moment he said, "I denied Avery's grant. I'm sorry for the things I said to you that night." He moved and sat on a rock nearby and looked out at the ships.

He was silent for a long time, and at last, because he

wasn't saying what she wanted to hear, Jean made herself be sociable. "Did you buy a new ship?"

He glanced at her. "Yes. It's a 130-foot minesweeper. It's called *Him*."

Jean smiled. "That's a funny name for a her." But she knew that *him* was the Korean word for the internal life force. She admitted, "I saw her when I was sailing today. What's that flag you're flying? Is it Korean?"

David stared at her for a moment, puzzled. Then, comprehending, he said, "Jean, that's the Blade Institute flag." For a moment he enjoyed the color flooding her cheeks. Then he said, "Actually I hoped you'd come out and see it tonight. The ship, that is. I still have your bonsai tree."

It sounded like it was something he'd been meaning to return. A wave of misery washed over her. She didn't want to be friends or kiss him casually on the deck of his ship or under the mistletoe or make love to him before he cruised away. She wanted him to take her along, forever.

He said, "Or we could go dancing. Isn't this a big night for parties here?"

It was. The twenty-fourth was Reveyon, the night of revelry, and there were dances everywhere. But it was also Christmas Eve, and Jean asked, "Where's Chris?"

David nodded toward an island, a landmass across the water to the east. "He's with Erika. He's made some little friends, and they want him to go caroling with them tonight. They go from house to house and play drums and ring metal triangles—"

Jean grinned. "And people give them money."

"Yes. He likes that idea."

Jean thought of Chris singing carols. Chris, whom she had wanted to be her son. She wouldn't know his voice if she heard it. She asked David, "How is he?"

"Great. He barks a lot."

Jean smiled, bent to rearrange a damp stone near her feet. "Playing Hank?"

He nodded. "I'm the cowboy, and Choong-Moo is Drover the deputy."

"Choong-Moo?"

"Ship's cat. A very fat kitten. You're not allergic, are you?"

Jean shook her head, wondering why he'd asked. *Please*, she thought.

David's eyes held hers in the sunlight, and Jean watched the emotion flicker over them. At last he said softly, "Jean, you've given me your forgiveness, but I know nothing can make up for what I've done."

Jean felt her throat swelling. She said, "It's okay." She realized she did want to hold him and be held by him, even if he was leaving. Not touching was too hard.

David said, "I was scared, Jean. Scared of what I felt. Do you understand?" When she looked into his eyes but didn't answer, he said, "This year I've tried to put things back as they were before I met you. But everything is too different." He thought of the long months, the nights when he sat in the dark with only her bonsai for company, listening to the indifferent water sloshing the sides of his ship. He'd ached for her body, and for a long time had convinced himself it was only that. He hadn't known his sadness was visible, tangible to those around him.

He said to Jean, "I think I told you once about a place I go to in Ventura to practice tae kwon do. The master is a very old Korean. He's taught me a great deal, and a few months ago he told me a story. An allegory. It was about a man who had a valuable vase he was always afraid would be broken. He kept it for years and years, never enjoying it as completely as he might have if he hadn't feared for it so. One day it did break, and he realized then that it had been broken all along, that its destructability was inherent and that he should have let himself love it and not worried about its safety.''

Jean was watching his face and he told her, ''Jean, you're the vase I've been afraid to have for fear you'd break. And now—I want to love you.'' He tried to read the expression in her eyes, and he saw she was near tears. Emotion threatening to close his own throat, he whispered, ''May I?''

She was huddling on the rock, biting her lip, and David wasn't sure if she was thinking of refusal or if she was simply vulnerable. She had given him her heart once, and he had stepped on it as he walked away.

Rising, he reached for her hands, and after a moment that seemed too long she gave them. He pulled her to her feet, then led her to a large flat rock on the ground nearby. When they both stood upon it, he said, *''Anj-oh.''*

Sit, thought Jean. Responding, she kicked off her shoes, knelt on the rock across from him and sat back on her heels. David knelt in front of her, his knees touching hers.

Closing her eyes, she listened to the sea and the creaking of the nearby docks and the silent chant of time. She felt him take her hands.

His voice was low, carried on the wind. ''Ma'am, you are precious to me, like the life you gave back to me. Your goodness is more than I deserve, your beauty more than I ever wanted. I love you more than I have ever loved a soul on earth. Please look at me and tell me now if you will make me the happiest of men by becoming my wife.''

Jean opened her eyes. David was there, eyes on her, the only man she had ever wanted. She said, ''Yes, sir. I will.''

He took her hand and slid a band around her finger, a band of gold for a pirate's maiden. As her hair blew around her in the breeze by the sea, she seemed like one to David. His maiden.

Jean looked down. A black pearl was set alongside a ring made by the curved body of a dolphin.

David said, "The wedding ring is the mate, another dolphin. They look after the pearl together."

Jean smiled down at the ring, then up at him. "It's a beautiful pearl."

"I found it."

Jean's eyes teared. "I love you, David."

He reached for her and drew her down beside him on the rock, then put his mouth near hers, wanting her as he had for so long. Now she was really his, and he was hers. His heart felt as though it would explode with the knowledge. He said, "Merry Christmas, Jean," and he told her again how much he loved her.

And he kissed her while they lay by the sea.

**He planned to decorate with Holly all year round...**

# Deck the Halls
## Heather MacAllister

# CHAPTER ONE

"I NEED A HUNDRED and fifty polar bears." Holly Hall paced as far as the phone cord would let her. "I need them right now!" She stopped abruptly then took a deep calming breath.

"Yes, I know you close at eight, but this is an emergency and right on your way and—" She listened, eyes shut tightly in annoyance. "All right...yes, I understand."

One eye opened to glare at the partially decorated Christmas tree. She plucked off an innocent brown teddy-bear ornament and glared at it, too. "If a hundred bears are all you've got, fine. I'm in the Meecham building—the penthouse—and please, please hurry."

Holly had begun to hang up the phone when a loud chattering made her jerk it back to her ear. "What? But Mrs. Bloom—" She stopped abruptly, not daring to antagonize her best supplier. Besides, she'd already exhausted all the others.

"Yes, I'll pay you now. Well, by check..."

"And have it bounce all the way to the bank?" Mrs. Bloom's grating voice screeched in Holly's ear.

"We're doing better this season, Mrs. Bloom." Holly ignored the familiar flush of humiliation that stung her cheeks. She gripped the receiver. "Deck the Halls hasn't bounced a check all year. And you know I always pay you back as soon as I get the money." Holly kept her voice coolly professional and took out her frustration by yanking off the bear ornaments.

"That you did," Mrs. Bloom wheezed. "But who's to say this check will be good? Your credit's shot. I gotta eat, ya know."

*You haven't missed a meal in thirty years,* Holly wanted to say. She also wanted to slam down the receiver and never deal with this cantankerous old woman again. And she would have, if she didn't need those darn polar bears.

"The bank's closed and I don't have that much money in my purse. I've got to have those bears tonight." She hated begging.

"Do you now?" Mrs. Bloom fell silent, making Holly wait. "Cash, or nothing."

Holly stared at the gorgeous but nearly naked white-flocked Christmas tree. "I'm doing the decorations for *Town Square*'s Christmas issue. People might want to know where I buy my ornaments." Holly swallowed and licked her dry lips, hoping her unspoken implication would be enough to sway Mrs. Bloom.

Silence.

"So, if you could bring those bears to me and some of the little black top hats—" she gulped in a quick breath "—I'd...I'd be willing to pay extra," she finished in a rush.

Mrs. Bloom cackled. "You must be in a spot, sure enough. Last-minute job?"

Holly raked her fingers through her curly brown hair and sent an agonized look heavenward. "No," she mumbled, wishing Mrs. Bloom wouldn't enjoy the torture so much. "Whoever is staying here," she explained glancing toward the nearest bedroom, "will be back at ten o'clock. The photographers are coming tomorrow morning."

"Get one of your sisters to pick 'em up."

Another deep breath. The smell of new fabric dye and fresh paint was beginning to give her a headache. "They're on another job right now."

Holly snatched the last bear off, threw it on a white silk sofa and kicked one of the boxes filled with tiny, medium and large brown bears. What idiot had chosen that theme for this elegant apartment?

A professionally decorated Art Deco penthouse, with a breathtaking view of the Dallas skyline, shouldn't have cutesy brown bears cavorting on the Christmas tree. This was a place of shiny black and white, punched with red and silver—and she had an absolutely *perfect* Art Deco tree in her portfolio.

Well, the scheduling sheet did say the law firm had chosen the bears, but at least she could change their color—if only Mrs. Bloom would cooperate. Detestable woman. At least she hadn't prattled on about how the "mighty had fallen" again this year.

"I said, maybe we could work something out." The voice boomed in Holly's ear.

Holly shook her head slightly, suspecting what would come next. Smiling wryly, she decided to get it over with. "Got a fancy party coming up?"

"Ruthie's wedding. Herman's niece? She's marrying the Battley boy. You know him?"

"No," Holly said faintly.

"Course you don't," Mrs. Bloom continued, undeterred. "I wanna look nice. Herman's people always look down their noses at me. So I wanna look nice. You know what I mean?"

Holly squinted at the bears and thought about the photo spread in *Town Square* magazine. Her biggest break. Free advertising... "You want to borrow Mama's necklace again."

Mrs. Bloom's smile was nearly audible. "Call it collateral until your check clears."

Holly thought briefly of the diamonds sparkling around her mother's neck and sighed softly. "Let me give you directions to the penthouse."

She allowed herself the luxury of slamming down the receiver—after giving detailed directions to both Mrs. Bloom and her husband, Herman.

"Old bi—" Holly stared at the phone. "No," she said thoughtfully. "Battle-ax." She tried the word again. "Battle-ax." *That* was Mrs. Bloom.

Now for the tree. Holly collapsed on the sofa, grabbed the teddy bear and absently tossed it from hand to hand. "You and your friends will have to go," she said to the ill-treated bear as she surveyed the boxes of decorations she'd brought.

The green plaid ribbon was also out for this room; there weren't even any plants. She got up and scanned the living area, trying to see it through the photographer's eyes. The tree would stay in front of the massive windows to capitalize on the fabulous view, no doubt about that. It was too bad the magazine people were coming in the morning; with the colors in this apartment, a night shoot would have been spectacular.

Holly glanced at her watch, then dragged both hands through her hair. Two hours wasn't enough time to do the kind of job she wanted. This Christmas tree had to be perfect. No, more than perfect.

Not that she was complaining. This was a good year, but it could be better—it *had* to be better. And she didn't need a couple of hundred cute bears giving her trouble, either.

Now, what could she salvage? Holly studied the tree. She'd keep the tiny white fairy lights. Thank heavens the tree was heavily flocked with white. Unfortunately the green plaid tree skirt was the only one she'd brought. It would have to go, and so would the gold beading. She ripped the strands from the tree, thinking furiously. Dumping the handful of beads into a box, she looked through the extra odds and ends she'd brought with her.

"Yes!" She pounced on the new silver ribbon she'd ordered. She'd use it to make the big bows that were a trademark of her Deck the Halls Christmas-decorating firm.

As her fingers flew over the ribbon and wire, Holly smiled to herself. Bows weren't that hard to make, but they didn't store very well. On the other hand, they were lightweight, which counted for a lot, and filled the gaps in nature's less-than-perfect trees. Deck the Halls couldn't afford to own more than a few artificial trees. In her typical fashion, Holly had turned this into an asset and boldly charged more for decorating "real" trees.

The buzzing of the intercom broke the silence. Holly collected her checkbook and the key to the private elevator on her way to answer the intercom. "I'll be right down," she told the security guard.

A couple of disgruntled Blooms stood beside the guard's desk.

"You and your sisters up to your fancy ways again, young woman?" Mrs. Bloom's nose was in the air.

"Everyone entering the building has to check in with the guard, Mrs. Bloom." Holly smiled sweetly. "As an employee, I just follow orders."

The thought of Holly as an employee apparently mollified Mrs. Bloom.

Holly gestured toward the two large clear plastic bags. "I hope the bears aren't all crushed," she said, then wished she hadn't spoken.

"And beggars can't be choosers, can they?"

"I'd hardly call it begging, at your prices," Holly muttered as she reached for the sacks.

"The necklace?" Mrs. Bloom snatched them back.

"I don't have it here!" Holly's patience was nearly gone. "Mama's necklace is at home. Come by tomorrow morning."

Mrs. Bloom eyed her shrewdly. "Thought maybe you'da run home and got it by now."

"Then I would've been able to get the bears, wouldn't

I? Besides—'' Holly looked her right in the eye ''—it makes me nervous to carry it around at night by myself.''

Mrs. Bloom snorted. ''Hmph. Your mama wore it at night. I still got that picture that was in the paper, the one of her and the governor dancing at the inaugural. Gonna take it to Ruthie's wedding.''

Herman Bloom winked at Holly. ''Nobody'd believe them sparklers was real otherwise,'' he said in an undertone.

*And they'd be right.* Holly kept a smile plastered on her face as she lugged the two plastic sacks of bears into the penthouse elevator. ''Mama's diamonds have more of a social life than I do,'' Holly complained to the bears as the elevator whisked them up to the penthouse.

Holly pushed up her sleeves and dragged the bears to the Christmas tree, then dumped them onto the floor. Hands on her hips, she surveyed the immaculately decorated room and the mess she left in front of the windows. She had managed to get the bears, hadn't she? Holly glared at them defiantly as the image of Mama's diamonds twinkling among Mrs. Bloom's chins came to mind.

Mama, of all people, would have understood. Laughing suddenly, Holly scooped up a handful of the bears and tossed them over her head.

IT HAD BEEN A LONG DAY. Adam Markland loosened his tie and leaned against the plush walls of the elevator. He closed his eyes and stood for a moment after he heard the doors swish open.

When he finally opened his eyes, he saw an angel—no, an elf—sitting in the middle of his living room. The sound of her laughter filled the quiet as fuzzy balls rained down on her curly brown head.

He smiled, revealing deep dimples. What was she doing here, this elf? This nicely shaped elf, he noted, watching her jump gracefully to her feet to gather the balls.

Holly turned off the lights, leaving the room in darkness except for tiny white lights twinkling on the Christmas tree. Nodding to herself, she flipped the room lights back on and turned in his direction.

"Oh!" She stopped and looked at her watch, then back at the dark-haired man lounging against the elevator door.

"I've been trying to think of something witty to say. With all of this—"he gestured as he advanced into the room "—there's bound to be a great line somewhere, but I'm so tired, I'm afraid you'll have to settle for 'Hi, I'm Adam Markland.'"

"Holly Hall, with Deck the Halls." Holly automatically extended her hand and looked straight into impossibly blue eyes. His dazzling smile, bracketed by deep dimples, made it unthinkable not to smile back. Her internal quality-control alarm went off.

Holly had a Texan's firm handshake. She noted the approval in Adam's eyes as he held her hand longer than good manners required. "What are you doing with the bears?" he asked, still smiling. She gently tugged her hand away, and laughed, then stuck both hands in the back pockets of her jeans. "I'm decorating for the photo shoot tomorrow." She quirked an eyebrow at him. "I don't suppose you were the one responsible for choosing these bears?"

Adam glanced down at the fuzzy brown sea at his feet. "No," he replied shaking his head, "I didn't choose the bears. Not that I have anything against bears," he added, covering all possibilities.

Holly frowned. "Neither do I, but brown bears don't go here and we had the perfect— Well, never mind. Anyway, I'm changing them to white—that's why I'm running late. I thought I had until ten o'clock." There was just a hint of accusation in her voice.

Adam gestured expansively. "As the sole occupant of the penthouse suite, I grant you permission to stay. How about some help? I'll be with you in a minute." He walked quickly to the nearest bedroom, ripping off his tie on the way, not giving her a chance to refuse.

Holly sank back into her pile of bears and stared at her fingers. Those couldn't be tingles. And if they were, it was because he'd gripped her hand too hard.

Mindlessly she grabbed a brown bear, pulled off the perky red bow around its neck and retied it to one of the polar bears. In spite of herself, she kept glancing toward the door through which Adam had disappeared.

The bow was crooked. Sighing faintly, Holly threw back her head and stretched her arms, then hooked her hands behind her neck. It had been a long day. Not for the first time, she wondered how Laurel and Ivy were doing with their tree. They'd insisted they could handle the decorating job alone. Holly smiled wryly. Her little sisters were growing up.

Adam paused in the doorway, tugging on a pullover sweater. "I've been doing that for the past hour, myself," he said, kneading the back of his neck before raising one hand and carelessly pushing back a lock of black hair.

Holly opened her eyes at Adam's approach and got another mental jolt. *Not now.* Not in the middle of the Christmas season. Besides, she thought she'd turned off quality control long ago.

"Are we tying bows here?" Adam squatted with difficulty. "Not broken in yet," he offered by way of explanation, grimacing at his jeans.

"Unlike these." Smiling, Holly gestured toward her own.

"Yeah." Soft from repeated washing, they hugged her lovingly. Holly studied him as his eyes unabashedly traced her curves, then flicked back to her face.

The pale blue of his sweater was a perfect foil for his cobalt-black hair and sapphire-blue eyes. Did he know that? Holly took inventory of his dark brows, his dimples and the tiny cleft in his chin. She liked the way his growing beard shadowed his face, giving it a rough look that contrasted with the soft sweater. Cashmere. Holly knew cashmere.

Adam picked up one of Holly's bears and she immediately realized she'd been staring. Feeling chagrined and a little embarrassed, she burst into speech.

"You don't have to help me if you don't want to. The law firm hired me to do this. It's my job." Now, why did she say that? She was desperate for him to stay. No, she wasn't. She didn't have the time or emotional energy to get involved with anyone.

"I want to," Adam said deliberately, his eyes holding hers.

All thoughts of insisting on her independence and self-sufficiency fled from Holly's mind.

They sat cross-legged, tying bear bows and exchanging unimportant tidbits of information about themselves. Holly decided there were enough red bows and began tying black and silver ones. She wanted to avoid looking at him. He sat there, surrounded by fuzzy bears, his long slim fingers tying elegant little bows around tiny furry necks. He seemed remarkably at ease.

"The brown bears and anything with green on it goes back in the boxes. How did you luck out and get to live in a place like this?" That seemed another in a series of safely innocuous questions. Holly knew that suites like this were often used for out-of-town clients, and she figured Adam would launch into a discussion of whatever company he worked for and its dealings with the law firm.

"The living arrangements are only temporary. Or they're supposed to be." He laughed lightly. "I'm the new partner at Swinehart, Cathardy and Steele. I came down from Boston a couple of months ago and haven't had time to find a place of my own yet." Adam was about to add more when Holly's rigid posture and frozen face stopped him.

Her eyes, a deep brown, were opened wide, and she

didn't bother to hide the dislike flooding them. "So you're one of the stealing swine?" Each word was an icicle.

Adam didn't laugh. "An odd way to refer to the name of the firm that hired you."

"A rather appropriate name, I've always thought."

"You've dealt with us before." It was more of a statement than a question.

He was treading very carefully. Just like a lawyer, Holly thought scornfully. She went back to strangling bears and didn't speak immediately, feeling a sharp disappointment. She'd been betrayed by blue eyes and a pair of dimples. "This is the first time...professionally." There was bitterness in her voice and she knew Adam could hear it.

She'd nearly choked when the law firm hired Deck the Halls, but she was a professional, and successful professionals didn't let emotions interfere with sound business decisions. Wasn't that what Mr. Steele told her when he'd refused to represent her case several lean Christmases ago?

Holly finished the last bear, tossed it at the others and watched as it bounced and tumbled down the mound. "A partner, no less," she said, looking at him directly.

"Yes." Adam nodded, his eyes assessing.

Holly hated it when lawyers did that, closed off their faces and gave nothing away, all the while conveying the impression they were privy to the secrets of the world. "I thought you might be a client. Or maybe a specialist here to testify."

"I'm not a trial lawyer," Adam offered, trying to ease the tension. "I'm a bankruptcy lawyer."

Holly's face whitened briefly and she turned away, gazing out at the skyline. "Lots of bankruptcy cases in Texas now."

Adam sat with his arms looped around his knees. "Not as many as there were."

Holly's eyes swiveled back to him. She owed him an explanation. It was just such a shock to learn he was one of *them*. "I haven't had very good experiences with lawyers."

Adam studied her. "Nasty divorce?" he asked in an impersonal tone. "Or was your husband the lawyer?"

"I've never been married." She said it without apology, but her staccato tones warned him not to pry.

Adam felt inwardly cheered at finding out that she was single. So, she hated lawyers. From the tight look of her lips, it was going to take an abundance of charm to melt away the icicles.

With that thought in mind, he strolled over to the fireplace and lit the log he found there. It was one of those fake ones, the kind that didn't burn very long. He stayed by the fireplace longer than necessary, since the log caught fire so efficiently, and considered how to approach Holly. He wanted to get to know her. She had a direct quality that attracted him and her brown eyes had assessed him without coyness. He liked women who didn't play games.

She was the first woman he'd met who wasn't a fellow lawyer since he'd come to Dallas. He knew Holly hadn't been indifferent to him. Adam sighed, not caring whether or not she heard him, and poked at the log, which didn't need it. As he slowly replaced the poker, his fingers traced the elegant engraving on the pewter fireplace tool rack: S.C.S.—the Swinehart, Cathardy and Steele logo with its flowing script. The log shifted and the fire popped. It was a loud silence.

*Stop being such an ass, Holly*. Now that she'd created the uncomfortable silence, it was up to her to break it. She knew all lawyers weren't like the rich, parasitic vultures who had fought over the remains of her father's estate for the past four and a half years. And so far, Adam hadn't exhibited that cocky I've-got-you-right-where-I-want-you attitude, either. He'd even been helping her—without charge. That alone put him in a different category.

Gathering an armful of silver bows and garlands, she

approached him. "My parents always put colored sprinkles on our fires." She gave him a tentative smile and was rewarded with a breathtaking one in response.

"So did mine," he said his voice rich, velvety.

"A fire in the fireplace made it a special day." With difficulty, Holly dragged her eyes away from his and watched the dancing flames. Why was it so difficult to think all of a sudden?

Adam laughed. "Yes, it does take the chill off the air-conditioning."

Holly joined him in his laughter, her brown eyes reflecting the warmth of the fire, her brown curls glinting with copper lights from its flames.

"That's better. You have a nice laugh." Adam closed his eyes and inhaled. "You even smell like Christmas."

Holly grinned at him, revealing faint dimples of her own. "It's frankincense. It helps me get in the holiday mood." She indicated her armful of silver. "Want to help decorate a tree?"

"I'd like that," Adam said quietly. "I'll miss out on all that in Boston. Won't get home in time."

They stood in front of the tree and Holly handed Adam a bow triple the size of the rest. "This one goes on the very top."

Adam climbed the stepladder, leaning over as far as he could. "Is it straight? I can't tell from here."

"Yes, but be careful," Holly warned. "The tree is so full, I've been wondering how I was going to get the bow up there."

Adam finished securing the bow and gingerly straightened. "I assumed you'd have a giant bear sitting on the top."

Holly busily fed him more bows. "A Deck the Halls tree is always topped with a bow. We do make exceptions for angels, but then we have tiny bows surrounding them and ribbons hanging from those. But every other theme has a bow. I had a great one for the brown bears. It's just a simple bow with bears sliding down the streamers. Move that one over a bit."

"How's this?"

"Great!"

Adam looked down into her pleased face and caught his breath.

Holly was chatting merrily away, apparently putting her earlier animosity aside. "This is really going to work. I had my doubts and we don't usually go overboard on the bows, but I just couldn't leave brown bears on the tree, could I?" Holly looked to Adam for confirmation and flashed a quick smile.

"No." He loved hearing her voice. A pitch or two lower and it might be called a whiskey voice. It wasn't as rough as that, though. More bourbon cured.

Her movements were quick and precise, without wasted motion, as she flitted from one side of the tree to the other, anchoring bows. "Here." She pulled on one of his arms and draped long ribbons over it. "We're almost ready for the bears."

"Fine." He hopped down from the stepladder. "Have you eaten?" he asked suddenly.

"Mmm."

"Is that a yes or a no?"

"It's an I-had-a-late-lunch-and-I'm-too-busy-and-not-hungry-enough-to-stop."

"I suppose that's a good thing since I don't think there's any food in the kitchen."

Holly shot him an unreadable look. "Typical lawyer behavior."

"Hey," Adam protested. "There are all sorts of people who make a living delivering food to mean old lawyers."

"You don't get out much?"

"No. I flew to Boston for Thanksgiving last week. Other

than that, you're the first person I've met outside of the office."

"Business must be good." Holly's voice was muffled as she bent over the mound of bears. "Here, take these for me."

Adam took an armful of bears from her.

"Start hanging those on the back of the tree by the window."

Something flared in Adam's eyes. "Please," Holly added belatedly. "You have to watch me or I'll start treating you like one of my sisters."

Adam raised a black brow. "Not for long, you won't."

Holly watched him negotiate his way behind the tree, turning before he caught her at it.

"What do you think?" she asked a surprisingly short time later, her animated face filled with satisfaction as she checked the tree.

"It's...cute." Adam's half smile neatly displayed an engaging dimple. "Cute but simple. I like simple, but I thought you wanted extraordinary."

Holly sighed. "I do and you're right." She stared at the tree. "I'm not used to changing themes like this. I like to plan in advance." She was silent for a moment, going over her inventory in her mind. "I've got some white-and-silver-glittered snowflakes, and maybe some clear ones. If I had more time..." She looked at him. "I hate to impose—"

"It's no imposition," Adam assured her hastily.

"I was supposed to be finished by now. On the other hand, if I had a chance, I could get to a fabric store tomorrow morning. Silver lamé would make a great tree skirt. I could settle for white batting in a pinch..."

"But you don't want to settle when you could be outstanding."

Holly nodded. "If I could keep the key for another day..."

"Sure." Adam gestured negligently. "Come any time."

"Thanks." Holly ignored the extra invitation she heard in his voice. "May I use the phone?"

"Help yourself."

Holly was already reaching for the telephone when she jerked her hand back. "No, I'm not going to call them." She backed away from the phone clasping her hands together. "My sisters," she explained to Adam. "They're doing another tree and it's the first time I've let them handle a job on their own. I can't call them, or they'll think I don't trust them."

Adam slowly packed the boxes. "How about a toast to a job well done?"

"It's late…"

"But not as late as it would have been if you'd done this all by yourself." Adam smiled persuasively and headed toward the liquor cabinet. "This is bound to be well stocked. Yes," he confirmed, "it is. Now what would you like? White wine, sherry, scotch…bourbon?"

Holly didn't hear him. She had pushed the sleeves of her sweater above her elbows and stuck her hands in the back of her jeans, still studying her Christmas tree.

The room darkened just as Adam reached for a rich old sherry he thought matched Holly's eyes. He made his way toward her avoiding the nearly invisible black Steinway piano, guided only by the flicker of the fire and the twinkle of tiny white Christmas-tree lights.

Holly sat on the floor, leaning against the couch.

"Wishing for a bearskin rug?" Adam asked as he placed the bottle and glasses on the coffee table and sat next to her.

"Oh, Adam! Yes! Do you know where I can get one? I've got an idea, but it's a long shot." In her excitement, Holly grabbed his arm, preventing him from pouring their sherry. "Just think—the perfect touch!"

"No, I—"

"The *Town Square* people will love it. Maybe they'll

even use my tree for the cover." Holly hugged her knees to her chest.

Adam felt the potential mood slipping away. "Sherry?"

"Mmm." Holly was still dreaming of magazine covers. "It's good. Exactly right."

Adam shifted closer. "It matches your—"

The jangling of the telephone made them both jump. Adam was already off balance and managed to slosh a few drops of sherry onto his jeans. He looked around for something to dab it up, ignoring the phone.

"Aren't you going to answer it?"

"Why? The only calls on this phone are wrong numbers." Adam headed for the kitchen and a paper towel. "Calls for me come on the private phone line in the bedroom. But go ahead and answer if it bothers you."

"Penthouse," Holly said, wondering if she should add the law firm's lengthy name.

"Holly! There's been a terrible mistake. We're ruined."

"Laurel, calm down. Are you all right? Is Ivy?" Hearing the agitated voice of her normally placid younger sister upset Holly more than she would have expected. She was only vaguely aware that Adam had returned.

"No one's hurt—yet. But the sorority is furious. They said I switched decorations on purpose. I've never been so humiliated."

Holly took a deep breath. "What happened?" she asked with a sense of foreboding.

"The Alumnae Christmas Coffee is tomorrow and they said they picked the teddy-bear theme—you know bears are our mascot."

"And you've done a lovely Art Deco tree for them." Holly stared at the white bears—and the brown ones—in dismay.

"How did you know?"

"I've got the bears."

"Holly, you *can't*," Laurel wailed. "Listen, some of my

friends are here. They brought food by for the coffee. It's bad enough that they see me working, but they're being so nasty about everything. The Deco tree is classy.''

"But it wasn't what they chose. Is Ivy there with you?''

"Yes.''

"Get her to help you strip the tree. I'm on my way with the teddy bears.''

As Holly hung up the phone, she could feel a heavy fatigue settling around her. Her shoulders slumped and she frowned in disappointment. She had counted on them, *really* counted on them.

"That was my sister.'' Holly gestured to the phone as she turned to face Adam. He stood leaning against the wall, arms crossed over his chest. "It appears the design orders were switched. She has the Art Deco tree your firm must have ordered.'' Holly wearily rubbed her temple. "All that work—''

"Leave it,'' Adam ordered. "You're done in. I say the tree is wonderful. It stays as it is.''

Holly hesitated, wanting to believe him.

"I heard you tell your sister you were bringing her these other bears. Let's get moving.'' Adam began loading boxes onto the dolly.

"Thanks for your help.'' Holly secured the boxes with cords. "I'll try not to wake you when I get back here tomorrow morning to do the tree skirt.''

"I'm coming with you now.''

"Adam...'' It was tempting, really tempting.

"It'll be fun for me and you're too tired to enjoy anything right now.'' Adam lifted a hand to the base of her neck and kneaded it briefly. Then he swung her gently around and pressed the elevator button.

"No. I'll be fine.'' Holly shrugged off his hand and wheeled the dolly into the private elevator, realizing she sounded curt. She was tired and she was honestly sorry her younger sisters had botched the orders.

She turned—and saw Adam's expression. A frown had etched faint lines of concern around his mouth. "I'll see you tomorrow," she said to soften her refusal.

"Okay." Adam's smile didn't reach his eyes.

She had to face him until the padded doors whispered shut. She felt horrible. What was the matter with her? He had no business coming along. He was a *client*.

Her fingers hovered over the buttons, then pressed one. The doors opened. "Get in," she relented, "if you still want to come."

Adam did, and he entered the elevator with a blinding smile that temporarily banished all her misgivings.

"You won't regret it, ma'am. I'm an experienced tree decorator."

Holly laughed, feeling lighter and, well, merrier.

"Wait!" Adam stopped her from releasing the button and stuck his head outside the elevator. He gazed at the ceiling, then nodded.

"What are you doing?" Holly asked as the doors slid shut.

Unblinking, he regarded her lips and smiled slowly. "Measuring for mistletoe."

# CHAPTER TWO

HOLLY MANEUVERED her dark green van between the parked cars on the crushed-gravel drive and drove to the front of the white plantation-style sorority house. Two familiar figures sat beside a stack of boxes strapped to a dolly like the one in the back of the van.

Holly looked at Adam and sighed. "My sisters." She hopped down to unlock the van's double doors.

"Let me." Adam reached inside for the dolly, his shoulder brushing hers. Startled by the jolt of awareness she felt, Holly quickly backed away. Her sisters provided a welcome distraction.

"I'm *sorry*," Ivy apologized with an aggrieved look at Laurel. It obviously wasn't the first time she'd done so.

"It was humiliating," came Laurel's whiskey-voiced declaration. "And in front of my own sorority sisters. It'll be all over SMU by tomorrow morning. I never wanted to do this in the first place."

Holly quickly intervened before Adam was exposed to any more sisterly squabbling.

"Laurel, it was your idea to approach the sororities, since the students are busy with finals. And it was a good one," she added hastily. "With all the jobs we're doing this season, a mix-up was bound to happen sooner or later," she said, directing a reassuring look at Ivy. "Don't worry about it. I've got the right decorations, but we're going to have to trim the tree now. I know it's late—will it be a problem for the girls to have us working?" she asked Laurel.

But her sisters had noticed Adam. He flashed them a grin as he shut the van's doors. "Hi."

"Hello." They spoke in unison and turned questioning eyes to Holly.

"Adam is a temporary recruit. Adam Markland, my sisters, Laurel and Ivy."

Laurel sidled forward. "I hope you're aware of the honor, Adam. Holly never allows us to have guests on a job."

Every so often, Holly noticed, there was a drop or two of vinegar in Laurel's syrupy voice. "Adam lives in the penthouse that should have had the Art Deco tree. You remember—the one being photographed for *Town Square* tomorrow morning?"

If she hadn't been so tired, she would have been able to keep her own caustic remark to herself. She regretted the words even before Ivy's eyes filled with tears.

"I've ruined everything!"

Holly closed her eyes briefly as she geared herself up for another pep talk. "Are you kidding? This is nothing compared to what we've faced before. Hitches like this are going to happen. We just have to go on. We can make it work—we *have* to—and we will!"

Laurel and Ivy nodded as Holly spoke, responding to a litany they'd heard before.

Another crisis averted. Holly breathed an inward sigh of relief until she stood in the foyer. She came to a sudden halt, lips parted. "Did they steal the White House Christmas tree?"

The beautiful fir in the sorority-house atrium, soared two stories above them.

"We always got one like that when I lived here," Laurel said. Holly's shocked face didn't seem to faze her a bit. "You're worried about the top, aren't you? No problem. See, you can get to it from the balcony."

"I'm worried about the middle." Holly slumped onto the bottom step suddenly feeling very tired.

"I'll start unloading, Holly." Adam's voice sounded just above her.

"Wait. I need to think. We might not use these." Holly stared at the giant tree, elbows on her knees, hands steepled. Adam's hand rested briefly on her shoulder and he sat quietly beside her. The reassuring warmth of his simple touch relaxed the kinks in her upper back.

"Quiet! Genius at work!" came Laurel's snide remark.

"I'm open to suggestions," Holly countered. Couldn't Laurel behave herself just this once? "Even if you'd had the right decorations, there aren't enough for that tree. Didn't you tell them what size to buy?"

"We've always had a big tree here," Laurel said matter-of-factly.

"What did you decorate it with?"

"A mishmash. It never looked very good."

Holly rolled her eyes.

"That's why I was able to persuade them to hire us!"

Holly ran her hands through her curls. "That tree will swallow decorations. It needs more—that's why we charge extra for large trees."

"You always said simple was more elegant, that it was easy to overdo," offered Ivy in a small voice.

"That's not the problem here!" Holly said, her exasperation evident.

Laurel narrowed her eyes. "But you're oh-so-thrilled we had one, right? All evening, Ivy and I wondered when you'd show up."

"You called me," Holly reminded her.

"Just giving Mama hen an excuse to rescue her baby chicks."

"Laurel," Holly warned, acutely aware of Adam beside her. "We're all tired and edgy. Let's just do the best we can."

"If the tree in the penthouse is a sample of your usual work, your best will be more than enough." Adam leaned closer as he spoke, his words caressing both her cheek and her bruised feelings.

Adam had been so terrific, he didn't deserve to be subjected to this. Holly turned to him with a sheepish smile. "We usually get along just fine."

He smiled. "Sure you do. I've got a younger brother and sister myself."

She wrinkled her nose. "But you're not still living with them."

"Holly?" Ivy spoke hesitantly, her hands clasped nervously together.

Adam noted idly that Ivy's voice had the same low pitch as her sisters' and he'd run out of liquor to describe it to himself. Brandy? Holly jumped up and offered him a hand. He found himself grasping it, glad of an excuse to touch her again. He didn't let go, and for the moment, Holly was content to leave her hand in his.

Ivy continued, "If we've got the Deco *and* the bears here, what did you put on Adam's tree?"

Holly looked quickly at Adam and laughed. "Polar bears."

"We don't have them." Laurel began bumping the dolly down the two steps onto the tiled floor of the atrium.

"We do now."

Laurel shot her a shrewd look, which Holly met blandly. "Buy them from Bloomie?"

Holly swallowed. "Uh-huh."

Laurel and Ivy exchanged a glance before unsnapping the cords and opening the boxes.

The four of them stared at the contents of the boxes and then at the tree. "Okay, here's what we'll do," Holly said briskly. "Ivy, go back home and get the ribbons and bows left from that job where the tree was too small. And...don't we have some grapevine wreaths somewhere? Bring *lots* of ribbon. Any color." Holly closed her eyes to the wine-colored furniture in the public areas ringing the atrium. They didn't have time for the nuances of color coordination now.

"I've got it!" Laurel's dramatic declaration caught the group's attention. Holly sneaked a peek at Adam and wistfully saw that he seemed as fascinated with Laurel as every other man who'd met her. Even though she'd long ago accepted Laurel's effect on men, Holly had hoped Adam would be immune. Of course, she hadn't staked her claim or anything. And she knew Laurel wouldn't deliberately steal him—she gave her credit for that.

"You were going to tell us these bears were too small, weren't you, Holly?"

Holly gave her a lopsided grin. "Eventually."

"There are hundreds of teddy bears in this house. They're our mascot, remember? We'll borrow them and put them on the tree. We can use that pretty green plaid ribbon to tie bows around their necks. The unifying theme, right?" Laurel paused to note the group's approval.

Holly opened her mouth, but Laurel rushed on, "I know burgundy ribbon would be better with the furniture, but I don't think we have that much in stock."

Holly began to nod. "It'll work." She grinned at Laurel. "It'll work, don't you think, Adam? It's got to work." She seized his arm, looking up at him eagerly.

"Bear bows?" he asked faintly.

Holly noticed Adam was more enthusiastic about an hour later, when he found himself surrounded by several dozen pajama-clad young women clutching teddy bears.

"I like your job," he said to Holly as she whirled past him. "I'll bet," she replied, raising her brows at the line of nymphettes waiting to have Adam add ribbons to their bears. She hadn't missed the fact that when the girls returned upstairs to sort through their stuffed animals, many had exchanged voluminous football jerseys and ratty bathrobes for teddies of quite a different sort.

She could hardly blame them, she thought as she once again pushed the sleeves of her oversize sweater above her elbows. Adam had charm. He was older and had an innate sophistication guaranteed to appeal to the college women. And to her.

The tree-decorating turned into a party. No one had been asleep, even though it was approaching midnight. And clearly, no one had any intention of going to sleep now. Adam was definitely enjoying himself.

"I've got no right to be jealous. I've got no *time* to be jealous," Holly said softly to herself. They'd only just met, but she couldn't stop reminiscing about the quiet conversation in front of the fire, or stifle the tingle of anticipation she felt at the thought of seeing him tomorrow.

She was glad Adam had come with them, she realized, watching as he deftly fastened the bears to the branches in the middle of the tree. Not that she wouldn't have been able to handle it herself. She'd always managed before, and she wasn't about to go all mushy and helpless over an attractive man.

Of course, Adam's looks transcended mere attractiveness.

"Do you think we can get him to come with us to do all the other sororities' trees?"

"Laurel! You didn't tell me. That's fantastic—"

"Oh, we don't have them as clients yet," Laurel said confidently, "but we will. Just wait until word gets out about this."

"I think it already has." Holly motioned toward the disapproving housemother who had appeared on the scene.

"Never mind, this will make our reputation," Laurel said. "I guarantee they'll be talking about the Epsilon Eta girls for weeks."

"I thought you meant Deck the Halls's reputation."

"I did, but there *are* other things in life, as I hope you've finally noticed," Laurel replied with a nod upward at Adam.

Holly turned her direct gaze on Laurel. "I noticed." She chose another bear to hand up to Adam. "But right now, nothing can interfere with Deck the Halls. Nothing."

"A LAWYER? A bankruptcy lawyer?" Ivy looked at Holly in astonished surprise. Her sisters had fired the expected questions at Holly the moment they'd dropped Adam off at the penthouse. She had carefully sidestepped his occupation until now, though she didn't know why she'd bothered. After tomorrow, she wouldn't see him again. She couldn't.

"You made friends with one of those parasites?" Laurel looked at Holly as if she had betrayed national secrets.

"You mean vultures," Ivy corrected.

"What's the difference? Both feed off dead bodies," Laurel said caustically.

"Or dead companies," Ivy added with bitterness.

Holly felt relieved. Ivy and Laurel were helping her feel the anger and resolve Adam had dazzled out of her. He'd caught her at a weak moment, that was all.

She unlocked the front door to a home not much smaller than the sorority house they'd just left. "I'm glad you two didn't let your feelings show around Adam. It would be a novelty to have a lawyer on our side." Holly propped the door open with a box filled with odds and ends.

"We didn't know he was a lawyer then," Ivy reminded her.

"He could have made things very difficult. I was supposed to be finished and out of that penthouse by ten. I wasn't and had the wrong decorations to boot."

"Ah, yes. Bloomie to your rescue." Laurel rolled the dolly out of the van.

"Where's Mama's necklace going this time?" Ivy

slammed the van doors shut so that Holly could drive it around to the garage.

"Ruthie's wedding." It was difficult to meet Ivy's eyes.

"I wondered why she hadn't been working in their shop lately. Well, you better hope Bloomie doesn't dance with any jewelers," Ivy warned.

"Now that has possibilities," said Laurel, who'd returned for the second cart. "We could claim the real necklace was stolen. Is it still insured Holly?"

Holly shook her head as she started the van. "Too expensive. Mama only kept the policy so that Daddy wouldn't know she'd sold the real diamonds."

"Sure explains how she stretched the household money." Laurel dropped the last of the boxes with a soft thud. "I'm pooped. Let's unpack in the morning."

"It's already morning," Ivy said, heading for the stairs just as Holly came down the hall.

"Ladies, sleep will have to wait." Holly raised her voice to drown out the inevitable moaning. "The photo shoot at the penthouse begins at ten and that tree needs more more work. Ivy, why don't you look for those silver snowflakes? I've got some stuff I'd like to take over just in case they want some of the room decorated. You ought to see it, the Art Deco would have been—" Holly broke off and hoped Ivy wouldn't get upset all over again.

"Laurel, if you really think the other sororities would be interested, you should take the portfolio around tomorrow morning. We need to update our supply list so that we don't have any more mix-ups. After that, you can pack for the Stoffer's job. I've got two trees there. What do you think about doing an angel tree and the Deco one, now that the stuff's available?"

"I don't think. I can't think. I'm exhausted." Laurel pressed her hands to her head. "Holly, the main season's only a week old and look at us. We can't keep this up."

"We have to," Holly said grimly. "Look, we're so close

to making Deck the Halls support us for the whole year. You don't want to go back to Exemplary Temporaries any more than I do."

Laurel brushed her lightened, champagne-streaked hair back from her face. "Lord, I hate that place. Still can't pronounce it, but right now, it's looking better and better." She turned to go up the stairs, nearly tripping over a warm, inanimate object.

Ivy had fallen asleep, her head against the railing.

Laurel glared reproachfully at Holly. "It can wait until morning. Come on, Ivy."

Holly grabbed her arm. "The *Town Square* shoot is the biggest break we've ever had! If we play it right, we could have more clients than we can handle." Holly watched in vexation as Laurel ignored her, helping a groggy Ivy to her feet.

"Gotta get snowflakes for Holly," Ivy mumbled.

"Later," Laurel murmured to her. "She's exhausted, Holly!"

"We might get the *cover*. Don't you understand how important this is? You can sleep all afternoon!" Holly argued.

"I want to sleep now," Laurel said, each word distinct and final. "Tomorrow afternoon, you'll have something else for us to do."

"You're right," Holly said, making it sound like an accusation. "You two get some sleep. I'll come upstairs in a little while."

"Lay off, Holly. You can stay down here and play martyr by yourself this time." Laurel continued to guide Ivy up the stairs. "Besides, the Stoffer job is for charity and it's stupid to waste our two best themes on them."

Holly stared at her sisters and blinked rapidly. If they'd just work a little harder. That wasn't too much to ask. It wasn't as though it would be forever—just during the Christmas season.

She'd make it in spite of them. In spite of everyone. Holly ran her fingers through her curls and rubbed her neck and shoulders. She ached to follow Ivy and Laurel up the stairs.

The chirp of the telephone on the hall table startled her and she jerked up the receiver before the second ring. Who would call at two o'clock in the morning? Holly was tempted to hang up, convinced it must be a crank call. On the other hand, didn't relatives always call with bad news in the middle of the night? Memories of another middle-of-the-night phone call haunted her as she spoke softly into the receiver.

"Come have breakfast with me." The pleasant, honey-coated words instantly soothed her apprehensions.

"Adam." Holly closed her eyes and allowed her smile to sound in her voice.

"I'll cook."

"That's quite an offer."

"Is that a yes?"

The almost whispered words wrapped Holly in a sensation of warm intimacy as she stood in the dark hall.

"Yes."

"Sweet dreams."

Holly smiled and gently put the receiver down. Adam's words were a good-night caress. Had she already been in bed, she could have fallen asleep with their echoes. The thought was very appealing.

But not as appealing as a *Town Square* magazine cover.

Holly started walking briskly toward the laundry, hoping the plastic snowflakes were stored in what had once been the maid's quarters.


HOLLY HAD NEVER REALIZED how heavy a polar-bear rug could be. She enveloped herself in its musty warmth and leaned against the padded walls of the elevator, oblivious to the white hairs that rubbed off.

"I don't believe it." Adam shook his head as the private elevator opened and Holly and the bear emerged. "Where did you get that thing?"

"From the display window at a travel agency. They were promoting ski trips." Holly lurched over to the fireplace, heaved the bear off her shoulders and arranged it in front of the white-brick hearth. "Her name is Bianca."

"They just let you walk out with it—her? Or did you and your sisters do a little breaking and entering after you dropped me off?"

Holly's angry reaction caught Adam unprepared.

"We don't break the law." She gazed at him with a disturbingly intent look. It willed him to believe her.

The twinkle, usually present in Adam's blue eyes, was momentarily extinguished and his face became a pleasantly bland mask. Yet its mildness was purposeful and controlled. "I'm not implying that you do," he said in a voice that matched his expression. "I meant it as a joke."

Holly guessed this was his courtroom face, even though he'd denied that he spent time in the courtroom. It just seemed to be something lawyers knew how to do.

"Furthermore, I resent this unfounded hostility you have toward me. I was not involved in whatever legal problems you've had in the past, and I'm tired of tiptoeing around in case I step on your feelings." Adam stood above her, his face devoid of the warmth she'd come to expect.

Holly's lips parted slightly. She missed his smile with its outrageous dimples. "What was the question?"

"You three do a little breaking and entering after you dropped me off?" Adam repeated lightly.

"Nah. Would have been easier. One of us has to go back and redecorate their window."

Holly was wrestling with the bear and missed the look of tenderness on Adam's face. She looked particularly soft and touchable this morning. She wore camel-colored slacks and a creamy turtleneck sweater, and had negligently cast off a matching tan coat, which had slid from the sofa to the floor.

As Adam bent to pick it up, he noted the label and felt the extravagant softness that told him it was camel hair.

Holly was on her knees, turning the bear this way and that. Adam silently placed the coat on the sofa, next to the shoulder bag Holly had slung down beside it. A rich brown alligator. He shoved his hands into his pockets and checked her shoes. Matching loafers.

Adam began to piece together Holly's unmentioned past. Last night's visit to the private and expensive Southern Methodist University campus, accompanied by Laurel's references to her sorority, told him Holly and her sisters had come from a privileged background.

No wonder she was so defensive. He longed to tell her she wasn't alone. He'd seen plenty of Texas oil barons who had fallen on hard times.

"Mmm, is that breakfast I smell? Coffee in particular?"

"Uh, yes." Adam found it difficult to switch gears. "But that coffee has been sitting since six-thirty."

"That's only an hour and a half. It'll be great." Holly had preceded him into the kitchen and emptied the pot into two waiting mugs. She automatically removed the grounds and began to measure out more for another pot.

"I'll do that."

"Good." She relinquished the pot without argument. "I have a confession. I've already been here this morning and I left some boxes downstairs with the security guard. The travel agency wasn't supposed to open until nine, but I talked them into coming in early."

She was pleased with herself and had a right to be, she thought. How many cruises had that same agency arranged for her parents when they were alive? And the European "Grand Tour" she and Laurel had each taken the summer they turned nineteen—but Ivy couldn't. It was a favor for old time's sake.

"Better make a large pot," Holly said as she scanned the refrigerator for milk or cream. "I was up until four this morning." She found a white liquid in a cream pitcher, sniffed it and poured a generous amount into her coffee.

"Ah." She took a sizable swallow. "It's good. I'm glad you don't make wimpy coffee. I can't stand wimpy coffee." She drained her cup.

Adam glanced at her and added two more tablespoons of grounds to the filter basket.

"I'll be right back." Holly smiled breezily at him.

"I'll help you."

His eyes were even bluer this morning than they'd been last night. "Making the coffee is help enough."

When the elevator doors opened to the penthouse again, Holly had no trouble convincing herself to abandon the boxes and follow her nose to the source of the wonderful smells.

Adam heard her and had a cup of the milky coffee she liked ready for her.

"I could get spoiled," she sighed as she leaned against the doorway to the kitchen. "I see we're dining in state." She nodded toward the settings on the smoked-glass top of the dining-room table.

"No room in the kitchen." Adam handed her a bowl of strawberries.

"How decadent," Holly said before popping one into her mouth. "Strawberries in December."

"Imported from New Zealand. I got there just as they were unloading them."

"Got where? New Zealand?"

"I might have. For you." He met her eyes briefly before turning back to the stove. "As it was, I stopped by an all-night gourmet grocery not too far from here."

The only all-night gourmet grocery in Dallas was twenty miles away. Holly set the bowl on the table with hands that suddenly shook. Caffeine jitters, obviously—and not the disturbing intimacy of sharing breakfast with an attractive man she hardly knew. In fact, it felt perfectly natural to be here for breakfast. *That* was what concerned her.

"Eggs Benedict?" Holly watched as Adam carried in the plates and presented them with a flourish. "We'll have to do this more often." The remark just popped out and in less than a heartbeat, Holly realized exactly how Adam was going to interpret it.

His black brow raised; a half smile deepened a dimple. "Certainly."

Holly clutched her fork, determined to ignore all innuendos. It wouldn't be fair to flirt with him now. "I'm impressed. But does it taste as good as it looks?" With Adam watching closely, she took a bite, resolving to be complimentary even if it tasted like sawdust. At this point, she didn't trust herself to notice the difference anyway.

"I don't cook often," he warned.

Holly rolled her eyes and took another mouthful. "It's wonderful. Beginner's luck."

When Adam returned to the kitchen for more coffee, he tossed the empty jar of ready-made hollandaise sauce into the trash.

Holly nearly collided with him as she brought the dishes into the kitchen. "Do you have time for more coffee? Don't you have to get to work?"

"People can manage without me for a couple of hours."

Glancing at her watch, Holly wiped her mouth on a napkin. "Good. I want to help with the dishes, but it's nearly nine and I've got to get to a fabric store. Gus—he's the photographer—and the magazine people will come about ten. They had another shoot before this one. I'll probably have to beat on the shop doors, but I'm determined to have silver lamé for this tree."

Holly kept up her nervous chatter as she shrugged into her coat and grabbed her purse. "Thanks for breakfast. And please, if you have to leave before I get back, dump the dishes in the sink and I'll finish cleaning up later." She punched the elevator button.

"I thought I'd stick around and watch." The quiet words silenced her as she stepped inside the elevator.

The doors had already begun to close. Holly jabbed her foot between them and they shuddered apart. The look on Adam's face might have been the beginning of a smile. The sleeves of his crisp white shirt were rolled to the elbows, revealing the fine black hair on his arms, and he had a dish towel tucked in the waistband of dark charcoal pants. He still held the coffeepot, like a husband seeing his wife off to work just before he left for his own office.

A tiny lock of blue-black hair separated itself from the rest of the smooth wave across his forehead and Holly longed to push it back into place.

He'd be too distracting. She didn't dare allow him to stay, so this was goodbye. Even if he wanted to see her again, the timing was incredibly awful.

The profits Holly and her sisters made in December determined their standard of living for the next year. She was too busy to nurture a beginning relationship, never mind that he was a lawyer. Even when she'd first admired his appealing dimples and the brilliant laser-blue eyes, she had known the timing was wrong and would be for years.

Holly's lips were parted as she stared at him. Neither one had said goodbye. She took a deep breath; she was going to have to say it first. "I enjoyed breakfast. A lot. But..." Did he have to be so gorgeous?

The telephone rang. They glanced at it and at each other. "Here, hold this." Adam yanked her out of the elevator and handed her the coffeepot, then sprinted for the phone. Holly tried to convince herself to carry the pot back to the kitchen and quietly make her getaway. Her feet were fused to the Italian marble floor of the entry.

"Yes, Laurel, she's here." Adam waved an arm in her direction. "For you."

She set the coffeepot on the floor and practically flew to the phone.

"Holly? Do you have the fabric yet?"

"I was just on my way."

"Great. I'll be right up. You'll love this."

Holly turned to Adam as she replaced the receiver. "She's on her way up."

Adam walked over to the coffeepot she had left in front of the elevator. "Good. There's just enough for three more cups."

Holly grinned. It hadn't taken him long to figure out her vice. Off came her camel coat. She really did like Adam, she decided, even if he was a lawyer. What rotten luck.

"Not bad." Laurel entered the penthouse, looking first at the tree, then at Adam, who was bringing a third cup of coffee. "So you weren't a mirage." She took the mug from Adam and presented a Neiman-Marcus shopping bag to Holly. "See what you think of this."

Holly pulled out a long slink of a dress in silver lamé. "Laurel, are you sure?"

"I've got no place to wear it and you need the time." She sipped her coffee as Holly arranged the dress under the tree. "Here, stuff it with this." Laurel began to wad the tissue paper she'd packed in the bottom of the shopping bag.

"Thanks, Laurel. You're a lifesaver." The sisters exchanged a long look filled with understanding.

"I have my moments. What have you two been doing? I don't see any snowflakes."

Adam began opening the boxes Holly had brought earlier.

"You don't have to do that, Adam. Laurel can help."

"No, Laurel can't. I'm off to the Alumnae Christmas Coffee. I just stopped by here to deliver the dress—excuse me, tree skirt."

Holly sat back on her heels. Laurel's red silk dress and

the sisters' communal fur jacket registered at last. How could she think of going to a party when they had so much to do?

Laurel correctly read Holly's look. "I *was* invited to the Alumnae Christmas Coffee." She dangled a camera from her fingers. "I thought I'd go early and get some pictures for our portfolio, since Gus will be here."

"You're right." Holly offered a smile in apology.

Laurel bent down and ruffled her sister's curls. "It's okay. I left Ivy at home waiting for Mrs. Bloom."

"Oh, no! I completely forgot about Bloomie."

"You've got enough on your mind." Laurel slanted a glance at Adam and mouthed, "He's okay for a lawyer."

Holly nodded, with a wistful look over her shoulder as they walked toward the elevator.

"I'll be late getting back. I volunteered to be on the clean-up committee." Laurel adjusted her purse so it wouldn't crush the fur.

"Whatever for?"

"Leftovers," Laurel said succinctly.

"Good thinking."

"I told you I can think better when I've had some sleep. Just imagine what I could do with a whole night!"

Adam was on the telephone when Holly returned to the tree. "I need to go into the office," he said, rolling down his sleeves. He passed by Holly and disappeared into a bedroom, reappearing as the consummate lawyer, complete with briefcase. "I'll try to get back here for lunch. How about deli food and leftover strawberries?"

Holly's fingers raked her hair in the familiar gesture. "Adam, please don't go to all this trouble. I don't even know if I'll still be here." It was frightening to see how effortlessly he fit into her life, overscheduled though it was. She'd already caught herself mentally depending on him and she'd known him for less than a day. How could she allow herself to forget that the only person she could depend on was herself?

"I'll call first." He waved a hand as the elevator doors shut. "Relax for once."

Holly smiled to herself. He hadn't said goodbye.

# CHAPTER THREE

HOLLY FINISHED THE TREE, added Christmasy touches to the general vicinity and decided to take Adam's advice. Who knew when she'd get another chance to relax?

Maybe next year Deck the Halls could hire some part-time help or sales staff. It would depend on whether the exposure from this layout resulted in more jobs. A *lot* more jobs.

In theory, Holly and her sisters lived year-round on the profits from the Christmas season. In reality, they usually ran out of money by the summer and worked as temporary office personnel for a few months. Holly counted progress in terms of when they had to call Exemplary Temporaries. This year, they'd made it all the way to August. Of course, Holly wasn't about to let them come close to going broke. So they'd been working as temps since March.

Next year would be different. It would take only a few more jobs now to squeeze in September's and October's expenses before they began full-time preparations again in November. She'd have to be firmer with Adam. She literally couldn't afford to get involved.

Holly closed her eyes and thought of her parents. This would be the fifth Christmas without them. Five Christmases of struggle. Why did it have to be such work?

The faint click of a shutter startled her into wakefulness.

"Great! I'll call it Christmas Beauty. I could sell it like that." The man with the camera snapped his fingers.

"Make your fortune, babe. And the less you wear, the more you make."

Holly straightened on the sofa. "Gus, the only thing that's going to get exposed around here is film."

"I think I'll call it Christmas Cactus."

"I won't sign the model release."

He shrugged. "Pity."

People poured out of the elevator, dragging lighting equipment and extension cords.

"What time is it?" Holly still felt bleary-eyed from her interrupted nap.

"'Bout ten-thirty, give or take a few."

"Ugh." Holly shook her head slightly. "You look like I feel."

Gus grinned down at his fraying jeans and worn plaid shirt. "I'm workin'." He tossed back long, lank hair and rubbed his scraggly beard. "Didn't get around to shaving this morning."

"Or any other morning."

Gus shrugged his thin shoulders.

"I brought some extra stuff, in case you need to do some wide-angle shots. Who's in charge? Will you introduce me?" Holly studied the half dozen people in the *Town Square* entourage.

Gus pointed to a striking brunette in skinny black pants topped by a tunic sweater, then turned away to consult with one of the technicians.

"That's it?" she exclaimed in an accusing undertone. "You promised a lot of contacts."

"Look, babe, I opened the door. You gotta walk through."

With a look of exasperation, she thought of Gus's unabashed seediness and decided she might do better on her own.

"Hello, I'm Holly Hall," she said, approaching the brunette.

"Beth Robinson, with *Town Square*. Are you Swinehart, Cathardy and Steele's representative?"

"No, but they hired my firm to do the decorating. Let me give you my card."

The other woman nodded as she glanced at it. "The tree's unexpected, but I like it. It adds a touch of whimsy. I'll admit I'm rather surprised at the firm's choice. They have such a...formidable reputation."

"Yes." Holly smiled widely, frantically trying to think of something to say.

"I suppose the rug gave you the idea for the theme." Beth Robinson made notes on a clipboard.

Holly miserably wondered if Beth would put that in the accompanying article. It should have occurred to her before now that the law firm might object to the change in decorations. But Adam had told her the tree was great, hadn't he?

"Um, not—"

"Beth!"

She smiled dismissively at Holly and walked over to a man positioning umbrella reflectors.

"Classy place. Funky tree." Gus appeared beside her, taking light readings. "Weird choice."

"Gus," Holly said through clenched teeth and a broad smile. "There was a slight miscommunication, but everything's fine now. Did you spread the word that Deck the Halls has a few openings left this season?"

Gus smirked. "Only a few?"

"The tree's over here."

"I know." Gus crouched down, glanced impatiently at the white light from the windows and took some readings of the fireplace. "Holly, go stand over there, will ya?"

She complied, wishing the fireplace had a mantel and that she'd decorated it, since Gus seemed to find it so fascinating.

"Sit."

Holly sat.

"No." Gus waved her down. "On the rug. I see ashes, so the thing works, right? But you probably wouldn't know."

Holly stared at the telltale ashes, remembering. Half-smiling, she carefully unwrapped her memories of Adam: images of dimples, a bewitching cleft in his chin, and blue, blue eyes. She felt again the warmth radiating from the fireplace and saw the glimmer of crystal catching the light.

"Okay, thanks, babe."

Holly nodded at Gus. Before she got out of the way, she took the brush from the tools by the fireplace and swept the coating of fine powdery ashes from the white brick. It was an unusual fireplace set. Holly positioned the tools so the engraved logo of the law firm was visible and would get into the photographs of the tree. The name would add prestige to her portfolio.

WHY COULDN'T THE GUY have stayed hidden one more day? Of all the times for there to be a break in the embezzlement case... Adam loosened an already loose tie and waved the courier into his office. Simultaneously dictating information into the phone, he thrust a sheaf of papers into a nine-by-twelve envelope, scrawled a name and address on the outside and handed it to the waiting teenager.

With his now free hand, Adam plugged his ear, trying to concentrate on the tinny bureaucratic voice at the other end of the line. A few feet away, Bernard Steele, of Swinehart, Cathardy and Steele, spoke into the other telephone in Adam's office.

Hanging up the phone, Adam glanced at his watch, surprised to find that it was only ten-thirty. He wondered how Holly was getting along with the photographers.

"Do you think we can get those extradition papers in time? Joe's booked on the next three flights to Mexico City." The older man turned weary eyes toward Adam.

"It'll be close."

"Yeah." The other man stared at nothing. "I suppose it would be too much to hope for that lowlife to stay put. His embezzling might cost a good friend of mine his company." He sighed, then smiled. "Next time you talk to your dad, thank him for letting you go."

"I'll convey your greetings," Adam said after a moment, "but it was my decision to come here."

"Must have been a tough one—you being the first Markland to leave the family firm. 'Course, you have a different style."

Adam's blue eyes gave nothing away. "We weren't getting too many bankruptcy cases." He stood, but Mr. Steele showed no inclination to leave.

"Not enough for two of you? Isn't it also your sister's field?"

The expression on Adam's face warned Mr. Steele that this had better be the last question about the Marklands. "We each have our preferences. Hers is real-estate law— she likes the hours better now that she has children."

Mr. Steele nodded. "Children." His knees creaked audibly as he struggled from the small sofa. "You never know how they're going to turn out." He sighed again and faced the window. "I feel responsible, you know."

Adam glanced at his watch. He wanted to call Holly before she left. "Pardon?"

"How old are you now, Adam? Twenty-nine? Thirty?"

Adam reached for some papers he didn't want and sat down again. "Thirty-one."

"Eh?" Mr. Steele turned from the window to look at him. "I guess you've turned out all right, then. So far." He faced the window again. "Our embezzler is a friend's son like you. Younger, though. I recommended him for his job. Supposed to be a financial whiz, by reputation. Didn't really know him, though any son of…"

Mr. Steele lapsed into silence and Adam stifled his impatience.

"None of that matters now." The man by the window couldn't see Adam's irritation. "He betrayed a trust and shamed his daddy and we're gonna get him."

Adam didn't doubt it as he watched the wistful old man become the shrewd and ruthlessly razor-sharp lawyer the world knew.

"In my time a man's handshake was binding and he stood by his word. It's time we brought those days back."

Adam censored a cynical thought. "If we did, we'd all be out of a job," he remarked lightly.

"Not you, Adam. Now, I don't know what differences you and your people had and I don't care." Adam couldn't tell whether Mr. Steele had deliberately misunderstood or not. "I need people I can trust. They're rare, they're rare. But—" he whirled from the window, shattering his pensive mood "—a firm is its reputation. Without that, you have nothing."

Adam picked up his suit jacket and walked Mr. Steele to the door. "Speaking of reputations, it's time I got back to oversee things at the penthouse."

Mr. Steele blinked. "Is there something I've forgotten?"

"The photographers?" Adam prompted.

"Ah." Mr. Steele took a deep breath. "That's today, is it? Well, damn. We'll have to cancel."

Adam caught his breath. Holly would be devastated. He couldn't let that happen. "It may be too late. The photographers are already there. The tree is ready."

"We can't have them running all over the penthouse."

"I agree. I'll be back as soon as I can." Adam opened the door of his office for Mr. Steele.

"The timing on those extradition papers is critical. One of us needs to be here." Neither man moved. "And I'll be in court."

Adam felt a surge of anger. The old man was testing

him. This recent bit of nastiness must have affected him more than Adam had realized. He faced Mr. Steele's watery-blue unwavering stare, magnified by thick glasses, and thought of Holly's warm brown eyes. "Canceling and throwing the magazine people out after they've already got there is going to get you some bad press," he pointed out.

Mr. Steele winced. "Just what I was trying to avoid in the first place."

"I'll contact the decorator and have her oversee them." If he couldn't see Holly for lunch, at least he could save the shoot for her.

Mr. Steele's hand crept into a pocket of his baggy pants. "That'd work, I suppose. Tree look good?"

Adam nodded, remembering the mix-up. "It's... approachable. Friendly." He sat at his desk again, his mouth curved in a determined smile.

"Good, good. We're trying to soften our image a little. People seem to think we're too formidable and aloof." Mr. Steele shook his head as if wondering how such strange ideas got started. "Clients have been afraid their cases weren't important enough for us. Get too many people thinking that way and you won't have any clients at all."

Adam smiled, a real smile this time. "Yes, sir, it's a friendly tree, all right."

"Good, good. Doug Hall's gal did it. Got herself quite a little business. Would have made her daddy proud, even if she is a female child. He had all girls. Never seemed to bother him."

Mr. Steele pursed his lips in thought. "His death was a real tragedy."

Adam, who had been about to dial the penthouse, glanced up. "I don't know the story."

"Had some dealings with Doug Hall, like a lot of folks." The old lawyer jabbed a finger at Adam. "Now there was a man who did business by handshake." Some of the vigor left him. "And shouldn't have."

"What happened?" The leather chair sighed as Adam leaned back.

"Douglas Hall and his wife were killed in a light-plane crash on their way to an oil-well fire about four or five years ago. Worst possible time." Mr. Steele shook his head. "He was overextended and the oil recession was on. His affairs were a legal nightmare—or fantasy, depending on your scruples. Some of it's still in litigation. There was nothing left for the girls, but that oldest one wouldn't give up. I felt real bad when she came to me. I had dealings with other parties in the case and frankly, there was no money there. No trust fund—Doug Hall didn't have anything to put in one."

Adam began to get a horribly clear picture of Holly's experiences with lawyers—and with this firm. "Lots of publicity?"

"Oh, my, yes. There was the insurance suit and the fraud thing—some said he set fire to his own well. Nothing was proven, and it's still on appeal."

No wonder Holly hated lawyers. He'd just have to make her change her mind. "I'll give her a call then—since you know the family and you want the publicity."

Mr. Steele studied Adam for a moment and nodded slowly. "That'll be fine, Adam. We can trust Doug Hall's girl to keep an eye on things."

"PHONE'S RINGING." Gus dropped the light meter that dangled from his neck and glanced over his shoulder at the softly purring telephone less than two feet from Holly.

Holly fussed with a bowl of silver and red balls she had brought for the coffee table. "I know." She supposed she had as much right as anyone there to answer the telephone. She tried to make her "hello" sound authoritative.

"Holly? It's Adam. Photographers there yet?"

"Yes." Even with all the commotion, she had instantly recognized his voice.

"I can't get back for our lunch." His voice vibrated with genuine regret and she found it matched her own. "Listen, Mr. Steele wants someone there to supervise, or he'll cancel. I told him you could. Do you have time?"

She'd planned on staying during the actual shoot, anyway. It was nice to know she was now there in an official capacity. "Thanks. It'll be tight but I'll stick around till everyone leaves."

"Good. Can you squeeze in dinner tonight?"

The silence on the phone line was the only silence in the room.

"Holly, move! You're in the way." Gus waved her aside, but the phone cord didn't stretch behind the lights and her shadow was in the picture.

"Adam, let me go to the kitchen phone." She handed the white receiver to Gus. "Hang this up for me?"

"Okay, Gus!" she called when she reached the kitchen. The few moments had given her time to subdue the emotional rush she felt and put Adam's dinner invitation into perspective. He was obviously attracted to her and goodness knew, she was attracted to him. But putting him on hold on the telephone was radically different from putting him on hold in her life. It was better not to start anything; her life was in balance right now—just barely. One more commitment would tip it over.

"Adam..."

"You're going to say no. Don't." His voice was quietly compelling.

She leaned her forehead against the cool white tile in the kitchen. "Adam, I can't. I really can't tonight, but even if I could, I shouldn't."

"Holly, Mr. Steele told me about your parents. I'm sorry, but don't turn me down because I'm a lawyer. I want a chance to prove that not all lawyers are alike."

"You've already done that," Holly said. "That's why it's so difficult to say no."

"You've got to eat. I've got to eat."

He wasn't making this easy for her. "That's right, and tonight I'm eating sandwiches in a furniture store. I've got two trees to do." *And all these breakfast dishes,* she thought as she surveyed the monument to their meal. She added a mental reminder and wondered where she'd steal the time to check the boxes of decorations Ivy had packed for tonight.

"Fine," he said easily. "I'll bring the sandwiches and a few other goodies and meet you there. What time?"

"Adam..." Holly sighed in frustration.

"We've established the fact that we're both going to eat. I'm merely proposing that we do it together." He paused while she absorbed that piece of logic. "I've had too many lonely meals lately."

The rat. He was pulling every emotional string she had. "As long as you understand the ground rules," she said firmly, planning to review them herself.

"Sure," he agreed. "I get to work while I eat."

Holly laughed. "You're incorrigible."

"Absolutely," he said in a voice that sent chills down her spine as it warmed her heart. Her resolve had wavered and they both knew it.

"What furniture store?" he asked in the same persuasive voice he'd used during their entire conversation.

This was it. Holly closed her eyes. Decision time. "It'll be a late night," she stalled, hoping she wouldn't have to turn him down again. Knowing she couldn't.

"I do my best work at night."

Her lips quivered. "Stoffer's near Central Expressway. Six o'clock."

And this would be the absolute last time she could see him. It had to be.

"Haven't you started yet?" Holly asked Gus as she returned to the living area.

"Uh, had some trouble finding enough outlets." Gus faced her, but his eyes didn't meet hers.

"Didn't you bring extension cords?" She looked pointedly at her watch. "You're already an hour behind schedule, aren't you?"

"That's my problem," Gus sniffed, fiddling with his camera.

"It's mine, too. That was the law firm on the phone and they want me to stay until you're finished."

This time Gus's eyes did meet hers. "Good, I've got a favor to ask. Stick around."

Whatever she thought of him as a human being, Gus was a superb photographer, Holly marveled as she watched him work. She felt really good about things for once. Gus photographed from all possible angles, with Holly watching from the sidelines. Beth Robinson and her crew had taken over the penthouse. Holly didn't object. For one thing, she didn't want to sabotage her chance at landing this design on the cover of the weekly magazine, and for another, Beth had a good eye.

While the crew loaded the elevator after the shoot, Gus tracked her down in the small kitchen. "How's about you and me teaming up for a little something on the side?"

"Gus, why is it that you can make what is probably a very reasonable request sound lewd and suggestive?" Holly shook her head as she loaded the dishwasher.

Gus grinned and slouched against the doorjamb. "Just keeping all my options open. Which," he continued, "is what I wanted to discuss with you." He looked down at the cameras slung around his neck. "I'd like to take some more photographs."

Holly gestured through the dining area into the living room. "Go ahead."

"Not now." Gus squinted his eyes. "We're running late…"

"And you thought that your old buddy Holly would let

you skimp here so you wouldn't be so late to your next appointment.'' She gave him a disgusted look. ''Thanks a lot.''

There was a brief flicker of something in Gus's expression. ''No, no. You've got it wrong. You know how I am. All these people.'' He shrugged. ''I like working alone.''

''What do you want from me?'' Holly gave him a hard stare and began wiping the white-tiled counters.

Gus shifted and fiddled with his light meter. ''Look, I want some night shots. This place would be great, and there's a bonus if I land the cover. I want you to make sure that the guy who's living here stays away for a while tonight.''

''You listened on the extension!''

''So?'' He took in her outraged expression and gave her a little shake. ''Come on, I'm trying to do you a favor—''

''With a tidy profit for yourself,'' Holly interjected.

''—and I get shot down. What happened to Holly the Hustler? This might be the cover. Can't you just see it?''

Holly could, and had a thousand times. ''I've got to clear it with Adam,'' she said, ignoring his crack. She dug the key out of her purse and dropped it into his slightly grimy hand. ''If he says no, then leave the key with the security guard. Where can I reach you if it's not okay?''

''You can't. Keep him outta here until ten.''

''Wait a minute—''

''Thanks, Holly!'' Gus ran for the elevator.


''DRAT!'' SHE'D FORGOTTEN all about Gus's request to return to the penthouse, Holly realized in the middle of unpacking her angel tree decorations. It had slipped her mind in the rush. Maybe there was still time to alert the guard. Holly stared at her watch, then buried her fingers in her curls. Adam would have left his office by now.

''Hello.''

She jumped. ''Adam, you startled me.''

He looked around at the dozens of people working on their various trees in the mock living rooms. The sounds of crushed tissue paper as ornaments were unwrapped, the scrape of boxes, the squeak of Styrofoam and an occasional tinkle of breaking glass surrounded them. He smiled quizzically. "I did?"

"I was thinking."

"About me, I hope." He knelt quickly and placed a rattan basket before her. "Dinner, as promised."

"In a hamper?" Holly smiled delightedly. "Just like in the movies."

"Of course, just like in the movies. Where do you think I got the idea?" he admitted unselfconsciously.

It was so elegant that Holly felt guiltier than ever.

"How did everything go this morning?" Adam began to unpack the basket and Holly caught the whiff of fresh bread.

"Fine," she chirped, feeling miserable.

"Did they like the tree?" Adam turned one of her boxes into an impromptu table as he covered it with a small cloth.

"I think so." She swallowed. "The photographer told me that he'd like to go back for some night shots. I meant to ask you. Do you mind?"

"When?"

"Tonight? I lent him the key." Holly bit her lip.

Adam studied her for a moment. "Will a lot of people be with him?"

Holly was relieved she could tell Adam no. "He said he'd be working alone."

Adam shrugged. "You obviously trust him, so it shouldn't be a problem."

"Gus is all right." Her eyes brightened. "That tree looks so good against the night skyline, we think they'll use it for the cover shot. It's becoming one of my favorites."

"Mine, too." His eyes held hers.

It was getting more and more difficult to remember that

she didn't want a relationship with anyone. "What have you brought to eat? I'm starved," she said quickly, trying to ignore the moment they'd just shared.

"You didn't eat lunch, did you?"

Holly shook her head.

"I was afraid of that. How do you propose to get the energy to keep up this hectic pace you've set for yourself if you don't eat?" Adam set a poor-boy sandwich in front of her and opened a plastic container of crudités.

"Someone special fixed a marvelous breakfast for me." Her voice was soft and huskier than usual.

When she saw the expression on Adam's face, she was almost sorry she'd spoken. It wasn't fair to encourage him.

"The competition is gaining." Adam gestured to the trees taking shape next to them.

"It's okay. As a pro, I'm disqualified. This is all for charity. Different organizations decorate trees and the public votes on them. A dollar a vote and the winners get theirs matched dollar for dollar by the furniture store."

"That doesn't seem fair to you. Your time is worth as much as anyone else's."

Holly shrugged. "It's good exposure and I asked to do it. I figure some of the groups would drop out at the last minute and I was right. Don't worry, I'll make the most of this."

Adam unearthed a small container of dip for the vegetables. "You always play all the angles, don't you?"

"I have to," Holly snapped, irritated. "You know, if I were a man, I'd be admired for being a real go-getter. But that's not considered an attribute in a woman."

"I didn't mean it to be a criticism," Adam stated quietly. "Just a comment. You put quite a lot of pressure on yourself. It must get tiring."

"I can't afford to get tired." Holly stood and brushed the crumbs from her camel slacks. "You're good with treetops. See if you can get this angel up there. And please...don't tangle the ribbons.''

''I haven't eaten my sandwich, yet,'' Adam protested.

''You can eat later.''

''Slave driver,'' he complained as he rewrapped his sandwich.

Holly whirled around, her brown eyes intense. ''This is exactly what I was afraid of. I didn't ask you to come. In fact, I specifically told you not to. I'm *working*, Adam. Working. This is what I do for a living. How well I live depends on how hard I work.''

She took a deep breath, conscious that her voice was louder than it needed to be. ''And I've got my sisters to consider, too. Everything depends on me. My business is seasonal. I'm trying to expand, but for now, I've got three income-producing months out of the year. That means one of my working days is worth four of yours. If you can't accept that, I understand. But if you want to see me, it will have to be on my terms. It's selfish and I know it. But that's the way it has to be.''

The emotional torrent of words ran out about the same time as her breath. She faced him, breathing quickly and waited for him to tell her off, pack up all that lovely food and stalk out of the showroom.

''Want a hug?'' he asked softly, already reaching for her.

Holly's face crumpled as his arms closed around her and held her tightly.

''Been rough, has it?'' One of his hands gently caressed her curls as she rested her head against his shoulder.

''Yes.''

''Tell me about it some time?'' His voice was gentle.

''Yes.''

''Holly?''

Holly shuddered and lifted her head.

Adam's hold relaxed. His fingers tilted her chin until she

was forced to look at him. "Have I complained about your work?"

"No," she answered honestly.

"I won't. You've come into my life at a time when I have emotional energy to spare. To give. It won't always be that way." He noted the wariness in her eyes and let her study him. "I don't think you know how to be a taker."

He surprised her. "What does that mean?"

"Just what it sounds like. The world is full of givers and takers. You've been a giver for so long, you can't take without feeling guilty."

Holly disentangled her arms from his and ran a shaky hand through her hair. "You sound like a pop psychologist." She couldn't believe he was still there. Anyone else would have left long ago. *She* would have left long ago. Well, she'd warned him. He knew exactly what he would be getting into. Okay. Fine.

"Thanks for being so understanding." Holly took a deep breath and smiled. "Now, would you hang that angel?"

"No."

Her smile disappeared and her jaw wore a militant look.

One of his dimples appeared. "I'm going," he said with quiet finality, "to eat my sandwich. Now."

# CHAPTER FOUR

"WHY CAN'T YOU USE a bank like everyone else?" Laurel followed Holly into the large walk-in pantry and watched as her sister sorted foil-wrapped packets.

"I do. Where do you think I get money? Open the freezer for me, will you?"

Laurel yanked up the heavy white door. "I was getting lunch out, anyway. Holly," she began as Holly placed the packets into neatly, but misleadingly, labeled plastic bins. "Don't you think the money would be safer in a bank?"

Holly smiled grimly. "I happen to like cold hard cash."

"Give me a break."

"Shh. I'm counting and my fingers are freezing."

"Well, hurry up. I'm hungry."

Holly looked pointedly at Laurel's statuesque curves. "You're always hungry. Thought about going on a diet?"

"Cheap and miserly, that's what you are."

"Yeah, but that's twelve tax packets. We've got a roof over our heads until next December, but we can't eat after April. Although—" Holly studied her sister consideringly "—we could feast well into May if one of us would try to lose a few pounds."

"I lost five pounds in October!"

"We *all* lost five pounds in October." Holly moved aside as Laurel reached into the freezer. "What's for lunch?"

Laurel gave her a smug smile. "Alumnae Coffee leftovers again. This will be our third free meal, so no more comments on my appetite."

Holly nodded. "Point taken."

Laurel dug around in the freezer. "What's that?" she gestured to a frosty container.

"Ivy's college money. If all goes well, she can enroll for the spring semester."

"Finally." Laurel pulled out a bag of frozen sandwiches and meat tarts. "We've got to finish the raw veggies today. They're looking grim."

"Make soup."

"Out of what?"

"Don't we have a can of tuna or something?" Holly glanced at the bare shelves around them.

"Yuck. I'll send Ivy to the store." Laurel slammed the freezer door shut. "Seriously, Holly, I feel nervous having that much cash around."

Holly gave her a wry smile. "It isn't that much. Besides, I'd rather have my assets frozen here than in the bank."

"It wouldn't happen again," Laurel said quietly.

Holly turned out the light in the pantry and headed back into the kitchen. "It *won't* happen again. Anyway," she said after spending a few minutes at her ledger, "it cuts out impulse spending. Why do you think I made the American Express card into an ice cube?"

Laurel muttered something about microwaves as Ivy burst into the kitchen carrying their fur jacket on one arm and the black skirt, which one of the sisters usually wore daily, on the other.

"I just wanted to let you know I took these out of your closet, Laurel. I'm going to wear them tomorrow."

"Sorry. I'm going out to lunch after church."

"I've been invited to the Cowboy game. On one of my *rare* outings," Ivy said with a significant look at Holly. "I ran into a bunch of my friends. They're home for Christmas break. They've got extra tickets, so it won't cost anything."

Holly's sigh went unheard by either sister. "Maybe you can both wear the outfit. What time is kickoff?"

"Two. Tony's picking me up at noon."

"Noon!" Laurel glared at Holly. "What are you suggesting, that Ivy just strip me on the church steps?"

"Please, Laurel?" Ivy looked pleadingly from sister to sister. "Wear the red silk. Holly probably doesn't need it."

"Wear Holly's camel outfit," Laurel countered. "It still looks chic."

"It looks chic on Holly. It looks dumb on me. The pants are too long and I don't have the right shoes. At least with the skirt, I can wear my boots. I need the jacket to keep warm." Ivy hugged the furry softness to her cheek.

"Huh-uh."

"Come on! It's supposed to be *our* jacket." Ivy held it out of Laurel's reach. "How come I never get to wear it?"

"But to a football game?" Laurel looked to Holly for support. "She'll probably spill mustard on it."

"Laurel!" Holly ran her fingers through her curls. "It's okay, Ivy. Why don't you go put everything on and we'll help you pick your jewelry."

Ivy beamed. "Thanks, Holly!"

"She'll look like a little kid playing dress-up." Laurel shoved the cookie sheet with the leftovers into the oven.

"Laurel, she wants to wear the jacket to impress her friends. You know how they all but dropped her when they went off to college. And *they'll* be dressed to the teeth."

"That jacket was never meant to be hers," Laurel said resentfully.

"There wasn't any name on the package." Holly said quietly. "We'll never know which of us Mom and Dad intended to have it."

A howling from deep in the house made Holly roll her eyes. "What now?" she asked herself as it grew louder.

"It's not fair! Look what she did!" Ivy began crying with deep anguished sobs as she thumped down the stairs.

Holly ran to the bottom of the steps. "What's wrong?"

"Look!" Ivy pulled at the folds of sweater hanging on her slender frame. "She...she stretched all the sweaters!"

Holly sighed. "That one probably needs to be cleaned, anyway. We'll have the cleaners block it back into shape," she said soothingly.

"But what'll I wear?" Ivy wailed.

"You know that new red turtleneck we got on sale? You can be the first one to wear it."

"Really? Gosh, thanks, Holly!" Ivy smiled through her tears and whirled back up the stairs.

Holly felt a gut-wrenching twist of guilt, regret and a flare of the old anger, which melted into pity. Little Ivy had been hit hardest. Teenagers could be so cruel.

Holly sat on the bottom step, head on her knees. "Little" Ivy was nineteen. Nineteen and thrilled to be the first to wear a sweater they would all share. How pathetic.

She sat that way until she heard Gus's distinctive tapping on the front door.

"Are those the proofs?" Holly asked when she noticed the brown envelope Gus held.

"Hello to you, too, pretty lady." He sniffed. "What do I smell?"

"Lunch," answered Holly, resignedly gesturing him in.

"What? That time already?" Gus exclaimed in mock surprise.

"As you well know, moocher."

Gus eyed her expectantly. "Didn't Beth Robinson call you?"

"No, why?" Holly gripped his arm. "Gus, is it the cover?"

"Sure 'nough. Take a look at these." He handed her the envelope.

Holly fumbled with the clasp a fraction of a second before ripping open the flap and drawing out the photographs "Gus, they're gorgeous!"

Gus pointed to the photograph on the top of the stack. "This one is Beth's choice for the cover. Said she was going to call you for some more information about Deck the Halls."

"You sweetie!" Holly restrained her impulse to plant a kiss on his fuzzy cheek and settled for a careful hug.

"Look here." Gus took the pictures from her and shuffled through them. "I sold this to your boyfriend's law firm. Can you believe they were going to go the smoked-turkey route for Christmas? When they saw this, they ordered copies for a bunch of their clients."

"They didn't mention the change in design?"

"Huh?"

"Never mind. There's the bearskin rug." Holly pointed. "You got the fireplace tools with the logo. Nice touch."

"Profitable touch. You ought to get some business from this, too."

Holly felt a weight lift from her shoulders. "Gus, dear friend, are you free for lunch? Laurel should have it ready about now."

Gus grinned, his teeth showing bright against the unshaven face. "I can work it in."

Holly entered the kitchen, more lighthearted than she remembered being in ages. "We're setting another place, Laurel. A soon-to-be-famous photographer is dining with us."

"Such an occasion will necessitate a trip to the freezer." Laurel raised her eyebrows in a silent question, which Holly answered with a quick affirming nod. "And what's the occasion?"

Holly swept her ledgers off the table. "The cover of *Town Square* magazine! Take a look at these." She handed the packet to Laurel and went to get the silverware.

Gus grabbed her elbow. "Holly? You think I could use that set for some more pictures?"

Holly shrugged. "You'll have to ask Adam." She tried to tug her arm away.

"Hol-ly." Gus sighed impatiently. "I don't want to give him a chance to say no. I…already signed a contract."

"Gus!" She regained possession of her elbow.

"Oh, come on. You know you can't get ahead by following rules." He gave her a disgusted look. "Just let me know when the Yankee's going to be gone and I'll pop in then."

"I *don't* have the key," Holly pointed out.

"Get it." Gus threw out his arms. "You're palling around with him. Or haven't things progressed that far?"

"Holly, weren't you thinking of asking Adam over for a thank-you dinner?" Laurel inserted smoothly.

Holly deliberately took a deep breath. "Yes, sometime—"

"You and Adam would have more privacy at the penthouse and Gus could take his photographs while you're cooking."

"We won't need—"

"You could get the key from Adam and have a nice dinner waiting for him. It would leave you plenty of time to chitchat about his…briefs, or whatever else was on his mind." Laurel composedly turned back to the stove.

Holly ignored Gus's snicker. She did owe him a favor. He'd suggested her company when *Town Square* first approached the law firm. His photographs were first-rate and he'd always been willing to finish out a roll of film and let her have the photos to show prospective clients. Now, thanks to him, one of her designs would be on the cover of the popular city magazine.

"So-o-o—" she endured the brotherly arm he put around her "—all I want is a little time in an empty apartment. Nothing illegal—I'll come in the front door and march right by the rent-a-cop downstairs."

"Gus," she sighed, "I don't want to bother Adam with this."

"He doesn't need to know. You give people too much information and it clutters their mind."

"Gus, it isn't that I don't appreciate what you've done—"

"I'd be crazy not to stay on the right side of three gorgeous babes." Gus released her.

Holly laughed. "You just want to make sure you have some place to stay when things are a little tight."

"Hey, I pay for it in pictures. You think film is free?"

"Speaking of which, have you got a couple of extras here? That was a new design."

His teeth gleamed in a sarcastic smile. "That's my girl. Always hustling."

"I've got to, Gus." Holly flipped through the pictures, selecting the ones for her portfolio.

"They're still in the kitchen, I think," Ivy's voice called from the hallway. "Hey, look who I found at the front door."

Holly looked up as Adam followed her youngest sister into the kitchen. His eyes sought hers immediately and the dimpled grin flashed. Dinner alone with Adam? In the penthouse with the glorious view? Well, she owed him, too, didn't she?

"I rang the bell and knocked," he explained.

"That's okay." Ivy went to investigate the lunch possibilities. "The doorbell doesn't ring in this part of the house anymore. Next time, come around to the back."

"Adam, we were just discussing you," Laurel announced in her best sultry movie-queen voice, ignoring Holly's outraged warning glare. "And your marvelous penthouse."

Adam's smile included all of them, but lingered on Holly. "Just temporarily mine, I'm afraid."

"Have a seat." Gus shoved a chair toward him. "And take a look at these." He snatched the pictures from Holly.

"We were just having lunch," she said loudly. "Would you care to join us?"

"I had no intention of inviting myself," Adam protested, but not too strongly.

"That's okay, we're used to it." Ivy set a bowl of fruit on the table and tore off a couple of grapes for herself.

"Anyway, this guy I know went really wild over the shots," Gus was saying, and Holly cringed.

"We're having a light lunch, Adam, but Holly will make it up to you, won't you Holly?" Laurel gave her a sisterly hug and scooted out of the range of Holly's elbow.

"Naturally, I planned—"

"I'd like another crack at it before Holly takes the tree down." Gus used his earnest voice. "You know...to make some pocket money."

The best she could hope for, Holly decided, was that Adam wouldn't think what was turning out to be the world's most blatant setup was her idea.

Laurel slipped into Holly's usual place at the round table, leaving the chair next to Adam vacant. An oblivious Ivy quietly devoured the grapes.

"Fine with me," Adam answered as Holly sat down beside him. "What day?"

"I'm flexible," Gus shrugged. "Anytime."

"How about when Holly fixes you dinner, Adam?" Laurel bypassed Gus and pushed the sandwich plate toward Adam.

"I haven't had a chance to discuss it with him." As Holly spoke, Adam caressed her wrist and laced his fingers through hers. Holly felt an instant jolt that shot up her arm and lodged deep in her stomach. "Yet." She turned widened eyes to the man beside her. His brilliant blue eyes regarded her steadily.

"She'd planned to have it at your penthouse," Laurel

prompted, since Holly had apparently lost all power of speech.

Adam gently squeezed her hand. "What about Wednesday?"

Holly squeezed back. "Wonderful."

IF SHE HADN'T BEEN dreaming about blue eyes and a funny feeling in the pit of her stomach, she wouldn't be in this mess, Holly thought, as the Wednesday-morning job ran late. And she was having trouble making the simplest decisions, like what to have for The Dinner. Laurel and Ivy had cheerfully donated Monday and Tuesday's meal money, which made Holly suspicious. Not of Ivy, who was a sweetie, but of the ever-ravenous Laurel, who was not.

Holly quickly walked into the lobby of the building where her next job was scheduled and headed for the telephones.

"Laurel, I'm running late. Can you go to the store for me?"

"Sure."

"You're being awfully nice. Why?"

"The more time you spend with Adam, the less work I have to do. What are you cooking?"

"I don't know," Holly said irritably. "How about Rock Cornish hens? Get a couple, plus some wild rice—"

"Feed the man some meat, Holly. Does he look like a wimp to you?"

A vision of Adam instantly flashed into her mind. She sighed.

"Right," Laurel said in her syrupy drawl. "You don't feed prissy food to a man like Adam. I figured you'd run late, so I already got a couple of steaks and some potatoes."

"That's not very impressive," Holly protested.

"But easy." Laurel's sultry laugh sounded in Holly's ear. "You don't plan to spend all your time cooking, do you?"

Holly swallowed, her mouth dry. This dinner was going to get her into trouble. On the other hand, how threatening could steak and potatoes be?

Two and a half hours later, Holly rode the plush elevator up to the penthouse, pleased at having made up some lost time.

At least she was pleased until the doors whispered open.

"Hey, babe!" Gus's jaunty smile was strained around the edges.

"What is this?" Holly stared in disbelief at the remnants of the once-elegant room, too stunned to realize immediately what was going on.

Gus turned his back to her and brazened it out. "Don't worry, you won't bother me." He waved negligently. "I won't need the kitchen."

Holly climbed over the back of an armchair, which was jammed into the foyer, along with most of the living-room furniture.

Gus, visibly nervous, watched her progress. "Look out for the cords."

"Relax, Gus. They're too heavy to use for strangling you." Holly's foot caught on a tripod supporting an umbrella reflector. It teetered and Gus leapt to steady it. Then Holly saw the rest of the room. Mounds of feathers and filmy lingerie were heaped on the white silk sofa. Holly peered into a cardboard box. "What is this stuff?" She grabbed a handful of minuscule scraps of fabric and some leather...things, momentarily diverted. "How do you wear this?" she wondered aloud.

"Which one?"

Holly's head jerked up and she dropped her handful "Bianca!"

"Who?" Gus croaked nervously, prudently remaining out of reach.

"My bear. She's wearing glasses and has an apple in her mouth." Holly glared at Gus accusingly.

He shrugged. "Back to school."

Holly repeated the words silently. She bent down and picked up an Easter basket, a couple of American flags and a stray shamrock. "You...you took all the snowflakes off my tree!"

"Just borrowed 'em." Gus gestured toward Holly's tree. "I've been putting 'em back."

Holly followed the trail. She found a bow and arrow with a heart at its tip. "Too bad August doesn't have a major holiday, Gus." She rescued a pilgrim hat from the corner.

"Oooh! These feathers tickle!" A bright giggle preceded the entrance of a flaming redhead. "Hi, honey," she warbled as she passed Holly. "Oh, good. You found the hat. Just put it on the bear, will ya? Oops!" She giggled again and grabbed a slipping turkey-feather boa. "Gus, I don't know if these pins will hold."

"Get out!" Holly's eyes blazed furiously. "Now!" She threw her armload in the general direction of the cardboard box.

"M-my stuff." Sweat beaded on Gus's forehead.

"Here!" Holly picked up the entire box and heaved it toward him. Gus lunged for it and the umbrella reflector crashed to the floor.

"I should have known you were up to something scummy!" Holly snatched up a handful of white netting from the sofa. The tiara attached to it provided a nice weight and the whole thing arced like a comet as it went zinging through the air.

"Hey—that's rented!"

Holly vented her fury by throwing the rest of the lingerie. The flimsy fabric couldn't hurt anything. She wasn't so angry she didn't consider that.

"Holly—babe—I've never seen you like this." Gus swatted at the sheer materials.

"And you, too, turkey." Holly threw a handful the redhead's way.

"Now wait a minute, honey. We haven't done November yet and I went to a lot of trouble to fix this cute feather bikini."

"Holly! Have you gone completely insane?" Laurel shouted from the elevator.

"You!" Holly gulped air and glared at her sister.

Laurel tossed her mane of streaked hair. "Come into the kitchen and we'll discuss this."

"There's nothing to discuss." Holly took one more deep breath and then bent to gather some of the littered props. "Do you realize that Adam could be here any minute?"

"Nonsense," Laurel said, briskly carrying a grocery sack into the kitchen. "It's only four-thirty."

Holly hesitated, glaring at Gus. "Get out." Her voice trembled with anger. "You, too." She pointed at Miss November and followed Laurel. "Did it occur to you that Adam might take off early to be with me?"

"No," Laurel said, unconcerned. "If Adam takes off early, it will be to buy you flowers, or a bottle of the perfect wine. That man knows how to make the most of an opportunity and he's been holding back too long."

Holly blinked. "You knew about this, didn't you?"

"As much as you did." Laurel began unloading the sack.

"I did *not* know Gus was taking sleazy pictures of some turkey." The corner of Holly's eye caught a flash. "I suppose he's doing November now."

"He might as well finish."

"Adam's been really great to us. He trusted us. Me. And how does he get repaid?"

"A fabulous steak dinner. That is, if you ever cook it."

"Gus shouldn't have been here alone," Holly protested.

"He wasn't. The redhead works as a receptionist for Adam's firm. Gus met her when he sold them the other pictures."

Holly moaned.

"You are just determined to be unpleasant about this

whole thing, aren't you?'' Laurel slammed a jar of cinnamon on the counter. ''After shopping for *your* groceries, I got here and checked the cabinets to see if you needed spices or anything. You didn't have any flour.''

''So?''

''You can't make an apple pie without it.''

''Is that dessert?''

Laurel smiled slyly. ''If you've got time. I got a couple of pastries as backups in case you get distracted and the pie burns. I thought they could double as breakfast, if dinner drags on later than you planned.''

''This is *not* a seduction,'' Holly said firmly.

''It should be,'' Laurel retorted as she drifted out of the kitchen.

Holly sank onto the stool by the telephone and stared into the narrow kitchen. How could she tell Adam any of this? She ran both hands through her curls. It made them all look like opportunistic users. And maybe Gus was like that, but she and Laurel weren't, not deep down.

Adam had been so... Sweet was the word that popped into her mind, but that didn't describe Adam. He'd been tolerant of them, so far. Holly knew it was because he was attracted to her.

She slowly emptied the plastic sack of Granny Smith apples and began to peel them. Adam had allowed her to set the terms of their relationship. She winced, uncomfortable that everything so far had gone her way. Holly heard Gus and Laurel leave and went out to inspect the living area. It wasn't too bad. She spent a few minutes straightening and putting knickknacks back as she remembered. The tree was a mess, of course. Holly shrugged and returned to the kitchen to roll out pie dough.

Twenty minutes later, she grudgingly admitted that Laurel's instincts hadn't failed her. The penthouse kitchen was tiny and not intended for elaborate meal preparation. The pie made a big mess, but the rest of the meal would be simple to prepare. Holly's breath caught at the price of the steaks. Did Laurel have to be so extravagant?

Wasn't Adam worth it? countered an inner voice as she slapped the meat on the fancy countertop grill. The potatoes baked with the pie and Laurel had included a slice of pâté, crackers, but no wine.

Holly had just carried the pâté out to the living area when she heard the elevator. Adam was later than she'd expected and she was glad she'd had the extra time to compose herself. She stood in the foyer, feeling slightly awkward.

Adam's face lit up when he saw her. He *was* worth it. Surprising herself, Holly reached for him. "Hello." Her voice was low and husky.

It barely registered that his arms were full of elongated brown sacks and a bouquet of flowers. He quickly set them on the floor in time to wrap his arms around her.

Holly wasn't sure what she'd originally intended, but it hadn't included fusing herself to him. She wasn't ready for the incredible melting sensation, or the excitement that seemed to sparkle through her whole body. Amazed at her response, Holly shakily attempted to disengage herself.

"Don't stop now." Adam lightly brushed her lips with his.

"I think I'd better." She laid a trembling hand on his shoulder.

"Not yet." He spoke quietly, all the while inching his lips closer and closer to hers.

Holly's first thought was to resist; then she remembered the explosive sparkles of a moment before.

An instant later, Adam's lips touched hers. He gradually, but deliberately, increased the pressure, unhurriedly moving his lips against hers until he felt the last of her resistance melt.

Holly felt it, too. Her will drained out of her, leaving her insides shaking so much, she knew Adam had to be aware of it.

They broke the kiss simultaneously, each breathing in quick shallow breaths.

"I—" Holly stammered, not having any idea what to say next. "I had no idea you could kiss like that!" she blurted.

Adam threw her a sexy half smile. "I know."

In a daze, Holly found that, yes, her legs still worked, and led Adam toward the pâté.

She sank, wordlessly, onto the white sofa. Adam retrieved the paper bags and the flowers. "These are for you."

"Thank you." Her voice was a husky whisper.

Adam smiled perceptively. "I'll put them in water."

"That's my line." She managed a short laugh.

Working at Exemplary Temporaries wasn't so bad, she began to rationalize as Adam walked toward the kitchen. And maybe the business boom they'd been expecting wouldn't materialize anyway.

What was she thinking? She gave herself a mental shake. She wasn't about to let a few kisses jeopardize Deck the Halls. In spite of her recent actions, Adam had better realize that.

"I saw the steaks and smelled the pie. Dinner's going to be great." Adam poured her a glass of wine, then sat beside her, casually stretching his arm along the back of the sofa.

This was going to be harder than she'd thought. Adam's hand on her shoulder gently urged her to relax against him. She did, enjoying the warmth of his body next to hers. The fire Gus had built flickered gently, reducing itself to a bed of glowing embers.

"I...didn't mean to get quite so carried away earlier." She spoke slowly and quietly, easing her words into the companionable silence.

Adam rested his head against hers and she could hear the steady beating of his heart. "There's no going back, Holly."

Holly felt a choking lump in her throat. She nodded, unable to speak.

"I'm willing to be patient—not forgotten."

Holly smiled sadly. Adam might think he could be patient, but she knew better. He'd interfere, resent her work and become more and more demanding. Then they'd have a big fight and that would be the end of it.

The timer on the stove went off. "I'll bet that's the pie." Adam planted a kiss on her forehead. "I'll go change while you take it out of the oven."

Holly sat up, then turned and gave Adam a fierce hug. *Please wait for me,* she pleaded silently, because if he wouldn't and she had to choose, Holly wasn't so certain that Deck the Halls would win.

The aroma of warm apple pie surrounded her as she tore lettuce for their salad. She concentrated fiercely on her task and avoided thinking about the man changing his clothes. She succeeded so well that she didn't hear Adam's approach. She had only a momentary warning as gentle fingers pushed aside the curls at the nape of her neck and soft lips kissed it.

Holly reacted immediately. Her stomach contracted, pulsing with each of the butterflylike kisses Adam placed on her neck.

"Adam." She sighed his name.

Hands on her shoulders, Adam slowly turned her to face him.

What had happened in the minutes since he left her? She thought they understood one another, that they'd agreed their relationship would have to wait until...until what?

"Adam," Holly whispered again. He wore the blue cashmere sweater and she couldn't resist sliding her fingers over the inviting softness covering his chest, up to the firm muscles of his shoulders and neck.

Their lips met as Holly's fingers entangled themselves in the blue-black hair curling behind Adam's neck.

All her ideas about controlling their relationship were swept away. She pressed closer to Adam and found herself held in a bone-crushing embrace.

It was Adam who parted her lips and Adam's tongue that met hers in a slow leisurely dance. It was Adam, in fact, who was very much in control and Holly who was fast losing it.

At the precise moment when Holly felt she would faint if the two of them didn't throw themselves onto the kitchen floor, he set her from him.

Smiling tenderly, he gently caressed her cheek, then reached around her and shut off the grill where the sizzling steaks hissed and popped. Only then did Holly notice the slightly charred smell.

Adam placed his hand on the small of her back and gently urged her through the door. Holly took a step and stumbled.

"My knees," she said with an apologetic laugh.

"Ah, my cue," Adam slipped an arm under her shoulders and lifted her against his chest. "I've always wanted to do this," he said as he carried her into the bedroom. He stopped by the edge of the bed and looked down at her.

"Now what?" Holly whispered.

A muscle worked in Adam's jaw. "In a move of exquisite finesse, I shall set you gently on the bed. Isn't that how it's supposed to go?"

Uncertainty warred with passion. Holly's teeth tugged at her lower lip. "Maybe not."

"Okay." Adam tossed her unceremoniously onto the center of the bed.

Caught off guard, Holly bounced a couple of times as Adam crawled toward her.

"Why did you do that?" Her face was a portrait of confused sensuality.

Adam propped himself on one elbow. "I don't want to be predictable."

Holly pushed Adam squarely in the center of his chest and pinned his arms to the bed. "Neither do I."

She felt his muscles tense slightly just before he freed himself and pinned her in an identical position. "Yield?" Without waiting for an answer, Adam covered her mouth with his.

It had been so long since a man had held her in his arms and kissed her. Had it ever felt like this? If so, how had she been able to numb her feelings?

"Holly?" Adam nuzzled the side of her neck.

"Hmm?"

Adam raised his head so he could study her face. "What changed your mind?"

"About what?" Puzzled, Holly shook her head. Adam smiled and reached toward the floor beside the bed, bringing up a handful of red chiffon.

Holly blanched.

"I got the message." Adam held the nightie up by the straps. It was completely transparent, except for three strategically placed patches of black lace.

It was hideous.

And it meant she'd have to tell Adam about Gus's latest project. Furthermore, she was not flattered to realize Adam thought she ordered her sleepwear from trashy catalogs.

"Quite a departure from your usual look."

"Yes, uh, no. It's…not mine." She didn't want to explain. She felt guilty and embarrassed by the whole episode.

"You borrowed it?"

"Kiss me, Adam."

Holly put everything she had into that kiss, determined to turn Adam's brain into putty, or at the very least, make him forget about the garish nightie he'd discovered.

He held back, not responding the way she'd hoped. His insides should be jelly by now.

She'd show him. She reached under the softness of the cashmere and splayed her hands across his chest, feeling a tremor. Holly was so caught up in her determined seduction of Adam, she failed to realize that she was the one who was trembling. Her brain was putty; her insides were jelly.

Adam felt the tremor, too. Enjoyable as the last few minutes had been, he wasn't fooled. Holly was trying to convince herself that she was still entangled in a web of passion. But she wasn't now. That vulgar scrap of material had changed everything, and Holly was obviously trying to overcome second thoughts.

He couldn't go through with it. Holly was much too special for him to indulge in a lusty fling. No, he was going to be noble. He'd wait just long enough to give her something to think about—and then he'd do the right thing. If he could.

Holly eased the sweater off Adam's shoulders and over his head in a quick movement that caught him by surprise.

Adam's heart thundered in his ears. Any minute now he'd be noble and stop this. He exhaled sharply as Holly moved against him, fitting herself against his length. Any minute now, he told himself as his arms pressed into her back, pulling her even closer. Any minute.

Holly raised her lips to his once more and then, incredibly, Adam's hands were on her shoulders, pushing her away.

He breathed heavily, his eyes closed, as she watched in dazed puzzlement. With a sigh, he rested his forehead on hers.

"Enough."

"It doesn't have to be," Holly whispered.

Adam dropped a light kiss on her forehead and rolled to a sitting position on the bed. He drew one more deep breath, opened his eyes and smiled crookedly at her.

Holly lay on the bed, her lips full and parted, her hair charmingly mussed.

Adam reached for the discarded red nightie. Holly immediately bolted to a sitting position. "Adam," she began determinedly, "I'd like to explain."

He shook his head. "No. You're entitled to change your mind. No reason necessary."

"*I* didn't!"

"Yes, you did, and it's okay." Adam paused for a moment, staring at the black-and-red chiffon. A brief flicker of his imagination had Holly wearing it. "Holly," he began slowly.

"It's this stupid thing." Holly snatched it from him, wadded it up and flung it into the wastebasket. "It was a mistake."

"It isn't stupid," Adam disagreed. "And it doesn't bother me that you've changed your mind," he said again. He ignored the frustrated ache in his belly. "Though I'll admit this isn't your style."

"I should be apologizing to you." Holly hesitated uncertain how to begin the embarrassing explanations.

"Don't." Adam placed a finger over her lips. "We don't have to rush into a physical relationship. I told you casual affairs have never appealed to me. I want to get to know you better. Then sex becomes a communication of the soul, as well as the body."

*I don't deserve him,* Holly thought as guilt tore through her again. "That's beautiful." She reached out to draw her fingers along his cheek.

Adam caught her hand, turned her palm and placed a kiss in the center of it. "I don't want to rush you. And I'm not prepared for this just now, in any way. I'm all for spontaneity—not recklessness." One of his dimples appeared. "Of course later we could renegotiate."

# CHAPTER FIVE

"THIS HAS GOT TO BE the classiest warehouse around."
Laurel stood, hands on well-rounded hips, surveying the
living room.

"Can't beat the rent." Holly smiled briefly and went
back to her notebook. In the distance, the telephone rang.

"I'll get it," shouted Ivy.

"You don't suppose that's another job, do you?" Laurel
stopped at the bottom of the stairs.

"I hope so."

"You would. I don't understand all these people who
wait until the last minute."

"Isn't it great?" Holly's face creased in a smile. "Anyway, two weeks before Christmas is not the last minute.
December twenty-fourth at one o'clock in the afternoon
is."

"That's still a possibility."

"Another Chili Christmas!" Ivy yelled from the study.

Holly groaned. "That's the last one."

"Holly, that one and Merry Texmas are our most popular
trees this year." Laurel started up the stairs. "Bloomie said
she could get as many crystals as we needed."

"They're costing us a fortune. We have to rent each tree
twice before we break even. What if nobody wants it next
year?"

"Quit worrying. Next year, you take off the chili-pepper
lights, leave the crystals and call it New Age Christmas or

Crystal Christmas. Merry Texmas isn't about to go out of style and you can use the chili-pepper lights on that."

"But we still won't make a profit until the year after that."

"Okay, don't take off the chili-pepper lights and call it Fire and Ice."

Holly scribbled in her notebook. "That's great, Laurel."

"Some of us think about things other than money."

Ivy came into the room in time to hear that last exchange. "Is she still going on about profit margins?"

Laurel nodded.

"Holly, just think about the four sorority-and one fraternity-house trees we're dismantling tomorrow and the fact that so far you've rented two of those for a second time this season. Twice the profit. That's a first."

Holly flipped to the scheduling calendar. "I can't believe it's already the middle of December."

"I can!" Laurel and Ivy said at the same time. They chattered amiably as they climbed upstairs to the bedrooms where the decorations were stored.

Holly scheduled another Chili Christmas, wincing at the cost and number of ornaments.

"Time for a dinner break?" Laurel asked hopefully as she and Ivy lugged another box downstairs. "I wonder what Adam will bring tonight."

"It isn't right to expect him to bring us food all the time," Holly protested.

"But he does," Ivy said.

On cue, the doorbell rang. "Ah, dinner!" Laurel said softly, an arched eyebrow directed toward Holly.

Holly gave her a warning glance.

"I'll go get some napkins and drinks." Ivy dropped her box and hurried into the kitchen.

Holly made an exasperated sound as Laurel flung open the front door.

"Why, Adam, what a nice surprise! Holly, honey," Laurel drawled, "It's Adam. Isn't that nice?"

Holly opened her mouth to protest.

Adam walked in, carrying flat cardboard boxes, exuding the mouth-watering aroma of pepperoni and Italian spices. "Hey, busy night! Congratulations. Let me save you some time, here, Holly." He headed toward the kitchen.

"Bring your sister," he instructed Laurel. "Where were we? I know—you tell me I shouldn't have. I say it's no trouble, just a couple of pizzas. Then I say I like to spoil you, and no, I won't take your money. Okay, next time it's your treat, et cetera, et cetera."

Silence.

"Laurel and Ivy want pizza, don't you?" Adam asked with an amused look at them.

"Please, Holly, please, please? Pretty please with pepperoni on top?" Laurel and Ivy pleaded, with outstretched hands.

Holly bit the insides of her cheeks. She would not encourage them.

Adam picked up one of the boxes and waved the aroma toward her. Nothing.

"Relax, Holly," he said as the others helped themselves. "I used coupons."

"I knew you were incorrigible," she said at last, taking the gooiest piece of pizza she could find.

"And you love it." Adam grinned.

"Yeah." Holly grinned back.

"So how goes the season? Are you ahead or behind projected income?"

"Ahead," Laurel answered. "You were an unexpected help with the food budget."

"Laurel!" Even though they all realized it was true, Holly hated to hear it admitted aloud.

"How many jobs do we have to pack for tomorrow?"

Adam began clearing away the remains of their pizza dinner.

"Seven," Ivy replied.

"Hey, they're really beginning to pick up, aren't they?"

"And we take down five trees tomorrow. The semester has ended and all decorations have to be cleared before the dorms and houses close for winter break." Laurel followed the last two pieces of pizza over to the kitchen sink. Holly watched as she edged toward Adam while he sealed the leftovers in plastic wrap. Laurel grabbed at the pieces and Adam whisked them out of reach.

"That's tomorrow's breakfast, Laurel. You'll hate yourself in the morning."

He already knew all their little foibles, Holly realized.

"More boxes need to be hauled downstairs?" Adam asked.

"Adam, you don't need to help," Holly said automatically. Another ritual.

"I know." He smiled.

"You're going to anyway, aren't you?"

"Yes."

This time, instead of waving him up the stairs or assigning him some task, Holly tilted her head to one side. "Why?"

Adam tugged on one of her curls, hiding the fact that his fingers briefly caressed her cheek. "Because I want to be near you," he said in a low voice only she could hear. "And because I keep hoping you'll get caught up on the work and we can have some time alone."

Adam watched the guilt flash through Holly's expressive brown eyes. "You asked."

"So I did. Make an appointment for March. It's a quiet month."

"I like my plan better." Adam turned and walked into the living room. Approaching one of the seven piles of boxes and ornament cartons, he picked up the inventory sheet and began checking off the items.

Holly watched pensively. He knew the whole routine. What would she do if he quit coming after work every day?

HOLLY'S ALARM SCREECHED and she reached out to silence it. Every muscle in her body screamed in protest. Seven trees up and five down had meant a lot of lifting and stretching and bending…. She was still exhausted. Her eyelids scratched her eyes, which squinted from the bright winter sunlight pouring through her window. She'd never had a hangover, but suspected this was close to how one felt.

Coffee! She smelled coffee!

There was a tap on her door. "Holly?"

She opened her mouth to answer and managed a hoarse squeak.

"Holly?" Adam's voice sounded raspy. "I heard your alarm. I brought you some coffee."

Holly groped around for the jeans and baggy sweater she'd been wearing last night, or rather, early this morning when she'd collapsed on her bed. She hobbled toward the door, voice creaking. "Minute, Adam."

He stood there holding two mugs of coffee, one black, the other heavily laced with milk. He thrust the milky one at her. "Drink."

"Thanks." She drank.

"You look like I feel," she said, and discovered that her voice worked again.

Adam rolled bloodshot eyes at her and drained his coffee mug. He wore the same clothes he'd worn all day Saturday, too.

"You go through this every year?"

"No." Holly shook her head and looked inquiringly at the bottom of her mug.

"There's more downstairs."

"Anybody else awake?"

"Nope." Adam appeared disinclined to fetch her more coffee, so Holly reluctantly began to make her way downstairs.

They reached the kitchen after a silent procession from the second floor. Holly refilled their coffee mugs and slumped at the kitchen table. Adam slid into the seat next to her. He needed a shave.

"Yesterday was incredible," Holly began.

"Incredible is one way to describe it, yes. Hideously overscheduled even for a masochist like you is another."

"You didn't have to stay."

"I couldn't abandon you and your sisters." Adam took another sip of coffee. "Besides, my car was back here, remember?"

"So much for chivalry."

"I made coffee this morning. All you managed to do was hit your snooze control three times and wake me up."

"I did? Three times?"

Adam held up three fingers.

"Sorry." Holly sneaked a glance at Adam's disgruntled face. "You make great coffee."

"You always say that." He gave a tired smile. "I would've started breakfast, but…" He waved at the refrigerator and pantry.

Holly shrugged. "No time to shop and we're not much on breakfast."

"Figures." He sent her a stern look. "You don't have any more days like yesterday scheduled, do you?"

"I didn't do that on purpose. I didn't realize that when the university said all trees had to be down by the end of the term, they weren't going to make an exception for us."

"Why would they?"

"Because we're hired professionals. Since the students have to leave, it makes sense to have that rule for them. I assumed that since we're an outside business, we'd have more leeway."

"Now you know."

Holly grinned. "I know that seven up and five down in one day is about all we can handle."

"Next time, I *will* abandon you."

Holly wavered, then hesitantly touched Adam's arm before giving in to impulse and hugging him. It was the first physical intimacy she'd initiated since their dinner a few days earlier and she felt momentarily awkward.

Adam hauled her onto his lap. "Fair warning," he said, running his fingers along his beard. "You are about to be kissed."

His beard was rough and he tasted wonderfully of coffee.

"I see someone woke up and smelled the coffee," Laurel drawled as she padded across the kitchen floor to the pot. She pulled the ties of her silk kimono tighter and skimmed her fingers through expensively layered hair. It responded by framing her face in artful disarray. Pouring herself a cup of coffee, she leaned against the counter and silently regarded the two of them.

Holly tried to get up, but Adam held her fast. Rather than engage in an undignified struggle, she relaxed.

"Well." Laurel sipped her coffee and looked at them. "Did I see a blank day today, by chance?"

"Not by chance," Holly replied. "The *Town Square* magazine with our cover comes out tomorrow and I scheduled today as a buffer. All we have to do is check the light strings and load the van."

Adam's hand absently caressed her back. "Anticipating a flood of business?"

Holly looked down at him. "I hope so and I hope we get some party jobs out of it."

Laurel joined them at the table. "What's more likely to happen is that we'll get a whole batch of calls right near Christmas from frantic people who haven't left themselves enough time to do everything."

Adam didn't say any more. Holly knew he was disappointed that their work wasn't winding down. After yesterday's marathon, even she was beginning to get sick of it all.

"Got it." Laurel set her mug down. "We're having a lazy day today—no arguments from you, Holly. Adam, you're invited."

"For what?"

Laurel grinned. "There'll be food."

"Naturally," Holly murmured.

"We'll get a turkey—they're on sale this week, Holly—and have a big dinner with all the trimmings. You know, cranberry sauce and the whole bit."

"Sounds like work," Holly said, but she smiled.

"Not with the four of us." No one had noticed Ivy's appearance. "And we'll move the television in here and watch football all afternoon, right?" She went to the cabinets by the pantry and pulled down several cookbooks. "After lunch, we'll make Christmas cookies."

"We haven't done that in ages." Holly began to look forward to the rest of the day.

"Up," Adam ordered.

Holly climbed gingerly off his lap. "Leg numb?"

Adam's eyes twinkled as he pounded feeling back into his leg. "It was worth it."

"I'd better get to the store." Laurel rinsed her mug on the way out.

"Don't we have any juice? Hardly any milk... You caffeine addicts can't see beyond your morning fix," grumbled Ivy from the refrigerator. She grabbed a can of soda. "I can't believe I'm having Diet Coke for breakfast."

"Laurel will see to your nutritional needs for the rest of the day," Holly reassured her as another layer of guilt settled on her shoulders. When would she stop letting people down?

After a last look in the refrigerator, Ivy slammed the

door. "I'll be in the pantry making a list. Think I'll go with Laurel to buy groceries."

"And I," Adam said, testing his leg, "will go home to shower and change."

Holly walked him to the door. "Hurry back. It won't be the same without you," she added, surprising herself.

Even worse, she thought, as she watched Adam's car follow the circular driveway to the street, nothing would ever be the same again. And she didn't *want* it to be the same again. "Watch it, Holly," she murmured to herself, "you're falling in love with him."

Her realization didn't spoil the afternoon, but it did make her intensely aware of Adam's every movement. When he approached, she felt the back of her neck prickle; her eyes darted to his constantly. More often than not, she found him watching her. He was never the first to break contact.

How could he be calm if he felt even half of what she did?

This was terrible. No wonder she'd avoided relationships for the past few years.

"Dishwasher is loaded and running," Laurel announced. "Ivy and I'll start the cookies."

Adam and Ivy were discussing what kind of cookies to make. Holly smiled benevolently as she finished the dishes left in the sink. Adam fit in with their family. Adam was kind to her sisters and a hard worker. Adam's touch melted her insides. She was obsessed with Adam.

What was the matter with her? How could she have allowed him through her defenses?

The back of her neck prickled. "I'll dry," Adam said softly standing right behind her.

They worked in companionable silence. "You've been really sneaky," Holly said at last.

"How so?"

She dipped a pot in the rinse water. "I've started to take you for granted. When I plan jobs, I assign you something to do and just assume you'll be there to do it. And you always are.''

"Do you mind?'' Adam tilted her chin until she met his eyes.

"I'm afraid,'' she told him.

"Of what?''

Holly dried her hands and wrapped her arms around Adam, unconcerned whether her sisters saw or not. It was frightening to realize how right it felt to be held by him "I'm afraid of depending on you too much. Deck the Halls is almost there—we're just about to make it. And when we do, I want to say that we did it all on our own, without anyone's help.''

"And you're worried I'll negate that achievement. You've got to do it all by yourself, or it doesn't count? Is that it?'' For the first time since she'd met him, Adam's blue eyes were cold. Holly's arms slipped down.

He was exactly right, but he made it sound petty.

"Yes,'' Holly avowed. "And I have to prove I can make it on my own to everybody, especially the vultures who destroyed the business it took my dad a lifetime to build.''

"And you lose points for accepting help?''

Holly's eyes flashed. "I don't want to be helpless anymore. I don't want to be helpless ever again.'' Her eyes burned, but she was an expert at fighting off tears.

"Hey!'' Laurel exclaimed. "Now Adam, honey, Holly can be a—'' Laurel hesitated, obviously bypassing the first word that came to mind "—slave driver, but you have no idea what she went through.''

Holly's eyes widened at Laurel's unexpected defense.

"In the first place, she was just out of school with a brand-new shiny business degree and no job. She couldn't even look for one, because she ended up spending all her time with lawyers. I was still in college, Ivy was in high school and the bottom had fallen out of the price of oil. Even if Dad hadn't died, the company might have gone bust. Holly fought. Hard. But against those oilmen and their lawyers…'' Laurel shook her head.

''They auctioned off everything. You know that Texas lets you keep your house, but you saw the rooms when you stayed last night.'' Laurel's expression dared him to comment.

''No furniture.'' Adam's voice was clipped.

''No food, either, for a while,'' Ivy added.

Adam threw her a startled glance, seeing her words confirmed in the faces of the other two.

Holly shrugged. ''They froze the assets. I just didn't know how…'' She splayed her hands expressively.

''But your lawyer should have seen to that!'' Adam protested even as he remembered with sickening clarity Mr. Steele's refusal to help her. ''You aren't supposed to starve!''

''We shopped for food in a certain department store's gourmet section, Adam. They very kindly issued us a brand-new credit card and never bothered to bill us.'' Holly's chin tilted.

''It was kind of fun, though, charging all that ritzy food. Now that we can pay for it, we can't afford it.'' Ivy laughed, and it broke the tension.

''I paid them back—every penny,'' Holly said.

''You would.'' Adam forced himself to smile. ''I didn't know all the details of what happened. Now I understand why you so badly want to succeed—just don't overdo it, okay?''

Holly smiled back. ''Okay.''

''Well, now that you've finished your little spat,'' drawled Laurel, ''let's make cookies.''

''I miss making these for the hospital,'' Ivy said, a complete football game later.

''I think I've got a real artistic flair for sugar cookies.'' Adam gestured to his precisely decorated creations.

''It's peaceful sitting here doing this. You don't have to

think." Holly looked around the kitchen, absorbing the warmth and inhaling the smell of vanilla.

"Cheap therapy." Laurel licked icing off her fingers. "Any more rejects?"

"Laurel!" Three voices protested in unison and dissolved into laughter.

"Holly, why can't we decorate the children's wing this year?" Ivy glanced at her sister as she reached for the icing.

Adam observed Holly's expression, choosing to remain silent. There was the guilt again. It was never far below the surface. Holly tried to do everything and if she achieved anything less than perfection, she felt she had failed.

"I left fliers at the hospital, Ivy." Laurel brought another rack of cookies to be decorated.

"No, I mean the way we did when Mom and Dad were alive."

"We can't afford to donate our time and supplies to the hospital anymore." Holly bit off each word, sounding harsher than Adam knew she intended. Her head was bent over the Christmas-tree cookie she was decorating, but Adam saw the stricken look. Here she was, decorating Christmas trees even during her time off.

Laurel looked from Ivy to Holly's bent head. "We could take over our leftovers on Christmas Eve, Holly. We won't get any more jobs after that."

Adam watched Holly compose her face. "We could," she said evenly, "but why would the hospital, or anyone in it, hire us if they knew we'd come by on Christmas Eve, anyway?"

"We wouldn't have to tell them," Ivy pleaded.

Holly dragged in a deep breath. "It took three years for them to stop expecting us to pick up as usual. We do it now, and we can write them off as a potential client."

"Money! That's all you ever think about!" Ivy ran from the kitchen.

Laurel scowled at her. "You never quit, do you?" She turned toward the door. "I'll go to Ivy."

There was an uncomfortable silence. "Aren't you going to leave, too?" Holly stared at Adam defiantly.

"No." Adam put his arm around her and pulled her toward him. "I'd waste a perfectly good opportunity." He kissed her, then drew back reluctantly. It wasn't what she needed now.

"You don't think I'm heartless?" She looked up at him, hurt visible in her brown eyes.

Adam cuddled her reassuringly, as he might a small child. "You've had to make some difficult and unpopular decisions." Holly laid her head on Adam's shoulder. He could smell the unusual scent she wore and satisfied himself with resting his cheek on the top of her head.

It was so rare to be alone with her, to be this close, that he found her nearness sweet torment. "Tell me why decorating the hospital is so special."

"You know how my parents were about Christmas. Well, this was one of Mom's charities, and we started decorating the children's wing for Christmas each year. It got bigger and bigger. My...birthday is Christmas Eve..."

"Figures." Adam laughed softly. "How did your parents manage that?"

Holly raised her head. "They were always well organized," she said, smiling. "Noelle is my middle name. They thought it was fate."

"This is too corny to be believed."

"It is not. I always felt special. Anyway, I never regretted having my birthday so close to Christmas. We'd be at the hospital and bring presents for the kids there. It was like a giant birthday party and I always felt happy I could go home and not have to stay at the hospital. Which is probably just what my parents were trying to teach me."

"I wish I could have met them," Adam said, regret vibrating in his voice.

Holly just nodded, unable to speak. "At any rate," she continued after a few moments, "it was the hospital decorations I used to start Deck the Halls, and Laurel and Ivy…" Her voice trailed off. Lifting her head, she scooted her chair away from Adam.

"You, sir, are addictive," she said in an attempt to lighten the mood.

"That's the whole idea." Adam handed her a cookie.

"Seriously, you've been a good friend. I didn't know how much I needed one until I met you." Even as she spoke, Holly knew he was more than that.

Adam's raised eyebrow, as he took a recently iced cookie for himself, told her he knew it, too.

# CHAPTER SIX

"ADAM WOULD DO IT—I know he would!" Ivy held up a red velvet Santa costume as Holly shook her head doubtfully.

"Probably, but let's not ask him."

"Holly, honey," Laurel drawled, hands on hips, "you are going to have to decide how you feel about that man and go with it."

"Laurel, *honey*," Holly drawled back, glaring, "what does that have to do with asking him to wear Daddy's Santa suit while we decorate the hospital?"

"You're wearing Mama's Mrs. Claus outfit," Ivy stated as if that explained everything.

"Let's give him a break. Adam is around here all the time!"

Laurel raised her eyebrows. "Which ought to tell you something."

"Yes. We take advantage of him." Holly returned to her ever-present notebook.

"He doesn't mind—remember Sunday? If we don't ask him to come with us, he'll be hurt." Ivy shook out the costume, apparently hoping five years worth of wrinkles would magically fall away.

Holly relented. "Come with us, yes. Wear the Santa outfit, no."

Laurel poked through the hanging clothing bag. "I wonder if I can still get into my elf outfit?"

"Don't even try."

Laurel threw Holly a venomous glance. "I will overlook that remark. Holly, honey, your halfhearted protests aren't fooling anybody. Including Adam."

"Probably not, but I feel obligated to make them."

"That's the dumbest way to hook a man I ever heard of."

"I'm not trying to hook him!" Holly grabbed the phone. "I'm going to let him know when we're leaving."

"On the other hand, maybe it's pure genius. Maybe he likes the challenge."

"Oh, for heaven's sake, it's busy." Holly slammed down the phone. "I'm going over to his office," she announced, thinking it would be a good excuse to do so.

"Ask him about wearing the outfit?" Ivy grinned hopefully.

Holly bit her lip and tried to imagine Adam in the huge red suit. "Have the pillows ready." She got her coat. "And don't forget to pick up replacement bulbs for the two jobs we've got this afternoon."

It had been five years since Holly had been to the Swinehart, Cathardy and Steele offices. She'd asked for legal help. Not only did they plead conflict of interest—which she had heard countless times—they'd presented her with another in a mounting pile of bills.

She'd learned a lot that day. Old Mr. Steele had looked her right in the eye as he denied her request. Most of the other lawyers hadn't been able to do that, hiding behind a barrage of papers and legal terminology.

The typewriters were silent as Holly opened the glass doors and stepped into the muted gray of the outer office.

"Adam Markland?" she asked the flamboyant redheaded receptionist, whose eyes widened apprehensively.

"I'm Holly Hall," Holly introduced herself, adding dryly, "I don't believe we've met."

"Thanks." The woman sagged with relief and flicked a glance at the phone board. "He's on the telephone."

"He's still here, then."

"He never goes out for lunch." The woman answered one of the blinking lights on the switchboard.

The sound of Adam's voice as he spoke on the phone guided Holly to his office. She peered around the half-open door and slowly walked in.

Adam cradled the receiver between his ear and shoulder, scribbling furiously. Without looking up, he waved her in and stood up to feel for his wallet. He withdrew some money and shoved it toward her, never removing his eyes from his notes.

"Just a moment." Adam covered the mouthpiece. "Make it roast beef today, Darlene—" He looked up finally, and saw Holly, his face registering pleased astonishment.

In the few moments Holly stood by Adam's desk, she had a chance to see the stacks of file folders and bundles of papers covering every chair, sofa, filing cabinet and shelf in the office.

"Adam, you're busy so..." She waved and turned to leave.

Adam stretched across the desk and grabbed her arm, shaking his head. He held on, looking at her as he finished his phone conversation.

"Holly! What are you doing here?" Adam smiled delightedly as, still holding on to her arm, he walked around his desk.

"I—" Holly stopped, looked around the room and back to Adam. "You're very busy aren't you?"

"Oh, always," Adam replied cheerfully.

Holly was silent, absorbing the unpleasant implications. She folded her arms and tapped her foot. "You haven't been doing your homework before coming over to our house to play."

"Have so. I'm a morning person, anyway." Adam lounged against his desk, grinning.

Holly wagged a finger at him. "You are not. And the receptionist says you don't go out to lunch."

"Don't want to."

They eyed each other.

"What's up?" Adam continued to lean against his desk—no chair was available for Holly—extremely relaxed, considering that moments before, he had been a whirlwind of activity.

Holly deliberately rested her weight on the desk, side by side with Adam. "An anonymous philanthropist just hired us to decorate the children's wing of the hospital. He must have seen our stuff in one of the *Town Square* magazines they leave in the waiting rooms. Laurel and Ivy are thrilled and, uh, they insisted I come to invite you along, since you got to hear all about it last Sunday."

"I'd be delighted."

"But Adam!" Holly gestured at the mess around them. "You can't leave this."

Adam started to say something, but didn't. Holly suspected he was about to admit that he left it every night and cringed.

He shrugged. "I'll come in early tomorrow."

Holly walked around until she stood in front of him. "Like you do every morning?"

"Best time of the day," he said softly.

Holly gave him a long look and started for the door. "I'm going to get you some lunch. *Healthy* lunch. When I get back, I want you to tell me how I can help you."

"Thanks for the offer." Adam smiled. "I'll accept the lunch, but you're not a lawyer."

"No, but Exemplary Temps taught me how to do office busywork."

"Holly." Adam crossed the room. "You don't have to do this." His hands cupped her face and he placed a kiss on her forehead.

"Sure I do," Holly said as Adam released her and she hurried out the door. "I didn't tell you about the Santa suit yet."

HOLLY COUNTED IT a major achievement when she cleared the leather sofa in Adam's office after several hours of tedious work. She rewarded herself by stretching full-length on it. Her eyes drifted shut as the intercom buzzed.

"Hey, move over." Adam nudged her feet onto the floor. "I want to sit here and enjoy the thirty seconds before another load arrives."

"Adam, what are you? The garbage dump for the office?"

Adam chuckled wearily as he rubbed his temples. "I mediate nonroutine controversies and assign cases."

"You haven't assigned very many cases."

"I like to keep the difficult ones."

Holly sat up. "You're doing all the behind-the-scenes work and other lawyers are getting all the glory."

Adam rested his head on the sofa back and stared at the ceiling. "I don't want that kind of glory. I do not enjoy tearing apart the remnants of people's lives just so I get a mark in the win column. I like sitting around a table with two opposing sides and hammering out a way for everyone to get on with their lives. I've won if people resolve their differences and are still speaking to each other." Adam closed his eyes in a slow blink, then turned his head toward Holly. "Understand?"

"No."

Adam wore his bland face. When he spoke, his words were barely above a whisper. "If I'd been mediating for you, your father's estate could have been sorted out in a quarter of the time. There might even have been something left for you."

"I don't want *something,* I want it all. I'm entitled to it."

Adam shook his head. "That attitude clogs the courts

and makes lawyers rich. With compromise, everybody wins.''

''That's giving in, admitting you're wrong.''

''You see? When people let their emotions interfere—''

''Oh, no,'' Holly interrupted. ''I learned, right here in the glorious offices of Swinehart, Cathardy and Steele—'' she threw her arms out in an all-encompassing gesture ''—that emotions have no place in business.''

''And you don't think anger and bitterness are emotions?''

''They're reminders.''

''Great.'' Adam reached out and put his arm around her shoulder. ''Wouldn't want you to go soft.''

Holly heard the faint sarcasm in his voice and didn't care. ''If I'd gone soft, we wouldn't be getting paid to decorate at the hospital tonight. But,'' she added, trying to lighten Adam's flat mood, ''I've been known to mellow a bit.''

''How?''

''I just spent the entire afternoon here with you.''

''I have a feeling I'm going to pay for that in some way.''

''No, no. It's an honor, really.''

''Mmm.'' Adam absently caressed her shoulder, his eyes closed.

Just when Holly thought he had drifted off to sleep, he opened his eyes, training his blue gaze on her. ''You mentioned children and a Santa suit within moments of each other.''

''Oooh. You're good. I thought you missed the bit about the Santa suit.''

Adam raised an eyebrow at her.

Holly stared down at her hands, finding some imperfection on her thumbnail and examining it. ''It was Ivy's idea. I'll be wearing Mom's Mrs. Claus outfit and...''

A dimple deepened in Adam's cheek. "Finally asking for help?"

"This isn't help, it's atmosphere." She glanced up at him, trying to gauge his reaction. He was back to the blandly pleasant lawyer again. She hated that. He did it so well. She flung her hands apart. "Ivy is…Ivy's trying to make everything like it was."

"*Ivy* is."

Holly took a deep, exasperated breath. "The children like it."

Adam nodded. "The children."

"Adam!"

"Holly?"

They stared at each other.

"Are you worried that I'll get lascivious notions at the thought of you playing Mrs. Claus to my Santa?" He leered at her.

Holly began to laugh, a deep throaty laugh. "You'll do it, won't you?"

"Ho ho ho."

"YOUR FATHER was a *big* man." Adam stared at the folds of red velvet pooling around his ankles.

"Yes," chorused three female voices. There was one Mrs. Claus, one elf and one red designer jumpsuit.

"Don't worry, Adam," fussed Holly. "No one will know when we stuff the legs into the boots.

"Ho ho."

"Adam, honey, say that with more conviction. You're the darlingest Santa we've ever had." Laurel handed him another pillow.

"Okay, ladies, that's it for the pillows. I can't bend as it is." Adam hitched the belt tighter, looking at himself in the mirror with resignation. Only the bubbling happiness of the three sisters made this worth it.

Half an hour later, as they went from room to room,

Holly experienced a wide scope of emotions. There was the inevitable jerking on her heartstrings when she saw the children and their concerned parents. There was happiness and nostalgia and unexpected memories of past Christmases. She almost wished she could hand the hospital's check right back. Almost.

"These outfits remind me of the final scene in *White Christmas*," Adam said, catching their reflections in the windowed corridors of the hospital.

"That's because they're copies of the costumes in the final scene of *White Christmas*." Holly flicked her muff under Adam's nose—the only part other than his eyes not covered in whiskers.

And those eyes. Holly sighed inwardly. They'd been sending her wicked messages all evening. Most unSantalike messages.

They passed the nurses' station. Holly was sweltering in the heavy costume and could only imagine how Adam felt. He'd been the perfect Santa. Rather than a boisterous, booming character, he'd been gentle and low-key. He talked quietly to the children who could talk; other times he simply sat next to the beds while Holly and her sisters quickly put up small twinkling trees.

It wasn't too late when they finished the children's rooms and began the large tree in the children's wing waiting room.

"The angel tree, I see," Adam said as he opened one of the boxes.

"*An* angel tree. I didn't have enough notice to save one of the others, but I think this one is better here. The angels are all different. Like the children."

"See, you are a softie." Adam took off his hat and beard. "I'd like to get out of this suit," he said, loosening his belt and removing the pillows. "Then I can help you."

"Adam…" Holly wanted to tell him how he'd made the evening special for her, that having him there, wearing the silly suit, had meant a lot to her. She'd just realized it herself.

"Be back in a few minutes," Adam said, and the moment was lost.

Holly watched Adam on his way down the hall. He walked with a grace her bear of a father had never had. For just a moment, the thought of her father brought hot tears to Holly's eyes. She didn't know why she was so weepy this evening.

"Got it bad, huh, Holly? Here, untangle these lights. Why did you bring so many, anyway?" Laurel handed her a snarled string of fairy lights.

"Quit jerking them out of the box and they won't tangle." Holly handed the string back to Laurel and got the rest of the lights out of the box herself.

The next time she looked for Adam, he had stopped at the nurses' station and was opening a canned soft drink.

"That looks good. You all want something to drink?" When her sisters nodded, Holly headed for the station. Several of the nurses were talking with Adam.

"...will just love it," she heard as she approached.

"It was sweet of you to do it."

Holly missed Adam's reply. One of the nurses noticed her. "Y'all did a really great job."

Holly smiled her thanks. "It was more fun than work. Please thank whoever hired us."

"Thank him yourself. He's standing right here."

Holly's eyes flew to Adam just in time to catch the slight shake of his head. She heard a soft groan from behind the desk. "Adam?" she whispered.

"Sorry. I'm just getting off a twelve-hour shift. Otherwise I wouldn't have..." The nurse shrugged.

Adam quirked a half smile at her, not certain how Holly would take this. "It's a couple of days early, but happy birthday."

"Oh, Adam." And the stoic Holly Hall burst into tears.

"I'LL MAKE SOME hot chocolate," Ivy offered as the Deck the Halls van pulled into the driveway.

"Trying to avoid unloading duties?" Laurel asked, slamming the door.

Ignoring her sisters, Holly looked up at Adam. "Can you stay? You don't really have to go in so early tomorrow, do you?"

Adam drew her closer. Holly had let Laurel drive, choosing to sit next to Adam. "Have you got any jobs tomorrow?"

"Just two. The omigosh-it's-nearly-Christmas-and-I'm-not-ready-for-it kind. And that's it. We'll do them tomorrow morning."

Adam nodded. "I'll have a cup of hot chocolate."

Ivy had the hot chocolate ready when they finished unloading the boxes. Adam followed Holly into the kitchen. She'd been quiet ever since her outburst at the hospital, content to hold his hand on the drive home. He hadn't minded.

Adam hadn't intended for the sisters to find out that he'd arranged for them to decorate the children's wing at the hospital. Holly hadn't said anything about it to Ivy and Laurel and he hoped that she wouldn't. He didn't want to change the easygoing relationship he had with them. On the other hand, he intended to disentangle Holly from her family right after Christmas.

"Where's your tree?" he asked suddenly.

"We don't get one for ourselves anymore." Ivy's voice was clipped.

"This time of year, there isn't money left for *unbudgeted frivolities.*" Laurel sipped her chocolate and eyed Holly over the rim of her cup.

Adam watched as the guilt flashed across Holly's features, then turned his head to face Laurel. Laurel's gaze flicked from Holly to him, was caught and held. Her eyes, brown like Holly's, widened.

With Laurel, Adam didn't choose to be gentle. When he looked at Holly, his eyes were warm. As family, her sisters had been included in that warmth—until now. A muscle worked in his jaw and he knew his expression was hard—he intended it to be. *If you hurt Holly again,* his eyes said to a wary Laurel, *you deal with me.* The look on his face left no doubt that the experience would be an unpleasant one.

His eyes briefly left Laurel's to direct a piercing glance at Ivy, who blushed, then went back to Laurel. Adam reached for his mug of hot chocolate and took a sip. Laurel set hers on the table as the slight trembling in her hands became perceptible.

Holly noticed nothing. She was embarrassed and furious with her sisters and took a few moments to compose herself. She fervently hoped that Adam would not interpret their remarks as a hint that he buy their Christmas tree.

"Usually we're too tired to decorate our own, anyway." Holly dredged up a smile. "But this year, why not?"

"Ivy and I'll buy one after the last job tomorrow," Laurel said hastily.

"I'd like to come by and see what sort of tree the professionals choose for themselves," Adam said, finishing his chocolate and getting to his feet.

Holly laughed. "Whatever is left over."

"I could come by your office tomorrow after we finish," she offered as she walked Adam to his car. "Help you with some of the paperwork. Then you could have dinner with us."

"Very tempting," Adam said softly, admiring her face in the moonlight.

Holly shivered and wrapped her arms around herself.

"Let me." Adam opened his coat and held it around her while she snuggled against his heart.

"Thank you for my birthday present," she said softly,

not wanting to disturb the stillness of the night. "It was wonderful." She looked up at him. "You are wonderful."

Her mouth was only inches away from his and he closed the distance quickly. Their lips were cold, and Holly and Adam drew apart, laughing, before melting together once more.

Holly was surrounded by Adam, by his warmth and scent. She worked her arms out of the cocoon of his coat to wrap them around his neck as she pressed herself closer.

He tasted of chocolate.

"Holly." He filled her name with all the pent-up yearning he'd felt for weeks. She'd warned him she didn't want to become involved and he hadn't believed her for a while. A very short while. Just until he'd spent long stretches working next to her, learning all about her. He lived for moments like this one, when she seemed to want him as much as he wanted her. He'd gone so slowly, never cornering her into choosing between Deck the Halls and Adam Markland. He'd tried to fit into her life. Now he was going to find out how successful he'd been.

"Holly," he said again, his breath warming her face. "I'd enjoy a quiet evening with you—alone," he added, deciding to drop some early hints. "But I'm only going into the office for a couple of hours tomorrow. I've got an afternoon flight home to Boston."

"Boston?" Holly searched his face. "You won't be here for Christmas?"

The dismayed surprise on her face was an encouraging sign. "I'm spending Christmas at home with my family. My brother and sister will be there with their kids." It occurred to him that she might ask him to stay. He could; after all, he'd just been home for Thanksgiving. No, if Holly was ever going to think about him and what he meant to her, she needed time alone. Christmas was that time.

"Of course." Holly recovered quickly and gently pushed

herself out of Adam's circle of warmth. "I forgot that you aren't a free agent." She shivered.

"Get back in the house," he directed softly. "I'll drop by tomorrow on my way to the airport with something to put under your tree."

A Christmas present! Holly had thought she'd have two more days. She'd always been a last-minute shopper, finding that her impulse buys were usually the best. Besides, she never knew until Christmas Eve how much money she could spend.

This year, she had money, but no time.

"Do YOU THINK he'll like it?" Holly looked at Laurel, panic in her expression.

"It's real cute, Holly," Laurel drawled.

"He'll hate it." Holly dropped her head on the kitchen table beside the small box she was measuring for paper.

"I don't know," Laurel picked up the little glass bear. "You've decorated it real nice."

"Oh, cut it out." Holly snatched the bear back and polished off Laurel's fingerprints.

"It *is* Steuben glass. You've still got some taste, I see," Laurel muttered.

"What'll I do?" Holly wailed. "He'll be here any minute."

"I could help you select a nice tie."

"I couldn't give Adam a tie! It's too...impersonal. Bears are special to us."

"Special to us?" Laurel repeated with heavy emphasis. "Is there an 'us'?"

"I don't know." Holly studied the little bear. "I saw this and it reminded me of the night we met. You remember—"

"Yes, and I'd rather forget. I don't mean Adam," Laurel added when she saw the look on Holly's face.

"We tied these little ribbons around all those bears

Bloomie got for us." Holly smiled to herself as she placed the bear back in its nest of tissue paper.

"How sweet."

"I thought so."

Laurel drifted toward the refrigerator, opened it and peered inside. "Holly," she said, extracting an apple and closing the door. "Has it occurred to you that Adam isn't a *sweet* man?"

"No, it hasn't." Holly ripped off tape with a snap.

"Honey, you've hooked more man than you know." Laurel gestured to the glass door behind Holly. "Let me know if you decide to throw him back."

"What?" As Holly stared at Laurel, she heard the slam of a car door and barely had enough time to stash the wrapping paper in the pantry. "Stick this under the tree," she said, thrusting the box at Laurel as she watched Adam's approach.

"You came around back," Holly said, a little breathlessly, when she opened the door.

Adam flashed her a smile. "Lunchtime?"

"Uh—" Holly looked around the kitchen "—we were trying to get the tree up before you got here." True, but she neglected to tell him that their morning jobs took longer than scheduled because she was Christmas shopping instead of helping.

"How about a turkey sandwich?" she offered, trying to ignore the large red-and-gold package Adam held.

"Sounds fine, but lead me to the tree first."

Holly led Adam through the house into the living room.

"Oh, no." It slipped out before she could stop it.

"Hi!" Ivy grinned at them from her perch on the ladder. "Well Adam, we've done our part." She finished tying the last of at least two dozen bunches of mistletoe and hopped down. "Think I'll go into the kitchen and start lunch." She gave Adam an exaggerated wink in passing.

"Think I'll go with you." Laurel and her husky laugh followed.

"That's an interesting shade of pink," Adam commented, tilting Holly's chin.

"I can't believe they're so obvious."

Adam laughed, took her hand and led her to the tree. "I rather like it," he said and positioned her under one of the bunches.

"They poked holes in the ceiling," Holly grumbled before Adam claimed his kiss.

Afterward, she didn't mind the holes at all.

"Now, about this tree…" Adam regarded the jumble in front of them.

"We each have our favorite ornaments," Holly explained.

"It isn't coordinated."

"We like it that way."

"Good." Adam sat on the carpet and nudged the red-and-gold package under the tree. It joined one small silver box.

Holly sank down next to him, besieged by nerves.

"Tomorrow's Christmas Eve." Adam leaned back against a chair, totally at ease. Although he didn't smile, his eyes held a secret amusement. "Do you want to open your present now, or wait?"

"I—" Holly broke off as she considered whether she wanted to prolong the suspense or get the embarrassment and the explanations over with.

"Personally, I like to watch people's faces when they open my gifts." His dimples deepened, but he still wasn't actually smiling. The wretch was *laughing* at her!

"Here." She grabbed the silver box and shoved it into his lap.

"Here, yourself." Adam thunked the large box on Holly's legs.

Her heart pounded. He'd think her present was goofy.

She was convinced that she was about to open a five-or ten-pound box of chocolates. She hoped they were Godiva. If she got fat, it wasn't going to be on cheap chocolate.

She couldn't stand his staring at her, and plucked at the sticky tape. "Let's open them at the same time." She had magnified this out of all proportion. They were just friends, for heaven's sake.

She couldn't look at him. He was obviously of the paper-ripping school, while she liked to unwrap slowly.

The tearing sound stopped. Holly sneaked a quick peek as Adam took off the box lid.

Hearing his delighted laugh, she exhaled. Adam crawled over to her. "Look—his bow is crooked." He retied it. "Brings back memories."

"It's supposed to."

The blazing look Adam gave her made Holly catch her breath.

"Open yours," he urged softly.

Holly ripped the rest of the paper. Inside the box was a framed copy of the *Town Square* magazine with their cover.

"Adam!" Holly reached up and threw her arms around him in a great hug. "Thanks," she whispered softly.

She leaned against him, admiring the cover. "I wish you weren't going back to Boston for Christmas, but I know you want to be with your family."

It took all Adam's self-control not to cancel his flight instantly. He'd better leave now, while he could still convince himself to go.

He squeezed Holly's shoulders briefly. "I'm going to take a rain check on the turkey sandwich. I need to get to the airport. Walk me to the door and stop under some mistletoe on the way."

Giggling, Holly hopscotched out of the living room and into the foyer. Adam followed and they broke in as many bunches of mistletoe as they could.

"Your car's around back," Holly reminded him.

"I know. I want to say goodbye in private."

Holly smiled wickedly and planted herself under a particularly large bunch of Ivy's mistletoe. When Adam dutifully bent his head, she locked her arms behind his neck and sinuously pressed herself against him. Extremely satisfied with herself as she felt a shudder pass through his body, she backed him against the front door and began to undo the buttons of his plaid shirt.

Holly trailed kisses after her fingers, enjoying the feel of the softly curling hair on his chest.

"Holly!" She heard the hoarse rumble in his chest and stopped abruptly as two strong hands firmly set her away. "No more games." Adam closed his eyes and took a deep breath.

Holly was ashamed when she realized how affected Adam was by her caresses.

"Sorry," she mumbled, quickly buttoning his shirt once more. "I guess I was hoping you'd decide to stay."

The corner of Adam's mouth lifted in a half smile and he managed a credible drawl. "Holly, honey, I'll be back."

## CHAPTER SEVEN

WHEN WAS HE COMING BACK? How could she have let him leave without telling her when he'd be back?

Boston. It might as well have been the moon. He'd only been gone two days, but it was Christmas and Holly missed him. She thought she'd handled everything so coolly, being very straightforward about her intentions. No time for relationships.

How was she supposed to know he'd take her at her word?

She should be scheduling their tree dismantlings. At least that's what she told Laurel and Ivy when she escaped to her room after the Christmas dinner dishes were done. Ivy would spend the rest of the day watching football and Laurel was doing who knew what. Probably eating.

She ought to have done the books and typed the statements by now. Instead, she'd spent all day mooning about Adam Markland. This was ridiculous. Maybe if she went downstairs to the office, she'd get some work done.

ADAM CHECKED HIS WATCH, calculating how soon he could break away and call Holly. He had decided that he would—a quick Christmas greeting. He wanted her to think about him, after all.

His father gently cleared his throat. "You've been rather tight-lipped about the cases you're handling at Steele's, Adam."

Adam glanced quickly toward the head of the table and met his father's querying look. "Testing me, Dad?"

"Not at all." The elder Markland blotted his mouth with a snowy damask napkin. "Confidentiality is understood. But there is nothing ethically wrong with consulting your colleagues for another opinion."

His family called it consulting, but it was nonstop talking shop. The only way Adam could avoid it was to play trains with his nephews.

"Yes, and we'd like some tips on handling bankruptcy cases," his brother said with what Adam knew was complete sincerity.

That was the problem. His family lived and breathed law, celebrating victories and agonizing over defeats.

There were more victories than defeats. A client didn't hire one Markland—he hired all of them, with their combined specialities and driving desire to win at any cost.

"I'm mediating my cases." There was silence around the dinner table. Adam looked into the faces of his mother, father, brother and sister and sighed inwardly. His brother-in-law and sister-in-law looked at him pityingly. They were also lawyers.

"You mean you haven't won any." Stephanie Markland Brandt's blue eyes regarded his knowingly.

Adam bit back a harsh retort. "Our definition of winning isn't the same. Don't worry—business is good. I'm not starving." He reached for his coffee.

Four pairs of Markland-blue eyes assessed him, and he responded with the pleasantly bland face Holly hated.

Shouting erupted in the kitchen. "I'll go referee," Adam said, glad to leave the dining room. It would give them the chance to talk about him, but he didn't care.

"Tell you what," Adam said as he served his boisterous nephews and niece their Christmas cake, "Come upstairs when you finish these and we'll play trains."

Figuring he had about five minutes, Adam dashed up the back staircase and into the upstairs library.

The phone on her desk rang loudly, startling Holly. Her heart began to pound and she forced herself to let the phone ring twice before she pounced on it. "Hello?"

"Merry Christmas, Holly."

Holly grinned like an idiot. "Merry Christmas, Adam."

She knew he was smiling, too; she could practically hear it. A few seconds slipped by while every rational thought escaped Holly's mind.

"Do you miss me?" Adam prompted.

"Of course we miss you! Laurel and Ivy haven't forgiven me for not convincing you to stay. We got so used to having you around." Holly paused, conscious of how awful that sounded.

"I asked if *you* miss me."

Holly heard shouting in the background. "I—"

"Uncle Adam!" It echoed right in her ear, along with Adam's laughter. "The troops found me. I promised them we'd play trains— Hey! Don't jump on me—"

The phone crashed to the floor and Holly could hear laughing and shrieking. A breathless Adam finally retrieved the telephone. "Holly, I've got to go. Talk to you later."

She still didn't know when he'd be back. It would serve her right if he *didn't* come back. Why should he rush away from his family? At the very least she should have admitted how much she missed him.

Work. That would take her mind off Adam Markland. Holly scanned her client list, checking for those who had scheduled a tree-dismantling in advance. Not one for December 26.

She threw down her pen. How could she concentrate? Her life was a mess.

No, it wasn't. She had never been as financially stable as she was this season. She hugged her knees to her chest in the great leather chair that had been her father's. Burrowing down, she could still smell the horrible cigars he used to smoke in here after dinner. Holly inhaled deeply, then straightened, reaching for her pen, which had bounced across the massive oak desk.

Financial stability. Security. She could relax, pull back some, right?

Okay, so exactly how much of this season's success did she owe to Adam? As long as she couldn't stop thinking about him, she might as well find out.

Holly unfolded her scheduling calendar and began to list the jobs Adam had worked on. Grinning to herself, she decided to allocate minimum wage to his work hours, which had been nearly every evening and every Saturday since they'd met.

She'd been selfish, she admitted, remembering the late nights and the condition of his office.

Holly gritted her teeth when she finished calculating Adam's work hours. Suspecting was one thing, seeing it confirmed was something else. She pushed herself out of the leather chair and found last year's records.

No wonder this had been a good year. Holly fought back tears of censure. Look at the jobs she'd scheduled from the middle of the month on. Twice as many as before. They couldn't have handled the work load without him. She had calculated Adam's unpaid help into their job times.

She added in the profits from the hospital job. Feeling masochistic at this point, she figured in an arbitrary amount for the pizzas and deli food Adam always brought with him.

Holly felt horrible. She must be in love.

"When have I had time to fall in love?" she asked aloud. When people fell in love, they saw it coming. They went out to eat, they danced, they took long walks together. They went to movies, to the symphony and a few charity functions, right? They prepared for it—nurtured it. They allowed it to come into their lives.

This couldn't be love. She wasn't ready for love. She had to put Ivy through college first.

In an unreasonable panic, Holly began to feel angry. How dared Adam allow her to fall in love with him?

A night's sleep improved Holly's outlook. Work should make it even better. Some people, somewhere, wanted to get rid of their tree today. She was going to call until she found them.

Holly had her hand on the telephone when it rang. Startled, she jerked her hand away, then laughed. "Deck the Halls," she answered.

"Oh, which sister have I got?"

"Holly."

"Holly, dear, I need help. It's dreadful, but it's actually an honor, but a terrible imposition, but how could I turn them down? Where else could they go?"

The disjointed ramble in the cigarette-hoarsened voice could only come from Claudia Fitzhugh. "How can we help, Mrs. Fitzhugh?" Holly asked, trying to infuse her voice with reassuring calm and not giving in to an urge to laugh.

"Oh, I knew I could count on you, Holly, dear. You're just like your mother and I could always count on her when things got in a tangle."

"What's wrong?" Holly prompted, becoming impatient.

"Martha is in such a tizzy about it all. She accused me of being jealous, which is true, because I'm a human being and there isn't a person alive who wouldn't be, and after all, I'm Bernard's sister, but just because I'm not invited doesn't mean I can't tell her she shouldn't have canceled everything even if she isn't going to be here."

"Mrs. Fitzhugh!" Holly managed to interject when the woman stopped for breath. "I've been out of touch for a while and I don't know what you're talking about."

"Oh, dear. I think I'm having a New Year's Eve reception in my home."

"You don't know?"

"Well, I'm not having it if I can't make the proper arrangements. It's the Music League's reception for the symphony musicians and the Green Room donors."

"The one after the New Year's Eve pops concert? Mother and Dad used to go."

"My sister-in-law, Martha Steele, was having it this year. She got a call last week from the White House, and she and Bernard have been invited to a New Year's Eve gala with the president! It was a telephoned invitation," Mrs Fitzhugh stressed, "so there must have been a cancellation."

Holly bit back a smile.

"And the silly woman only tells me this morning! She *canceled* the caterer and the room designer! I called immediately, but of course they were booked." Mrs. Fitzhugh let out an exasperated breath. "And having Mr. Kelly was such a coup. Now, dear, please tell me you aren't booked for New Year's Eve, too?"

Holly's heart began to pound. "We don't do food, Mrs. Fitzhugh."

"I realize that, dear, but when you did my tree, you did say you wanted to expand into social events. And, frankly, the better-known names will already be hired."

"Mrs. Fitzhugh, Deck the Halls would be thrilled to decorate your home. What about a budget and a theme?" Holly flipped through the pages of her phone book, looking for Mrs. Bloom's number.

"Whatever you've got." Mrs. Fitzhugh was realistic when she needed to be.

Holly hung up the phone and let out a yell that brought Ivy and Laurel running.

She spent the rest of the week happily preparing for the party. She wanted to share her good news with Adam, but he didn't call, which was fine with her. She didn't have time to be in love, anyway.

Late in the afternoon of the thirtieth, the doorbell rang.

Holly's hands stilled as one of her sisters answered it. A moment passed, and she continued slowly making a bow out of silver netting.

Adam appeared in the workroom doorway and leaned a leather-clad shoulder against it. His cheekbones wore a ruddy stain, due to the recent cold snap. The lock of hair, still untamed, fell across his forehead.

Holly wanted to stand up and throw herself into his arms. But he'd been gone a week and had only called her once for about two minutes. She didn't know what to think. "Hello, Adam," she said, trying to sound nonchalant.

"Hello, yourself. I just got back."

"Did you have a good time?" Couldn't she come up with something better than that?

"Yes, I did," Adam answered politely. "I'd like to take you out tomorrow night."

"That's New Year's Eve."

"I know. People go out on New Year's Eve all the time." There was amusement in his voice.

"We're booked this New Year's, isn't that great?" In trying to sound enthusiastic, which she was, Holly overdid it.

"No." His blue eyes turned stormy.

Holly ignored him. "Claudia Fitzhugh hired us to decorate for the symphony's New Year's Eve reception. Isn't that fantastic? Think of the contacts we'll make."

Adam crossed his arms. "It's after Christmas, Holly."

"I know," she answered quietly.

"I thought things were going to slow down after Christmas."

"They did."

Adam watched as her fingers fumbled with the netting, taking longer with this bow than any of the others. "Is your presence required for the duration of the party?"

Holly gave up on the bow. "Adam, it's our *first* society

function. We have the opportunity to make incredible contacts.''

"I thought your family was a member of the upper echelon.''

"Was. The upper echelon has a short memory.''

Adam's stern expression made Holly uncomfortable. "Mrs. Fitzhugh invited us to stay. Laurel and Ivy will be there, too. Laurel needs your tree skirt to wear.'' Holly tried a light laugh.

Adam's blue eyes were unreadable. "How many other parties are you doing?''

"None…yet.''

"Black tie?''

"Of course.''

"Of course.'' Adam turned, obviously leaving.

"Adam—wait.''

He turned back, raising an eyebrow.

"I missed you,'' Holly said, barely above a whisper.

Adam's lips curved in the smallest of smiles, but he shook his head slightly and left.

"YOU NEED SOME PEACE and quiet,'' Adam said as he opened Holly's front door.

"Everything looked all right at the party, didn't it?''

"Yes,'' he reassured Holly smilingly. "It was perfect.''

"Well, not perfect—''

"Holly.''

She looked at him, recognizing the warning note in his voice.

"It's a new year. We're alone, with each other, and I have a plate of party goodies and a bottle of champagne. Getting some ideas?'' He nodded his head toward the family room.

Holly grabbed two glasses and followed him, sitting on the sofa as he opened the champagne.

"To the future.''

"It's going to be great, isn't it, Adam?" Holly set her champagne on the coffee table and leaned back.

Adam didn't kiss her the way she'd hoped. Perhaps she'd better make the first move.

He held a finger to her lips. "Not just yet. Are you only after my body, or will you respect me in the morning?"

Holly was surprised into a laugh. "Adam, you lunatic, kiss me."

Adam's even white teeth tugged at his lip as he shook his head. "Answer."

"You're serious!" Holly said, amazed.

"I have a right to know." She obviously didn't understand, so he elaborated. "I told you before that I don't go in for flings. Where are we headed?"

"Adam," Holly protested, running her hand through her curls, "it's only a kiss."

"Is it?" Adam cupped her chin with his hand and pressed his lips against hers.

At least that was the physical description of what he did. But how it *felt* was something else altogether. Being confronted with her feelings for Adam frightened Holly. He would start making demands—already his lips were demanding a response from her. Her blood became liquid fire, making her achingly aware of him.

She gasped when he broke the kiss.

"You see?" he asked, softly triumphant, mouth slanted in a half smile.

Holly was too bemused to answer.

"You can slow down now, can't you, Holly? I'm not asking you to quit work so you can be at my beck and call. Just make room for me—for *us* in your life."

Holly wound her arms around his neck. "I love you, Adam."

To her astonishment, a look of pain and anger flashed across his face.

"But you're not *in* love with me."

Before she could reply, Holly heard the unmistakable sounds of the front door opening. She stared at Adam's tight face. "What's the difference?"

"You haven't been alone with me long enough to find out," she heard him say as Laurel and Ivy burst into the room.

"This has been the most wonderful evening!" Laurel proclaimed, her eyes bright and her cheeks flushed.

"Champagne will do that to you." Holly was glad of their company. What was with Adam? She'd just told him she loved him, for heaven's sake!

"Not champagne—a man."

"Who?"

"Bart King. He's a member of the Southwest Film Commission and I think he can help me in my career."

"What, they want Deck the Halls to decorate for some films?" Holly leaned forward eagerly, missing the bitter smile on Adam's face.

"Holly, honey, he couldn't care less about Deck the Halls."

"What help could he possibly be, then?"

Laurel glanced at Ivy. "My acting career."

"Your acting career," Holly repeated immediately, unaware she had done so. "You don't have an acting career."

"I'm hoping to change all that."

Ivy prudently remained quiet.

"You don't have any experience," Holly pointed out.

"Don't you think this has been one big act for the last five years? Living here—" Laurel gestured all around them "—with the impeccably decorated front rooms and the rest of the house gutted? Sharing our clothes, bringing home all those sugar packets, crackers and doggie bags from the restaurants? Gorging ourselves at salad bars so there would *be* doggie bags? Even Mama was acting." Laurel reached out and tugged at the necklace Holly wore. "Keeping up appearances has been one long act, hasn't it?"

Holly took a deep breath. "It is cheaper for us to live in this house than anywhere else. If you'd remember any of your business training, you'd know that. The real-estate market is in the toilet and this house is paid for. All we do is pay taxes, which are deductible. Rent isn't."

"Okay, okay. You probably don't remember, but when I was at SMU, I loved my drama classes. It's what I want to do. I think things could finally begin to happen for me."

Holly turned to Adam. "It's the champagne talking."

"Holly." Laurel was so intense she forgot to drawl the "honey." "I'm almost twenty-five. I want a job of my own—"

"Deck the Halls is better than a job! We own the company."

Laurel changed tactics. "We've finally got some money. Ivy is going to college, so you'll need to hire someone, anyway. It's a new year. New beginnings."

"How could you even *think* of wasting your business degree after all we've sacrificed for it!" Holly's patience was gone.

Laurel looked as if she'd been slapped. "You don't need a business degree to rent Christmas-tree decorations."

"There is a lot to running your own business."

"How would I know?" Laurel asked caustically. "*You* keep the records; You make the decisions. You didn't even trust me to decorate a tree by myself until this year."

"You can't earn your living acting!"

"*I want to try!*"

The room went horribly quiet.

"I can't allow it, Laurel," Holly said unyieldingly.

"It's her life, Holly," said Adam's calm voice behind her.

"You, too?" Holly was stung. "She doesn't know anything about acting."

"She can learn."

"She'll ruin her life. I didn't work this hard so she could

waste everything on a whim.'' How could the man she loved take Laurel's side?

"This isn't a whim," Laurel said.

"It's her life," Adam repeated. "And she's old enough to know what she wants."

Laurel nodded regally. "Thank you, Adam."

Holly's lip quivered and no one was fooled into thinking it was from impending tears.

Laurel put a hand on Holly's shoulder and Holly shrugged it off. "Holly, nothing will happen right away. I just wanted you to know, because I won't be spending as much time with Deck the Halls. Mr. King offered me a job as a receptionist, so I'll work there and save money for acting classes."

"Thank you for telling me," Holly said icily.

Laurel stood there a moment more, then she and Ivy left the room.

Holly whirled on Adam. "Traitor!"

"Now who's the actress?"

"I know." Holly squinted at him. "You took Laurel's side because you think I'll give up the business then."

"Holly…" he began with exasperation, but she ignored him.

"Nothing can interfere with Deck the Halls. I won't let it. I will do anything to make it succeed." Holly shook her head. "Anything."

"Thus proving you aren't in love with me." Adam's voice was cold. "You'd sacrifice us to Deck the Halls. But I wouldn't choose my job over you because nothing is as important as what we have together—what we *could* have together."

"Being a success is *important* to me, Adam," Holly said urgently. Why wouldn't he understand?

Adam's eyes searched her face. "You're trying to be a success at Laurel's expense."

"That's not true," Holly lashed out, hurt at Adam's betrayal. "For two years, Ivy and I worked so Laurel could get her degree. Now she wants to throw it all back in our faces."

"Let her go, Holly." Adam reached out to caress her cheek, but Holly batted his hand away. He sighed. "People have different definitions of success. For me, achieving happiness is success."

"If I'm a success, I'm happy," Holly shot back.

"Then I'm sorry for you."

"I don't want your pity!" she snapped.

At Adam's silence, Holly began to feel uncomfortable.

"You remind me very much of my family," he commented at last. "It's money, power and winning. Nothing else matters."

That was easy for him to say. He'd never been poor or powerless. "You'd better believe it."

Adam looked directly into her eyes. "You don't mean that."

Holly met his gaze unflinchingly. "Oh, yes, I do."

Now Adam's eyes mirrored Holly's feeling of betrayal. "Then we have nothing more to say to each other, do we?"

# CHAPTER EIGHT

"I DON'T WANT to go to SMU," Ivy stated flatly. "It's too expensive. I had no idea you were trying to save up that much money." She followed Holly into their office.

Why were both her sisters being so unreasonable all of a sudden? Holly wondered, tired from a day of tree dismantling and decorating for a client's dinner party. "Actually, if you live at home, it won't cost that much more than going to a state school." Holly sat back in her father's leather chair, unconsciously echoing a posture he'd assumed many times.

"Laurel got *her* degree from a state school. She didn't finish at SMU and—"

"And she's been upset ever since."

"I'm not Laurel. I'm not the sorority type," Ivy said. "I know our whole family went to SMU, but I don't want to. You should be glad—my plan's cheaper. I'm going to register at the college next week," she said resolutely.

Holly gave up. "If you change your mind about SMU, let me know. We've booked some parties for January. Little ones, like tonight, but it's a start."

"Have you and Adam made up yet?" Ivy asked.

Holly shook her head.

"Why not? You and Laurel have." Ivy handed Holly the phone. "Call him and take him with you when you go check on things tonight. He'll add to the decor."

Holly snatched the phone from Ivy and glared until her unrepentant sister left the room.

It didn't help that Ivy was right. She owed Adam an apology. She'd overreacted just because he disagreed with her.

Holly slowly punched out Adam's office number.

"Markland." Adam's voice was impersonal.

She squeezed her eyes shut. "Adam, it's Holly. I'm sorry. Laurel and I made up. Mama's diamonds and I are going out to check on a dinner party we did today. If you and your tux would like to come with us, I'll pick you up at seven. We'll stay there during cocktails and then we could get coffee or dinner or something."

There was a silence of several heartbeats—interminable to Holly. It made her realize how much she hoped Adam wasn't the kind of man who carried grudges.

"I think I'll choose the something," she heard Adam say at last.

In the end, they did have dinner, in a chain restaurant where they were overdressed.

"What's the story behind those?" Adam tugged at Holly's necklace, mimicking Laurel's gesture on New Year's Eve.

"You mean Laurel's reference during her dramatic scene?" Holly swirled the coffee in her cup before answering. "Dad bought Mama this necklace. It was her only piece of 'important' jewelry."

Adam raised his eyebrows. "She didn't need anything else."

"She didn't want anything else." Holly bit her lip and went on. "I tried to sell the diamonds and replace them with fakes before the auction." She looked at Adam defiantly. "We needed money for lawyers. Someone had to fight for us before everything was taken away. But guess what?"

Adam watched the bitterness cross Holly's face and tried to imagine how he would have reacted if his world had fallen apart when he was only twenty-two. "Do you think that necklace might be a copy? It isn't unusual to have copies made for insurance reasons. There could be a real one somewhere.''

''That's what we thought, but it appears Mama had been selling diamonds out of it for a long time. We found... papers.'' Holly gestured expressively. ''I guess things weren't going well in Dad's business.''

She fingered the necklace. ''Anyway,'' she said, lightening the mood, ''I'm making this black dress and the diamonds my signature look—like Lillie Langtry. I'll stop in during parties and eventually everyone will recognize a Deck the Halls design.''

Adam raised his coffee cup. ''To new ventures.''

IT BECAME A ROUTINE that on a party night they went out after Holly's appearance. It wasn't like any relationship Adam had ever had before. The barrier of Holly's responsibilities still came between them, frustrating him enormously. At least, he had to acknowledge they were spending time together—without her entire family looking on.

''My social life has improved markedly,'' he commented one evening. ''I kind of miss the trees, though.''

He poured Holly a glass of red table wine. They'd found a small Italian restaurant they now thought of as ''theirs.'' It reeked unashamedly of garlic and tomatoes and fresh baked loaves of crusty bread. They rarely ate a complete meal, having nibbled at parties, but Holly immediately became addicted to the oversize mugs of cappuccino, topped with an extraordinary amount of whipped cream.

''You miss all that work, huh?'' Holly dipped her spoon into the whipped cream. ''We've still got one tree left to take down.''

Adam raised his eyebrows in mock horror. ''It's January!''

At her happy face and throaty laughter, Adam ached with a sweet yearning. ''It's Mrs. Fitzhugh's,'' Holly was saying. She left town right after New Year's and just got back. I'm taking it down tomorrow morning.''

"So you are slowing down a bit." It was time to push their relationship forward. During his week in Boston at Christmas, Adam realized the only way to keep Holly from thinking about her sisters or her company would be to take her away from them. Not forever, just a weekend. A weekend for the two of them.

"A bit," Holly replied cautiously. "We have to do inventory and get rid of damaged ornaments, and check our books and—''

"Come away with me." Adam reached across the table and held both her hands in his.

"I can't," Holly protested automatically.

"You can. For a weekend. I'll plan everything."

Holly gazed into Adam's brilliant blue eyes and was lost. His voice was quietly mesmerizing. "You won't have to think. You won't have to do anything. I want to take care of you—just for a weekend. Let your soul heal."

Holly closed her eyes. "When?"

It was barely a whisper, but Adam caught his breath. Holly opened her eyes and looked at him with so much longing, his hands began to shake. He released hers before she noticed.

"The last weekend of the month," he said with such certainty that Holly asked why.

"Where's your optimism?" Adam scolded her gently. "Deck the Halls will be booked for Valentine Day. I'm allowing plenty of time."

The next morning, a dreamy fog enveloped Holly as she tackled Mrs. Fitzhugh's tree. She suspected that Adam would have been gratified, if he'd been there to see it.

Her daydreams shattered at the sound of Mrs. Fitzhugh's scream.

Holly scrambled down the stepladder and raced into the

study, where Mrs. Fitzhugh sat at a cherrywood escritoire, clutching her heart.

"No, no," Mrs. Fitzhugh moaned. She held a letter crumpled in one hand.

"Mrs. Fitzhugh!" The matron turned to her and Holly was alarmed at the gray tinge in her face. "I'm calling an ambulance."

"No!" Mrs. Fitzhugh visibly composed herself. "This has never happened to me before and now twice in one month... Martha is completely insane."

She handed the letter to Holly. "This probably came the day we left. I should have had our mail forwarded."

Holly recognized the pale green engraved notepaper instantly. Mr. John Kelly, Event Designer, regretted that he would be unable to keep his commitment to the Ballet Guild's Winter Ball due to his hiring by the Heart Foundation for its annual Valentine's Heart Ball.

"Martha and I had words," Mrs. Fitzhugh explained. "The committee and I were shocked at her behavior over the New Year's Eve reception. I expressed my concern at her unreliability, and she resigned as chairman of the Winter Ball. I, of course, was elected to replace her. And now this."

Holly leaned against one of the floral chintz chairs. "She hired him out from under you."

Mrs. Fitzhugh pulled a check for five hundred dollars out of the envelope. "His donation to a worthy cause," she said dryly. "Oh, you can hardly blame the man. Our ball is more select, but he'll get better exposure at the Heart event. Diseases are always more popular than the arts."

"I can do it." Holly took a deep breath. "Deck the Halls will do the Winter Ball, Mrs. Fitzhugh. We'll donate our services to the Ballet Guild."

"Oh, Holly, dear." Mrs. Fitzhugh smiled and shook her head. "You are so like your mother. Much too generous. I can't let you."

"How much time have I got?"

Mrs. Fitzhugh pressed her lips together. "Less than three weeks," she said crisply. "The ball is the twenty-ninth, the last weekend of the month."

The date jarred Holly's memory. She had something scheduled. Well, whatever it was, she'd cancel. This, so close to the New Year's symphony party, was a gift from fate. Fate, which had treated her horribly, was making up for lost time.

"Please, Mrs. Fitzhugh."

Mrs. Fitzhugh gazed at the determined woman before her. "Sit down, Holly," she said, all traces of flighty society matron gone. "I'm going to be very frank. You don't have the experience and you're not going to get it at my ball." She went on, softening her words. "We start planning a year in advance. We've been working with Mr. Kelly for weeks, contacting florists to donate flowers, underwriters for caterers, door prizes, the printers—"

"You won't be able to find a big-name decorator," Holly interrupted flatly. "They don't have enough time to start from scratch, and they're not about to link their name with anything less than successful."

"There you go!" Mrs. Fitzhugh flung up her hands. "If a professional can't do it—"

"*I* am a professional, Mrs. Fitzhugh. And I won't be starting from scratch."

"What do you mean?" Mrs. Fitzhugh was quick to grasp the lifeline Holly threw her.

"John Kelly isn't stupid. There's going to be publicity over this. Now, if I were Mr. Kelly, I would hope that you and your committee plan to keep his defection quiet so you'll still sell tickets."

Holly had Mrs. Fitzhugh's complete attention. "Go on."

"I'll pay a call on Mr. Kelly," Holly said, her mind working furiously. "He'll cooperate and give me his lists and discuss his plans in return for stories about how helpful he's been.''

''And if he doesn't?''

''After several articles about how he backed out at the last minute, do you think anyone will ever hire him again?''

Mrs. Fitzhugh hesitated, obviously wanting to believe Holly.

''Would *you*?'' Holly asked, pressing her point.

''It could ruin you.''

Holly smiled. ''Or it could send me right to the top.''

Mrs. Fitzhugh studied Holly a moment longer. ''So help me, I think you might just do it.'' A sly smile curved her lips. ''Martha will be very annoyed.''

Her sisters weren't home when Holly breezed in after her meeting with John Kelly. In her office, she began to schedule what had to be done and who was going to do it. When her sisters finally came in from who knew where, she was ready.

''Have you lost your mind?'' Laurel snapped. ''We can't do it. Certainly not in three weeks.''

''Not by ourselves, no. But I've got a list of florists and caterers and others who are donating to the ball. There's a committee to oversee everything. We'll coordinate and do the decor.''

''But Holly, my classes begin that week,'' Ivy protested.

''We can do this!'' Holly insisted. ''Can't you two see that this is the chance we've prayed for? We'll never have to waste our time on small jobs again. We can hire help. We won't have to struggle—we'll hire Exemplary Temporaries for a switch!''

''I've started drama classes,'' Laurel announced quietly.

''What is the matter with you two?'' Holly stared in disbelief. ''Don't you understand? This is it, our big chance!''

Both of her sisters sat in the office and stared back at her stonily. ''Our chance for what?'' Laurel asked.

Holly couldn't believe they didn't see the possibilities. "To make a lot of money," she said distinctly.

"How much are they paying you?" Laurel asked quickly.

Holly took a deep breath. "Nothing. I'm donating our services."

"Forget it, Holly." Laurel stood up. "You can donate *your* services."

"You could have asked first," Ivy said, preparing to follow Laurel.

"There wasn't time. Listen to me." Holly hurried to the door to keep them from leaving. "I'm doing this for the contacts. The Winter Ball is big news. It gets national coverage." Holly emphasized the last two words and saw interest in Laurel's eyes.

"That's right, it does," she mused, looking fixedly over Holly's shoulder.

"Now do you understand? People all over the country will hear about Deck the Halls. You two can help me and we'll make this the best Winter Ball Dallas has ever seen, or I'll do what I can by myself. Either way, we'll be noticed."

Ivy and Laurel exchanged glances. Ivy shrugged.

"Okay," Laurel said slowly, "but the next time you get the chance of a lifetime, check with us first."

"I will, I promise." Holly hugged them both. "You won't regret this, you'll see."

The days slipped by, with Holly spending most of her time on the telephone. She redid the theme. There was no way she planned to use a secondhand theme. She did like Mr. Kelly's idea of covering the ballroom in white silk, though. The room at the Landreth was heavily ornate, decorated in multihued reds. A huge quilted hanging, glorifying the Alamo, was displayed on the back wall.

Finding that much silk was a problem. Holly called a

number of fabric mills to locate the hundreds of yards needed. All wanted a deposit.

Holly had just hung up the phone after talking to a sales rep at one of the mills. She was going to have to buy some and rent a lot. But she couldn't spend thousands of dollars on draping the walls without considering the rest of the room.

"Holly, I've got the snow-making machine from the amusement park confirmed. They want to know where and when you want your snow." Ivy stood in the doorway.

Holly stared at her without answering.

"Holly?" Ivy entered the office uncertainly. "The snow? They asked if you have a permit. Shall I check on that for you?"

"Ivy..." Holly hesitated, then ran her fingers through her curls. "Ivy," she said again, "you remember the ballroom at the Landreth..."

"Uh-huh. About ten shades of red and orange. Clashes with everything."

"So you realize the problem."

Ivy looked at her with the first hint of suspicion. "Yes. That's why you're covering everything in white."

"I need at least three thousand dollars for a deposit on the silk," Holly said baldly.

"Wow. What does the ball committee say?"

Holly pretended to study the papers on her desk. "Nothing. I can't bother them with—"

"Then keep the room dark. The walls will look black that way. Too bad the carpet—"

"We could do it if we borrowed your college money," Holly interrupted quietly. "The ball committee can't reimburse me until afterward."

There was painful silence in the room.

Ivy's lower lip began to tremble. "I'm supposed to register next Tuesday."

"I'm sorry," Holly whispered. "I need the money for

Mrs. Bloom, too. She's renting us the lights, the trees and the polar bears.''

"What about all these people who are donating money and stuff?"

Holly winced at the bitterness in Ivy's voice. "It costs thousands of dollars to put on a ball like this. They hope to make hundreds of thousands."

Tears began to flow down Ivy's cheeks. "Can't you find a way to do it that doesn't cost so much?"

Holly felt horrible. "We decided to do this only if we made it spectacular. Otherwise, it won't do us any good."

"*You* decided."

Holly exhaled heavily. "Now I'm asking. If I could find another way to borrow the money, I would. Listen, after this, we'll be set for life. We'll never have to worry about money again. I promise you can enroll in the summer. You can go to any school you want. It's only four more months, Ivy.''

Ivy wiped her cheeks and stood, clutching her papers. "I'll check on that permit for you."

"Ivy!"

Ivy, long black hair swirling around her, paused in the doorway with her back to Holly.

"You didn't say whether or not we could use your college money."

Ivy glanced back, her lips twisted in a bitter smile. "I understood my agreement was a mere formality. You're going to use it, anyway."

"Don't, Ivy."

"You want my blessing? Will that make you feel better? Or are you even capable of feeling guilty?"

Holly's stomach curled into a knot, as if she'd been punched. "If you tell me not to, I won't use your college money," she said evenly.

"Right," Ivy said, flinging up her arms, "so if anything goes wrong, it's my fault!"

"I'll be getting it back this time." Holly tried to smile. "In fact, why don't you check with the admissions department and see if there's a way to delay payment?"

"Don't treat me like a child, Holly. I'm not one anymore. You and I both know the college won't wait for payment, for the same reason no bank will lend you money. Bankruptcy and no tangible assets."

Holly sat at her desk for a few moments after Ivy left. Ivy was angry now, but she'd come around. She'd be grateful. Holly dialed the fabric mill. Ivy would go to the best school in the country. With a wardrobe to match. And a car.

And Holly would have a winter wonderland like no one had ever seen.

It was time to defrost the American Express card. Holly finished talking with the mills and had a rather tedious discussion with Mrs. Bloom. The concept of donating was foreign to her. They were arguing over whether she would supply a hundred white trees at cost, or at cost plus ten percent, when Holly noticed a shadow in the doorway.

"Mrs. Bloom, I'd like to stay on good terms with you, so I think I'll go with someone else." Holly hung up the phone with a feeling of great satisfaction. Let Bloomie call *her* for a change.

"So your telephone isn't out of order." The words were spoken with a deceptive mildness.

"Adam!" Holly exclaimed a little breathlessly. "What are you doing here?"

Adam walked over to her desk, leaned across it and tilted her chin with his fingers. "You haven't been sleeping," he said sternly. "You need this trip more than I thought."

Holly's face froze, then flushed with guilt. She tossed her head defensively.

Adam cleared a spot on her desk and spread out a travel brochure. "Warmth and sun, white beaches and our own cabana. Breakfast served on our private beach. No sight-seeing, no responsibilities, no worries.''

Holly studied the brochure, feeling Adam's gaze on her bent head. He folded the leaflet and put it back in his breast pocket. "And no trip?"

"I..." Holly couldn't say anything else.

"I thought your phone was broken," he said conversationally. "I called. Several times. I haven't heard from you in three days."

Holly plastered a determined smile on her face. "The most incredible thing has happened. We're decorating for the Winter Ball. It's a chance I never thought we'd get. I happened to be in the right place at the right time."

Adam broke into her babble. "When is the Winter Ball, Holly?"

"The twenty-ninth."

"The day we're supposed to leave on our trip."

Holly felt uncomfortable with this quietly solemn Adam. He had the same look on his face that Laurel and Ivy had on theirs. He didn't understand. No one did. "I forgot."

"Forgot." The word hung between them.

"I'm sorry—I didn't mean that the way it sounded. Couldn't we postpone the trip? It sounds perfectly lovely and after this, I'll need it." Holly laughed shakily and ran her fingers through her hair. "Be happy for me. We'll get national coverage in the society pages. It'll be wonderful. You'll see."

There was no warmth in Adam's face. "Will I?"

"Yes." Holly looked at him in surprise. "You'll be there, won't you?"

"When were you planing to invite me?"

Holly threw down her pencil and sighed in exasperation. "I'm telling you about it now, okay?"

Adam strode around the side of her desk, withdrew the glossy leaflet with the ocean sunsets and private cabanas and thumbtacked it right in the middle of her scheduling board.

She had no warning. He grasped her shoulders and lifted her to her feet. He gazed at her an instant before crushing her slightly parted lips to his. Passion flared briefly within her before he set her roughly back in the chair. "Next time—ask."

# CHAPTER NINE

HOLLY HALL WAS A WRECK, but a happy wreck. With her mother's diamonds glittering around her neck, Holly watched from her post near the ice-tunnel doorway as each group of people entered. Without fail, the newcomers gasped and exclaimed with delight as they left the twisting tunnel and entered a frosty world of enchantment.

Holly couldn't believe all the hard work was over and she had managed to pull it off. Fueled by caffeine, her brain had concocted a fantasy that had taken the carpenter and his crew a week of time-and-a-half to create.

The city of Dallas had graciously permitted artificial snow in front of the Landreth Hotel. Thousands of lights twinkled in white leafless tree branches as guests entered the hotel lobby. Outside the ballroom, they entered an igloolike tunnel with swirling fog, courtesy of a dry-ice machine. The tunnel twisted and turned before opening into a glittering white world.

Holly's only disappointment had been the silk. Who cared about its lovely draping qualities when the hideous color scheme of the ballroom showed through the thin fabric? Holly ended up shining colored lights on it like a theater scrim. She told everyone they were the northern lights.

"You know," Laurel remarked, noticing Holly studying the room, "it would have been less expensive to cover the walls with cheap dark fabric, hang lights and call them stars."

"Yes, it would have," Holly snapped. "That's a great

idea. Why didn't you mention it?'' How dared Laurel try to spoil her evening?

"You wouldn't have listened. You were determined to do it all by yourself." Laurel waved across the room. "There's Gus."

"That's not true! You had plenty of time to speak up!"

Laurel raised an eyebrow. "Really? Listen to yourself."

Holly brought a hand to her curls, jerking it back before she could succumb to her nervous habit. "We were all in this together."

Laurel adjusted the bodice of her silver lamé dress. "Whether we wanted to be or not."

She didn't expect gratitude, Holly told herself as she watched Laurel slink off. She took a deep breath, mentally composing herself and letting the feeling of triumph return.

This was her night. Holly Hall was back on top. She touched the necklace around her neck, knowing that it—or at least parts of it—was no stranger to opulent charity functions like this one. Amazingly, the few people she'd greeted didn't seem to remember the sordid accusations surrounding the financing of her father's last oil well. After dealing with the tedious legal processes for years, Holly felt everyone knew about the insurance company's claim that her father had deliberately set the well fire that had ultimately led to his death.

Dallas accepted her without question. Holly was lightheaded with happiness as the last possible barrier to her success fell.

She beamed as she noticed Ivy approaching her through the crowd. Never mind Laurel. Ivy had come through for her. "Isn't this—" Holly hesitated "—perfect?"

The edge of Ivy's lips barely curved. "Here." She handed Holly a piece of paper.

Holly scanned it quickly. "He doesn't want to be paid right this minute, does he?" she asked tersely. How could the workmen present her with an invoice during the ball?

"It's a time card. The carpenters need you to sign it."

Holly frowned. "Hey, this is double time."

"You insisted that the men stay on call all night."

Holly scribbled her name on the sheet of paper. "Insurance. If anything collapses, help will be close by."

"Of course." Ivy took the paper from her and walked regally away, the daring white beaded dress she'd borrowed from Laurel earning her admiring looks.

So Ivy was angry at her, too. Great. Silver Siren and the Ice Princess. Sighing, Holly wandered over to the table where she'd left her coffee cup. Her polar bears, some recycled from Adam's tree for luck, cavorted on rock crystal.

Where was Adam, anyway? The crowd thickened. Restlessly Holly wandered around the perimeter of the ballroom, unnecessarily checking on the activities, her eyes darting to the tunnel entrance every few seconds.

A flash of light caught her eye, telling her Gus had begun photographing. Holly approached the sleigh set in front of a snowy backdrop. Gus had agreed to split half the profits of his souvenir photos with the Winter Ball committee. Mrs. Fitzhugh had accused Holly of a high-school prom mentality, but Holly had insisted on the photo gimmick. Couples posed in the sleigh, either as they were, or with the men borrowing a cape and top hat, and the women a fur-trimmed cloak.

Laurel, perched in the sleigh, leaned forward and crossed her legs, the clinging silver dress parting to reveal an inordinate amount of skin. Holly's eyes narrowed.

"Lighten up, Holly. They're supposed to be attracting attention." The Ice Princess had returned.

"And succeeding admirably." Holly smiled stiffly. "What are you eating?"

"Champagne ice from the Ice Palace." Ivy licked her spoon. "Do you think you might have overdone the ice theme a tad?"

"No!" Holly said sharply.

Ivy backed away. "Just asking."

Holly touched her sister's arm,. "Look…I didn't mean to snap at you. I just want everything to be perfect."

Reaching out, Ivy gently took Holly's coffee cup and set it on a table. "No more of this for you. Makes you jumpy."

"I can handle it."

Ivy shook her head. "Nope. You look like a hag as it is."

"I didn't spend all day getting ready, unlike some people." Holly darted an accusing glance toward Laurel, who had draped herself next to an older man she'd coaxed into posing with her.

"That's not fair!" Ivy lowered her voice. "Laurel traipsed all over town for you. Whose idea was the diamond ice, anyway? Who got the diamond gift certificates?"

Holly's shoulders sagged. "You're right. I'm sorry." Her buoyant spirit collapsed. "I don't know what's the matter with me."

Ivy's voice softened. "Too much caffeine. You'd be in worse shape, but Adam sent over some decaf beans and we've been mixing them in with your coffee."

"Adam did that?" Holly's spirits rose again.

"Yeah, remember him?" Ivy placed her empty glass next to Holly's coffee cup.

Holly exhaled forcefully. "Adam knew how it was going to be. I didn't make him any promises."

Ivy fingered the white silk of Holly's dress. "It wouldn't have mattered if you had, would it?"

A numbing pain started in Holly's chest and radiated outward. Ivy met her look without apology. There was a bitterness in Ivy's eyes that recalled the day they'd quarreled about the money.

Holly took a deep breath as the pain lessened. "Things don't always happen the way we'd like them to."

Ivy's gaze shifted to just over Holly's shoulder. Holly turned and saw Adam striding toward them.

He'd come! With the way her sisters had been acting, Holly had half expected not to see Adam tonight. But here he was, coming to share her success.

It was the first time she had seen or spoken to him since he'd walked out of her office that day. Holly felt a rush of pride as she watched his approach. His tuxedo fit perfectly and was an elegant, unadorned black. The errant lock of hair, which usually fell onto his forehead, had been tamed. He looked wonderful. She'd missed him so much. Maybe they could take that trip together next weekend....

"Adam!" Holly laughingly threw herself at his chest.

Knocked off balance by Holly's unexpected greeting, Adam held her close, steadying her before gently unwrapping her arms.

"I knew you'd come!" Happiness shone in her eyes.

"Did you?" Adam asked quietly, his blue eyes cold.

Holly's smile froze. Not Adam, too. Everyone who meant anything to her had abandoned her during this project. Hadn't she learned she could depend only on herself?

"Ivy." Adam's gaze warmed as he greeted her sister. "You look stunning." His eyes flicked over Holly. "You look horrible."

"Thanks a lot."

"White isn't your color."

"Black isn't either, anymore," Ivy commented. "She ran herself down so much, her dress didn't fit, so we sewed her a new one out of the leftover silk."

"Figures." Adam's face softened slightly as he saw beneath Holly's indomitable facade. "When was the last time you ate?"

Without waiting for an answer, he propelled Holly toward the kitchen. "Are those mascara smudges or circles under your eyes?"

"Why did you bother to come?" Holly jerked her arm away. "You're spoiling everything. Leave me alone."

Adam ignored her. "Sit." He pushed her into a seat

among the white branches ringing the room and started to go through the doors into the kitchen.

"Hey, don't bother the caterers," Holly called after him even as the scent of food wafted through the open door.

Adam gave her a disgusted look and disappeared through the doors. He returned in moments, bearing a plate of food. "Eat."

Holly clenched her jaw mutinously.

Adam set the plate on her lap. "Eat, or I'll force-feed you, creating precisely the kind of scene you wish to avoid tonight."

The shrimp looked delicious. Suddenly ravenous, Holly tried one. She reached for the glass Adam patiently held for her, drank and grimaced. "This isn't champagne."

"Apple juice."

Adam sat back on the silk-covered folding chair and watched Holly devour the food. Had she been trying to kill herself?

Adam's fury had faded the moment he'd seen Holly. Her eyes were enormous in a sallow haggard face. Even her curls had lost their bounce. He wondered if she'd thought about him at all during the past two weeks. He wondered if she'd guessed he had decided not to see her again.

It was too painful to dream about what they might have had together. His lips tightened. Too painful for him. Holly didn't appear to be affected one way or the other. But she needed him, couldn't she see that?

Just as he needed her.

"Ivy was right." Holly stared at her empty plate. "I've been drinking too much coffee."

One corner of Adam's mouth lifted just enough to hint at a dimple.

"I'm glad you're here." Holly leaned her head against Adam's shoulder, causing him to sigh with resignation. "What's the matter?"

"I'm glad I'm here too."

Holly nestled closer and Adam curled his arm around her. A passing waiter took her plate and they sat for several minutes listening to the soft music from the harps and watching people discover the grottoes and explore the Ice Palace.

"This is beautiful, Holly. I hope it brings you every success." Adam waited for an acknowledgment and some comment on her future plans.

The harpists finished their piece on a rippling chord. As they changed their music, Adam heard Holly's slow even breathing. She was asleep.

Chuckling to himself, Adam retrieved her purse from the floor, turned her in his arms, picked her up and carried her out the door to the corridor outside the kitchen. Swiftly ducking into a meeting room, Adam gently set Holly on a mound of leftover silk and closed the door.

He shrugged out of his tuxedo jacket and laid it over her. With luck, she could sleep undisturbed for a few minutes. All the extra chairs, tablecloths and crockery were stored in here. With hors d'oeuvres just now being served, this stuff shouldn't be needed for about half an hour.

Adam watched Holly sleep. She was noticeably thinner and must have been completely exhausted to collapse during her big evening. He shook his head, smiling wryly. He didn't dare let her sleep through the whole thing.

The unflattering fluorescent light and stark white material leeched color from Holly's already pallid skin. She still looked beautiful to Adam. Beautiful and independent. Strong and stubborn.

He'd noticed his polar bears, too, and strongly suspected that was Bianca, the polar-bear rug, making another appearance, this time on a Styrofoam ice floe.

So Holly felt something for him, right? But was it enough?

The harp music had stopped and Adam listened to the

sounds from the ballroom. Within moments, a string quartet began playing, the music muted by the walls.

Adam reached out and ran a finger over Holly's cheek. There were men who would be noble in situations like this. He didn't plan to be one of them.

Time for Sleeping Beauty to awaken. Adam bent over her and kissed her lightly. No response. At least she hadn't bolted upright and crashed into his head.

He settled next to her, gathering her into his arms. For several minutes he was content just to hold her, savoring their first peaceful moment alone in almost a month.

They should have been on a beach tonight, their bodies caressed by warm sea breezes and pillowed by sand. Adam closed his eyes for a moment, almost able to smell the salty tang of the ocean.

Eyes still closed, he began a gentle trail of kisses from Holly's temple down the side of her neck, where her pulse beat slowly and steadily.

Holly was zonked.

Sighing heavily, Adam jiggled her slightly. "Holly?"

Someone shattered her lovely dream. "Go away."

Adam tugged at his jacket. "If I did that, you'd never forgive me."

"I will, I promise." Holly drifted back onto her cloud and waited for the lovely sensations to begin again. But now the cloud was cold and wet.

"Hey!" She wiped her forehead. It hadn't been raining in her dream.

Holly opened her eyes. Adam stood over her tilting a pitcher of ice water.

"Stop, you'll ruin the silk." Holly struggled to sit up.

Adam knelt and gently wiped her face with some of the napkins piled in the room.

"Did I fall asleep?" Holly took a napkin from Adam and finished drying off.

"Yes," Adam affirmed, smiling affectionately. "Feel better?"

"Kind of groggy." She looked at him in alarm. "How long did I sleep?"

"Twenty minutes or so." Adam sat next to her. "Don't worry, I wouldn't let you miss your big night."

"Oh, Adam." Holly's shoulders sagged. "Why do you put up with me?"

He gazed at her steadily before clasping her shoulders and drawing her toward him. "Because, Holly, I love you."

"You do?" She looked up and found the love radiating from his eyes. "I thought you were mad at me."

"I was—am." He gave her a rueful smile. "But as I discovered in the last two weeks, it is very possible to love someone and feel like strangling her at the same time."

"I always feel that way about my sisters."

"I do *not* think of you as my sister!"

Holly smiled and settled back onto the silk. "Prove it."

A split second later, Adam covered her mouth with his. If she thought she could say something like that and get away with it just because they were in a not-so-private room surrounded by hundreds of people, any one of whom could, and probably would, burst in on them...well, Ms. Hall was about to learn a thing or two about men who had been deprived of their weekend in the sun.

Adam kissed her for all the days he'd spent working himself into a stupor at the law firm, trying to forget her. Then he kissed her for the days they'd been apart, the hours of their lost weekend and the exasperating trouble Holly had been. Then he kissed her for the heck of it.

In the back of his mind, Adam was aware that unleashing the emotional torrent raging inside him was not a good idea. He began to pull back before his voice of reason drowned completely.

Holly's already had. The rising tide of passion swept her away. As Adam pulled back, Holly moved forward, nudging him backward until he was enveloped in masses of white silk.

He could stay like this forever, Adam thought, breathing in the unique scent Holly wore. The string quartet's music serenaded them, changing from fast-paced Vivaldi to a slower lusher sound.

Their kisses changed, too, from frantic caresses to deeply sensual ones.

Adam buried his face in the side of Holly's neck, his hands stroking the shoulders left bare by the cut of her dress. He wanted her so much he ached. Wrapping his arms around her in a tight embrace he tried to calm his breathing.

"Ouch."

Adam released her instantly. "Did I hurt you?" he managed to ask, his voice hoarse.

Holly propped herself on her elbows above him. "Mama's necklace," she gasped, looking down at her neck.

Adam's gaze followed hers, fastening on the deep red marks made by the stones as they pressed into her soft flesh.

"I'm sorry," he whispered, raising his head and gently kissing the worst of the marks.

Holly sighed and rolled away from him. "It's just as well, don't you think?" She smiled sheepishly.

"Ask me again in a few minutes." Adam lay on the silk, his eyes closed.

Holly got to her feet, ineffectively brushing at the wrinkles in her dress. In a few minutes, Adam stood beside her, shrugging on his coat.

"I told you once that I loved you, but you didn't believe me." Holly tried to keep the hurt out of her voice.

Adam gave her a wicked grin. "I know exactly which parts of you love me. I'm holding out for all of you."

Puzzled, Holly watched him straighten his tie and cummerbund. "What do you mean?"

"How many brothers and sisters do I have?"

Holly blinked.

"What's my favorite food? Where's my home?"

"Boston," Holly answered quickly.

"That's where my family lives—do I live there? What's my address?"

"I don't have it. You live in Dallas now."

Adam nodded. "I'll concede that. What are my favorite sports? Where did I go to school? What's my favorite color?"

"Blue," Holly guessed, desperately.

A smile lit Adam's face, making her feel worse. "How did you know?"

"All men like blue," she mumbled.

Adam sighed. "What are my plans for the future?"

Holly glared at him. "All right, you made your point."

"Did I?" he asked, quietly.

"I'm free all day tomorrow. Want to find out?" Holly held out her hand and Adam took it, lacing his fingers through hers.

They stood, smiling at each other, until the rumble of dish-laden carts reminded them where they were.

"Dinner," they both said at the same time and laughed. Adam opened the door, beckoned to her and they escaped down the hall away from the kitchen.

"Where have you been?" Laurel whispered when Adam and Holly slipped into their places at the table reserved for them.

"Checking on this and that. You know Holly." Adam's smile included everyone around him—especially Laurel.

"Welcome, friends and patrons of the arts." Mrs. Fitzhugh began to speak from the head table. Laurel narrowed her eyes suspiciously at Holly before turning to listen.

Mrs. Fitzhugh informed them that this Winter Ball was the most successful ever. "And I understand that as of this moment, several diamonds have not yet been discovered. Waiters will be circulating with bags of ice. Ten dollars might buy you quite a rock. Be assured, the diamond you find may be exchanged for the real thing.''

"Whose idea was that?" Adam asked.

"Honey," drawled the voice on his left, "don't you know that diamonds are a girl's best friend?" Laurel gave him an outrageous wink.

Mrs. Fitzhugh continued, "Among the many who made this evening possible, none worked harder than Holly Hall of Deck the Halls, who stepped in at the last minute to create this winter wonderland. Thank you, Holly!''

The applause was thunderous. Holly rose to acknowledge it, grasping Adam's hand tightly. Instead of quieting, the noise swelled in a crescendo as the ball committee stood, followed by everyone at the tables.

As she soaked in the sweet sound of the applause, Holly knew she would never forget this moment. It had taken more than five years of scrambling to reach the top and now she intended to stay there.

Adam tightened the pressure on her hand so much that she glanced at him in surprise. He nodded slightly toward her sisters.

Belatedly, Holly gestured toward them and applauded. Ivy, wearing a tight smile, inclined her head. Laurel threw kisses to the crowd.

Holly floated through the rest of the evening. She sparkled, she bubbled and she worked the crowd like a pro. Throughout the night, Adam was at her side. She held his hand or her arm, her eyes seeking his every few minutes.

At last, it was over.

"Holly, you saved the ball for us. We won't forget it."

Holly smiled at the venerable society matron. "Just think of Deck the Halls the next time you entertain."

"I will, dear. Martha's and Claudia's tedious rivalry has done some good, after all."

As the hotel workers moved in to clear the room, Holly and Adam stood arm in arm. "It *is* great, isn't it?"

Adam laughed. "Haven't you had enough compliments for one evening?"

"Never. I hate to undo all that work, but I'm paying a crew double and it's time they earned it." She looked at Adam. "I'm going to change into some jeans and pack up the rented stuff. Want to stay and help?"

Laurel and Ivy had already changed and begun dragging boxes into the room. "Hey, Cinderella, it struck midnight," Laurel said.

"More like 1 a.m." Adam removed his jacket and tie.

"Holly, it looks like a bunch of Mrs. Bloom's bears have disappeared." Ivy had a worried frown on her face.

"Yeah, pretty light-fingered for a well-heeled crowd." Laurel stood, hands on her hips, and surveyed the room. "I'm going to check in the kitchen and make sure the caterers know not to throw anything away until we look through it first. Maybe I'll find some of the bears in the trash."

"Not to mention leftovers," Holly murmured to Adam. "Ivy, keep a count of the missing bears and I'll add it to my expense sheet."

"What about all these trees and lights?" Adam asked.

"The work crew will dismantle those. Why don't you get Bianca? I think we used a hanging bag to transport her."

Holly grabbed her jeans and headed for the restroom.

"Holly!" Mrs. Fitzhugh and her committee were adding up receipts from the diamond ice and Gus's photography. "We're just getting a preliminary tally, but the ball has been a tremendous success."

"Oh." Holly set her jeans on a table and dug in her purse. "You'll want this then." She handed Mrs. Fitzhugh an envelope. "It's just an estimate right now, but it will help you figure your profit."

"Goodness." Mrs. Fitzhugh glanced at the long list and initialed it. "We'll send you a formal letter for tax purposes, of course," she said, handing the paper back to Holly.

"Don't you need these numbers? I have to warn you, some of the table decorations seem to have walked off and the rental company will have to be paid for those."

Mrs. Fitzhugh nodded absently and went back to tallying the cash.

"Mrs. Fitzhugh? It's very late, so I'll leave this with you to look over and we can discuss the expenses tomorrow or Monday. I have some statements here." Holly reached into the envelope and handed them to Mrs. Fitzhugh.

"What are these?" Mrs. Fitzhugh looked at Holly blankly.

Maybe she was tired. Holly certainly was. "These are invoices from the rental company, some fabric mills, the amusement park for the snow-making machine out front and the work crews, who are dismantling the sets." Holly waved a hand around the room. Adam was a few feet away and came to stand beside her.

"They're your responsibility, Holly." Mrs. Fitzhugh handed her back the invoices. "I thought you understood."

"You'd rather I pay them and you'll reimburse me." Holly nodded, wondering how she'd manage that. She'd just have to figure everything up and submit her bill pronto.

But Mrs. Fitzhugh shook her head. "There is no question of reimbursement. You agreed to donate your services."

"And I did. These are my out-of-pocket expenses. I didn't charge you for my time." Holly's eyes flicked to the piles of cash the women were counting. Cash they wouldn't have if she and Laurel hadn't come up with the photos, the diamond ice and the wishing pond in the Ice Palace.

"I should hope not. We're a charity organization, dear. We raise money. Everything is donated, otherwise we wouldn't have such successful fund-raisers."

"It is understood that all fund-raising events generate expenses, Mrs. Fitzhugh," Adam said in his lawyer voice, and Holly laid a warning hand on his arm.

"*Reasonable* expenses."

"I had less than three weeks, Mrs. Fitzhugh." This couldn't be happening! "If more time had been available, I might have found companies willing to donate materials and labor." Holly swallowed as five stony society faces glared at her. "Under the circumstances, you should expect some extra expense this year."

"We certainly didn't give you carte blanche to spend all the profits!" Mrs. Fitzhugh's hoarse voice began to carry.

Holly's temper rose, along with her panic. "If I hadn't stepped in, you wouldn't have had a ball!"

"While we are certainly grateful, you must understand how it is if you want to continue to work at this level of society. You gain the exposure and write your expenses off to advertising or charity or something. We've never had to pay for anything but the room and a minimal amount for food." Mrs. Fitzhugh shook her head. "I was afraid of this when I agreed to work with an amateur."

A cold feeling settled in the pit of Holly's stomach. "I am a professional."

"Mr. Kelly would have understood." The others murmured and nodded.

"Mr. Kelly backed out," Adam inserted, but Holly gripped his arm.

"I apologize for the misunderstanding, Mrs. Fitzhugh." Holly's tight smile included the crones seated around her. "And I look forward to working with you all in the future."

# CHAPTER TEN

"DON'T BE A FOOL, Holly!" Adam paced in front of the wing chair where Holly sat, tightly curled up. He'd been saying the same thing, or a variation of it, all night long.

"Stop badgering me." The dull resignation in Holly's voice alarmed Adam more than if she'd snapped at him.

"Let me help you. Legally, you're in a strong position to—"

"No."

Adam rubbed the back of his neck as he glared at Holly. Impossible woman. Sighing audibly, he paced to the front window and drew back the curtains. A pinkish-gray dawn greeted him. "How much did you spend?" he asked, without turning around.

"Everything."

The breath hissed between his teeth as Adam let the curtains fall back into place. "Look." He crossed the room swiftly and knelt in front of her. "You're playing right into Mrs. Fitzhugh's hands." His lips tightened. "These women all compete with each other. She wants this ball to raise the most money, and anything she has to spend takes away from the profits."

Holly turned her eyes to him. His once immaculately crisp shirt was a network of wrinkles. She reached out a finger and ran it over his stubble-shaded jaw. "That's a sexy look for you."

"Holly." Adam pulled her hand away and held it between both of his. "Mrs. Fitzhugh is treating you as a social equal."

"And I'm just the hired help?"

Adam spoke very gently. "In essence, yes. She wouldn't have tried this with anyone else."

"I'll make it back." The fire was missing from her voice.

"How many jobs is it going to take before you do? Wait a couple of hours and call the Fitzhugh woman and insist that she reimburse you." Adam could see Holly had no intention of following his advice. "Better yet, I'll do it— as your lawyer."

"No." Holly tugged her hand away. "If I do that, no one will ever hire me again. I'll be blackballed."

"Hardly. You're a terrific bargain." Adam got to his feet and looked down at her. "You're supposed to be running a business. Now act like it. That is, assuming you have a business left."

Holly huddled in the chair. "I built it once. I can do it again."

Adam wanted to shake her. "Listen to yourself! You're allowing them to wipe out five years of work."

"I won't be starting over completely. I have the Christmas stock and I have *contacts*." The word was a talisman.

"That Fitzhugh woman has some kind of gall. You saved her neck." Adam shoved his hands in his pockets—another gesture he'd been repeating for hours. "I suppose it's pointless to ask if you had a contract?"

Her eyes briefly met his.

"Great." Adam jiggled the change in his pockets for a minute. "Did you ever discuss a budget?"

Holly shifted her legs. "No. I kept her informed of my plans, but she never questioned anything I spent."

Adam stared at her in disbelief. "That's no way to run a charity ball. Then again, it was brilliant. Poor Holly. Don't you understand? She set you up right from the start."

"Actually, I got the idea she was so happy just to *have* a ball that anything I spent was all right."

"Unbelievable." Adam began to pace again. "What are you going to tell Ivy and Laurel?"

Holly's laugh was mirthless. "Big sister miscalculated."

"Let's see by how much." Adam glanced around the living room, before sitting down at her mother's writing desk. "When you said you spent everything, did you mean a lot or…everything?"

Holly gave a crack of laughter. "I spent it all and then some. I have bills coming in and I defrosted the charge card."

Adam didn't laugh. "Get your receipts and any outstanding bills. I assume you kept records."

With a contemptuous look, Holly unfolded herself from the chair. "Start on this," she said, handing Adam her notebook.

Adam was working on that when Holly returned and dumped the contents of a file folder, a calculator and a frosty foil-wrapped package on the desk, then returned to the chair.

"What's this?" Adam held up the frozen package.

"I overlooked that one. We found it last night when we put all that food in the freezer. It's money."

Adam's dimples appeared. "Your total, uh, liquid assets?"

Holly nodded, watching as Adam studied the receipts and bills. She supposed she should feel really horrible, but she didn't. She'd make all the money back, and it wouldn't take her five years, either. This was an expensive lesson and one she didn't intend to repeat.

"Okay." Adam stared at the figures. "Here's what we're going to do."

"Oh, really?"

"Be quiet. We're transferring some of your expenses. Today, you're going to have a chat with the hotel conference manager. The dishes and the tables—where did you get those?''

For the first time, there was a brief flicker of interest in Holly's eyes. "From the hotel."

Adam held up a piece of paper. "This is a bill for white dishes. There isn't anything unusual about white dishes— why did they charge you for them?"

"The hotel's had colored bands. I asked for plain white."

Adam smiled. "Fine. But supplying dishes is the hotel's problem or the caterer's problem—not your problem. You're going to instruct them to add that to their bill to the Winter Ball committee." He put it aside. "See how painless that was?"

"But—"

"Tables and chairs?"

Holly began to smile. "The hotel."

Adam added to the small stack. "Labor?"

"I used a set designer from a theater group."

"Did he hire the workers?"

Holly sat up. "No, the hotel got them for me."

"Then let them bill the hotel. Claudia Fitzhugh isn't about to tangle with the Landreth."

Holly slipped out of her chair and came across the room to stand beside Adam. "How does it look?"

Adam turned the sheet he'd been writing on toward her. "That takes care of half your expenses right there."

"Thank you, Adam." Holly bent down and wrapped her arms around him.

The phone rang. Holly jerked. "You see? It's started. I'll pull out of this."

She ran to answer the phone, waving a piece of paper triumphantly when she returned. "A Valentine luncheon— what did I tell you?"

"Is it for charity?" Adam asked cynically.

Holy shook her head. The phone rang again.

"Don't these people go to church?" Adam grumbled.

Holly skipped back. "I'm getting booked for all the holidays. Fourth of July at the country club."

"Have them sign a contract, which I'll draw up. Then call Mrs. Fitzhugh, apologize for not making it clear that you were donating your services in a professional capacity, and offer to split your expenses."

"Adam..." Holly began, a warning in her voice.

"That's called compromise, my dear. My specialty. Everybody walks away with something."

The phone rang a third time. And a fourth.

"I'm going home," Adam announced, when it became apparent that he wouldn't get any more uninterrupted conversation with Holly. "I'll draft a standard contract for you so you won't be in a mess like this again.

"What mess?" A rumpled Laurel put in her first appearance of the morning.

"That's my exit cue." Adam kissed Holly on the cheek. "Hang in there," he whispered and let himself out the front door.

Her sisters handled the news the way Holly had expected they would. Laurel screamed and Ivy cried.

"I don't care what Mrs. Fitzhugh and those other biddies think," Ivy declared. "We should go and demand our money. My *college* money."

Laurel nodded. "You always said we were in this together. Well, I'm with Ivy. You can't decide all by yourself to write it off." They'd moved to the kitchen and Laurel poured them each another cup of coffee. Ivy wrinkled her nose and diluted hers with three sugars and a generous slug of milk.

"Look at this." Holly picked up the notes she'd made from the morning's phone calls. "We're booked for most major holidays for the rest of this year. If I raise a stink, they'll cancel."

Laurel stared at her a moment. "That might not be so bad."

Holly's protest was cut off by the telephone. Laurel stood up quickly to answer it.

Holly took another sip of coffee, careful not to gulp it down, as she observed Ivy's stormy face. "I know what I said about your going to college and I'm sure that by September, you can."

"Really?" Ivy gave Holly a disgusted look and went to raid the refrigerator. It was packed with last night's leftovers, which Laurel had sweet-talked out of the caterers. "Work on the Christmas trees now and go to college later. Look where that got me."

"Gripe, gripe, gripe. Adam says to check the society section and call Mrs. Fitzhugh this afternoon. She'll be mellower then," Laurel said, hanging up the phone.

Ivy emptied a bag of once-elegant, slightly wilted party food as Holly dug out the Sunday newspaper society section.

Laurel spread the paper on the table. The center two pages were devoted to candid photographs of the Winter Ball.

"You see!" Holly stabbed the paper triumphantly. "There are as many pictures of the decor as there are of the personalities. That's why I can't sabotage this kind of exposure by whining about the money to Mrs. Fitzhugh."

"Whining!" Ivy protested. "We're talking about thousands!"

Her sisters were impossible. "That's what we're talking about if I lose these new jobs."

"Hey, here I am. Laurel Hall, Our Town's aspiring actress—"

"*Actress?*" Holly leaned over the paper and scanned the text. "You were interviewed and didn't mention Deck the Halls?"

Laurel looked surprised. "Admit I was the hired help?"

"Would have solved a few problems," Holly said dryly.

"There are three pictures of Laurel posing with those old men in the sleigh." Ivy pointed to them.

"Oh, no," Holly groaned. "She looks like she's about to fall out of that dress."

"Oh, piffle," Laurel said. "Those men were sweet. Their wives are on the committee."

Holly winced. "I'll bet they just love this." She sighed. "I'd better get to Mrs. Fitzhugh before they do."

As Adam had predicted, Mrs. Fitzhugh was all smiles, until she saw her caller was Holly.

"Enjoying your success?" Holly asked as she led the way into Mrs. Fitzhugh's study.

"I was." The unblinking matron declined to sit, forcing Holly to stand, too.

Holly handed her a brown envelope. "This is a revised list of the ball's expenses." When Mrs. Fitzhugh made no move to take it, Holly carefully placed the envelope on the cherrywood desk. "I apologize for not making it clearer that you were dealing with me in a professional capacity." The words nearly stuck in her throat.

"I find that, in your inexperience, you have been wildly extravagant. The Winter Ball committee authorized none of the expenses." Mrs. Fitzhugh's smile was a mixture of triumph, pity and smugness.

"I hoped we'd be able to reach a compromise," Holly stated, looking into a watery blue gaze that was the twin of Mr. Steele's.

"It will cost you more than it's worth." The threat was implicit in each well-modulated word.

Holly walked out of the study. "I'll have all further invoices directed to the Winter Ball committee."

"Do that and you won't work in Dallas again."

"I BELIEVE YOU'VE MET my sister, Claudia Fitzhugh."

Adam smiled and nodded, taking in the rigid posture of

Mrs. Fitzhugh and the rest of the Winter Ball committee, stiffly perched on the leather furniture in Mr. Steele's plush office. No one returned his smile.

"Have you seen this?" Mr. Steele whirled around and thrust something at Adam, obviously hoping to catch him off guard.

"A pinup calendar?" Grimacing with distaste, Adam shook his head and tossed the calendar back on the desk. "Not my style."

Mr. Steele retrieved it, flipped through the pages and turned it around to face Adam. "Care to comment?"

It was the penthouse with the skyline view, Bianca, the fireplace tools and, unfortunately, Darlene, the receptionist.

Mrs. Fitzhugh sniffed. "It appears Bernard has a penchant for hiring floozies."

"Claudia," Mr. Steele warned as he awaited Adam's reaction.

Adam, drawing on years of lawyer-family upbringing, kept his face carefully neutral. "I know nothing about it."

"Kinda thing you find in army barracks—or service stations," Mr. Steele said. "In fact, one of our clients found this in a service station. One of his. Wanted to know why he got a picture of a tree and his employees got her." Mr. Steele laughed, but Adam wasn't deceived. "We look like fools."

"Darlene is an excellent receptionist. This shouldn't—"

Mr. Steele waved away Adam's comment. "I don't blame her—it was that Hall gal. Brilliant. I underestimated her. She's still mad 'cause I wouldn't represent her after the crash. Purely a business decision, but she was too green to see it that way. Stood right where you are now and told me she'd never forget it. That I'd regret my...betrayal, I think she called it." Mr. Steele smiled in remembrance.

"Are you implying that this is her revenge?" Adam forced amusement into his voice.

"Superbly planned, too." Mr. Steele thrust out his lower lip and stared at his shoes. "Too bad she's not a lawyer."

Claudia Fitzhugh could remain silent no longer. "My ball, Bernard! That girl and her strumpet of a sister used me and embarrassed the committee. And your new partner's involvement in this entire—" She stopped abruptly as she noted the anger in Adam's eyes.

"Be very sure of yourself before you make accusations." Adam's words were chiseled, his face like stone.

"It's obvious to anyone!" Mrs. Fitzhugh thrust the Sunday society section at Adam and pointed a jeweled finger at the pages of color photographs of the ball. "Look how she insinuated her sister into these pictures. Look at that dress!"

Adam found it difficult to control his mounting fury. "You should complain to the newspaper. They chose the pictures."

"It says she is an *actress*." Mrs. Fitzhugh said the word in a tone that indicated she felt it was synonymous with call girl. "The ballet is hardly mentioned."

There was a whispered comment from the committee. Mrs. Fitzhugh nodded her head. "Do you know how many of the men were forced to pose in the sleigh with her instead of their wives?"

Adam's gaze flicked over some of those wives. "No," he said blandly. "But it was for charity, wasn't it?"

"Tainted money," Mrs. Fitzhugh declared. "And speaking of money—" she imperiously held out a hand and an envelope magically appeared in it "—this…this is a demand for payment. Not only did Ms. Hall use our ball to further her sister's career, she actually wants the committee to pay for it!"

Adam took the envelope from Mrs. Fitzhugh and glanced at the papers inside. Holly hadn't varied from the figures he'd calculated. He nodded and handed the papers to Mr. Steele. "Everything appears to be in order."

"How can you say that?" Mrs. Fitzhugh quivered indignantly. "She was outrageously extravagant!"

"Just on the silk, but she's offering to split expenses down the middle there. You must admit, the room was spectacular."

More whispering from the committee. "Nevertheless, she must pay for her exorbitance. We'll sue her if she refuses."

"Claudia," began Mr. Steele heavily.

"Stop waffling, Bernard. Are you with us or this poor besotted young man?"

The challenge hung in the air. Mr. Steele's faded blue eyes traveled from his sister and her friends, whose husbands represented some of his largest corporate accounts, to Adam.

"Ladies." Adam turned to the disapproving women, making an effort to sound conciliatory without being patronizing. "Let's meet in a couple of days when tempers have cooled." He smiled the devastating smile that could turn Holly's bones to water. "I'm sure you want to avoid dragging this into the public eye."

"It's already public." Mrs. Fitzhugh abruptly changed targets. "Mr. Markland, since you are living in the penthouse, tell us when *this*—" she walked to the desk and picked up the calendar, holding it as if it threatened to contaminate her "—was photographed."

Barely controlled fury radiated from Adam. "I have said I know nothing of it." His voice rang with the authority of two generations of Markland lawyers. "I will remind you that I am unaccustomed to having my word questioned."

"I believe you, Adam." Mr. Steele's attempt at conciliation failed with his next words. "But not everyone does. It looks to me like we'll have to take this case. I'm still going to let you handle it though." Mr. Steele's jowls stretched into a smile as if he had handed Adam a gift.

Adam turned his piercing gaze on him. "I'm no longer

a trial lawyer." The brilliant blue eyes shaded by thick black brows were an intimidating Markland weapon. Adam used them now. "This can be settled out of court."

Mr. Steele backed off, as others had before him. "You're right, Adam."

"Are you refusing?" trilled Mrs. Fitzhugh, with a furious look at her brother. "It appears you have something to hide, Bernard. A penthouse tryst with your receptionist, perhaps?"

Adam watched Mr. Steele's face turn a dull redbrick color. Mrs. Fitzhugh, bolstered by her committee, was in fine form. When he recovered, Adam knew Bernard Steele would bend to the wishes of his sister.

"I've heard enough." Adam's voice sliced through the heavy silence. "I want it understood that before you accept this case, I am resigning my partnership in Swinehart, Cathardy and Steele. You'll have a letter within fifteen minutes."

"Adam!" It was the first time Mr. Steele had raised his voice. "You're thinking below the waist."

Adam lifted an eyebrow and turned to leave, quietly closing the door. He stood for a moment, his eyes tightly shut. Holly. He had to go to her.

HOLLY SAW ADAM'S CAR from her bedroom window.

"Hi," he said softly, when she answered the door.

He stood looking at her, but not really seeing her. Holly noted the lines of strain around his mouth and the bleakness in his eyes. Wordlessly, she opened her arms and he came to her, hugging her fiercely.

"Let's go sit down." Holly began to rub his neck and back.

Adam relaxed. "Feels good." He smiled wearily at her and drew a gentle finger along her cheek.

Holly turned her face into his palm and kissed it.

Words began to pour out of Adam as Holly listened silently. He told her about his lawyer family and the challenge of growing up a Markland. He liked law, he said, but wasn't a fanatic about it. He refused to separate the law from people and preferred arbitration over going to trial. His family had been subtle and then overt in their disapproval.

Holly listened, conscious that she was learning more about Adam now than in the months she'd known him. As he talked, she began to understand what he'd meant about her not being *in* love with him. Quite suddenly, she realized she wanted to spend all the evenings for the rest of her life listening to Adam discuss his work and his feelings, and sharing hers with him. Adam was right—there was a difference.

"What happened today?" Holly asked softly. For once, she forgot about Deck the Halls. There was only Adam and right now he needed her.

Adam released a lungful of air and closed his eyes. "I resigned my partnership today."

"Why?"

He hesitated. "They're about to take a high-profile case that has no business in court. I'm trying to prevent it. They wanted me to handle it."

"Couldn't you win it?" Holly asked, trying to understand.

"Yes." He opened his eyes, but didn't look at her. "I could win it."

"Then why not accept it? Adam, you've spent hours negotiating behind the scenes. This would put you in the spotlight." Holly unconsciously began a pep talk like the ones she'd given her sisters hundreds of times.

"I'm not a trial lawyer." A touch of irritation entered his voice.

"But you said you could win it."

Adam turned toward her. "Winning isn't everything,

trite as that sounds. People would get hurt. It might destroy a family business.''

"So? Someone has to lose. Is this another bankruptcy case?''

"It's headed that way.''

Holly didn't like feeling disloyal to Adam, but she owed him her opinion. "People and businesses go bankrupt all the time. It happens. It happened to us and nobody was worried about where we'd get our next meal.''

Adam opened his mouth, then closed it abruptly, obviously changing his mind. "There's a little more to it than I've told you,'' he commented at last.

"I still think you should take it. If you don't, another lawyer will and get all the publicity.''

"Holly— I resigned,'' Adam said, biting off each word.

Holly was trying so hard to encourage Adam to grab the opportunity, she missed the warning tone in his voice.

"Don't you have any ambition?'' Holly asked, filling her voice with amazement. Maybe he'd try to prove her wrong.

Adam got to his feet. "I have principles and I refuse to sacrifice them on the altar of money.''

"Glad you can afford them,'' Holly said dryly. "Not everyone can.''

Adam stared at her, his face drained of color. "It was a mistake to come here.'' He started for the door.

"I don't believe this!'' Holly shouted, running after him. "You're leaving just because I disagreed with your decision?''

Adam paused at the door. "I…wanted your support.''

Holly gripped his arms. "I'm not ever going to agree with you when I think you're wrong.''

"I thought you'd understand. You've made decisions everybody thought were wrong, but you believed in yourself. This time, I expected you to trust my judgment,'' Adam said quietly.

"Even when it's wrong?''

The bleakness returned to Adam's eyes. His gaze roamed over her features, as if committing them to memory. He leaned down and kissed her on the forehead. "Goodbye."

His goodbye made her very nervous, even though Holly told herself she was right to give Adam her honest opinion. He was just stewing over it for a while, but she was confident he'd come around. He ought to know she wasn't some fluff-brained creature who would agree with anything he said or did.

Guilt, her favorite emotion, settled in the next day. Mrs. Fitzhugh refused to take her calls, but the hotel and caterers agreed to bill the committee directly. Mrs. Bloom howled about losses and damages. Holly wearily promised to pay for the bears, but not for normal wear and tear on the white trees.

"Holly? Lunch." Laurel popped into and out of Holly's office.

At least there were no surprises there—party leftovers.

"How's the money situation?" Laurel asked.

"I can't get through to Mrs. Fitzhugh, so I don't know if our suppliers are getting paid or not. We have one month's expenses in the freezer, but we've got credit-card balances." Holly smiled with false brightness. "Fortunately, I already paid our taxes on the house, or we'd be out that, too. Thank heaven Ivy went back to Exemp Temps. I'm still working on Bloomie."

"And the silk?"

Holly shook her head. "One mill offered about ten cents on the dollar to take it back—"

Ivy burst into the kitchen, clutching papers. "Holly, we're being sued!" She thrust the papers at Holly and sat at the kitchen table trying to catch her breath.

"What is this?" Holly tried to make sense of the papers.

"Exemplary Temporaries sent me to a law firm and I've been typing. This was in the stack."

"Are you at Swinehart, Cathardy and Steele?" Holly began to feel sick.

Ivy nodded.

"That's Adam's firm," Laurel whispered.

"Was," Holly corrected.

"No one told me anything. I didn't even see him there!" Ivy turned bewildered eyes on Holly. "What happened? Why didn't Adam tell us about this?"

With hideous clarity, Holly remembered every word of her discussion with Adam. "I think he tried to." She quickly scanned the papers. "It's Mrs. Fitzhugh and the Winter Ball committee. They're suing us over the bills."

Holly wanted to throw herself on her bed and bawl as she remembered the look on Adam's face. He'd quit his partnership for her and she'd criticized him for having principles. "Does anyone know you have these?" she asked Ivy as tears blurred the words on the documents.

Ivy shook her head. "I waited until lunch and took them. There's a whole stack of court papers and I put ours on the bottom. I can pretend I never saw them. Maybe by the time they remember, you can talk to Adam. He wouldn't let them sue us."

"I'm not so sure." Holly stared at the papers and her hands began to shake. "Fraudulent business dealings? That's absurd." She threw the papers on the table.

Laurel picked them up. "We could destroy these."

Holly got wearily to her feet. "I'll take them back. Don't worry, Ivy."

Ivy looked ready to cry. "You'd better let me. I can sneak the papers back and no one will know they've been gone."

"No." Holly smiled sadly. "I've got some groveling to do."

Adam's office was cluttered with signs of packing. Holly tapped on the open door before walking the miles to his desk.

His face was expressionless as he watched her approach.

It seemed best to dispense with the social amenities. Holly carefully unfolded the slightly rumpled papers and smoothed them on his desk, brushing aside a take-out food container. The crackling was the only sound in the room.

"Where did you get these?"

Holly stood, like an errant schoolgirl in front of the principal's desk. "It's quite a coincidence, actually. Ivy's working here as a temp. She was given the papers to type, panicked and brought them to me."

Adam flicked a glance at her before picking up the documents Holly would have given anything to burn. He put them in his out basket, then returned to his writing.

Holly wasn't about to let him ignore her. "This is the case you were talking about yesterday, isn't it?"

Adam dropped his pen and steepled his hands. "Yes."

He obviously wasn't in a charitable mood. "Did you unresign?"

"No."

Holly made a vague gesture that silently asked what he was still doing there. "Just tying up loose ends," he answered.

"I knew Laurel's chummy poses wouldn't sit well with those women, but fraudulent business dealings?"

"Going to play it that way, are you?" Adam leaned back in his chair and reached behind him. He tossed the calendar at her. "Seen that before?"

Bianca, the penthouse, Darlene and…the fireplace tools, logo clearly visible. Holly closed her eyes and exhaled shakily.

"Did you know about that?" Adam asked, his voice rising.

"No!" Holly protested. "Well, afterward," she amended.

"Check February."

Holly saw the notorious red scrap of lingerie and dropped

the calendar as if she'd been scalded. Her face flamed. "I didn't know what Gus had planned. You told him he could use the penthouse that day," Holly reminded Adam.

"Good point."

"I didn't tell you about it before because I was ashamed at the way Gus set us up. I walked in on the photo session and threw them out."

"During what month?"

Maybe he didn't hate her completely. "November. Gus must have done December first."

Adam didn't smile, but his face seemed softer. "The calendar gave Mrs. Fitzhugh ammunition to convince her brother to take the committee's case."

Holly bowed her head. "I'm sorry."

"So am I." Adam studied her. "Steele thinks you planned this whole thing as revenge."

Holly shook her head. "Please get them to drop the suit and…and…talk or compromise or whatever you do."

Adam raised one black brow.

"It'll ruin us," Holly pleaded.

"Probably."

Holly waited for a hint of compassion. If she had ever meant anything to him… "Help me."

The bland mask cracked just a little. "I did when I resigned, because I'm very good and I would win."

Holly gasped slightly. "And now?"

"You need a good trial lawyer." Adam cleared his throat. "I'm available, as it happens." His lips curved slightly.

Holly stood a little straighter. Now she understood. It was his career or hers. And Adam didn't hesitate to sacrifice his.

But Holly did. Hours of mind-numbing work, petty humiliations, nagging, cajoling and pushing couldn't be dismissed in an instant. It took two. "Hiring a lawyer would be a pointless waste of money I don't have," she said, deliberately misunderstanding his offer. "I'll just make a simple statement to the judge. That should clear everything up."

"You'll be committing financial suicide." The coolness in Adam's voice was replaced by concern.

"No." Holly gave him a bitter smile as she turned to leave. "I did that last week."

# CHAPTER ELEVEN

THEY WERE DESTROYING the woman he loved.

Adam sat toward the back of the courtroom, directly behind Holly, so she'd be unable to see him out of the corner of her eye. He stared at the solitary figure in the conservative navy suit and the unrestrained brown curls. Too stubborn and too proud to accept his offer of help. And he loved her, anyway.

The trial had been scheduled quickly, with Mr. Steele calling in his markers. Adam thought disgustedly of the hundreds of plaintiffs who waited years for their cases to come to trial. Mr. Steele's justification was that the ballet couldn't function without their money from the ball.

He knew that Holly hoped a quick resolution would allow the publicity to die down so she could start over.

Adam shifted on the hard wooden bench as he examined the battery of lawyers clustered around Mr. Steele. So, who was the crown prince chosen to lead the attack against Holly and her small-time business? Joe Longoria.

Adam brightened. Joe was thorough and methodical, but too slow to recognize when a particular strategy wasn't working.

However, this time, his strategy appeared to be working.

Adam mentally winced each time a witness appeared. With no defense lawyer to object, Joe gained confidence as he flirted with the gray areas of courtroom procedure. Adam gritted his teeth until his jaw ached. Anyone who had ever watched television trials would have been tempted to scream. "Objection—leading the witness," or, "Objection—irrelevant."

Right now, Mrs. Herman Bloom was testifying.

Joe was posturing. "Describe your dealings with the Hall sisters."

Mrs. Bloom, an ample woman with small eyes, preened self-importantly. "Those girls were always looking down their noses at people."

*Objection,* sighed Adam mentally.

Joe, in one of his ponderously choreographed moves, looked to where the jury would be—if there had been a jury. "You had a business relationship?" he prompted.

Mrs. Bloom sniffed. "Those girls were just playing at business, you know?"

*Objection.*

Joe leaned against the witness stand. "No, you tell us."

"They bounced checks all over town. It didn't matter to them that I had to eat and they had their trust funds. They figured I could wait for my money." Mrs. Bloom looked righteously indignant.

Joe strolled over to the exhibit table. "Bank records."

Those were duly entered as Adam got out a small notebook.

"They offered to let me wear their mother's vulgar diamond necklace, like I was a peasant or something."

Adam's heart twisted for Holly. The necklace, even in its present almost valueless state, was more than a piece of jewelry to her.

Witness after witness, some who'd had dealings with Holly and some who hadn't, was called. It seemed at times that not only Holly, but her family and entire way of life was on trial. Surely she could see that she was wrong not to have a lawyer?

After lunch, the courtroom was packed with reporters. News of the juicy trial had leaked out. Holly appeared calm, but Adam noticed her back wasn't quite as straight and her head drooped until she remembered to jerk it upright. Only her hair remained a defiant curly halo around her head.

At least Laurel had taken Adam's advice and stayed home. It would be bad when Joe got around to her sleigh poses, and judging by the expression on Claudia Fitzhugh's face, he was just about to.

"And so out of the generosity of your heart, you gave Holly Hall her big break."

Mrs. Fitzhugh bowed her head modestly. "Her mother was very dear to me." She directed a look of eloquent disapproval at Holly.

"Was Ms. Hall grateful?" Joe assumed his deferential demeanor.

"Apparently not."

"Could you be more specific?"

"She spent thousands of dollars on decorations for the Winter Ball. I'll remind everyone that the primary purpose of the ball is to raise money." Mrs. Fitzhugh addressed the room at large, effectively donning her Old Guard Society Matron guise.

Adam glared at Mrs. Fitzhugh as if he could mentally remind *her* how Holly had come to her rescue twice.

Mrs. Fitzhugh was speaking. "It became like a…like a commercial for her sister. And then—" Mrs. Fitzhugh shot a withering look at Holly "—she had the effrontery to bill us for her expenses in promoting her sister's sleazy career."

"Objection!" Adam breathed a sigh of relief at the release he felt. He refused to allow this character assassination to continue.

The crowd of reporters murmured and the judge banged his gavel in the tradition of television dramas.

Adam missed all the looks directed at him, except one. After Holly's head swiveled in his direction in stunned surprise, a huge smile lit her face. Adam's eyes locked with hers as he made his way to the front of the courtroom, oblivious to the judge's beckoning.

Adam wanted to hold her and tell her everything would be all right, but contented himself with grasping both her hands in his. They were cold.

"What are you doing?" The words formed a question, but Holly's voice was a caress.

Adam's eyes searched her face, his lips tilted in a half smile. "I'm your knight in shining armor."

Holly shook her head. "Don't. Mr. Steele will never take you back."

Adam's lips parted with dawning comprehension. "That's why you wouldn't let me represent you?"

Holly dipped her head for a moment, then shrugged lightly. "I couldn't ruin your career," she whispered. "I'm in love with you."

Adam's smile was blinding. "So you were going to sacrifice Deck the Halls." The blood pounded through his veins. "Holly." His voice was husky and his arms ached to hold her, but conscious of their surroundings, he only squeezed her hands.

Adam felt a touch at his elbow. "Hey, man." Joe Longoria tugged Adam away to confront the stern-faced judge.

"Permission to approach the bench," Adam asked belatedly. Reaching into his breast pocket, he withdrew a card and his credentials and presented them. "Adam Markland, with Markland Associates."

The judge peered at the card. "Boston." He looked at Adam over the top of his glasses. "I don't need to tell you that I won't tolerate these shenanigans in my courtroom."

"No, sir." Adam turned icy blue eyes toward Joe Longoria.

"And your client chose not to be represented by counsel."

"My client came here to explain a misunderstanding, not to commit social and financial suicide. She expected matters to be resolved within a few minutes. This lengthy excuse for publicly humiliating her family has changed her mind.''

''I'll bet it has,'' the judge muttered. He banged his gavel and called for a ten-minute recess.

''Adam,'' Holly began, a few minutes before the recess was over. ''I know how you feel about being in the courtroom. It makes you…uncomfortable.'' She shook her head. ''It's okay. You don't have to do this. I wouldn't love you any less.''

Adam was surprised into a laugh. ''Good!''

''Maybe we could—''

Adam laid a hand over both of hers. ''Holly, dear heart, I choose not to be a trial attorney. I think there are better ways. But I've been one. Yes,'' he affirmed as her face registered amazement. ''In fact,'' he continued in a light conversational voice, obviously enjoying himself, ''I'm really quite good. No, I'm the best.''

He looked at her with such blazing intensity, in spite of his teasing tone, that Holly believed him instantly.

''It got so other attorneys didn't want to appear against me. They'd knew they'd lose and wanted to settle out of court. I began to prefer that, which irritated my family. They tried to pressure me, so I left. Steele offered me a partnership and I accepted, even though I knew he thought he could talk me back into the courtroom. Look.'' Adam pointed, his grin almost menacing. ''You can see Joe Longoria sweating from here.''

''Adam?'' Holly said uncertainly.

His face softened instantly. ''It'll be okay. Don't worry.''

Of course she was going to worry, Holly thought as she listened to more of Mrs. Fitzhugh's attacks. She stole a glance at Adam.

He wore his lawyer face and leaned forward attentively. Mrs. Fitzhugh, lulled by his deferential mask, continued to list her complaints against Holly.

At last it was Adam's turn. "Mrs. Fitzhugh, you sound very different now than you did before and during the Winter Ball. Then you were extremely grateful."

"That was before I discovered how I was used."

Adam straightened and fixed her with an unblinking stare. To Holly's astonishment, a faint pink tinged Mrs. Fitzhugh's cheeks. "How long does it take to plan the Winter Ball?"

"A year."

"Who was contracted to decorate for this year's event— before Ms. Hall?"

"John Kelly."

"Prestigious name—known for his lavish and unusual interiors. Yet he backed out three weeks before the ball, leaving you in danger of canceling, isn't that so?"

Mrs. Fitzhugh nodded reluctantly.

"Please answer audibly. The court reporter can't record gestures."

"Yes." Mrs. Fitzhugh answered through gritted teeth.

"Thank you. Mrs. Fitzhugh, to save time, I will summarize the events that followed. You may speak out if any differ from your recollection."

Holly listened as Adam calmly retold the story of her involvement with the Winter Ball, transforming her from an unscrupulous opportunist furthering Laurel's immoral career into a hardworking businesswoman, too generous for her own good. At Adam's prodding Mrs. Fitzhugh, whose eyes kept darting toward Joe Longoria, periodically confirmed his statements.

"Who pays for the Winter Ball?" Adam leaned back against the exhibit table.

"We sell tickets and there are several underwriters. Businesses donate food, flowers, that sort of thing." Mrs. Fitzhugh eyed him warily.

"And, in fact, Holly Hall donated her services, true?"

Mrs. Fitzhugh nodded.

"Let the record show an answer in the affirmative. Please tell the court what happened when Ms. Hall presented her list of expenses to you." Adam folded his arms across his chest.

Mrs. Fitzhugh's mouth opened and closed. "They were terribly high—higher than I'd expected. I'm sure that in other years John Kelly Interiors must have absorbed some of the costs—"

Adam cut her off. "John Kelly Interiors is an established firm that has an inventory of its own. They may or may not have done as you suggested. Did you pay Ms. Hall's invoice?"

"I..."

"Answer yes or no."

"No."

Even though Holly knew the answer, she, along with the rest of the courtroom, followed the exchange in rapt silence.

"Not only did you not pay Ms. Hall, you let her understand that if she pressed you, she would not work in Dallas again."

"Objection," Joe announced.

"I did not!" Mrs. Fitzhugh's chin began to tremble.

Adam ignored him. "Your exact words were: 'Do that and you won't work in Dallas again.' Correct?"

"I don't remember!"

"You are under oath."

"I can't..." Mrs. Fitzhugh sent a beseeching look to her brother.

"Words to that effect?"

"I—yes!" She covered her face with her hands.

Adam wasn't finished. "What other firm could put together a first-rate and—by your own admission—the most successful ball ever in three weeks?"

Mrs. Fitzhugh didn't answer. The judge motioned for her to, but Adam broke in. "She can't answer because no other firm could have done it. Holly Hall did the impossible for charity, knowing she wouldn't receive a penny for her labor and then got stuck with the bills because a greedy chairwoman knew she could get away with it.''

Adam strode toward Holly as Joe screamed in objection. Mrs. Fitzhugh and Holly wore identical stunned expressions.

Holly laid a hand on Adam's arm. ''Did you have to do that?''

Adam, the lawyer, answered her. ''Shall I have the court reporter read back all the things she said about you?''

Holly shook her head.

''Hang in there, we're nearly done.'' Adam went to the exhibit table and got a copy of Holly's invoice, holding it high over his head. ''I want it entered into the record that my client made repeated attempts to resolve this conflict and was rebuffed. She generously offered to absorb costs she hadn't expected to, putting herself in financial jeopardy. This trial is no more than blackmail.''

Adam strode back to sit with Holly as the courtroom erupted. The judge could no longer tolerate the noise from the reporters and declared a recess. When the trial resumed, half the press was gone.

Holly ran her fingers through her hair as she nervously watched the lawyers huddling around Joe Longoria.

''We've got 'em.'' Adam regarded the men contemptuously. ''The public is on your side now and these guys are exposed for the big bullies they are.''

''What's going to happen?'' Holly asked.

Adam shrugged. ''If they're smart, they'll get out of this quick.''

Joe approached the judge. ''Your honor, in light of recent developments and the explanation given by Ms. Hall's attorney, we withdraw our suit.''

''Bernie,'' the judge muttered, glaring at Mr. Steele and shaking his head in exasperation, ''I can't believe you called me back from vacation and pulled a stunt like this.''

He banged his gavel as the remaining reporters shuffled out the doors or ran to Holly. The shouted questions blurred together; the camera lights momentarily blinded her. She clutched Adam's arm until a microphone was thrust too close to her face and she released his arm to bat it away. The crowd separated them immediately.

Seeing that Holly was overwhelmed, Adam moved away, drawing half a dozen reporters with him.

In a few moments it was over. Holly dealt ably with the two remaining television crews as Mr. Steele approached Adam. "Reconsider that resignation, Adam?"

"Nope. I'll be vacating the penthouse today."

Mr. Steele shook his head as they walked toward the back of the now empty courtroom. "I knew having you with the firm was too good to last."

"MRS. FITZHUGH DROPPED the suit." Holly wearily set her purse on the kitchen counter and kicked off her pumps.

"I know." Laurel nodded her head. "It's been on the news."

"I expected more of a reaction from you." Holly looked at her sister in surprise.

"I have to talk to you about something. Bart King—with the film commission?—said my pictures have generated a lot of interest."

Holly opened the refrigerator door. "Mr. King has a flair for understatement." Seeing nothing cold to drink, Holly filled a glass with water and ice, collapsed into a chair at the table and waited for Laurel to continue.

"Holly, some casting directors have asked to see me." She tilted her head defiantly and swallowed. "I'm leaving for Los Angeles."

Nothing surprised Holly anymore. Laurel would have to find out for herself what kind of parts she'd be offered, if any. Holly opened her mouth to wish her well, but Laurel, apparently thinking she was going to get a lecture, cut her off.

"I don't want to hear any more about Deck the Halls! I'm sick to death of Deck the Halls! What about *my* life? Ever since Mama and Daddy died, I've done what *you* thought was best. I'm two years older than you were when you had to start running this family." Laurel stopped and took a deep breath. "I'm not going to spend any more of my life pandering to your ego by helping you build *your* business. You want to throw away your money on society snobs, go ahead. I'm not working like a slave to help you do it."

A month ago, Holly would have interrupted Laurel to argue, but the trial had taken all the fight out of her. She wasn't angry; she regretted that Laurel had held these feelings in for so long. "I'll miss you."

A look of disbelief, followed by elation, flickered across Laurel's face before it was smothered by concern. "The news reports were right, weren't they, Holly? It's over? We came out of it okay?"

"If you mean do we have to pay them any of our non-existent money, no. Whether we ever work again remains to be seen."

"I need to pack. Holly?"

"Take what you want, but be reasonable about it."

Holly sipped her water, wishing she had something stronger. Starting Deck the Halls again with just Ivy wasn't going to be the same. Laurel had contributed more than Holly had given her credit for, and she made a mental note to tell her so before Laurel left. And to send her off with the biggest hug she'd ever had...

"I'm glad I caught the news on TV. Didn't you think I'd want to know we're off the hook?" Ivy leaned in the doorway.

"Ivy!" Holly lowered her stockinged feet from the

kitchen chair and grimaced. "I'm sorry. So much happened, I forgot that you didn't know."

Ivy crossed her arms, but didn't come into the kitchen. "It wouldn't be the first time you forgot to tell me something important. Or is it that you think I'm too young to know these grown-up things?"

Holly very carefully lowered her glass to the table. "You're right. I should have told you immediately, but I saw Laurel as soon as I stepped in the door and she chose that moment to tell me about all the horrible things I've done that might not have come out in the courtroom where I've spent the entire day." Holly bit out the last words as she ran out of breath. She was close to tears.

"Adam turned out to be an old-fashioned hero, according to the news reports," Ivy said mildly.

Holly sank back in her chair. "He was incredible." It was disconcerting to discover she'd fallen in love with someone she didn't even know.

Ivy walked toward the table. "This came by courier a little while ago."

Holly reached for the envelope, but Ivy snatched it away. "Not yet. I opened it and it's a check from the Winter Ball committee signed by Claudia Fitzhugh. I don't know exactly how much of our expenses it covers, since you didn't bother to tell me how much they were."

"If you'll give it to me, I'll let you know." Holly held out her hand, but Ivy shook her head.

"I want one-third of this."

"Are you willing to take on one-third of our debt, too?" Holly regretted the words as soon as they were out.

Ivy hesitated, then handed Holly the envelope. Quickly doing some rough figuring, Holly said, "This will pay off everything but the silk, which we'll keep, and after paying for that, we ought to have four thousand left over. Total cash assets. You want a third of that now, or plow it back into the business and get all your college money later?"

"Now. I've been talking with some of my friends who are at the University of Texas and they have room for a fourth roommate in their apartment. I'm going to Austin now to get a job and then I'll enroll for summer school."

"You want to go to UT?" Holly tried to hide her dismay. "I assumed—" She caught herself. "They have an excellent business school."

"And journalism department, which is good since I plan to be a sportswriter," Ivy announced calmly.

"You've got it all planned." Holly knew she had to reach deep within herself and show Ivy some enthusiasm. "I'll miss you," she said with sincerity. "And I wish you success. But I'm going to get lonely with both you and Laurel gone."

"You won't be lonely," Ivy said, nodding toward the door behind Holly. "Laurel and I invited company."

Holly turned and saw Adam. He opened the door and shoved two suitcases inside. "Any damsels in distress here?"

"I think the other two can take care of themselves," Holly said, wondering about the luggage.

"Hi, Adam." Ivy gave him a hug, whispered in his ear and discreetly left the kitchen.

"What do you mean you didn't tell her?" Adam called after Ivy, as she scampered up the stairs.

"Tell me what?"

"I was on my way to a hotel, but Laurel and Ivy invited me to stay here." Adam went to the refrigerator, shook his head and got a glass of water. He sat at the table with her. "When they said 'we,' I assumed it included you."

"I'm sorry." She should have remembered that he was leaving the penthouse.

"I'm not." His blue eyes scorched her face.

Holly's numbed senses began to stir, warmed by his look. "There's certainly plenty of room. Laurel is off to California and Ivy is leaving for Austin."

Adam grinned. "Good for them."

"Are you on your way back to Boston?" Holly brought her glass to her lips, trying to fool Adam into thinking it was a casual question.

Adam waited until she set the glass down again, smiling a smile that told her he wasn't fooled at all. "Everything I want is here."

Holly clenched her glass, suddenly nervous. "What about—" she hesitated "—your work?"

Adam watched her with growing amusement. "I'm starting my own firm as I should have done in the first place. Got any space for rent?"

"Here?" Holly's lips curved in a slow smile. "I like that idea. Maybe rent some of the bedrooms to others who—"

"No!" Adam stated firmly. "I'll rent whatever you don't use as storage."

Holly sobered. "I don't know if I'll continue Deck the Halls." She swirled the ice in her glass. "I built it for Laurel and Ivy, you know."

"And for you."

Holly frowned. "They think I'm some kind of slave driver."

"Well, you are."

Holly turned hurt eyes toward him. "I had to be."

Adam smiled gently. "Had. You kept your family together until they could take care of themselves." He stood and offered her a hand, leading her to the family room off the kitchen.

Ivy had left the television on, and Adam turned it off before they were bombarded with more news flashes. He settled Holly on the sofa and drew her next to him. "The fight's over, Holly. You won. It's time they were on their own."

"I know." Holly leaned her head on Adam's shoulder. She pulled the check from her pocket. "From Mrs. Fitzhugh."

"It's a little short."

Holly shook her head. "The difference is about what the silk is worth. That woman doesn't miss much."

"You see? You've got all that silk. You'll have to keep Deck the Halls going," Adam teased gently.

In her mind, Holly replayed bits of the courtroom scene, contrasting that Adam with the familiar one who sat with his arm draped around her. "I don't know you at all, do I?" she finally burst out in a voice filled with self-derision.

Adam tilted her chin with his fingers. "Holly, look at me." Holly did and caught her breath at the expression on his face. "Yes, you do. I'm hardly Adam-the-Barracuda at all anymore. I don't like him very much. You know the real me. No one else ever did."

"I'm sorry you had to do that today—"

"No." Adam shook his head. "It's the best thing that could have happened. Not only did I get you off the hook, I've, uh, proven myself on the Texas battlefield. I shouldn't have to do it again. That day you told me I should take the case—you were right, but for the wrong reasons."

"A nice change from being wrong for the right reasons."

"Like trying to sacrifice everything you'd worked for to save my partnership at Swinehart, Cathardy and Steele." His eyes filled with tenderness.

"Lot of good it did," Holly mumbled.

Adam tilted her chin again. "Yes, it did," he said before his lips descended to meet hers.

The sweetness of his kiss flowed through her, washing away all the hurt and bitterness. "But loving you is right for all the right reasons," Holly whispered against his mouth.

"Definitely." Adam drew her closer. "I love you, Holly," he said, in a voice raw with emotion. "And I've wanted you for so long, but after what you've been through today—"

"Adam," she said, her voice huskier than usual, "*please* take advantage of me."

He laughed and kissed her forehead. "All right—will you marry me?"

"Yes," Holly replied immediately.

Adam's look of pleased surprise was followed by one of such blazing joy that Holly felt her throat tighten. He pulled her to him. "And maybe we could fill some of these bedrooms with little Marklands?" Adam searched her face as he asked.

Holly grinned. "During the off-season, of course."

"Of course," Adam agreed as he kissed her again, stopping abruptly with a stricken look on his face. "What's nine months from now?"

Holly began to laugh. "Christmas!"

# Tyler Brides

## It happened one weekend...

Quinn and Molly Spencer are delighted to accept three bookings for their newly opened B&B, Breakfast Inn Bed, located in America's favorite hometown, Tyler, Wisconsin.

But Gina Santori is anything but thrilled to discover her best friend has tricked her into sharing a room with the man who broke her heart eight years ago....

And Delia Mayhew can hardly believe that she's gotten herself locked in the Breakfast Inn Bed basement with the sexiest man in America.

Then there's Rebecca Salter. She's turned up at the Inn in her wedding gown. Minus her groom.

*Come home to Tyler for three delightful novellas by three of your favorite authors: Kristine Rolofson, Heather MacAllister and Jacqueline Diamond.*

# HARLEQUIN®
*Makes any time special* ™